SUZANNE, THE MIDWIFE

Book Three of
The Watertown Chronicles

Nancy Shattuck

Farmington Hills, Michigan

The Ardent Writer Press

Brownsboro, Alabama

Visit Nancy Shattuck's Author Page at
www.ArdentWriterPress.com

For general information about publishing with The Ardent Writer Press contact ***steve@ardentwriterpress.com*** or forward mail to:

The Ardent Writer Press,
Box 25
Brownsboro, Alabama 35741

Photo of Nancy Shattuck is by Devenand Ale.

Library of Congress Cataloging-in-Publication Data

Suzanne, The Midwife, Book Three of *The Watertown Chronicles* by Nancy Shattuck

p. cm. - (Ardent Writer Press-2020) ISBN 978-1-64066-131-8 (pbk.); 978-1-64066-132-5 (eBook epub)

Library of Congress Control Number 2021949841

Library of Congress Subject Headings

New England--17th century--Fiction.
New England History--Colonial period, ca. 1600-1775--Fiction.
New England--Social life and customs--Fiction.
Historical fiction--17th century.
Historical fiction, American.

BISAC Subject Headings

FIC014070 FICTION/Historical/Colonial America & Revolution
FIC014000 FICTION / Historical / General
FIC008000 FICTION / Sagas
FIC000000 FICTION / General

CONTENTS

ACKNOWLEDGMENTS

I began this project as a single historical novel, but as I wrote, the voices of the family emerged, each offering a divergent point of view on what happened in the years surrounding King Philip's War. They convinced me that history was more than a collection of facts; and I decided to follow where these voices might lead. The result was a series, *The Watertown Chronicles.*

I could never have progressed this far in the project without the aid and encouraging support of the members of my writing group, The Detroit Writers, who read through these novels as they streamed from my laptop to print. I owe thanks to Anthony Ambrosia, Dr. Anca Vlasopolos, Robin Watson, Alinda Wasner, Dr. Claire Crabtree, John Gallagher, Charlotte Varzi, Carol Campbell, and Patricia Abbott.

Early in my project, I was fortunate to meet Dr. Susan Parrish, who teaches American history at the University of Michigan, at a Washington University alumni dinner. She recommended that I contact the American Antiquities Society (AAS) and turned me on to Slotkin's *Regeneration Through Violence: The Mythology of the American Frontier 1600-1800.* That first meeting preceded Philip Shaddock's DNA findings that the Virginia Parrish family are genetically linked to the Shattucks; talk about synchronicity! Likewise, Philip Shaddock, who succeeds Lemuel Shattuck as the chief genealogist for the family, recommended Bridenbaugh's *Vexed and Troubled Englishmen 1590-1642* and *Cities in the Wilderness.* I must also extend special thanks to Philip because he wrote and published an exceptionally fine book review of the first book in *The Watertown Chronicles* on his website, www.shaddock.ca.

Following Dr. Parrish's recommendations, I was able to travel to Watertown and Groton in Massachusetts to begin my research. The wonderful receptions I received at the main libraries in Watertown and Groton, as well as that of The American Antiquarian Society in Worchester, Massachusetts are unforgettable. In Watertown, the librarians enthusiastically led me to a room where they pulled dusty boxes from shelves and opened them for the first time in perhaps years: we found original land grants and titles written in calligraphic script. In Groton, librarians led me on a wonderful search for books on early Groton. The AAS ushered me to a reading room where tables are covered in felt cloths and books are read on book stands and gave me access to digital archives. Imagine reading the Watertown and Groton council meeting minutes, which name the attendees and record the events of a day in 1666.

Lastly, I must thank my family, Polly Shattuck, Shelli Brown, and Mary Shattuck, readers whose encouragement is so important.

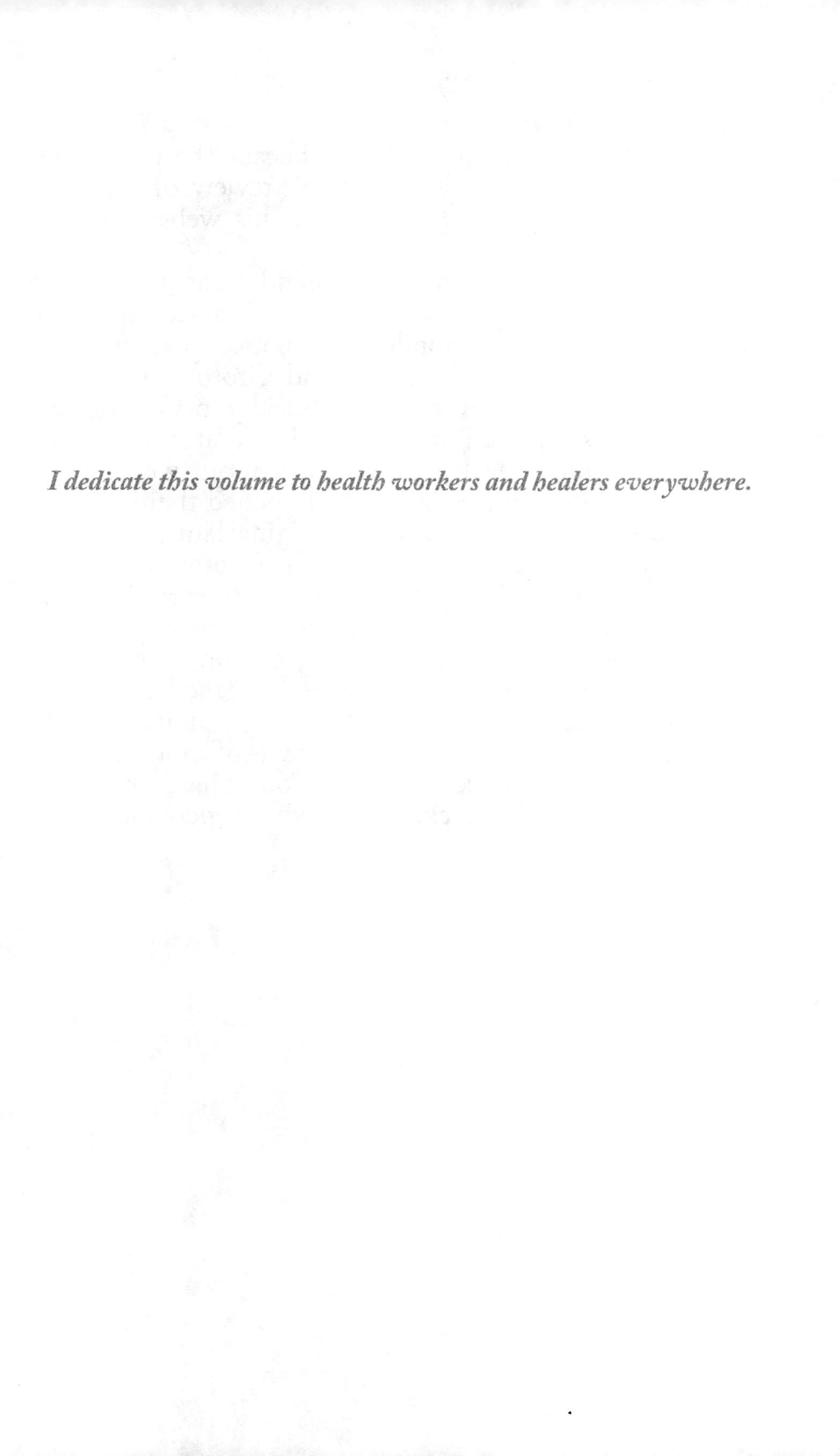

I dedicate this volume to health workers and healers everywhere.

INTRODUCTION

Suzanne, The Midwife, is the third book in *The Watertown Chronicles*, a saga of one of America's immigrant families. Suzanne is the oldest daughter of William Sherborn, an early emigrant from England to Massachusetts. The chronicles tell the story of this man, his wife, and their ten children, who live through the pivotal period in colonial history that surrounds the devastating King Philip's War of 1675-76 in New England. Suzanne's story (she's William's eldest child), begins in 1666, the year her youngest brother Samuel, the tenth child, is born. She has just moved from Watertown to Groton, a newly founded town forty miles away from her childhood home, with her husband and two children, and the pair are struggling to grow enough food for their first winter. She is the only midwife in a town that has no physician and only fifty households at its peak population in 1676. Her story ends in 1679 when she returns to her hometown, Watertown, after the catastrophic war, where she continues struggling to keep her family together.

Suzanne's place in history is bounded by her gendered position within the Puritan society. Most women were bystanders in war conflicts unless they were under direct attack. Unlike the men, they were neither conscribed nor had to drill for military preparedness. What Suzanne knows of the war is filtered through her husband, a farmer who bears arms to range and defend the town at the demand of the colony's local militia. He has no rank. However,

Suzanne is privileged through her work as midwife to glean the balance of news during the war from the many women that she serves.

Regarding the war, the reader needs to know King Philip's war ravaged more than half the New England villages, destroying eleven; its death toll was more than one thousand colonists (2% of the 50,000 New Englanders) and three thousand natives (15% of the 20,000 Algonquin Indians). After victory, the colonial government either executed or sold the remaining natives into slavery, nearly annihilating the East Coast native population, which was already fewer than half that of Europeans before the war started.

This war was also pivotal in colonial history. The Royal Charter for The Massachusetts Bay Colony was unique in that it didn't specify England as the seat of the governing board of stockholders. Board members not only could move to Boston, they bought out any stockholder who chose to stay in England. Unlike any other charter colony, The Massachusetts Bay Colony conducted regular meetings of company officers and stockholders—required of all colonies—in Boston instead of England. Beginning in 1630, the Puritans set up a theocracy in the Massachusetts Bay Colony. "Freemen"—white male church members who owned property and paid taxes—elected a governor and a single legislative body called the Great and General Court, made up of resident assistants and deputies. After the war, the colony lost this independence; in 1685, King Charles II revoked the Royal Charter, placed Massachusetts under the Dominion of New England, and appointed the governing body.

It's difficult to wrap our minds around those years of rising tensions between the emigrating colonists and natives because the complexity of competing nations and shifting alliances is unparalleled. The new colonizers were still tied to the wars and rivalries of the European nations they'd left while immersed in those of the Indian nations surrounding them.

English, French, Spanish, and Dutch immigrants were culturally more diverse than the Indian nations, tribal identity notwithstanding. European nations didn't share a language, dress alike, or even eat the same food, though they shared technologies. The Massachusetts tribes were homogenous by comparison. Christianity did unite Europeans, even as the Protestants splintered the creeds. The Puritan colonists made it their mission to convert natives to the faith, to unite with them. However, that intent politically divided the tribal people, complicating their alliances even more.

The English colonists banded together to meet their unified interests, forming the New England Confederation, a military alliance of Massachusetts, Plymouth, Connecticut, and New Haven. However, internal conflicts over boundaries, uneven contributions to the armies, and funding diminished its efficacy by 1662. The confederation no longer conducted regular meetings when the war began. Though it officially declared war on the Wampanoag and their allies in September 1675, conflict and resentment continued to erode its operation in the theater of King Philip's war.

The names of the Indians who were the chief players in King Philip's war are emblazoned brand names and place-names familiar to us, but featureless. One can buy Wamsutta towels, for instance, but never know that Sachem Wamsutta was the son of the Massasoit ("great chief") Ousamequin, who helped the Plymouth colonists survive their first winter. Nor would anyone know his importance in history, that his brother the Sachem (Chief) Metacom, or King Philip, wanted revenge for his death.

The Massasoit Ousamequin was a friend of the Plymouth settlers until his death. His treaty with the Governor was one of friendship and support; the colonists and the Wampanoag tribe even allied to fight the nearby Narragansett people. The Massasoit's sons and successors were given Christian names. Wamsutta, the oldest son, took the name Alexander; Metacom, the next son, took the name Philip. The treaty between Massasoit Ousamequin and Governor Prence of Plymouth unfortunately did not outlive its makers. After the Massasoit died and his son Wamsutta became Sachem, Governor Prence, threatened by the French and Dutch, began to make unreasonable demands on the Wampanoag people, who resisted. After King Alexander (Sachem Wamsutta) mysteriously died while in the hands of the British under suspicious circumstances, his successor King Philip (Sachem Metacom) began to build a fighting force. In 1671, Governor Prence responded by insisting King Philip sign a new treaty in which he declared he would sell no more land without the approval of Plymouth, would surrender all his guns, and pay tribute and fines. While Governor Prence instituted the moratorium on native land, conflicts continued, mainly over arms. However, after Governor Prence's death in 1673, the new Governor, Josiah Winslow, removed the moratorium, and reports are that in some instances he used illegal tactics to pressure natives to sell land. At this time,

The treaty between Chief Massasoit and Governor Prence of Plymouth unfortunately did not outlive its makers. After Massasoit died and his son Wamsutta became sachem (chief), Governor Prence, threatened by the French and Dutch, began to make unreasonable demands on the Wampanoag people, who resisted. After King Alexander (Sachem Wamsutta) mysteriously died while in the hands of the British under suspicious circumstances, his successor King Philip (Sachem Metacom) began to build a fighting force. In 1671, Governor Prence responded by insisting King Philip sign a new treaty in which he declared he would sell no more land without the approval of Plymouth, would surrender all his guns, and pay tribute and fines. While Governor Prence instituted the moratorium on native land, conflicts continued, mainly over arms. However, after Governor Prence's death in 1673, the new Governor, Josiah Winslow, ended the moratorium, and reports are that in some instances he used illegal tactics to pressure natives to sell land. At this time, Philip sold Wampanoag land recklessly to purchase guns and ammunition. He aimed to win back his lands, thereby ridding himself of the Europeans who waged war among themselves and pitted rivaling Indians against one another.

The conflict began in early summer when Governor Josiah Winslow executed three of Philip's men, convicting them for murdering a Christian Indian interpreter and spy in 1675. King Philip responded immediately, attacking Swansea in June, an act which coincided with a lunar eclipse. The Indians took this as a good omen and continued their offense on Plymouth towns; the New England Alliance officially declared war in September. King Philip's War raged for eighteen months, effecting Plymouth, Rhode Island, Connecticut, and Massachusetts, before the Indians were routed or sold for slavery in the West Indies.

The war nearly destroyed the economy; in the aftermath taxes rose so high colonists suffered hardships to pay them. Thousands of refugees who had lost their homes and all means of livelihood crowded into the towns the war passed over. The colonial government struggled to settle their debts to soldiers who'd fought in the war. Promises of land for pay weren't met until the eighteenth century, and land was often paid to the now-deceased soldiers' offspring. Charles II's brother, King James, dissolved the Massachusetts Bay Colony charter in 1691 and consolidated Massachusetts, New Hampshire, Plymouth, Martha's Vineyard, and Nantucket into The Province of Massachusetts, appointing a governor from England. With this loss of independence, thus began the ninety-year march to the revolutionary war to sever ties with the motherland.

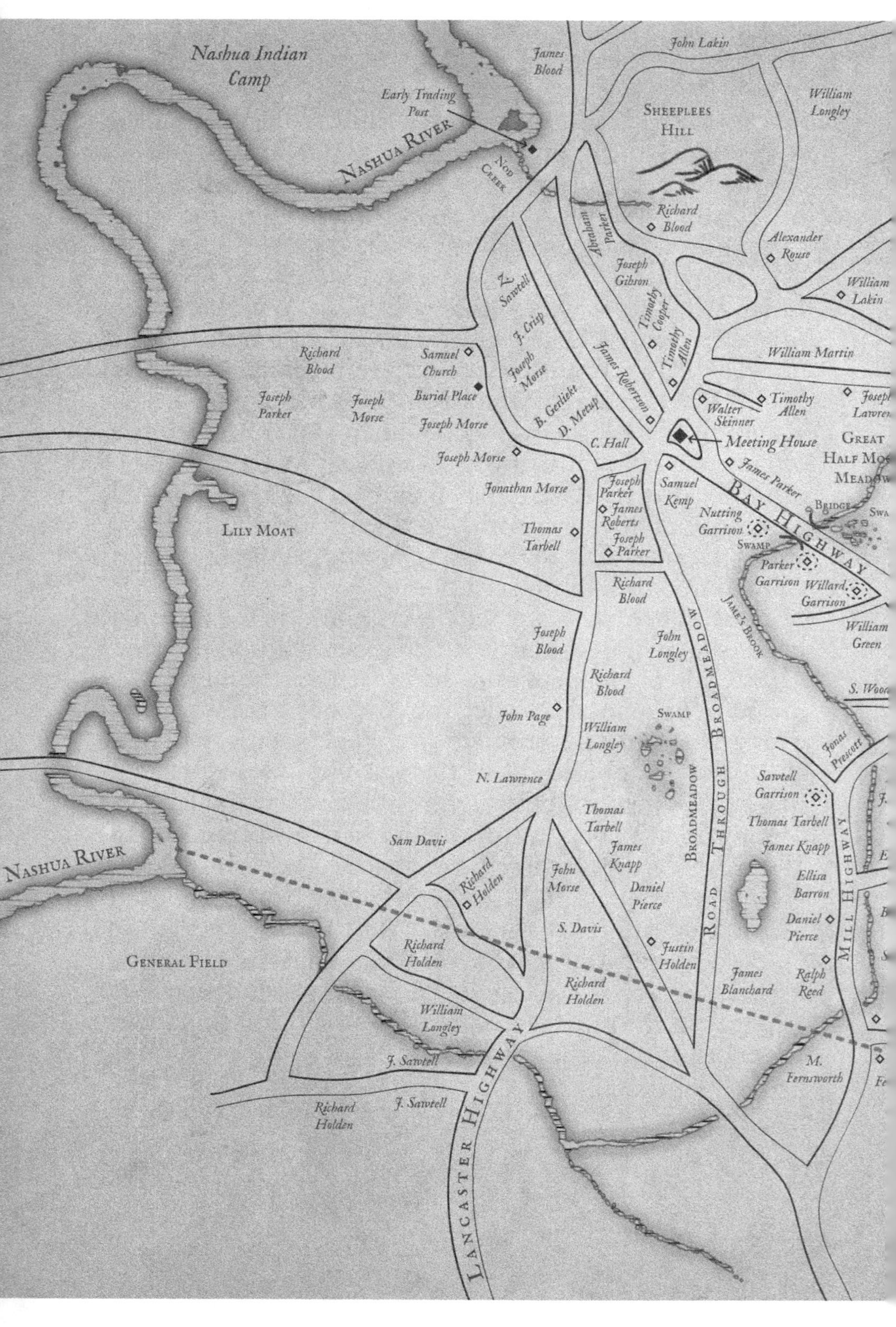
Nashua Indian Camp
James Blood
John Lakin
Early Trading Post
Nashua River
Nod Creek
Sheeplees Hill
William Longley
Richard Blood
Abraham Parker
Alexander Rouse
Joseph Gibson
William Lakin
Z. Sawtell
J. Crisp
Timothy Cooper
Timothy Allen
William Martin
Richard Blood
Samuel Church
Joseph Morse
James Robertson
Joseph Parker
Joseph Morse
Burial Place
B. Gerlieke
D. Metup
Walter Skinner
Timothy Allen
Joseph Morse
Meeting House
Great
C. Hall
Joseph Morse
James Parker
Jonathan Morse
Joseph Parker
Samuel Kemp
Bay Highway
James Roberts
Bridge
Nutting Garrison
Lily Moat
Thomas Tarbell
Joseph Parker
Swamp
Parker Garrison
Willard Garrison
Richard Blood
James's Brook
William Green
Joseph Blood
John Longley
Road Through Broadmeadow
Richard Blood
Swamp
John Page
William Longley
Jonas Prescott
Broadmeadow
N. Lawrence
Sawtell Garrison
Thomas Tarbell
Thomas Tarbell
James Knapp
James Knapp
Sam Davis
Nashua River
Richard Holden
John Morse
Daniel Pierce
Ellisa Barron
Daniel Pierce
S. Davis
Richard Holden
Justin Holden
Mill Highway
General Field
Richard Holden
James Blanchard
Ralph Reed
William Longley
J. Sawtell
M. Fernsworth
Richard Holden
J. Sawtell
Lancaster Highway

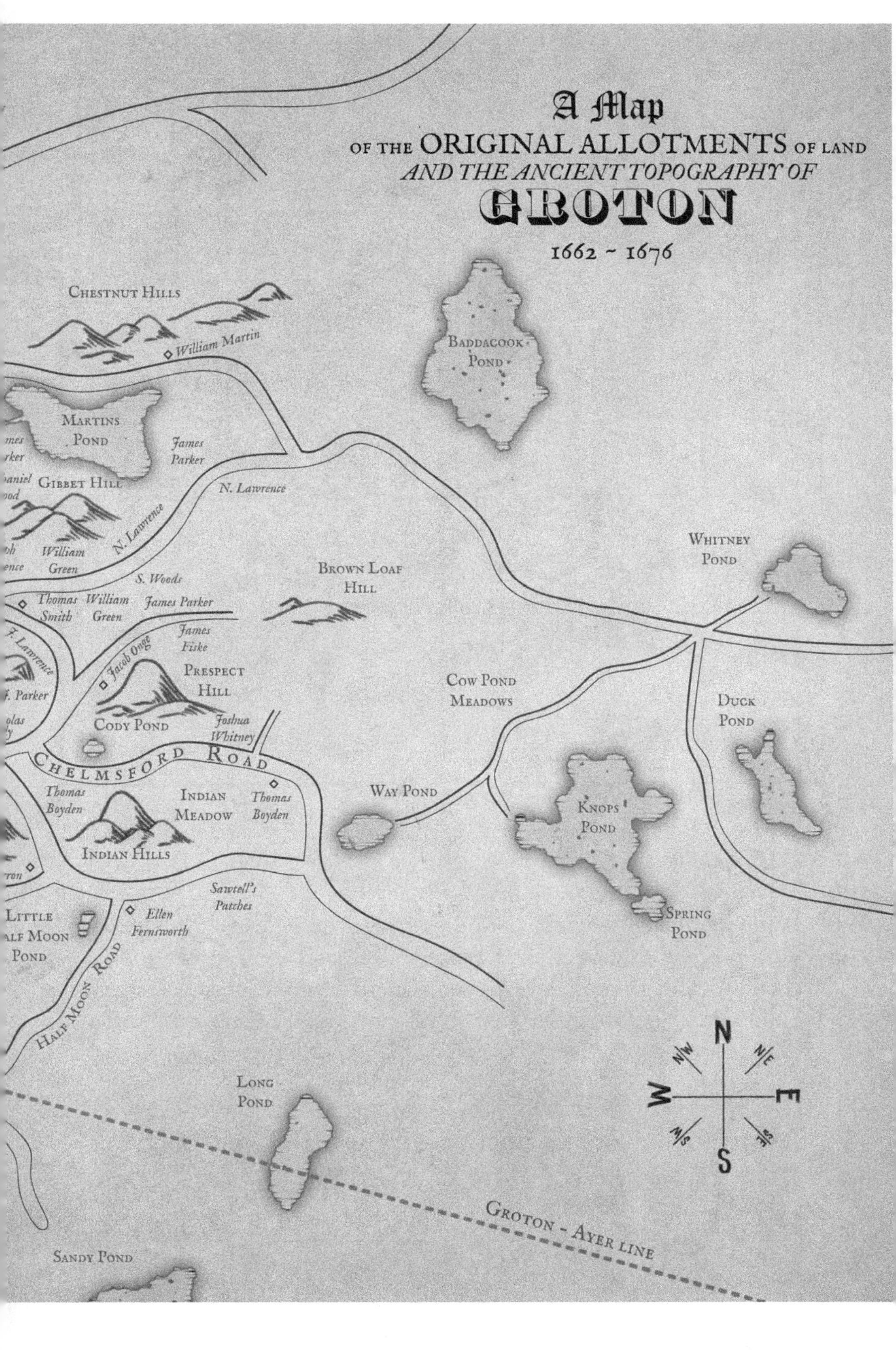

A Map
OF THE ORIGINAL ALLOTMENTS OF LAND
AND THE ANCIENT TOPOGRAPHY OF
GROTON
1662 ~ 1676
Chestnut Hills
William Martin
Baddacook Pond
Martins Pond
James Parker
Gibbet Hill
N. Lawrence
N. Lawrence
William Green
Whitney Pond
S. Woods
Brown Loaf Hill
Thomas Smith
William Green
James Parker
James Fiske
Jacob Onge
Prespect Hill
Cow Pond Meadows
Duck Pond
Cody Pond
Joshua Whitney
Chelmsford Road
Thomas Boyden
Indian Meadow
Thomas Boyden
Way Pond
Knops Pond
Indian Hills
Sawtell's Patches
Ellen Fernsworth
Spring Pond
Half Moon Road
Long Pond
N
N/W
N/E
W
E
S/W
S/E
S
Groton - Ayer line
Sandy Pond

Watertown, Massachusetts in the Seventeenth Century

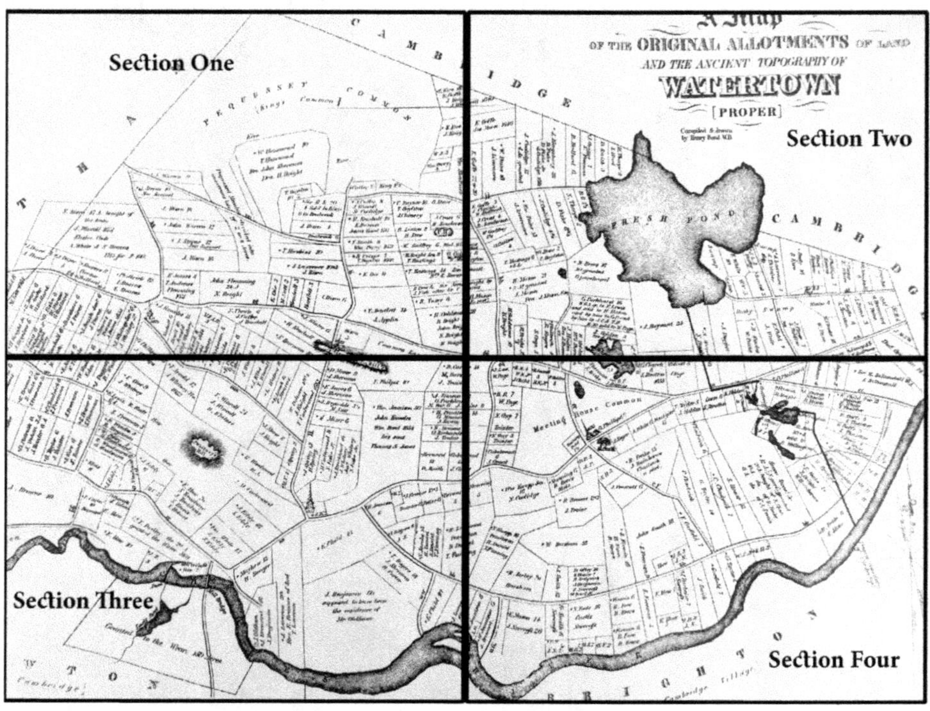

A Map of the Original Allotments of Land and the Ancient Topography of Watertown [Proper], Compiled and drawn by Henry Bond, M.D.

Note: The Sherborn/Shattuck's land is located to the right of the Pequuusset Common at the intersection of streets hh and jj (Hill Street and Road to the Pond). The homestead is perched near the crest of a steep hill labeled P.H., with a view east to the Fresh Pond and across Cambridge to Boston. The meetinghouse is one mile south on Hill Road in the commons.

Watertown Map on Successive Pages in Greater Detail Sections One, Two, Three, and Four

Explanations to the Map

The mark "+" prefixed to a name denotes an original grant. Two or more names on a lot show successive owners of it. The location and relative size of the lots are shown here, but the shape is conjectural because the early records indicate only the bounds and the acreage.

Key to the Streets

aa Mill Street: Cambridge Road: County Road: Mt. Auburn Street.
bb Bank Lane, a part of it now Walnut Street.
cc Water Street, to the landing.
dd Pond Road. ee Busby's Lane.
ef Ancient Road.
ff The way from the meetinghouse to Pastor Sherman's Arlington Street.
gg Back Road: North Road: Country Road from Cambridge to Weston: Belmont St.
hh Hill Street: School Street.
ii Stone Street: Pequusset Road: Common Street.
jj Road to the Pond: Washington Street.
kk Concord Road: Lexington Street.
ll Bowman's Lane: Common Street.
mm Ancient road without a name: Orchard Street.
nn Cartway to the Meadows.
oo Ancient road without a name: Hagar Lane: Warren Street.
pp Boundary between Great Dividends and Small Lots: Warren Street.
qq Way to the Little Plain: Way to Dirty Green: Howard Street.
rr Sudbury Road: County Road: Main Street.
ss Cartway betwixt lots: Way to Beaver Brook: Pleasant Street.
tt Driftway: Gore Street.
uu Driftway to the marsh.
vv Driftway opened to Washington Street in 1708.
ww Crooked Lane.

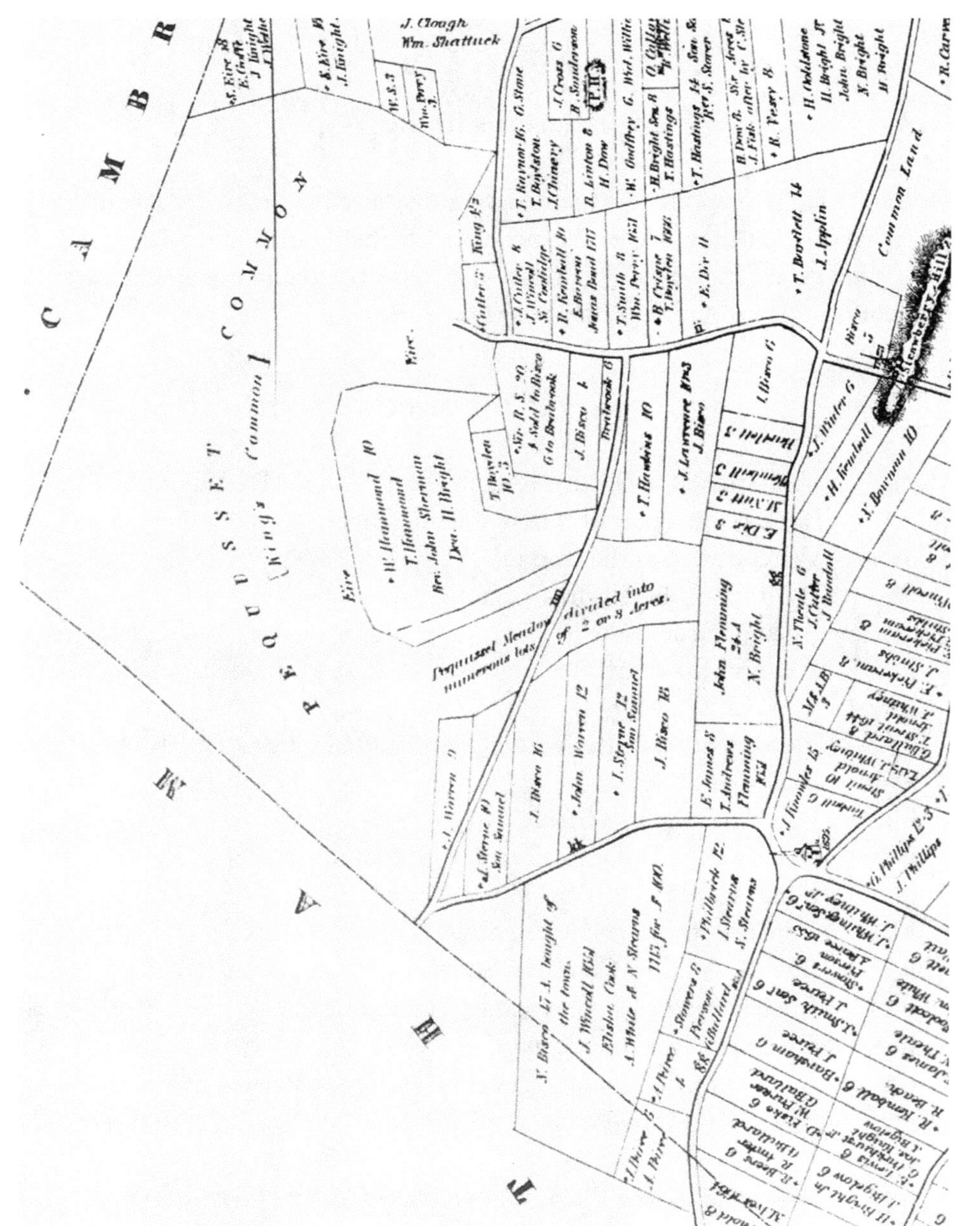

Old Watertown
Section One Detail

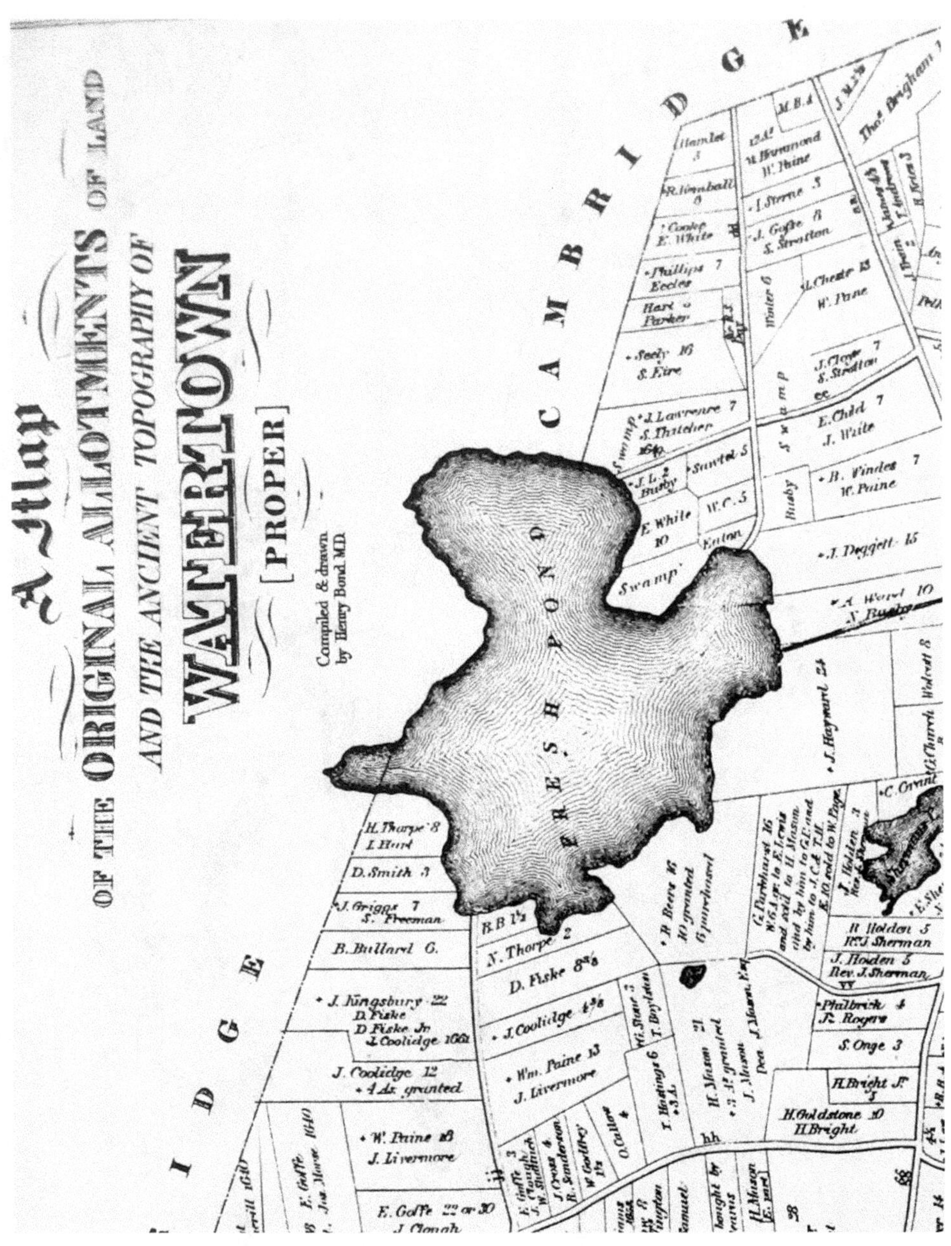

Old Watertown
Section Two Detail

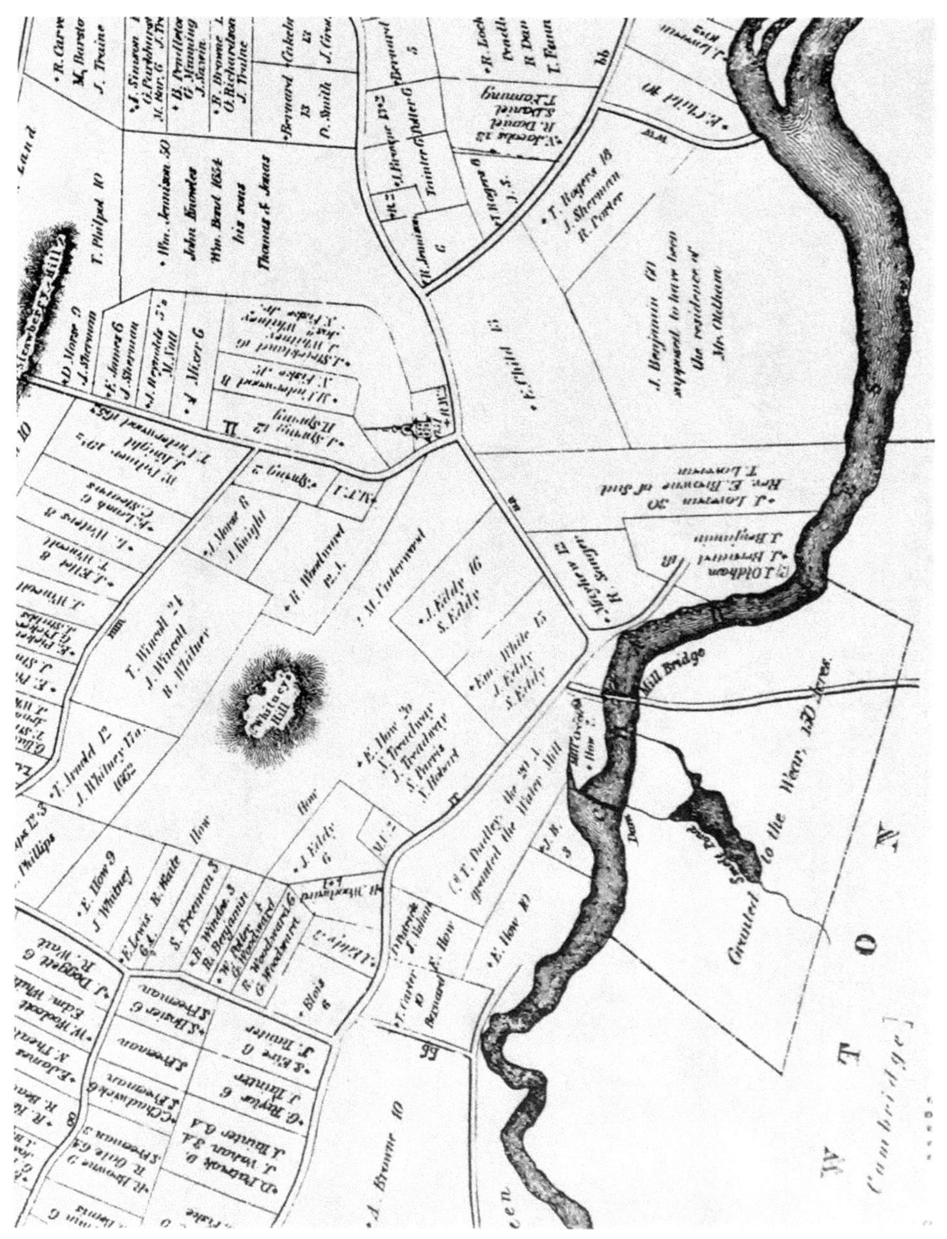

Old Watertown
Section Three Detail

Old Watertown
Section Four Detail

Chapter One

NEAREST NEIGHBORS

Groton, August 1666

Reverend Samuel Willard's most prominent feature was his nose–long, straight, narrow, with a hooked tip. He'd inherited it from his father, Major Simon Willard, veteran of the Pequot War of 1637. The son's nose was all that detracted from an otherwise handsome face. The young minister parted medium brown hair in the middle, and it fell in loose waves to his shoulders. Nature had evenly dealt out a broad forehead, high cheekbones, square jaw, and cleft chin. His wide mouth, which rarely curled in a smile, was belied by deep-set eyes that gave him a demeanor of quizzical kindness. The overall effect was the face of an intelligent and approachable young man. Suzanne Morse was surprised at how young. Accustomed to her previous minister in Watertown, who was older than her father, she found the man standing at her door disturbing. *Are we to seek spiritual counsel from a youth?* she couldn't help thinking.

"Goody Morse," he said, "I had hoped to visit when you first came to Groton, but with the meetinghouse still in progress, I've been about to visit other parishes. Now Abigail and I are back, we want to welcome you to our meetings." He pulled his wife forward, nodding as he spoke. Suzanne knew Abigail Willard as the Watertown minister's daughter, but Abigail had been a girl then, too young for more than a nodding acquaintance. She'd only a year ago married Reverend Willard.

His voice impressed Suzanne, a speech with a midrange resonance that pleased her ears; she'd find later that most of the parish would agree. "Honey tongued," they said of him.

"Welcome, Reverend and Mrs. Willard."

"Oh, please call me Abigail," she said. Abigail smiled genially, blue eyes squinting.

"If you wish," Suzanne said. "I'm so happy to meet you. Joseph is clearing the garden. I will call him immediately. Please, won't you sit?" She gestured to the bench at the rough table, uneven planks stretched across sawhorses. "I'll not be a minute."

Suzanne fit the mold for most of the Sherborn family: medium height, a stocky but well-proportioned, compact frame, and thick, wavy brown hair. Her most distinguishing features, inherited from her mother, were high cheekbones, a broad forehead, and a straight nose that gave her the look of a leader, a trait that she neither felt, nor claimed. Not inclined to assume authority, she found that people made the decision for her.

The day was hot, so she invited her guests to sit, though a mile walk was hardly considered a long distance. "We will, and thank you," Reverend Willard said.

Suzanne called Joseph from the back door. He rose from his work, cutting down yet another tree to clear his allotment, and wiped the sweat from his stinging eyes. "What is it?" he called.

"Reverend Willard has come," she answered.

A tall thin man with lanky limbs, Joseph Morse seemed disjointed in his long stride to the door. He'd bent over his sawing too long and was stiff. His dark curly hair bushed about his head where it had escaped from the leather thong that tied it back. His full sensuous lips curled in a smile involuntarily. Though they'd married four years ago, he still could not see his wife without smiling, which he tried to suppress in front of the most pious. Joseph joined the guests at the table while Suzanne carried the children to their play corner, handing each a crust and scattering toys. "Not a peep," she said, pointing at each one, making eye contact. She returned to her guests.

"Would you like some ale?" Suzanne asked. She had rum and applejack available in jugs, too, but she selfishly guarded these for medicinal purposes; she used alcohol to preserve tinctures.

"Yes," Abigail answered, adding "Can I help?"

"No. It's no trouble at all." Suzanne had a strict protocol when it came to serving guests. She dipped a pitcher into her fermenting barrel to fill it, then set out tankards and filled them. She added a platter of johnnycake for their fare, grateful she'd by chance baked it that morning.

"We've come from Lancaster," the minister said, "and thought we should stop to see you first. We have news that will affect you, Goody Morse."

"Please, call me Suzanne. My true name is Susanna; I was named for my mother and grandmother, but my family know me by Suzanne, and I like it."

The minister nodded. "Suzanne, then. You are a certified midwife, I understand."

"Yes, I worked with Joanna Morton in Watertown; I was apprenticed to her for ten years. Reverend Sherman certified both Joanna and me." She nodded to Abigail. "Your father."

Reverend Willard answered. "We're such a small community we've had to seek doctors in Lancaster or Concord. So, we thank God in His providence he's sent you."

Suzanne pushed the platter of cakes toward the couple. "Please, do have some."

"My father said it was Watertown's loss when you left," Abigail said. "He thinks highly of your midwifery." She stared appreciatively at the molasses brown corn bread, then reached for a square.

Suzanne couldn't help glowing with this praise, though she admonished herself; *It's what I am, not what I do.* She turned to the minister to air more important concerns. "I do want to know if you'll approve my practice in Groton."

"I'm not yet a voting freeman," the minister said, "so Reverend Sherman's approval will stand for now."

"I see." *Not only young, but not a freeman?* she thought.

"But you may expect my support at any rate," he continued. "Today, I mainly have news from Lancaster for you. Scarlet fever has come to Boston. Reverend Rowlandson told me it may spread as the weather cools."

"Thank you for that. I've heard of no illness here; indeed, no one has called on me since we've arrived."

"We must hope for the best." The minister turned to Joseph. "I understand from Suzanne that you are clearing land."

"Yes. I have a small plot cleared, but I need to enlarge it. Suzanne would use up all of our food lot for her medicines."

Suzanne answered her husband's challenge with an explanation. "Joanna Morton, my mentor, gave me seeds for many herbs not native to these shores. I must cultivate them to make my medicines."

Abigail sat forward, suddenly interested. "Of course. You must know so much. I learned a few common cures from my mother but would love knowing more. Could I offer my help? In exchange?"

"I could use help. The children are so young it's difficult to find the time." She nodded her head to the corner where her tow-headed daughters, Suzie, three, and Hester, going on two, continued their play. The thought of them brought with it the anxiety she'd been feeling since they'd begun homesteading in Groton. She turned to the minister. "Reverend, I fear I'm not a fit settler for this wilderness. I'm so anxious for my children because of the natives camped across the river. I hear their drumming and howling late into the night. It's frightening. Do you have word they might be dangerous?"

"I can assure you on that score." The minister smiled. "I've visited the Nashaway village many times. We know their sagamore to be peaceful, and reports say fair, too. Our neighbors are a friendly tribe, and while none are Christian, they worship a peaceful spirit of sorts. They avoid conflicts and stick to their own land, grow corn, beans, and squash, mostly."

"It's hard to believe anyone who howls with such intensity isn't possessed by the devil." Joseph wasn't challenging the minister but did signal he needed more proof of their nature.

"To the contrary, they're singing. Though I agree that harmonies are completely absent, I do admire their passion. They voice life from deep within. They put me in mind of cicadas!" He chuckled. "One day, I saw a cicada shell and was struck with the thought the tiny being had cried with such energy as to empty itself."

Joseph nodded appreciatively. An amateur poet, he immediately understood the offered metaphor. He was beginning to like this young pastor.

The minister continued, "I don't mean to suggest they are not humankind; you understand. The Godless are not devils, as some think. In fact, we could do better to find our own passion for the Lord from such a depth."

"You compare only their singing," Suzanne said. She was happy to hear his assurance. Suzanne's grandparents on her mother's side, who were the first to land in 1620, in Plymouth, had brought her up to believe the Indians were not animals or Devils. Suzanne's grandparents had left England and lived in Holland before they came to the colonies. She often thought that this self-imposed exile in Holland influenced the way they treated the Indians. Their experience made them open to different peoples, different ways. Her idea bore out if she contrasted their behavior to that of later arrivals from England, who thought of Indians as savages. A true granddaughter of Plymouth saints, she found those attitudes offensive.

The minister continued his reassurances. "Our nearest neighbors. A brave in their camp speaks a little English, as does their medicine woman. The tribesmen respect this *pau wau*, or medicine woman. I also heard she healed an English farmer who'd broken his leg. Delivered him safe home with medicine for the pain."

"Is she a midwife?" Suzanne asked, now filled with curiosity about the woman. In Massachusetts, all female healers were midwives.

"Dancing Light? She's a full *midewikwe*, a high-ranking healer. As far as I can tell, she practices halfway between physician and minister, although some think it's witchcraft."

"Dancing Light … northern lights?" Suzanne asked, alert to his comments on the medicine woman. *Don't all healers work with God?* she thought. *And a name that elevates her to His realm, at that.*

"Yes, I believe you are right."

"How lovely," Her curiosity whetted on the medicine woman, she pried him for more information. "What tribe are they?"

"Our Nashaway neighbors are Abenaki, a branch of Algonquians. Not all are peaceful, especially the northerners allied with the French. But Reverend Eliot converted many in our region; Nashobah, to our southeast, is the sixth Indian praying town he established. The other Christian town is a good deal northeast of that.

"How big is Nashobah?"

"It's about half the size of Groton. Ten families, maybe? *Our* neighbors are more numerous!"

Joseph stirred uneasily. "Have you heard of a sachem name of Monoco? He's a Nipmuk sachem?"

The minister nodded. "When we lived in Lancaster, he was our neighbor. We called him One-Eyed John. Reverend Rowlandson there said he's not trustworthy. He's in debt to the English for goods; traders overpriced them, trying to get more land."

"Right," Joseph said. "I've heard that too. And now there's a rumor he's been talking with Metacom, King Philip. Do our neighbors follow him?"

"Judge by their actions. Our sagamore is allied with the Nipmuk in Lancaster. but the sachem Monoco is Penacook, even though he rules from Mount Wachusett, Nipmuk territory. You'll find Nipmuk, Penacook, and Abenaki here; the borders overlap. Our Nashaway have traded and worked with settlers. We do well to treat them in kind. I know there are those who believe that all red men are savages, no better than animals. We can't forget, though, they are capable of reason. Many have converted to the Puritan faith, have formed congregations, live in English houses, and wear English clothes. Their ministers have attended our schools; John Printer even sets printer's type for Bibles. Indians have proved themselves to be Godly men, like ourselves. Though the Abenaki Nashaway are not Christian, their beliefs are not diabolical, merely naïve, animistic. They consider nature sacred and claim animals as brothers!"

"Astounding," Joseph said.

"Bears are sacred, more worshiped than honored it seems. But in the true faith, we know that God has given only mankind grace and reason. Only man can claim a soul and connection to the divine light of heaven. Animals will never be our kin."

At that moment, they heard a hearty call outside the back door: "Suzanne! Joseph!" Seconds later, the door swung open. John Morse stood there, ax in hand. Joseph's uncle John carried a family likeness; he was as thin and tall as Joseph. An elder, though, his hair was a thinning peppery gray; his eyes receded in skin creased with age; and his sunken mouth showed some loss of teeth. "What's this?" he boomed. "Reverend Samuel Willard? Abigail Willard, too? Ah, I've come to the promised land, a lucky man."

Joseph laughed at his uncle's flattery. He sometimes thought that his uncle John carried a continuous celebration with him everywhere he went. He always expressed such exuberance and goodwill.

"Uncle, you can't have followed your nose because we've not put the pot on to boil yet. Was it your ears burning?"

Uncle John had come with his ax to help his nephew clear the woods. Still joking, he held it out at arm's length, like a talisman against an enemy, and began to back through the door. "I can tell when I'm not wanted."

His nephew laughed louder. "Come, sit with us. Reverend Willard is telling of our neighbors, the Nashaway."

John Morse lowered the ax and stood it by the door. "I saw that you have another tree started."

Joseph nodded. "You came just in time. You can help me guide the stump down. I figure two more sections; the tree is gone. Meantime, some ale?"

Suzanne pushed the platter of cakes toward him, noting that he was eyeing it. "Johnnycake, your favorite."

His mouth already watering, he snatched a piece and immediately began savoring it. "The best," he mumbled, crumbs falling in his beard as he swallowed. He continued. "While Samuel and Abigail are here, I've a matter to discuss. I'm selling two acres at the edge of my meadow to raise money for livestock. Joseph what do you say?"

"I'm going to pass it on to Reverend Willard," Joseph said. "I've enough with clearing the homestead for now. What do you say, Reverend?"

"Where is it?" the minister asked.

"I'm on the road to Lancaster. South-east. I'll be selling meadow on the north edge." When John Morse had bought his land allotment from the Lawrence boy ten years before, few had settled in Groton yet. Only Goodmen Lakin, Tinkers, and Martin had built houses, and these were north of town, where the Nod Creek flowed into the Nashua close to the ford. So far from habitation, when the road to upstream Lancaster was no more than a foot trail, Uncle John delayed building several years. Now, the town had sprouted homes on nearly forty land grants. The town council had widened the roads to Boston and Concord and maintained them to allow carts to pass.

"A way from the river, then, below James' Brook?"

"Yes, that's right."

Reverend Willard shook his head. "I want to keep my holdings close to our homestead, so it won't work for me, either."

Joseph brushed crumbs from his place at the table. "Well, I guess that's settled. I'll ask Suzanne's brother tonight. He's talked about buying more land in Groton."

The Minister beamed. "Ah, yes. John. We met him yesterday when we inspected the meetinghouse; he's been laying the floors."

Suzanne nodded. "John is a carpenter. He's staying with us while he works in Groton." The Groton council had granted him five acres two years before, but John had just months before married, and his new wife was resisting the thought of leaving her home for a frontier town. Thus, his promise to occupy and improve the land in the agreed time lapsed, and the Groton councilmen hoped to speed that up. They'd hired him to join the crew building the new meetinghouse.

Reverend Willard turned to his wife, "We hope to see him at services when we start up."

Suzanne's face fell. "We will try our best." Her brother had stubbornly refused to attend services in his home, Watertown, and both he and his wife Ruth had paid fines for non-attendance. She was certain he wouldn't attend Reverend Willard's services either.

Joseph interceded. "It's likely that he'll be leaving as soon as he finishes his work here. His wife has a new-born at home. But we'll let him know you expect him."

Satisfied when her husband so deftly sidestepped the issue of her brother's chief failing, she nodded. "We will." *If the good Reverend should ask John's reasons....* She broke off the thought. Some had accused him of blasphemy.

Joseph stood up and extended his hand to Reverend Willard. "If you don't mind, Uncle and I have to finish a job while the light's still good. We'll talk more, soon. When will meetings begin again?"

"As soon as the roof and second floor are finished," Reverend Willard said. "You tell your brother to grease his heels."

John Morse stood, pocketing another piece of the Johnnycake. "Thanks, Suzanne."

"Soon, then," said Joseph. He reached and shook the minister's hand and left through the back door with John Morse trailing him.

Abigail stood, announcing it was time to go. "Don't forget, now. I would like to help with the herbs."

Suzanne beamed. "I won't, you can be sure."

Chapter Two

THE MESSENGERS

Groton, August 1666

Suzanne could never have predicted what the next day brought: events simply beyond her imagination, especially one that thrived on practical healing. She'd spent the early morning at household chores, skimming cream from the milk pail and adding it to the store she collected to churn butter, inspecting a pile of laundry. She'd need to remove dried dirt and draw grease stains before she could wash it. Though her house was small, newly built, the lingering tangy odor of fresh-cut timbers made it feel clean. Despite the lack of furnishings, Suzanne felt a sense of prosperity; it was the first house she and Joseph owned.

Suzanne was hot, and she'd tied up her skirts for air to circulate. Her girls, dressed only in their shifts, were so restless she gave up working. Finding a shady nook in the yard, she threw down a blanket and sat them there. While they played, she gathered corncobs, pine needles, flowers and grass stems, arraying them in neat piles on the blanket.

"Girls, shall we make dolls today?" She handed each girl a corncob. "We start with the corncobs." Suzanne always held back some corncobs when she stripped the kernels for grinding. Baby Hester thrust her cone into her mouth, first tasting and then examining it at arm's length.

"Momma," Suzie said, "Hester is eating her dolly."

"It won't hurt her," Suzanne said. We'll go ahead and make our dolls. How's that?"

Suzie smiled. "She's too little."

"That's right. Hester's too little. You can make a doll for her. I think she'd like that."

"I can," Suzie said cheerfully.

"So, take the cob like this. First, we're going to make a skirt for her." Suzanne picked up three leaves, catching their stems at the dolls 'waist,' winding the long grass around the waist and bodice, tying it off.

Just then, Hester looked up from her corncob and pointed with a dimpled hand at something behind her mother. Suzanne, turning to look over her shoulder, jumped, startled. Two bare-chested Indians had entered the yard. The first, dressed only in moccasins, a breach clout, an open vest, and adorned with a bear claw neckpiece and two-feather headdress that declared his high status, stepped forward, extending open hands to calm her.

"Good day," he said in clear English. "Are you Goody Morse?"

Shocked, Suzanne sprang to her feet and stepped in front of her daughters to shield them. She was unnerved that they'd approached undetected, but also that he spoke English. He must be the one that Reverend Sherman told me about, she thought. "Yes," she answered. "I am."

The man gestured behind him, pointing to his companion. "Running Fox," he said, "sagamore's son. I am Red Hawk."

Suzanne nodded to respond, instinctively knowing that any English greeting would be inappropriate. She could not offer her hand to a naked man, though she was no stranger to human anatomy as a midwife. She could not ignore that behind her shock was an appreciative eye; they were attractive, though she'd never admit it. Discomfited, she'd never directly addressed an Indian before this. Though Watertown had its share of Indians living nearby, often employed help or traders on the banks of the Charles, a woman, she'd not had commerce with them. Although she traveled more than most women in her duties as a midwife, she'd met few Indian servants. What could they want from me? she asked herself.

She directed her question to Red Hawk: "What do you want?"

"Willard say you have powerful medicine, white medicine. Sagamore's wife has white man's sickness, may die. *Widewikwe* has good red medicine, not white medicine. She asks you bring white medicine. Will you come?"

"Is that Dancing Light? Reverend Willard tells me you have a healer with that name."

He nodded to affirm this. "Great power. *Pau wau.*"

Suzanne didn't hesitate, even when the thought of treating an Indian repelled her. She was the kind of midwife that worked only face-to-face with her patients; she never entrusted any treatment to another. She wouldn't even send medicines. What's more, Dancing Light was a healer, and curiosity overcame all reluctance. *White medicine is God's medicine,* she thought. *Has God chosen me to be His instrument?* The thought humbled her.

"Yes, I'll come. Can you tell me more?"

"Hot." The man put his hand to his forehead and pantomimed shivering. He pointed to his armpit and neck. "Red spots."

Suzanne frowned. She was sorry to hear these classic symptoms for smallpox. Few natives could survive this fever. It had raged through their villages, killing so many they couldn't bury their dead. The first Englishmen to land in Massachusetts had walked through bone yards in some places. Given Reverend Willard's warnings from Lancaster, however, she thought it might be Scarlet Fever.

"Is the spot wet?" She pointed at her armpit. Open weeping sores would spell smallpox, but a dry rash might be scarlet fever instead. Still dangerous, but not nearly so deadly as smallpox.

"No," Red Hawk shook his head.

Relieved, she said, "That's good. Wait here." She picked up Hester, and grabbed Suzie by the hand, walking them to the side of the house where her husband worked.

He stopped when he sensed her presence. "What is it?"

"I'm called. I must go to someone's bedside and must stay the night. I need to go immediately. Can you take them?"

"Is it a delivery?"

"No, an emergency. The Nashaway need white medicine. The Sagamore's wife has been stricken with scarlatina."

"You can't mean it! I'll not allow it. You cannot go."

"Joseph, their medicine woman has taken care of a white man and is intelligent enough to know that she cannot heal a white man's disease. I must go. Making good neighbors is important to Groton. You heard what Reverend Willard said. It's God's will."

Joseph grunted. He was not happy about her decision, but he'd learned he couldn't fight her when she showed such determination. "I'll take good care of them."

"Thank you," she breathed a sigh of relief. "I must find help for the future. I cannot always expect you to take over the children; they are my duties."

"I'll ask around. Maybe Reverend Willard knows of someone we can hire." He followed her back to the house, where she packed towels, tinctures for the nausea and fever, a tea for the sore throat, and salve for the itchy shedding skin into a bag.

"Yes. They'll know someone." She embraced him. "I know how you feel, but I must go; it's my calling."

Joseph released her but said not a word when she bent to kiss Suzie and Hester. She straightened and strode from the house calling, "You mind your father now."

Chapter Three

WHITE MEDICINE

Nashaway Camp, August 1666

The river flowed around a tree downed at the far shore, creating eddies that swirled with debris from an early morning rain, and the sparkling riffles reflected on the undersides of leaves overshadowing the river's edge. Suzanne squinted from the glare. The Indians paddled swiftly across the rain-freshened current, skillfully using the eddies along the shore to maneuver the boat to the landing place. Pockets of water lined a path from the landing up to a rising bank. Two empty birch canoes, paddles stowed carefully in the bows, awaited the next voyagers. Uncle John had explained to Suzanne that empty canoes she saw along the river's edge were not abandoned vessels, there for taking. River traffic flowed freely; everyone had transport as needed in these shared canoes. Indeed, because the rivers penetrated the backwoods in a vast network linked by portages, they were the primary means of cross-country travel.

The sun was still high when the brave jumped from the hull and hauled the canoe to shore. It was a short walk north through a narrow strip of woods to reach their encampment. As many as thirty *wetu* (wickiups, wigwams) dotted the high meadow, and well-trod paths wound through the low, cedar bark huts. They passed by gardens that edged the village. High tassels of corn raised above the riotous jumble of rambling squash vines, where tendrils of beans climbed the cornstalks above them. Suzanne mentally registered the weeds that laced this mass of horticulture.

She couldn't help her critical thoughts: *How do they expect to reap a harvest from this choked garden?* An Englishman would have carefully planted in rows, leaving space for each plant to thrive. Beyond the garden, she could see another field was completely overgrown with weeds nearly waist high. *Had its owner not returned this summer? Why would they waste this meadow?* The more she looked about her, the more she felt they needed her "white medicine."

Scaffolded fire pits displayed a variety of clay pots and baskets; racks used to dry fish. *Outdoor kitchens*, she remarked. While that made sense in the heat of summer, it left their food open to insects, contamination from domestic animals and unsavory decay. A dark-skinned woman cooked at one fire, dressed from the waist down in skins folded artfully around her hips. She wondered that both men and women exhibited no shame, baring their chests. A similarly dressed, half-naked man stripped bark from a flexible wooden branch and stole glimpses in open curiosity at this white woman in their midst. Another woman close by wore a doeskin tunic and leggings. Suzanne was confused by the two costumes. *At least some of the squaws are modest.* A dog lay sleepily in the dirt-floored area, lifting one eyelid as she passed. Suzanne's progress did not pass unnoticed to a small band of children, who trailed them at a distance. While she reproved their immodesty, in the heat she couldn't help but envy their exposure to cooling breezes.

They led her to a large wickiup where a striking woman stood by the door. For one startling minute, Suzanne thought that she was looking into the face of her mentor Joanna. The woman was about Joanna's age, and had the same square-jaw and wide-spaced dark eyes, the handsome, high cheek bones of her friend. There, all likeness ended. The woman, dressed in leggings and a deerskin tunic embroidered with porcupine quills and graced with long fringes, wore a plate-sized ornament around her neck, a turtle shell cleverly made into a pouch. Other animal parts were pinned or tied to her mantle. A foot. A necklace of teeth. *An ear perhaps?* she thought. Even more repulsive, she wore a hood made of an animal's head. *A wolf?* The wide wampum belt signaled that she was important. That confused Suzanne for she'd heard squaws were mostly beasts of burden in their tribes, disrespected by their men. This woman's stance clearly revealed she was nothing of the kind.

The woman strode to meet her at once She extended her hand in white man's style and greeted her in heavily accented English: "Welcome, Suzanne Morse. I am Dancing Light."

The brave who had sought her attendance nudged her and declared, "Medicine woman. Big medicine."

Suzanne was too stunned to do anything but respond politely; her behavior was rote. When she tried to shake her hand, the witch doctor barely touched fingers and withdrew her hand immediately. Suzanne felt dissonant greeting a woman who resembled her friend and mentor but dressed like the devil itself. She muttered, "Pleased to meet you," and stood staring in shock.

Dancing Light spoke respectfully. "Reverend Willard say you are medicine woman. Sagamore's wife has white man's disease." Dancing Light continued, "Great Spirit sends dream. He say white man's sickness needs white man's medicine. I ask you teach me. You are medicine woman, pray to white God."

"I am a midwife, not a doctor."

"Midwife?" Dancing Light asked, uncertain of the meaning.

"A healer, yes." Suzanne realized her mistake. This medicine woman wouldn't understand the status that a doctor carried.

Reassured, Dancing Light continued. "I call Great Spirit, and spirit say I find white medicine, white God heal my sister."

"God willing, I'll do my best."*Ah*, she thought. *Her sister is the sagamore's wife. It's family, not politics.* The silent brave at her side, who she now realized was the son of the ill woman, rudely pushed her forward.

Dancing Light frowned, motioning to Running Fox to stand back. She would have his respect. She bent to pull aside the hide flap over the wickiup door and motioned for her to follow. Once inside, the two braves who'd brought her stood close on each side. It was so dark that she could see nothing for a long minute, but she smelled the disease. *Is it vomit?* she thought. *Feces?* The room was also so hot that she immediately began to sweat. *First things first;* she thought, *we need to breathe!* Gradually, the gloom dispelled, and she could make out the features of the woman who lay on a bed covered with furs. She was clearly related to Dancing Light, though her skin glowed a dark maroon with fever in the heated wikiup.

Suzanne set her bag down beside the bed and bent over her new patient, pressing her hand on her forehead, cheek and upper arm; skin so hot and dry alarmed her. The woman winced, turning her head away from her touch, murmuring with cracked lips. *She's delirious, too,* she thought. The fresh vomit in the bowl beside her contained no food; dry heaves had produced little more than dribbles of body fluids. Drained, she desperately needed water. Suzanne knew that she must work on two problems. She must get the woman's body temperature down. Second, she must work a miracle to get water into her before she died. The first was easy. With a woman too ill to cool in the river, they'd need to carry the river to her. The second was up to God. Her patient simply could not stomach water let alone an herbal remedy at this stage. Suzanne could only wet her mouth with any tincture or tea and pray it was enough.

Dancing Light stood back from the bed, and Suzanne was grateful she was giving her space. Her sister's condition was urgent, and Suzanne took on the mantle of her station at once. She barked out orders, without the respect due her hosts. "Put out that fire," she ordered. "Are there windows? Can you open the wikiup?" she asked Dancing Light.

Dancing Light bristled at first, but then tempered her natural reaction to taking orders from this younger woman. Suzanne waited, speechless, as the shaman shifted attitudes and lifted the bark panels so light shone in and a small breeze began to work its magic.

"Do you have pails, or skins to carry water?" she ventured.

Again, Dancing Light responded to the urgency of Suzanne's tone; her sister was in grave danger. She ordered her nephews, "Bring water from the river. Many bags. Fresh and cold." They left on the run.

Suzanne rummaged in her bag for linens she could use as compresses. There were conflicting views on the role a fever played in sickness. Some believed fever was the illness. Suzanne sided with the ancient wisdom that fever was the body's way of destroying the illness. The body heat was an army defending the sick ones from an evil attack, a belief that Dancing Light clearly shared, given the heat in the wickiup. But Suzanne knew that left unchecked, fever could destroy the host as well. She must bring it under control before it killed her patient.

When the braves returned with the water skins, she had removed the fur robes from the bed. Again, Dancing Light restrained her natural reaction to object, showing disappointment when Suzanne did not extract any medicines from her bag. Instead, Suzanne soaked the linens and wrapped them around her patient's neck and wrists and packed her armpits and groin. Then she fanned her. Suzanne knew the water would function as sweat did to cool her. As the woman's body heat dried the wet cloths, she again soaked them. She then soaked a cloth in the cold-water tea and wrung it so the solution trickled into the sick woman's mouth without causing her to vomit again. By nightfall, her body temperature fell, but she was still too ill to survive. Although her body showed the telltale rash of spotted fever, Suzanne could see the rash would never produce pustules. Relieved, she thought, S*he doesn't have smallpox, thank the Lord.*

Dancing Light left the wickiup when she saw that Suzanne had exhausted her medicine, and she entered a prayer circle by the fire to continue her own work. Later, as she explained to Suzanne, she drummed, calling Great Spirit to their home. She'd little hope her sister would survive and asked the attending spirit to show her sister the way, either way she might choose, the good red road or the spirit way.

Inside the hut, Suzanne sat by the bedside and prayed to her God but with little confidence. Her apprenticeship with Aunt Joanna had started when she was only ten. The midwife, who didn't practice Puritan faith more than the most superficial rituals, hadn't instilled a spiritual understanding of the world in her charge. While Puritans believed that God sent His children disease to punish them for sinning, and only contrition could cure them, Joanna Morton's world was practical. Her knowledge of it was calculated from measures of tinctures and crushed leaves, body temperatures and gushing wombs. Suzanne would have to rely on this most weak connection to her God as she prayed. In the night, augmented drumbeats became her own heartbeat. The Indian chants became more prayer than a devil's howl. Of her own humble words spoken in candlelight, she thought, *are we not praying the same? Inside out, like the cicada?*

By morning, Suzanne understood that Dancing Light was more like herself than even her nearest English neighbors. Dancing Light was a passionate healer. Both women celebrated the miracle that morning wrought. The chief's wife had slept. She could take liquids. She would live.

With her patient in recovery, Suzanne packed up her bag and made ready to cross the river with Red Hawk and Running Fox. She left the salve and cold-water roots; instructing Dancing Light in distilling "tea" should another tribesman become ill, which was likely. Groton might be spared the ravages of this contagious disease because the Indian camp was separated by the river, and the Nashua rarely mixed with the town's people. What's more, the minister's absence had suspended large gatherings; she'd be unlikely to pass it on, though she must take care not to expose her family.

"Steep the roots in cold water for eight days," she explained. "The tea must be sticky to sooth the throat and stomach." A midwife's miracle drug, it would also shrink carbuncles that sometimes appeared in patients with scarlatina.

Dancing Light then left the wickiup and returned with a wampum belt in her hands. "The sagamore thanks you," she said. "*Meeg-witch.* ("thank you")." She handed the wampum belt to Suzanne, who wondered, even as she accepted it, what she could possibly do with it. Wampum was no longer an exchange in the colonies. Once traders had exhausted the beaver and fur pelts, wampum had lost money value. Still, the beauty of the design of the beaded belt fascinated her. She would display it in her house, an eloquent gift.

"Meeg-witch?" Suzanne asked.

Dancing Light nodded yes with a suppressed smile at the corners of her lips and a light in her eyes. Suzanne felt warmly toward her, a feeling inspired as much by a sense of the strangely familiar as by her need for Joanna. Dancing Light and her former mentor were in no way related, but the likeness was remarkable, especially across races. "I would like you to visit any time. Reverend Willard told me that you have healed a broken leg. I would like to know what you use."

Dancing Light flashed the shadow of a smile and nodded. "I teach you. You teach me white medicine." The two women, having agreed to a future meeting, took leave of each other.

Chapter Four

DEVIL'S INVITATION

Groton, September 1666

Some herbs, like comfrey, which grew plentifully everywhere, tolerated the hot summer sun without withering, and remained green all winter. A mild comfrey tea never lost its efficacy, either. One mature leaf boiled in water would relieve head and chest cold symptoms for hours. Others, especially those that were not native to Massachusetts, or rare plants, needed special treatment. Suzanne dedicated one corner of her home to this apothecary. She'd used boards to fence the nook and mark it off-limits for her children. Bundles of drying herbs, cloth bags filled with medicinal roots, leaves, berries, hips, and stems hung from the rafters or sat on shelves out of reach. Today, she stooped to spoon water into wooden flats of shoots that were too tender to survive in the yard. Joanna Morton had sent her the seeds from her own supply, and Suzanne was eager to produce the salve from the mature plants. *I can't remember if I kept the recipe,* she thought. *I'll need to check my notes. Can I plant these now, or do I wait for a week?* She measured the height of a seedling against her thumb, testing a stem. Weak, it bent without springing back. *Better wait.*

"You need another week, I think," Suzanne said to her burgeoning seedlings.

She couldn't help herself. When she went without human company, plants, animals, trees, even furniture took on life, objects for conversation. She had few acquaintances beyond her husband's uncle because the meetinghouse was still under construction. She was about to clean up her mixing bench when she heard a familiar voice through the window.

"Suzanne, Suzanne, are you home?"

Suzanne opened the door, delighted at the visitor standing there: Abigail Willard, the minister's wife. "What a wonderful surprise; come in!"

Abigail handed her half a dozen ears of corn, and Suzanne laid them on the table. "Thank you so much." *I'll roast them in coals for dinner,* she thought. *We love corn right from the cob.* She salivated imagining an ear of it slathered with butter and salted. *I must be hungry.*

"I hope I'm not intruding," Abigail said. "I wasn't sure if you'd be home, but I thought I'd chance it. I know midwives can be busy."

Suzanne laughed. "You need not apologize. You alone have visited. I have yet to meet Groton women. Without the meetinghouse … well, I miss Sunday sermons and companionship. I'm not good by myself. I need people, you see."

Put at ease, Abigail missed no details in her hostess. "I see you've been gardening," she said.

"How did you know?" Suzanne said, startled. *Is she clairvoyant, like my sister?*

Abigail's eyes crinkled in a smile, and she gestured and nodded at Suzanne's hands.

"Oh." Suzanne stared at her own grime-creased knuckles and blackened fingernails. "Of course! You have keen eyes, Abigail."

"Thank you," Abigail said pertly. She had already caught sight of the plants growing in the corner. "Are these the herbs you use for medicine?"

"Yes. Come, I'll show you."

"Thank you. My mother taught me a few. We always kept comfrey and rose hips for colds. With so many children, she needed to know medicines. And she taught me how to make an ointment from camphor, while she could still get it. Mixed with rosemary and bay leaves, it soothes chest congestion."

"Camphor! It's rare in the colonies, precious even." Suzanne refrained from asking Abigail about her brothers and sisters. Everyone knew that Reverend Sherman had sired the largest family in Watertown, well over a dozen children. It struck her that Abigail's mother would have had little time to teach her much with eighteen on hand.

She stared at the profusion of drying herbs hung overhead in awe. "That's what she said. But I know so little." She bent to examine a stew of plants soaking in a wooden trencher. Black and red berries, green twigs, wilted blossoms and blackened leaves floated in the brownish water. "What is this?"

Suzanne showed her a jug labeled with the ingredients. "A tonic. It helps to strengthen the blood and ward off disease." She pointed to the bowl. "See? Rose hips. You recognize them! There's rosemary, milk thistle, comfrey."

"I would love to help you if you could show me more."

"You could help me put these trays out." Suzanne pointed at the flats. "I can't transplant them yet, but I'd like them to get full sunlight in a few days."

Abigail eagerly bent to inspect them. "What are these?"

"Yarrow. I make a salve of the flowers and leaves to treat bruises and bleeding wounds. I have some flowered already. I'll use this second crop for seeds."

"Oh, excellent. Living at the edge of nowhere, it's important if I'm to take care of my family."

Abigail's voice grew tense when she voiced the word "family." Suzanne could not help but notice. It didn't take intuition to guess Abigail had other reasons for coming than learning herbology. At her most discrete, Suzanne asked Abigail, "are you planning on a large family?" *I'll broach the subject,* she thought, *give her an opening.*

"It seems that is the case, planning or not." She blushed. "I couldn't say in front of the menfolk, but I think I'm with child. If mother was here, she would know what to do. But she's not. Can you help me?"

Suzanne smiled, taking both of her hands. *Poor Abigail,* she thought. *I know what it's like to miss a mother. I miss mine, too. And Joanna! With no one to talk to, she must be frightened.* "That's wonderful! Of course, I will help. Yours will be the first Groton baby I deliver. And I can show you some home remedies, too."

Abigail exhaled with a rush of air. "Oh, thank the Lord. I have worried. My monthlies stopped two months ago, and I am sick in the morning."

"You're coming at the right time. I'd like to examine you if it would be all right. I promise I won't touch you anywhere that makes you uncomfortable. Also, I can give you something for the nausea."

"Yes, oh yes. Whatever is necessary."

Suzanne signaled that she should sit on the bench at the table, facing her. As she probed, her hand flat on her belly, pressing gently, Abigail stiffened. Suzanne gently murmured, "I promise I won't hurt you."

Abigail, as though her complaint was more about the invasion of her privacy than about pain, sought to mask her embarrassment. "I spoke to my father about your brother's claim."

Puzzled about this sudden change to a subject of which she knew nothing, Suzanne exclaimed "What claim is that?"

"He did not tell you?"

"Apparently not."

"Oh, I'm sorry. Perhaps I should not have said anything."

Suzanne released her patient and stood. "There. That wasn't so bad, was it? You'll be happy to know that you are pregnant, about ten weeks along. Best of all, everything is as it should be. You are in good health."

Abigail sighed, her shoulders losing the tension. "Thank you."

"I have an herbal tea that can help you with your sickness. It can calm your stomach so that you can keep your breakfast." Suzanne bustled to her pharmacy and reached for the bundle of dried herbs hanging from the rafter. She talked as she worked. "I can't imagine that John would withhold anything from Joseph and me. We are close. I don't think you have overstepped your place in speaking to me. What did he claim?"

"He told my husband what John Ong had told him."

"John Ong. He's the carpenter working with John on the church?"

"Yes. That's the one. He said John Ong saw Jonathan Phillips molesting Mary Daniels. John thought Goodman Ong was afraid to report it and so, took it on himself. I confess that I overheard him tell my husband, but I felt I should tell my father because Jonathan Phillips is a member of the Watertown church, and it's his place to confront the man, not Samuel's."

Suzanne remembered Reverend Sherman, Abigail's father, as a man who stood on the side of justice. He would be obligated to report the charge to the magistrates in Boston.

"Jonathan Phillips? Reverend Phillip's son! How likely is that?" *John will be implicated as a witness,* she thought, her brow creasing with concern. *He's estranged from the church; that can't be good; Jonathan Phillips is the son of the first Watertown minister.*

"I know nothing of his character. Do you?" said Abigail.

"I don't want to cast stones. I am not one to gossip, you understand."

"Of course. We all hear rumors."

"Exactly. I will ask John tonight, to be sure."

Suzanne wrapped the herbs in a cloth and tied it with a stem of hemp. "Here you are. Drink a cup each morning when you wake. That should comfort you."

"Thank you." Abigail took her leave.

That night, when Joseph and John were home for dinner, she excitedly told them the news after they'd said grace. "Today, I had my first patient."

Joseph, who had heard Suzanne fretting about not meeting any Groton women, knew how much it must mean to her. "Good. Is it anyone we know?"

"Yes, Abigail Willard." She was proud that her first birth would be the minister's wife because Reverend Willard would eventually be called to certify her. It was an opportunity to promote her practice.

She sawed off thick slices of ham, added slices of bread, and passed the heaped wooden platter. They would eat a cold meal in the summer heat. The two men folded slices of ham around a slather of mustard and ate without speaking; they followed it with bread and passing a tankard of ale, carefully turning it to drink from the rim at the proper places, hurrying as they greedily eyed the large container of fresh berries and a dish of clotted cream that would end the meal.

John, still testy over an earlier conversation, growled, "She's not your *first*. The *first* was the Devil's sister."

Suzanne swallowed her first reaction and composed an answer. "Dancing Light is a healer, just as I am. You have no right to make judgments of someone you have not met."

"She's an Indian. The only good Indian is a dead Indian."

"I will not have you speaking so in my house," Suzanne exclaimed. "You may keep your opinions to yourself. I think that Captain Beers has poisoned your mind. God will punish you for it."

"Not so. You know I haven't much use for religion, but Reverend Sherman could tell you there are no Christian Indians."

"I don't attend the Watertown church anymore, and Reverend Willard says otherwise."

"True," Joseph said. "He did defend the Nashaway when he came by last week. That's a fact."

"What's more," Suzanne said, "you'll find no authority for those views in the Bible. God never said they were Devils."

"You know I put no store in the scriptures either. I'm not talking godly or ungodly. To me, Indians are animals, as likely to eat the heart of a man as to eat the heart of the animal they have killed. Only animals eat their own."

"You think they are cannibals!" Suzanne said.

"I know they are. It's a known fact if stories I hear are true. I'm only unhappy about you treating one of their kind because I'm worried about you."

"Well, stop worrying. The chief's wife survived, but it wasn't my doing. It was the Lord's providence… to a heathen. There! I've said it. God saved the woman."

"Enough," Joseph said. "You two will never agree. I don't think you should go back to the Indian camp, either."

"I won't need to. I have shown her white medicine. If another becomes ill, she will be able to treat them. It's why she asked for me."

"But you endanger your own? What's done, is done. Let's hear no more of it."

"Fine," Suzanne said, and began to dish out trenchers of berries. She plopped a scoop of cream on each dish, then dribbled it with maple syrup. These she handed around. *I'll catch more flies with honey,* she thought, mumbling her mother's often repeated homily. She swallowed her rancor before she bit into the first tart berry that burst to flavor the cream clot. *Delicious,* she thought.

"I'll be going back to Watertown as soon as I finish the first floor on the meetinghouse. Is there anything you want me to bring back?"

"I'm glad to hear it." Joseph scraped his bowl clean.

"And I. What for?"

"I promised Ruth I'd attend the christening for Mother's baby. You know mother. She's upset that we didn't name our first baby after father. Ruth thinks mother blames her."

"Probably." Suzanne knew that John and Ruth had hurt both of their parents. "I only wish I could be there. Joanna needs help what with the scarlet fever outbreak."

"Are you coming back?" Joseph asked. "I didn't think the meetinghouse was finished yet."

"It's not finished. I'll be coming back, so, I can fill any requests."

Suzanne, impatient to ask the question that burned in her mind, blurted out, "I heard today that you reported the misdeeds of Reverend Phillip's son Jonathan."

"Did you hear that from Abigail? I thought a minister would keep my confidence from common knowledge."

"Abigail overheard your conversation and told her father in Watertown."

John groaned. He'd not fare well in any dealings with Reverend Sherman. "It wasn't anything I witnessed. I was just reporting it for John Ong."

"I understand. It's like you. You *will* serve others but ignore *consequences*."

John huffed. "I'm not alone in that, now, am I sister?"

Suzanne took his point. He stood and yawned, then noticing that Hester had fallen asleep beside the fire, scooped her up and carted her to her bed. He plumped up the straw in her bolster and smoothed out the linens before he covered her with her sheet. It was a warm night, and she might throw it off before the night finished.

"You will make a wonderful father," Suzanne said. "I know we have our differences, but I know your heart, John." She knew at bottom, he thrived on serving others. His view of Indians estranged her, but she excused this fault. Captain Beers had bent the tree, and so it would now grow. Only God's enlightenment could bring him to realize his error.

Little Suzie followed her baby sister, yawning.

"Not without a hug and kiss," Suzanne said.

Dutifully, smiling sheepishly, Suzie crossed the room and hugged her mother, kissing her on the cheek. "Good night mother," she said. Then she turned to hug and kiss her father. "Goodnight father." She fell on her bed without straightening it. "Good night Uncle John."

John excused himself and climbed the stairs to the loft. He'd built the stairway to replace the pegs used to climb to the loft where he now slept. Though he was an extra mouth to feed, Suzanne felt that he had more than repaid his board. John was also company as she made the transition from

Watertown to Groton. He would be up before dawn in the morning, and the long day had exhausted him. Summer days stretched to eighteen hours at the solstice, and even the approach of autumn left scarcely enough time to sleep.

Suzanne could feel Joseph's presence as he scattered the coals in the hearth. When he turned and stood behind her where she sat, she felt his warmth before his hands began caressing her neck and shoulders. His kiss aroused her.

"Yes," she whispered and led him to the four-poster, drawing the drapes closed. They took their mutual delight in one another, though, even now that the days were shortening, it was only at the cost of needed sleep.

That next day, Suzanne sat at the table with pen and ink and wrote to her mother. Later, she gathered sumac from the edge of the common meadow for her father's dyes. John left on horseback for the trip to Watertown.

Chapter Five

THE PROFESSION

Groton, September 1666

Suzanne had not wanted to move a two-day ride away from her home in Watertown. Her husband, Joseph Morse, had insisted when his uncle John, a prominent landowner and selectman in Groton, made him a life-changing offer. He had added to the township's offering of a five-acre land grant, five more acres of his own bottomlands. In Watertown, they'd had to live with Joseph's parents, but in Groton, they'd own a house and farm. What's more, their status in the Groton congregation would be assured when Joseph, the new owner of ten acres, advanced to a voting freeman. Suzanne's first resistance wore away as Joseph spelled out what it would mean for their futures. No longer would she have to bear the slights and barbs of her sister Mary, who had married power and wealth. Suzanne's daughters, little Suzie, three, and Hester, one, would have a place in the newly incorporated village, though she had to admit they'd never have the advantages of Mary's two girls. Last, though Suzanne couldn't imagine working without her mentor Joanna Morton; she would have no competition for her midwife practice. There being no resident physician, Groton's women would sorely need her. It was this that mattered the most. She could be no other than midwife.

So, at the end of July, Joseph, and his brother Jonathan, with Suzanne's brother John, had loaded all her household belongings in a cart to follow the rough road that ended at the Nashua River in Groton. Joseph's uncle John Morse had joined them to unload two bedsteads, a rocking chair, two spinning wheels, a bench, and several trunks filled with miscellaneous implements, linens, and tools at their new house.

After they'd moved the furniture into place, Joseph installed pegs above the mantel and hung two prized rifles next to the peg for a large lantern, one a new flintlock, the other a matchlock. Joseph had trained for combat like all males over sixteen in the Massachusetts colony, where the military alliance in Boston required servicemen to own a regulation combat-ready matchlock musket. Muskets, which had smooth-bore barrels, were more readily reloaded in battle; gunpowder didn't clog them as it did rifled barrels. But he bought rifles because they were more accurate. He used the matchlock rifle for hunting; it had the accuracy and great range but was less sensitive to rain and damp weather than the flintlock. The newly invented flintlock served better in battle though it could misfire if he wasn't rigorous in cleaning it.

Suzanne had then conducted the last ritual. The mantel shelf would hold their library. She'd unwrapped the books from their linen covers and installed them to a place of honor: *The Holy Bible*, Jacob Rueff's *The Expert Midwife*, and the fragile and torn Thomas Raynald's *The Woman's Booke*. Joanna Morton had given the latter to her for finishing her apprenticeship. Her notebooks were indispensable. She recorded recipes for ointments, tinctures, salves, and teas as well as instructions, images, and records of studies with Joanna Morton. To this, she added her husband's most cherished books: a collection of the annual almanac, Milton's *1645 Collection of Poems, Paradise Lost,* and the newly published poems of Massachusetts own Anne Bradstreet. Joseph loved the poetry of Milton, the great defender of The Republic of England, and suffered from pen envy. In winter, he filled thin journals, scratching out his own rhymes with a quill pen by candlelight when his work was done. He longed to add Milton's latest collection published in 1663 to his one-volume acquisition but could not afford it.

The day after John left for Watertown, Suzanne was working in her apothecary, and looked up to find Dancing Light standing silently in her open doorway. She had the impression she'd been standing there for some time.

"Dancing Light," she exclaimed. "You startled me."

Dancing Light was not dressed in her ceremonial clothes. The deerskin dress was simple and draped her tall frame attractively, the quill work adding the interest of art. She was clad in moccasins and chaps to protect her legs. A heavy black braid draped over one shoulder hung nearly to her waist; two feathers tied to it signaled her leadership.

"I come," she said.

Suzanne hurried to the door and gestured to the medicine woman to enter. "A wonderful surprise. Please, come in." Remembering her hospitality, she offered, "Are you thirsty? Can I get you something to eat?"

Dancing Light stepped through the doorway of the front room, which faced a central hearth, and shook her head. "No." She pointed to the two girls playing by the settee. "Your girls?"

"Yes. Suzie is my first; she's three, and Hester is almost two. They are being so good today." Little Suzie smiled up at her mother. Hester stared at the Indian woman.

"Hello Suzie. Hester." Dancing Light nodded to them, then tapped her chest. "My children, old now." She swept her arm as high as her head. "All grown."

"Is Red Hawk your son?"

"Yes," she answered.

"And your husband," Suzanne asked.

Dancing Light shook her head. "No. Spirit take him. Then …." She paused, staring at the flats of dirt. "…better I am *midewikwe* alone. It's good." She pointed at the apothecary.

"Medicines," Suzanne explained. "I am growing medicines." She saw Dancing Light's eyes narrow keenly as she walked to the corner, scanning the chaotic collection. "You grow medicine? You don't gather?"

"Where would I find them? I bring many plants from England. They don't grow here."

"White man's medicine. I like to know."

"These are only seedlings. I have mature plants … grown plants …" She gave up on the words and signaled tall plants with her hands. "Would you like to see the garden?"

Dancing Light nodded but followed Suzanne, still looking over her shoulder at the apothecary.

In the garden, Suzanne pointed to the rows of blooming yarrow she'd planted. "Yarrow. I brought it from England."

Dancing Light nodded. "I know this. Grows in meadows. Flowers we drink; leaves for wounds. Stops blood flow."

"We too," Suzanne said, surprised. "We use it for women's cramps, too." She gripped at her stomach to sign a menstrual cramp.

Dancing Light nodded. Oddly, Dancing Light identified so many of the plants in her garden, Suzanne began to wonder if she needed to explore the nearby fields. Apparently, Joanna was wrong. Many of the plants they brought from England grew here as well. She began to feel grateful for this new friend. Gathering medicines would cut down on her work; she wouldn't have to plant them or tend a garden. Common herbs growing in the wild would also be well established and hearty; native plants made the strongest medicines. "Could you show me where this grows?"

Dancing Light nodded. "I will. Many more." She stooped and patted the dirt. "Our mother gives good medicine." She rattled off a list in her native tongue, that made no sense to Suzanne at all. She watched as the woman ran her hand over a plant, fitting her thumb beneath a blossom that hung limply from lack of water. "Grows in

England, not strong here. Better from our mother." She stood, brushing soil from her hands.

Suzanne had never imagined that an Indian might teach her, a trained midwife, anything. She had thoughtlessly begun to show Dancing Light "white medicine" from a position of authority. When Dancing Light gently corrected her, Suzanne realized that her new-found acquaintance might be her mentor as well. The woods in Massachusetts had much in store if what she'd said was right.

"I would like that," Suzanne said. "We can trade, then. Come. I'll show you white medicine." Suzanne led Dancing Light back into the house and stood before her library on the mantel.

"These are notes from my teacher. I studied with her for ten years. Did you have a teacher?" Suzanne asked.

"Learn my whole life," Dancing Light said. "My father is *midewini*, you say, 'medicine man.' Dead now. He teach me long time." Her voice trailed off. "*Midewikwe* ('medicine woman') learn many snows before healers. Know here." She touched her forehead.

Suzanne was impressed. Apparently, the Indians took medicine as seriously as the English did. She was now sure that this woman had knowledge. She brought out her notebook and opened it to show the Indian woman her notes. "I know here." She tapped the open page.

Dancing Light was impressed by the drawings of an herb, leaves and roots. "It's good," she said. "Draw plant like we do on *mide-wiigwaas*." She handed the notebook to Suzanne. "Remember here is good."

"What is *mide-wiigwaas*?"

Dancing Light returned to the mixing bench to examine more closely a utensil she'd noticed. She lifted the large stone mortar and pestle, testing its heft, then sat it down and moved the pestle in its track. "We make marks for medicine, plant, on birch bark to help us remember."

Suzanne picked up a small box filled with a waxy substance. "You keep notes too. This is yarrow salve," she said, "for wounds, to stop bleeding."

Dancing Light passed her finger across the surface and rubbed it on her skin. "It's good," she said. "*Aamooanbigiw-an*?"

"I don't know your language. I'm sorry," Suzanne said.

Dancing Light began to make a buzzing noise, passing her fist through the air. "*Aamoog-an.*"

"Yes," Suzanne laughed. "Bees. *AaMoog-an*. It's bee's wax. We use it to make a salve."

"*Anbigiw-an*. Salve," Dancing Light repeated. She pointed to the flowers and leaves in the drawing. "I fold on wound." She gestured smearing and then a wrapping motion on her wrist.

"Ah," Suzanne said. "We call that 'poultice.'"

"Pol-tis," Dancing Light repeated.

"You want to see white medicine for spotted fever?" Suzanne pointed to a drawing. "Marsh mallow. I make cold-water syrup from it. Added to tea, it soothes the throat and makes sweat; I fan to cool the fever."

"You not use this for my sister," Dancing Light said. "Why not?"

"Your sister was vomiting when her stomach was empty." Suzanne pantomimed throwing up." Even in a hot room, she had no sweat left in her body. I had to make sweat with water. Then I fanned her."

Dancing Light's eyes lit up. "I see. You treat fire." She held her hand to her forehead.

"Yes. First the fire, we say 'fever.' When she can drink, I give her water. Then, I can give her cold water tea."

"I know this plant. Grow in marsh."

"Yes. My teacher told me that many people will have spotted fever this winter. I can give you more if you need it. In a week, the red rash will peel and itch." Suzanne scratched her arm.

"We have medicine for skin," Dancing Light said. "I make water from *miizhishk-oon* of the bush."

"I'd like to see it."

"We must go, but soon. My people go to hunting land before first snow."

"When will you return, then?"

"We come back when tree sap runs."

Suzanne stared at the floor. *February*, she thought. *That's too long! I will have to give up a day or two from harvest.* "Then, we must meet soon."

The two women ended their exchange on a note of mutual delight. It was clear to Suzanne that she was to have a new friend, the strangest friend she could imagine, this native who danced around fires wearing a wolf's head. Suzanne had only seen a wolf's head nailed to the church wall, a symbol of the Devil. After Dancing Light left, Suzanne carefully noted the Algonquin words for bee's wax, salve, and yarrow. Then she drew a plant with roots, leaves, flowers, berries, and stems, making room for labels for each of the parts. *I must ask her how to say these,* she thought. *If I am to learn from her, I need to know her words. I don't want to make mistakes about medicines!*

When John returned from Watertown, he carried news of the family and a bale of rags for Suzanne's practice. Her father had been generous. Some of the remnants were large enough to sew dresses for her girls and a vest for Joseph. Those discarded patches too small to use as towels in her practice would serve well for quilts. She happily laid the fabrics aside until winter. No time to work with them now, immersed as she was in preserving food.

She found her days filled with drying, pickling, salting meats, and packing their cellar with the root vegetables, berries, and fruit she preserved. They'd moved to Groton in summer, too late to grow much, certainly not grains to sustain them and their animals, but they'd planned to trade for ground meal and grains. She also counted on her midwife practice yielding food; she accepted trades in lieu of money. While the almanac predicted that this winter would be severe, to supply food for the duration of a Massachusetts winter was a challenge in any event.

Everyone's harvest had to stretch for five months. April was dubbed "the starving month" for good reason.

In mid-October, her brother completed his work on the church and moved back to Watertown. Suzanne might have felt deprived at losing John's companionship had it not been for Abigail Willard. Joseph and his Uncle John began spending days away hunting. Long days alone, with only the company of her children, drained Suzanne's energy. One morning, though, Abigail stood at her door accompanied by a young woman she introduced as Martha Crisp. She was not a pretty girl because of an overbite and receding chin, but large and lively brown eyes made her face interesting. Fine brown hair that escaped from her cap and a broad smile spread a careless joy that made her attractive.

When she'd finished with introductions, and Suzanne ushered them to the great room, Abigail continued. "Joseph brought your request to council, and when Richard and I heard about it, we naturally thought of Martha. She'll be perfect for the help you need. She's willing to spend nights if you are called to midwife any birth. What's more, she lives nearby; Goody Crisp is your neighbor to the west."

Suzanne smiled in response to the girl's sunny face. "How old are you, Martha?"

"I'm fifteen, ma'am, and I've always taken care of my little brothers and sisters."

Abigail, who knew Martha's family were needy, promoted her. "Martha is also very knowledgeable about all manner of household tasks, and she'll work for room and board."

"Yes, ma'am. You won't have to learn me, neither. I know I'm small, but I'm stronger than I look."

Suzanne was pleased with the girl's eagerness to be of use. "I think you are big enough to take care of two very wee girls. Would you like to meet them?"

"Yes, ma'am."

"Suzie," Suzanne called. "Bring Hester. I have someone I want you to meet."

Martha beamed when the two girls sidled up to stand behind Suzanne, peering from her skirts. "Hello Hester. Hello Suzie!"

Suzanne pulled curly headed Hester forward. "Say hello to Martha. She's going to be living with us now, and I expect you to mind her the way you mind me."

Though bashful, Hester couldn't check her smile when she peeked at Martha, then quickly stared at the floor and giggled.

"Don't mind Hester. She's shy, but she'll come around," Suzanne said.

Suzie, who took after her mother more, stepped forward and gave Martha a summary head to toe, and spontaneously grinned. Then she turned to look up at her mother for approval. When Suzanne squeezed her shoulder, she squeaked out, "Pleased to meet you."

"Abigail, I can't thank you enough." Suzanne turned to Martha. "Can you start tomorrow? Early?"

Martha breathed a sigh of relief. "Yes, ma'am. First thing."

Chapter Six

PHOSPHORESCENT TRAIL

Groton, October 1666

The morning sun streamed in the front window, lighting a path across the uneven floorboards and the three-legged pan straddling the banked fire, now crusted with remains of oat-porridge breakfast cakes. Suzanne was concocting a salt and dill brine she would use for a pickle barrel; she and Martha had harvested the cucumbers the day before, the girls trailing after them. Suzanne's namesake always wanted to help and had carried as many as she could in her chubby arms. They'd all laughed when she'd dropped more than she managed to carry.

"Martha, taste this and see if it has enough dill."

Martha sucked the finger she swirled in the brine. "I like more dill."

"Then more dill it is." Suzanne threw a handful of stalks into the brew.

"Suzie, Hester, come here!" Martha said. "We're going outside now."

Suzanne noted that the girls had begun to prefer Martha's company to her own. She felt a tinge of jealousy from time to time that she squelched. This could only be a good sign once she started midwifing. There would be times when she was gone overnight, and the children must be comfortable with that.

Suzie skipped with excitement. "Let's play hide and seek."

Just then, Martha stopped in her tracks, staring at the door. She was speechless and threw out both arms to protect the girls behind her.

Suzanne quickly gauged the problem: Dancing Light stood at the threshold. She'd come as she promised. But Martha was so afraid, she was backing away, girls herded behind her. *I never thought to ask her what she knew about the Nashaway*, she thought. *This could be a problem*. She was thankful that Dancing Light was not dressed for ceremony. The only things in her appearance that said Indian were the porcupine decorations on the dress, the feathers, and the fringes.

"Martha, don't be afraid. Dancing Light, this is my help, Martha Crisp. Martha, this is Dancing Light, my friend."

Dancing Light had frozen at the door when she saw the girl. "Pleased to meet you, Martha Crisp," she said in a formal manner.

Martha let down her arms. "And I to meet you." She gathered the girls close to her sides.

"Today is perfect to gather herbs," Dancing Light said to Suzanne. "Will you come?"

Suzanne glanced at the barrel of pickle brine. Still on the trajectory of completing a task she had started, she assessed the invitation, but with little contest. The desire to escape the chores flooded her spirit, and she chafed at them, unruly as her children. "It's a perfect day, isn't it?"

Suzanne's knowledge of nature matched that of any farm girl born in the Massachusetts Bay Colony, but of nature in the larger sense, the wilderness and all it contained, she was ignorant. Suzanne, like her younger sister Mary, took the civil lives of their class in settled Watertown as God's providence. Neither of them would have chosen to pioneer at the edges of their known worlds. Watertown had been Suzanne's Eden, with its paths to the church, schoolhouse, and mill, with its roads to her neighbors and patients. Like all her neighbors, she complained of stinking swamps and tree fall that obstructed roadways; she feared deep forests.

When she'd moved to Groton, all that was familiar was stripped away; she faced an uneasiness she felt in her stomach. The fences were gone, and beyond the one road, virgin forests with their tangles of dank treefall and old growth light-devouring canopy flanked her house on one side. On the other, meadow marshes stretched vivid sunlit profusions of reeds and wildflowers, innocently beautiful to look at, rank and treacherous under foot. Wild animals encroached with no barriers. The frontier served to shrink the natural world for her.

Until her adventure visiting the Indian village across the Nashua River, she'd preferred her domestic sphere. When Dancing Light had visited and offered to show her new sources for herbs, she'd agreed eagerly. She leaped to the ends without reflecting on the obstacles presented by the means. She would have to face her fears, but the prospect still encouraged her.

Now that she had Martha to care for the children, she made her decision quickly. She nodded and turned to her helper. "Martha, Dancing Light and I are going to collect medicines in the forest today. I'll be gone past noon. I want you to feed the girls and make sure they get their naps."

Martha, who had somewhat relaxed, agreed to the task, although she couldn't help staring at Dancing Light and pretending not to stare, by turns.

"Dancing Light is a medicine woman, like a midwife for her people. She's going to show me some of the medicine that she uses."

Martha nodded, taking the girls with her, and Dancing Light made her way to sit on the settee.

"Not wear *them*," Dancing Light said, pointing to Suzanne's shoes. Footwear for women in the colonies was a narrow leather shoe with buckles and raised heel. "Must walk far."

"They are what I have. You will have me barefoot?"

"I bring moccasins." Dancing Light produced the pair of leather slippers from her deerskin pouch.

Suzanne took them from her, handling them as though they were dead animals. "They have no soles."

"They are soft, like earth. Put on; you see."

Suzanne sat on a bench to slip on the leather shoes, noting the fringe and quills that adorned them. She was surprised to find them lined with silky rabbit fur. When she put her foot on the floor, she could feel the floor through the soles. She stepped on an uneven floorboard, and the pain inflicted by the raised edge made her totter. "Ouch. The soles are so thin! Don't your feet hurt?"

"Only here." Dancing Light stamped on the floor to accentuate her claim, then changed the subject. "You need sack."

Suzanne lifted a cloth sack from its hook. "Will this do?"

Dancing Light snapped the cloth to test its strength. "This is good."

From the minute that Suzanne stepped from her doorsill, she realized what Dancing Light had been saying about the moccasins. Her feet reveled, freed of the hard shoe soles. They cleaved to the earth, which was soft under the pliable leather skins. For a moment, she could have sworn that the earth sent a jolt of energy through the soles of her feet up through her legs. She suddenly felt light as a feather. Her walk changed. No longer walking on her heels, she floated onto her toes like a dancer. "They are wonderful."

Dancing Light smiled, and led her, not to their road, but to the edge of the dark forest. There, parting the brush, she revealed a well-marked footpath that led over a low rise. They walked for some time before they passed from the runoff-scrubbed bottomland forest that flanked the Nashua river, and began to climb. The dank air bespoke molds and mildews, and she could make out no details in the gloom of the thick and still-green canopy. She did not breath easily, assailed by her fears. As the path rose, still in thick woods, Suzanne tripped over stones and roots in the path. Accustomed to walking on cleared roads, she hadn't learned to use these natural features as stairs at first. Soon, she learned that to avoid tripping, she must watch where she stepped. Staring at her feet, she began to note the trees and stones were coated with every shade of blue-green lichens. Lacy ferns, glossy ivies, and red berries at the trailside began to excite her sense of beauty. With her senses opening, she could feel the texture of the path change. One minute she was stepping on luxuriously spongy green mosses and, the next, on a smoothly worn boulder or a protruding bark of a tree root. The smell of the forest changed as they climbed from the wet riverside. Deeper breaths, drawn long, calmed her apprehensions of the wild. She described the air later as 'tasting green,' and she began to feel that it caressed her skin, even coddled her. Startling sounds—broken branches, dry rattles of foliage—at first frightened her, but finding only squirrels and chipmunks eased her hypervigilance.

The hills rose steeply, and inside them, the forested slopes opened like halls. From her path, she could view the other side of the valleys through the trees; the contours of the land determined the winding path, glorious where shafts of sunlight pierced the canopy of red and gold leaves. Patches of evergreen trees rose from the banks, their bare trunks like the columns of temples. The green wind shushed in their tops and her moccasin-clad feet registered the silky slip in drifts of fragrant pine needles.

Suzanne began to see that the moccasins were necessary. She could only imagine twisting her ankle on a stone in her old shoes. And the soft suede soles of deerskin clung to boulders. They didn't slip.

By the time that Dancing Light signaled her to stop, she had added stones and lichens to her collecting bag. Dancing Light stopped before one tree and broke off a large halfmoon of lichen. She cradled it in both hands and breathed on it with small puffs. Then she raised it above her head, singing a soft chant.

Suzanne looked at her as though she'd lost her mind.

When she'd finished, Dancing Light turned to her. "This plant is sacred. I sing to spirit, ask spirit to light way." She handed a piece, about the size of her hand, to Suzanne. "Sacred. Big medicine. Light path after dark. You see."

Mystified, Suzanne added the feather-light chunk of lichen to her growing collection.

Dancing Light stopped again at a yellow birch tree with a lump the size of a bunny growing on its side. The black misshapen outgrowth looked diseased to Suzanne, but Dancing Light pulled out her digging stone, and began to hack at the protruding mass. "Medicine," she said. "Strong medicine for winter."

"Are you sure?" Suzanne looked more closely. "It looks like a sick tree to me."

Dancing Light ignored her. "Chaga. I make chaga to drink." She broke the lump in two and gave Suzanne half.

Suzanne added the chaga mushroom to her bag.

As they began to ascend, the forest opened into a clearing. Dancing Light led her across and stopped at a bush. "This is *miizhishk-oon*."

Dancing Light helped her to break off branches, singing softly to the tree as she did so. Stuffing the branch into her bag, Dancing Light explained that boiling the twigs would give her a water that could help itching from insects or peeling skin.

"I use for fever spots." Dancing Light mimed scratching. "You take too. You try next time." She shoved half the twigs into Suzanne's hands. She then pointed out large areas of meadow where plants had died or gone to seed. "Yarrow gone now, but we cut in summer."

Suzanne marveled. The patch of plants covered a large area, more than ten times larger than her whole garden. She would never run out of yarrow, and she was betting that this meadow had other summer blooming herbs she could gather.

As they returned to trace their way back to the forest, Dancing Light knelt beside a plant with glossy round leaves and red berries. "For pain," she said, pointing to her head, patting her jaw. Suzanne took that to mean a headache or a tooth ache. Dancing Light snipped off a leaf, crushed it, and held it up to Suzanne's nose.

"What a wonderful smell."

"Green all winter. In your words, 'winter green.'" She snipped off as many leaves as she could, inviting Suzanne to do the same. "Boil these in water to drink." They returned when the sun had fallen midway in the sky. Dancing Light turned down her offer of refreshments.

"I not see you until spring. We go to winter camp."

"Where is that?"

"Three days." She pointed north. "Good hunt. Sap runs in trees, we come to plant our three sisters: squash, beans, and corn."

I will miss her, Suzanne thought. In truth, she could hardly wait for another day in the woods."May God go with you."

Dancing Light turned to continue her way.

Martha was relieved when Suzanne showed up again. Suzanne laughed to herself. *Did she think I'd be kidnapped or scalped?* She had already forgotten how much the Nashaway Indians had frightened her when she first came to Groton. Setting foot in her house, she realized that she'd forgotten to give back the moccasins. She hoped Dancing Light would not need them.

That night, she emptied her bag and placed mementos on the sill of her window. She carefully drew images of the plants she had gathered and noted the Algonguin names for plant stems (*miizhishk+oon*), flowers (*waabigwan+iin*) and berries (*miinens+an*).

When Joseph returned for a late dinner, she couldn't stop talking. The adventure and companionship ignited an energy he'd not seen in a long time. Suzanne had missed her days with Joanna Morton, and the Indian woman was showing her a new world. She couldn't get over the beauty of the forest. When they'd extinguished the last candle, Suzanne gasped when she saw a faint blue light across the room. She had forgotten Dancing Light's gift, the lichen.

She walked to the window where it sat, emitting a phosphorescent, moonish-blue light in the dark. She could almost believe it *was* a spirit. She touched it lightly, reverently. *So pale! It is magic*, she thought. *An Angel who lights the way of souls lost in the woods? Do I blaspheme?*

Chapter Seven

COMMUNITY AT LAST

Groton, October 1666

Reverend Willard needn't have sent a messenger to announce regular services would begin at their new meetinghouse the next Sunday; rumors ran faster. When he threw open the doors of the meetinghouse on the first Sunday, Suzanne and Joseph followed the line of people shuffling into the bright interior, herded Hester and Suzie before them. She nodded to Martha, who had the day free to attend church with her family; however, she noted that Goody Crisp, Martha's mother, avoided her greeting and gave her a cold shoulder. It wasn't a good sign. The community expected everyone to attend the Sunday sermon. Now that Reverend Willard had restored regular services, it was the law. Suzanne could not afford enemies in Groton. Not on the Sabbath. It didn't take long for her to figure out the cause. Martha must have told her mother about Dancing Light. If Goody Crisp hated Indians as much as her brother John did ... her heart sank. *I will need to talk to her,* Suzanne thought. *May be Reverend Willard can help.*

The aisle down the center of the meeting house showed their muddy prints the more because the wood was new. The church smelled, too, of vinegary sawn lumber and iron nails. Three windows, left and right, brightened the room, and the morning sun lit the men's pews on the east side. They followed greeters, who had been posted to help them find their places. The gallery pews at the front were for the wealthy. Suzanne had not met anyone who might sit there, though she'd heard Uncle John speak respectfully of Richard Blood, James Parker, and William Longley.

The six rows of general seating for men and boys over sixteen flanked the left, and six for women and children on the right. Joseph joined the men and Suzanne pushed Hester and Suzie ahead of her, motioning them into their pew. She fluffed out her skirt as she sat, wriggling into her seat with happy relief that the plank pews had high backs. She had been apprehensive that they would be forced to sit on planks, as was the case for many frontier communities. *But not in Groton*, she thought. The Town Council had voted that each family should pay for its own seats. Not only did their pews have backs, but racks for hymnals.

Notwithstanding the cold greeting by Martha Crisp's mother, she was impressed with the friendliness of this congregation. Smiles and greetings, covert laughter, and a hum of conversation spread through the crowd, and with much stamping, nestling, and shushing, the people settled for the first sermon in their new meeting house.

Reverend Willard ascended the pulpit, which was placed high so that his voice could reach everyone. His white collar was so bright that it reflected upward, at once disguising his prominent nose and revealing his handsome face. He cleared his throat and read from the Book of Haggai.

Suzanne knew this story because she had heard it from Reverend Sherman in Watertown. The short book spoke to the duty of a professing people to keep the covenant with an omnipotent and sometimes inscrutable God. The Prophet Haggai answers the Lord's calling and tells them the Lord promises His people that He will reverse their bad fortunes if they rebuild his house of worship. When they do, their God rewards them, but not without warning. If they break their covenant, they will lose his goodwill. Reverend Sherman had focused on that last element of the story. If God was to reward their Puritan congregation, they must not suffer sin in their midst.

She nodded when Willard read the two verses from Haggai. *How fitting for our dedication today*, she thought. *We have a new place of worship, too, and he's telling us we will prosper.* He dashed her expectations when he skipped to passages from the Book of Jeremiah. She knew the entire book was about Jerusalem falling, with the most alarming descriptions! *We're in for a fiery sermon*, she thought. She smoothed Hester's hair when she laid her head in her lap. Suzie was already fast asleep, slumped at her side.

Suzanne followed only half of the sermon, which lasted for two hours. The first two doctrines he discussed–God's leniency and the difference between expedient and true repentance–were so familiar to her that she drifted into her own thoughts. She was dismayed when the greeter had to dangle the feather in her face to wake her.

She jerked awake to hear the last of what the minister said: "… when men speak of their privileges, and rest on them, they deceive their own selves." He preached the opposite of Reverend Sherman, who so often said their prosperity was a sign of divine favor. That brought her to full attention.

Reverend Willard raised his voice and pronounced: "They thought if they did but come to Gods house, and perform a few ceremonies there, offer sacrifices, they might take the liberty to steal, murder, swear, and what not. Hypocritical service is no better than robbery, pretended service to God."

This last struck home with her because she'd been guilty of backsliding while the meetinghouse was under construction. Not a spiritual person, her worship had dwindled to Reverend Willard's home visits and bible study with Joseph on Sunday mornings (well, more of the psalms than of the good book). She'd ignored God's commands that forbade work on the Sabbath. The New Testament excused work on Sundays for emergencies, but she'd worked household tasks into her Sunday. If Reverend Willard thought the meetinghouse was an empty symbol of their faith, God would, too.

Reverend Willard ended his sermon for the lunch break, asking them to read Chapters 1 and 2 in the Book of Jeremiah before the men discussed the sermon for the day.

Despite the cold of late October, the sun brought enough warmth to the closed meetinghouse to heat the room. Suzanne quickly settled her girls, who were fidgeting in their seats, hungry. She brought out a sandwich for Suzie and spoon-fed Hester a mashed sweet potato. Her baby seemed almost precocious if she compared her to her sister Suzie, who had nursed more than a year. Hester had eagerly switched to solid foods and was too restless to nurse by the end of her first year.

"Slowly," Suzanne complained to Suzie. "Chew your food before you swallow it." Her words were to no benefit, and the white-haired blue-eyed three-year-old smiled angelically, continuing to gobble her food. When she climbed down from the pew, she pushed the half-eaten crust of bread away.

As Suzanne wrapped up the remains, she could see Martha headed to her pew to help. "Martha," she said, "Could you take them?" Martha immediately grabbed Suzie, who began to run from her.

"No, you don't." Martha laughed and grabbed the squealing girl. Suzanne lifted Hester to stand her on the floor. "She's eaten, but she's wet herself."

Abigail waved from the aisle. "Suzanne, Goody Roberts and Goody Greene are anxious to meet you." Goody Roberts smiled from a ruddy, good-natured face with naturally red lips. Already short, her girth made her appear more so. Suzanne was sure Goody Roberts was in the last months of pregnancy. Goody Greene was as young as Abigail, of medium height, with dark brown hair pulled back tightly under her cap. Wide-spaced eyes under arched brows arrested onlookers; she had beauty.

"Wait," Suzanne said, "and I'll join you." She bent and shook her finger at Suzie. "You mind Martha, now." Then she made her way to the aisle.

"Adelaide and Anna," Abigail Willard said. "I'd like you to meet Suzanne Morse. She's my new midwife. Suzanne, meet Adelaide Roberts and Anna Greene. Adelaide lives close by you, south, on the Lancaster road."

Suzanne was aware of the plantations on their road but hadn't yet visited them. She and Joseph had worked hard to get settled before winter set in, feeling no time to spare.

Adelaide pulled Anna forward. "We are so happy to meet you. Abigail has been telling us what a wonderful midwife you are to her. As you can see, I'm only two months away from a birthing. Having you practically next door! This is great fortune! I've had to visit Lancaster for any women troubles."

"Yes," Anna agreed. "The women in Groton have no one. Boston assigned Dr. Knox to the soldiers regimented here, but he's a Chirurgeon, of little help to women, and admits it. He sends us to Lancaster or Concord."

"While I'm still getting around," Adelaide said, "I'd like to come and see you. Would that be all right with you?"

"Yes, of course," Suzanne said. "I've only seen Abigail so far, so I am rarely gone. Please do come."

"Your girls are the same age as mine," Anna said. "Two are always into mischief. I don't know how Adelaide does it."

"How many children do you have?" Suzanne asked Adelaide.

"I have seven." Adelaide turned to Anna. "Anna, when your girls are older, they can take care of the younger ones. Big families take care of themselves."

She addressed Suzanna. "I am no stranger to labor, and I'm always available to help when others are giving birth. Experience counts for something."

"Indeed! Experience is the best teacher of all. Then I can count on you?"

"And I," Anna said. "I was hoping that you could come to look at my three-year-old. She has a strange rash that I cannot get rid of, try as I might."

"Yes, I can make house visits, thanks to Abigail." Suzanne nodded to Abigail. "Abigail found Martha Crisp for me, and she comes to take care of the children when I must work."

Two more women pushed their way forward in the aisle to get a glimpse of Suzanne. Word had gotten around town, and the women were eager to make her acquaintance. A tall, middle-aged woman shouldered her way into the circle and extended a gloved hand. "Hello, I'm Goody Tarball. You can call me Ann. We've all heard about you and are eager to meet you. I live down the road from you, too."

She extended her hand warmly to Ann Tarball, and said: "Then, Ann it is. Pleased to meet you, Ann."

"I don't stand much on formalities," Ann Tarball said. "Here in Groton, we're all one family. May I call you Suzanne?"

Behind her stood Mary Parker, a brown-haired, blue-eyed woman who Suzanne recognized; her Uncle John had introduced her when she'd first come to Groton.

Mary Parker, Suzanne thought. *She's married to the son of the wealthiest man in Groton.* Mary Parker opened her mouth to speak, but just then, the Elder, Ann's husband, Thomas Tarball, called the meeting to order. "Yes," Suzanne said hastily. "We'll talk later."

Once the women sat in their pews, the Elder opened his Bible to the passage he'd read aloud. But before they would begin their discussion, he aired the announcements.

"Today, our first day in our new meetinghouse, I want to welcome our newest homesteaders. Joseph Morse and his wife Suzanne. Also, the ladies tell me that Goody Morse is a midwife who comes highly recommended by Reverend Sherman in Watertown. I know it's caused much excitement at our house. Goodman Joseph and Goody Suzanne, will you please stand?"

Murmurs and shouts of welcome circled the room as Joseph and Suzanna stood. The meeting commenced for the afternoon. At sundown, the Sabbath ended.

Chapter Eight

SKUNK CABBAGE

Groton, February 1667

As the almanac had predicted, the winter of 1666-67 was the worst winter in decades. Daily through November and December two or three inches of snow fell, drifting up to five feet deep where the wind swept across meadows into roadways. A cruel Nor'easter took out trees that blocked roads and damaged houses, and reports came from Boston the monstrous storm lifted storm tides that flooded the coastal towns from north to south.

Martha Crisp, who had turned out to be a responsible fifteen-year-old, stayed with the children whenever Suzanne had to make a house call, but when winter came, moved into the Morses' house. When the snow was too deep to return home, Suzanne often spent the night with her patrons. When she made calls to distant north or east homesteads in Groton, which always meant an overnight stay, people who lived nearby would come with their complaints. She turned her host's dwellings into temporary infirmaries. While the community relied on Dr. Knox for conditions that needed bleedings or amputations, Suzanne was the healer of choice. She learned to pack various medicines to cover all manner of common winter maladies—chest colds were universal. Chilblains and frostbite, rashes, wounds, whooping cough, and measles were common. In the elderly she found arthritis, apoplexy and rheumatism; in women: pregnancy, births, lactation, and menstrual problems.

The town had been spared more serious plagues, such as smallpox. However, Suzanne had four cases of scarlet fever after she'd treated the sachem's wife. One of these had been Martha Crisp's baby sister, and afterwards, Martha's mother was more cordial to Suzanne. She thought that Mary Crisp's change was due as much to Dancing Light's absence as her daughter's recovery from scarlet fever. But Suzanne didn't care which; Martha's ingratiated mother now treated the Morses like family, and the Morses adopted Martha Crisp, in turn.

As the winter wore on, with the added mouth to feed, their supplies dwindled fast. They were on the last of their oats, and a few wrinkled apples, potatoes, and carrots remained in their cellar. They were lucky if the hens produced more than three eggs in a week. The cow, too, began malingering in the fall, when Joseph was still putting her to pasture each day. Now, Bessie gave less milk, despite being a good age for a milk cow. Often, women paid for Suzanne's services with a cabbage or turnips, sometimes a rabbit or slab of frozen venison, a sack of grain. Joseph was still hunting, of course, but even the turkeys were hard to find by February. She had already begun to ration their meals, making it difficult to tell whether the children fussed from hunger or another complaint.

One morning, Hester began to whine, despite Martha's attention. "Hester is teething again," Martha said. "She's been fussing. Do you have something for her?"

"Yes." Suzanne thought she looked flushed and tested her forehead. "How do you feel sweetheart?"

Hester whimpered.

"She's a little warm," she said to Martha. "Dancing Light gave me a tincture you can use."

She strode to her medicine corner and rummaged through a collection of containers until she found the willow sap. "You want one drop in a spoonful of water. It's bitter, so you might add a drop of maple syrup. It will dull the pain a few hours. Give her another spoonful when she starts fussing again."

The family had finished their lunch—a thin bone broth with a few dried vegetables, minced to stretch them out–when she heard shouting at the front door.

Suzanne was sure it was the oldest Roberts boy. She nodded to Joseph. "I'll be needing the horse," she said. Adelaide Roberts was due to deliver her baby in February, and Suzanne had already prepared her bag with supplies she would use for the birth. Joseph followed her to the door and opened it to swirling snow. Jimmy Roberts stamped his feet and pounded his hands on his sides. Clouds of steam poured from his mouth as he spoke.

"Mother's having her baby," he said, "and she wants you to come."

"Come in here," Suzanne said. "You're freezing." She caught his upper arm and pulled him across the threshold.

"Yes, ma'am," he said. "It's really cold!" He bent to remove his snowshoes.

"You came here on foot!" she exclaimed. "Where is your horse?"

"Mother said I'd be here in the time it took to saddle up," Jimmy said.

"She might be right at that," Joseph said. "I'll saddle the mare. You can ride double."

"Come, let's get you something warm to drink before you have frostbite," Suzanne said.

She led him to the great room where Martha worked with Suzie and Hester at her side. Jimmy stood by the fireside warming his hands, which were swollen and burning from the cold, while Suzanna poured a hot herbal tea into a mug. "Here you are," she said, handing him the tankard. "I'll just be a few minutes; I have everything ready to go."

"Thank you, Ma'am," he said. Jimmy ducked his head shyly when he saw Martha and held the hot mug in both hands, as much to shield his stealthy glances as to thaw his aching fingers. The mug was inadequate, however, and Martha couldn't help but notice his attention. She blushed.

Suzanne collected her bag and then joined Martha, stopping on the threshold when she felt, rather than saw, the attraction between the two youngsters. She noted the scene for future action and strode into the room, resetting her priority. *First things first*, she chanted to herself. "Martha, you have the children tonight. I'll be at the Roberts' house for a day, maybe two. Jimmy will let you know if it will be longer. Is there anything you need before I go?"

Martha, suddenly shy, shook her head.

"Come, Jimmy," Suzanne said sliding on her cape, hat, and scarf. "We need to hurry." She stopped to get her snowshoes, which she never was without in deep snow, even when she rode horseback.

Ann Tarball, who lived directly across the Lancaster Road from Adelaide Roberts, had already arrived and was collecting an assortment of containers to boil water when they arrived.

"Mary Parker is coming, too," Ann said. "I stopped at her house before I came. She had to prepare food for the family before she could leave."

"I hope she can come," Suzanne said. "The road is nearly impassable now! The drifts are so deep." Suzanne was grateful that all Adelaide's closest neighbors were able to pitch in. It would make the birth easier for the family as well as shorten her stay. Of course, she'd have preferred that Abigail Willard had come, but that was out of the question. She was in her eighth month of pregnancy and needed to stay at home.

Adelaide's oldest daughter, Deborah, who was two years younger than Jimmy, tried to corral her younger brothers and sisters, who clustered about the visitors. All were grimy after weeks in a closed house with wood burning fireplaces. The three-year-old, who clung to his sister's skirt like a burr, looked like a painted Indian where mucus ran down his upper lip and streaked his grimy chin. Another girl, around five, standing near, also had a glassy flow from her nose. Suzanne could hear from their coughs and sneezes that all seven had colds. She'd come prepared for this.

Suzanne called Deborah to her side. "I'll need your help in keeping the children quiet. But first, take this napkin and have them blow their noses. And I have tea to make them more comfortable. Come, I'll show you." She led Deborah to the fireside, where she instructed her on how to make a strong tea from comfrey leaves. Deborah was charged with making each child drink a cup and helping the youngest blow their noses. Suzanne knew their immediate relief from runny noses and coughing would only last a few hours, but it would give them enough comfort for naps. Ann Tarball helped Deborah lead the youngest to bed upstairs.

The birth went easily as Adelaide had given birth seven times before. This baby, a little girl, was born underweight at the end of winter, but that made her labor go quickly. Mary Parker joined them after an hour, and the three women stayed up late in the night visiting. Suzanne's midwife service was spread thinly over the community, so her overnight exchanges often became teaching opportunities. Frontier women needed to know quick remedies; often they were the first to respond to injuries and the last to retire from tending the sick.

Suzanne gratefully accepted a sack of Adelaide's dwindling supply of potatoes and carrots as payments for the delivery. Adelaide explained that with seven children, she always put away twice the amount she thought she would need each harvest and had enough to spare. Suzanne rode home the next day, leaving Ann, who volunteered to attend to Adelaide's lying in.

One sunny day a few weeks later, she again heard the drums and chants of her Indian neighbors. The Nashua had returned to their summer camp as Dancing Light had said they would. A week later, Dancing Light showed up at her door.

Drifts of yellow crusted snow still dotted the yard. Thin layers of frozen mud coated the remaining ragged patches of melting snow; the earth was hard beneath the spongy surface. It was still too early for the geese migrating north, but the longer days were promising spring.

"Boo shoo," Dancing Light called. "Suzanne?"

Suzanne went to the door immediately, shielding her friend from Martha's sight. "Kwey! ('welcome')," she exclaimed. "So happy you're back."

Dancing Light tilted her head, with a hint of a smile. "I come show you medicine," she said. "You come?"

"In this mess?" Suzanne exclaimed. "The snow's melting. Mud everywhere."

Dancing Light stamped her foot several times on the hard ground. "Not today. Cold. No mud. Swamp is ice. Come. I gather skunk cabbage."

All Suzanne knew about skunk cabbage was that its name described its smell. The swamps were full of this aromatic plant that smelled like rotting meat, but she didn't know it could be used for medicine. Her curiosity was roused. "Yes, I can," she said. She glanced at her friend's feet to see what she wore in winter. Dancing Light wore moccasins with fur interiors and had turned up the high tops and stuffed them with straw; she carried her snowshoes on her back. *I wonder how deerskin does on ice?* she thought."Do we still need snowshoes?" Suzanne was surprised her friend carried them, because the temporary thaw had melted most of the snow.

"Some drifts deep. Not melt."

Suzanne followed her friend's example and stuffed her moccasins with straw, but she didn't put them on. "I almost forgot. I have something for you." Suzanne had knitted a pair of wool stockings for her friend and went to retrieve them from her bedroom.

"These are to keep feet warm." Suzanne handed the stockings to her friend. "Wool is warm even when it's wet."

Dancing Light fingered the stocking. "Wool."

"From sheep." Suzanne pointed to her spinning wheels, beside which hung skeins of wool.

"I'll show you." Suzanne stripped off her shoes and showed her the proper way to pull them on and tie them at the knee. Then she pulled the moccasins over the top.

Dancing Light sat and changed her footwear. When she pulled on the woolen stockings, she smiled, and ran her hands up and down her legs. "It's good."

Suzanne reveled in the sunlight, which warmed her even in the chill wind. Dancing Light led her through the woods on a trail they'd followed before, now nearly unrecognizable. The leafless trees let in light where shade had obscured the ground's features before. Now, the tree roots, bared of all moss and lichen, were easily crossed without stumbling or tripping. The entire forest had turned a dull, dunnish gray, contrasting little with the leaves that covered the forest floor. In bright sunlight, Suzanne could readily distinguish the bark of different species, though she knew only the maples by name. Her knowledge of nature was bounded by its use to her; colonists loved maple syrup and thus learned to identify sugar maples easily. They had walked for more than an hour before Suzanne noted the air began to stink. When they reached the edge of the swamp, she saw the cause: a wide swath of yellow blooms stretched before her. At her feet, she noted that a single bright yellow sheath, nearly six inches tall, had melted the ice around it. From the spathe poked a four-inch green finger that looked like it might generate seeds. The entire swamp was still frozen, but the flowers had bloomed anyway.

Suzanne was astounded. "The ice. How can they bloom?"

Dancing Light bent over a plant and motioned her to step closer. She thrust one finger into the sheath and removed it, then gestured to her to follow. "Spirit."

Suzanne was even more astonished. The interior of the plant was nearly as warm as a summer day. Clearly the plant was making heat enough to melt ice. The close look also revealed a swarm of insects inside the sheath. *Do they breed here,* she thought?

Dancing Light pointed to a group of ragged plants, their flowers and leaves obviously chewed up. "Bears eat in spring. Mother hungry. Bear medicine for bear babies. Teach Abenaki."

"You eat skunk cabbage too?" Suzanne asked.

Dancing Light shook her head. "Leaves burn mouth. When no food, *very* hungry, woman boil yellow stem to eat." She chuckled. "*Very* hungry."

Suzanne laughed, not understanding how often that occurred in her friend's band. She felt embarrassed to admit that her own family was needy, and she wanted to try them. "Will you gather stems now?"

Dancing Light again shook her head. "I show you powerful medicine. First, we dig roots. Not easy. Skunk cabbage powerful spirit. Melt ice, melt here." She pounded her chest and coughed to communicate chest congestion and followed the gesture with mimicking a whooping cough.

Suzanne caught her meaning: she was showing bronchial conditions and whooping cough. She kept silent about gathering the stems. Paying full attention now, she watched Dancing Light extract a digging stick from her sack and begin to attack the root of the plant before her. "Great power. Strong root. Deep." Suzanne couldn't help wondering how she planned to dig in the frozen ground, but soon saw the entire plant, roots, and stems, had melted it. Dancing Light dug to expose the root, working it from all sides until she had a hole more than a foot deep. She extracted a large woody rhizome six inches thick from the thawed, heated soil, brushed it off, and stowed it in her sack. Then she repeated it with a smaller plant and handed the root to Suzanne.

"You keep. I show you medicine."

Suzanne didn't budge but stood staring at her feet, too embarrassed to ask but knowing she needed to speak. Dancing Light stood with the root in hand, puzzled when Suzanne did not respond. "What?"

"We are hungry." She passed her hand across her stomach. "*Very* hungry. I need to gather the stems." She couldn't look Dancing Light in the face.

Dancing Light caught her hand and pressed the Skunk Cabbage root into it. "Take this." She stared at Suzanne, waiting for her to speak. When Suzanne was silent, Dancing Light relaxed and turned to lead the way. Only a few plants had matured leaves, but they worked their way across the ice, cutting stems, dropping them in Suzanne's bag. "Boil until water gone. Long time."

When the two women returned to Suzanne's house, Dancing Light showed Suzanne how to prepare the roots for medical use, washing, cutting, boiling, and storing the strong syrup to mix.

While the root was boiling, Dancing Light again stressed how strong this plant was. "Strong medicine. One drop, two in one day."

When Dancing Light left to return to her camp across the river, Suzanne couldn't help wondering how she could ever repay her. The stockings were only a beginning; Dancing Light was generous in a way that made trading impossible. At dusk, she heard a noise at the front door, as if someone had thrown something. Opening the door, she found a rabbit skinned and gutted hung from the tree beside her house. No one was in sight. Gratitude swelled, stiffening her throat, moistening her eyes.

Chapter Nine

FRIENDS AND MENTORS

Groton, October 1667

The summer passed, beginning to end, with growing food, preserving food, and storing it. Suzanne mused that every conversation with her neighbors, even greetings in passing, contained some reference to food. "We have potato and carrot sprouts if you need them." Or "Has your squash blossomed yet?" or "The barley's planted." Remembering the long spring during which they'd struggled on rations that included boiled skunk cabbage stems, she understood why. In a frontier town, trade was a luxury no one could afford because they couldn't grow enough in their cleared fields to reserve for trading; everyone needed to be self-sufficient as well as resourceful.

She also had other reasons to be concerned. In May, she found she was again with child. They would have another mouth to feed before the next winter began. She was determined to not be caught short as they had when they'd moved to Groton so late in the growing season. Suzanne started her garden early and taking her neighbor Adelaide's lead, grew twice as much as she estimated. The space she had used the previous summer for medicinal herbs, she planted with carrots, parsnips, turnips, cabbage, corn, potatoes, and beans. Since she had foraged with Dancing Light, she now knew that she could gather most of her medicines from the wild and didn't need to cultivate them. She'd gathered enough wild raspberry and yarrow, so important for women in labor, to keep her supplied for the year, and she'd located sources for peppermint, tansy, and comfrey as well.

Ann Tarball and Adelaide Roberts coached her with gardening tips, kept her on schedule with planting and weeding, choices in what to plant. As life unfurled in her gardens, she marveled that she quickened with all of nature at the same time. *This child*, she mused, *will have a life in spirit without end.*

Adelaide's son, Jimmy Roberts, had volunteered to help with preparing the garden beds. Suzanne knew neighborly love hadn't inspired his gesture; he had a crush on Martha. Her neighbors showed her how to pickle vegetables and preserve berries, items her mother had traded for in the more populated Watertown. They helped her plant apple and pear trees, which they'd carefully nurtured from seeds. Though her orchard wouldn't bear fruit for many years, it promised God's providence; she watered her newly planted trees faithfully until they could survive on their own. Joseph had tapped maples and they'd boiled a bit of syrup to sweeten their porridge.

This year she'd hung the loft larder with salted fish and meat, filled bins in the dark cellar with her harvest and rutabaga and apples she'd taken in trade for her services. She'd stored sacks of white beans and grains in the loft. Once winter had frozen the ground, Joseph would store the game he'd hunted in a lean-to outside. They'd bought barrels at the trading post to store ale and spirits, such as hard cider. Vats held pickles and condiments. Baskets of dried vegetables and wild berry preserves, honey, and maple syrup crocks lined the cellar shelves. At the same time, Joseph piled hay in the barn to feed the cow and horse, stacked wood up to the eaves. By October, Suzanne felt the relief that comes from such long and hard labor; they were ready for winter.

After the long days of summer and September had passed, the fall had come in a whirl; dark now came earlier and earlier. Suzanne felt the winter approach in her bones;

the daylight disappeared at the same speed her pregnancy ripened. She was now only a month from delivering her third child; she hardly knew where the time had gone.

Joseph sat in an armchair nearby, where a lantern lit the text of his most precious belonging, Milton's *Paradise Lost*. She heard the rasp of the pages turning. *Is it his fourth reading*, she wondered? *No, not reading. Studying.* She knew that he read as much to improve his craft as he did for knowledge. Joseph had ever been poet-scholar in temperament, though a farmer in pocket. It wasn't until winter that he had the leisure to spend crafting his own verses.

"It's late. Time to put them to bed," Suzanne said to Martha, who sat near the hearth, where a fire warmed the room.

Martha sighed; it was her job to put the children to bed. She swept up Hester. "Come on Pickle Toes. Time for bed." Hester, already nodding off after their evening meal, didn't complain.

"Yeah, Pickle Toes!" Suzie followed Martha, giggling and grabbing her sister's toe. "I'm going to eat this pickle toe." She made a gobbling sound and Hester screeched, grinning, pulling her foot out of her sister's reach.

"Say good-night now," Martha said. She trooped by Joseph and Suzanne, letting Hester—who eyed her sister, her defenses on high alert–kiss them each in turn, and Suzie followed, pecking them on the cheek.

"Goodnight, Mama. Goodnight, Papa."

"Don't forget to say your prayers." Suzanne smiled, again grateful that she'd found Martha. The children adored her.

After Martha had voiced her own goodnight, she climbed the steep stairs to the loft; little Suzie followed on all fours. Her legs were not yet long enough to take the stairs in stride as Martha did. A large sheet of canvas partitioned their sleeping room from the stores, and the bed they shared occupied the center of the room, the only standing place beneath the slanting roof in the loft.

Suzanne knitted in silence, studying Joseph's face, that glowed a warm color in the lamplight. She could see his full lips move as he silently pronounced the words he read. Occasionally, he puffed on a long pipe that sent out an aroma of spice and fruit, exotic as a tropical island. She wished he was reading aloud; he'd courted her with that deep sonorous voice of his. Her other impulse was to still his lips with a kiss, though she restrained herself. Puritan women who showed such affection in public were pilloried, and the prohibition held in private. Suzanne had fallen in love with Joseph when he'd read aloud for the Watertown congregation during their prophesying on Sunday afternoons. She kept her secret for months before her younger sister caught her suppressed glances at the targeted Joseph, who sat in the men's rows. Mary had begun to tease her, making fun of the stick thin young man who was a nobody in Watertown. Mary was attracted to money and power in a way that Suzanne, admittedly a hopeless romantic, could never understand. Suzanne always said she'd marry only for love, and what she loved were qualities of intellect and sensitivity.

Suzanne set down her knitting and crossed to the chair where Joseph read, bending down to read over his shoulder in the flickering light. "Are you beginning again?"

Joseph nodded, then drew on his pipe, smoke puffing from his mouth with each word. "The first book has the most memorable quotes. I have memorized some of them, but that does his poem disservice. Memorizing a couplet without the text surrounding it changes Milton's intent."

"Will you read one for me?"

He smiled with pleasure and reached up to caress her arm. He uncrossed his leg, sat forward, and read a most famous quote.

"The mind is its own place, and in itself / Can make a Heav'n of Hell, a Hell of Heav'n."

Suzanne had heard it before and related it to her favorite quote, Shakespeare's 'nothing is but thinking makes it so.' Puritans had condemned all theater, but her teacher in Watertown, Master Norcross, had insisted that reading one Shakespeare tragedy and comedy would have more benefit than harm for his older students. "Does he mean that our minds make our reality?"

Joseph said, "I think Milton's meaning is the opposite, Satan's words. Satan philosophizes over God casting him from Heaven; he congratulates himself. Now I'll read the whole passage."

Joseph read,

'The mind is its own place, and in itself

Can make a Heav'n of Hell, a Hell of Heav'n. *Here* at least/

We shall be free; th' Almighty hath not built

Here for his envy, will not drive us hence:

Here we may reign secure, and in my choice

To reign is worth ambition though in Hell:

Better to reign in Hell, than serve in Heav'n.'

Milton sees Satan as the rebel, whose sin is pride. Hell is a flaming circle, but Satan boasts he can make it Heaven with his mind. To his way of thinking, he's free and secure in Hell, and that's better than serving God in Heaven. He believes he's God the Creator's equal."

"So, Satan sees heaven as a kind of prison?"

"Yes, as long as God rules it. It's an ironic idea."

"Perhaps this Satan is more human than fallen angel. Aren't all humans guilty of the same pride?"

"True. We can make a comparison to Puritans if you leave God out. They couldn't serve the King in England and chose to move to the wilderness and tame savages. Many elders still think the colonies are Hell and long to return to England. They denounce our generation as fallen and rude."

"Not my father. He told me he came here to create a Heaven, something new, something pure."

"Has he succeeded in creating Heaven?"

"I think he's a happy man," Suzanne squeezed her husband's shoulders. "Don't you?"

"You and I were born here. It's our Heaven because we know no difference. But your father? He was a Pilgrim, like Uncle John and my father."

"Your Uncle doesn't live in Hell. I've never known a happier man."

"I'd agree, if I weren't even happier." Joseph closed the book and reached for Suzanne's waist, pulling her onto his lap. He ran his hand over her belly, searching for movement. "He's quiet tonight. Have you decided who will deliver the baby?"

"If the weather holds, Joanna may still come, but it's unlikely. And Dancing Light has gone for the winter. Of course, my neighbors would protest if she was to deliver me. You know what the talk has been at Sunday meetings."

"You need to be more careful. Will Dr. Knox come?"

"He always turns women down; he will come if I need surgery. No, I think that Ann Tarball and Adelaide Roberts will do; they will have my instruction. We can always tap on Mary Parker and Abigail Willard, who have also volunteered. They live too far away; I don't want them to come out in November with the weather so uncertain. And Abigail's still nursing her Abby. Martha can help my lying in. I don't think I will have a shortage of help." Suzanne laughed nervously. "Don't worry," but she knew *best* that her assurance was a thinly disguised wish. Women faced mortality with every birth, even experienced midwives. God willing, she would deliver safely; children truly were gifts of God.

Joseph was silent.

She slid off his lap and led him to the bedroom.

On November 11, 1667, Suzanne gave birth to her first son and third child. Before Dancing Light had left for the Nashua winter grounds, she had insisted that Suzanne save a length of the *awigiwin* ("umbilical cord") for a *nitaawigiwin* ("birth rite") for her child. Suzanne had complied out of curiosity. She'd asked Adelaide to snip a piece of the cord and save it for her. Adelaide had glanced at her sharply, but relaxed and complied with her request.

Ann Tarball, though, confronted her. "Why?"

"It's for my medicine bag," she explained. *It is for medicine, just a different kind of medicine,* Suzanne reasoned. *Nashaway medicine.*

Ann Tarball was suspicious, knowing that Suzanne spent time with the Native American witch. Ann and Deacon Thomas Tarball had discussed her with others at church. "Is it for your witch doctor?"

Suzanne reassured her that it was for the baby, no one else. But Ann wouldn't take her word. "It's witchcraft. I know you think the world of this *pau wau*, but she's not Christian. The Lord stands behind you and your medicine, but a heathen who practices magic is a witch."

"Ann, the Lord has healed Dancing Light's sister. The Lord doesn't put little signs on people, 'this one's mine,' but 'let this one go.' The Indians are God's children, too. All creation, in fact. Rest easy. I am not the Devil's target today."

Suzanne's reproval had silenced Ann Tarball for the present, but Suzanne knew she hadn't heard the last from her. Later that day, Abigail gingerly put a thumb's length of cord to dry on a sunlit windowsill.

They named the baby Joseph, after his father; he was healthy, a mid-weight child with long legs, a lusty cry, and a strong grip. Although she had to forego midwifing for three weeks, she was soon back on her feet, thanking heaven for her continued strong constitution and physical health.

Joseph's Uncle John had been elected Clerk for the Groton Council again in December and, hoping to secure a position for his nephew on the council, he began to invite Joseph to meetings. Joseph didn't have enough acreage to become a freeman yet, but his uncle assured him that would come in time. For now, he recommended that Joseph become a contracted member of the church. Though Uncle John was critical of Suzanne's friendship with the Nashaway *pau wau* as he thought it might impede his nephew's chances with the church membership, he kept silent on the matter. John Morse could see that although the town's women were put off by her visits to the Nashaway camp, they would never denounce her for losing faith. Suzanne was the only midwife in town, and they needed her.

Chapter Ten

BOUND IN SPIRIT

Groton, April 1668

April was unusually mild, which brought everyone out to sow the fields and take in the lengthening days. By May, every colonist had outlasted their winter food supplies. Having exhausted their winter stores, they relied on the fish running in spring before they sowed crops again. Though she'd planned well and worked hard to put up enough food, Suzanne learned the advantage of living near the Nashua River, the source of food in late spring.

Dancing Light, who had returned with the tribe in March, could not tell Suzanne what day she would hold the *nitaawigiwin* ("birth rite"). Usually, the Nashua people performed the ritual when the baby had survived for one month, but she couldn't be there for Suzanne and her baby in December. Her tribe had migrated north to their winter grounds and wouldn't return until spring. Because of this, Dancing Light said the ceremony day had to be right, that Great Spirit would let her know. When the day came, Red Hawk and Running Fox stood at Suzanne's door.

Red Hawk cleared his throat. "Mistress Morse, we come to take you to *nitaawigiwin*."

"Wait here." Suzanne smiled at the two young men, who were already dressed for summer; having shorn their shirts, they wore deerskin leggings, breechcloths, and English vests. Their black hair glinted blue in the sunlight. She would need the small dried piece of umbilical cord Dancing Light asked her to prepare for a baby blessing.

And her son, who was now nearing seven months. She'd start weaning him soon.

"Martha," she called out, "I'll be leaving. You'll need to take over while I'm gone." Suzanne rummaged through a trunk for the ceremonial birth cord.

Martha came in the room, wiping her hands on her apron. "Where will you be? What can I tell Joseph?"

"I'll be at the Indian camp. I'm back before dark."

"I'll let him know." She glanced over her shoulder at the two young Indian men standing in the doorway and blushed. To her, they were naked.

"Hello," Red Hawk said. He added as an afterthought. "Martha."

Flustered, the girl mumbled a hurried "Pleased to meet you."

Suzanne wrapped the baby in her carrier, a heavy cloth, hoisting him to her back and tying the band in front. Baby Joseph had napped and now awake, was peering over her shoulder, cheerfully gurgling. She followed them on foot to the river, hoping her neighbors were not out in their fields. Just knowing that she visited the village across the river was enough to raise their suspicion without giving them the evidence of this single-file march to the riverbanks.

They quickly boarded the canoe, and her guides skillfully paddled across the speeding current, engorged by spring melt. The water had risen so high that it swamped the trees on the riverbanks, and branches swept underwater created strong currents where they impeded the flow. The spring melt also carried a hazardous cargo of deadwood and debris swept from the flooded riverbanks. Suzanne stepped from the canoe with gratitude that they'd landed safely.

This time, Dancing Light met her on the path and led her through the village and a woods beyond it to a narrow clearing. There, Suzanne noted a large circle at one end. Stones piled about a foot deep marked the rim and two transverse lines divided the circle into four parts; Suzanne thought it must have some ceremonial purpose but could only guess what that might be. *I must ask Dancing Light*, she thought. She was impatient with her own ignorance. Piles of rocks were randomly placed at the edges, interspersed with piles of wood cut for burning. At the clearing's other end stood a low, wide domed structure covered with animal hides; its opening on the west side faced a large and deep fire pit piled high with burning logs. Suzanne could make out the edge of a large stone that glowed red in the licking flames; it was a hot fire. Just in front of the opening to the *mide-wigaan* (medicine lodge), a staff ribboned with deer hide strips, shells, and feathers flanked a small oblong altar of raised earth. Arranged there were an embroidered pouch, artfully-tied herb bunches, and a small basket of tobacco atop the earth mound. A hide carrier full of water sat near a wooden dipper.

Dancing Light motioned to her. "Please sit." She gestured to the embankment circling the fire pit. "Do you have *awigiwin*?"

Suzanne nodded. "Yes." She dug into the purse that hung from her waist, unwrapping the twisted dried cord, which Dancing Light took. Suzanne sat, pulling Joseph to her lap. He was just beginning to show rooting behavior, and she knew she'd have to feed him to keep him quiet.

Dancing Light sat in front of the altar, and Suzanne watched her make an offering of tobacco to the fire and add some to the embroidered pouch.

While Suzanne nursed, Dancing Light began the ceremony. She murmured prayers above the birth cord, then placed it in the pouch and sewed it shut.

Suzanne was so intent on Dancing Light's actions that she didn't at first notice the women who were undressing beside the medicine lodge. Dancing Light's sister, the sachem's wife was the only one she recognized. Suzanne had healed her with white medicine two years ago. The *squa-sachem*, woman sagamore or chief, nodded, smiled, and invited her to follow them. They each held up a pinch of tobacco, and saying prayers, threw the tobacco on the fire. Suzanne felt awkward at first but remembered that

Dancing Light had told her they would hold the ceremony in the medicine lodge. She'd explained the ceremony would cleanse them; they'd bathe in steam. She wouldn't want to get her dress wet.

Offering tobacco was familiar to her; she'd watched Dancing Light offer it for every plant she'd dug. Suzanne wasn't sure if God would understand, but she said a prayer nevertheless. When Suzanne had removed clothing down to her shift, one woman picked out an herb bundle and lit it from the fire. She fanned it until wisps of smoke spiraled up, then circled each woman, smudging them with the fragrant sweetgrass smoke. When Dancing Light took the bundle, she waved a feather fan to direct the smoke. "Clean for great spirit," she explained. She motioned for Suzanne to turn while she smudged her, back and front.

Then, each woman knelt and kissed the ground at the lodge door, muttering words Suzanne didn't understand but understood to be honoring sacred space. When she crawled into the narrow opening and sat cross-legged in their circle, Red Hawk handed Joseph to her. She sat him in her lap. He was wide-eyed with curiosity about the strange surrounding. The lodge had no vents or windows; it's only source of light was the open door. Once they were seated, the fire keeper brought rocks, pushing them into a hollowed round pit at the lodge's center. Dancing Light and a drummer sat on each side of the door.

The lanky Joseph, who even in infancy was clearly to grow as tall as his father, let out a squeal. She held him squirming by the waist, so he could stand on his feet. Dancing Light signaled to the drummer, and the woman began a slow rhythm, a thumping heartbeat. She spoke the next words in English, so her guest could understand, but directed her words to a spirit. She held the embroidered pouch in both hands, like an offering.

"*Awigiwin* tie Suzanne to her boy Joseph; give him life." She passed the pouch in one hand from Suzanne's stomach to Joseph's stomach. "Now is cut, child in danger. Great Spirit, we give you mother cord. I ask Great Spirit, make Standing Heron new son." She passed the pouch from Joseph's middle up into the air. "Keep Standing Heron safe when he walks good red road. Keep him like mother."

The women passed the pouch, and Dancing Light's sister looped the medicine bag around the newly named infant's neck. Suzanne remembered suddenly that Dancing Light explained the baby blessing was so late that they would combine it with a *waawind-aasawin*("naming rite".)

Dancing Light spoke to her. "You keep medicine bag close to boy. One year. Put in bed at night, he wear it every day." She gestured to the drummer, who started up a new rhythm.

The women began to sing a chant that sounded unlike any Indian song she'd heard from across the river; it was clearly a lullaby. Sweet, gentle. "*Neeta, neeta, neeta, kai-o-me-yo*," she heard. The chant was simple enough to join in their singing, though she didn't understand a word. Joseph, now Standing Heron, began to bounce, dancing to their tune. The sentiment of offering the symbolic umbilical cord to God touched her. They asked that God be a mother to her son. At the same time, she felt uneasy, as though disloyal to her own father God. *Am I practicing witchcraft?* she wondered. *What would Reverend Willard say if he knew I asked a heathen God to take care of my son?*

The ceremony continued when Red Hawk brought four molten red stones to the door, placing them in the pit. Dancing Light again lit sweetgrass and passed it over the stones, which threw up arcs of star-like sparks in the gloom. She intoned what Suzanne thought might be a blessing of the stones. When Dancing Light poured a dipper full of water on the rocks, steam burst from them, quickly filling the lodge. Suzanne felt as though the lodge itself became a womb in which she floated, safe and warm. At this point, the baby's face puckered, and he began to fuss.

"Enough for Standing Heron." Dancing Light motioned to Suzanne that she was to pass the baby to her, which she did. "Red Hawk, take him until we finish."

Once she'd passed Joseph from the lodge, Dancing Light called to Red Hawk to close the door. It was pitch dark when she began to pour dipper after dipper on the rocks. Soon the air was so filled with the clouds of hot steam that it was difficult to breathe, and Suzanne felt her skin was scalded. She fell to the ground, pressing her face against the cooler earth. Sweat poured from every pore on her body. She was drenched in mere minutes. The women continued to chant, song after song. When the steam scattered, Dancing Light again poured a dipper on the rocks, again bathing them with the scalding mist. Sometimes they stopped to speak. Suzanne hoped it was prayer. *For all I know*, she thought, *they could be calling the devil.* Dancing Light had explained that sweat lodges were to cleanse the body, and she now knew what that meant. She would be clean from the inside out. *What did Reverend Willard say about their singing? Like cicadas. I've been cleaned inside out.*

At the end of the ceremony, Dancing Light called Red Hawk to open the door. Clouds scented with sage poured out. As the women crawled through the door, they again bent to kiss the ground in gratitude.

Suzanne would never forget the experience. The lodge had impressed her; she even smelled different after she'd wiped herself dry and changed from her shift to dry clothes. More than that, she knew she was opening herself to experiences that were making her think differently. She felt guilty, a little like a tippler who didn't want to stop. She wouldn't be able to tell her husband, or Reverend, or even Martha.

Red Hawk and Running Deer brought her back across the river, dropping her on the shore, and she made her way with her baby up the bank and down the road to her house. Once there, she had a chance to examine the medicine bag the women had placed around her baby's neck. Dancing Light had decorated the pouch with porcupine needles and fiber. It was the flower, leaves, and stalk of yarrow, drawn in imitation of her own journal sketches. Dancing Light had produced the stylized rendition from her memory. Suzanne gasped and held the pouch to her chest. Her son would always be Standing Heron in her heart now. She wanted to repay her friend more than ever.

Chapter Eleven

TRADE WORRIES

Groton, June 1668

Late in May, everyone was talking about an incident at an Indian trading post near Concord. In a drunken brawl, a Penacook native murdered the English agent at a trading post near Concord, not far from Groton. It opened Pandora's box. Though their nearest neighbors, the Nashaway, had nothing to do with it, the settlers' latent apprehensions about Indians began to swarm.

Suzanne had put the girls to bed, and they were just sitting down to their evening meal when John Morse, Thomas Tarbell, and Adam Blood stopped by for Joseph. Common courtesy made it compulsory to invite the men to stay and eat.

Suzanne hurried to set three more places at the boards: the homely wooden trenchers and the towel-sized napkins. She had mugs now for ale; the riches of having enough for company made her proud. She poured ale from the pitcher as the men sat, and she listened as she loaded a platter with roasted meat and vegetables.

"Joseph, you heard about the murder?" Uncle John said. "Boston's calling Thomas and Adam here to witness."

Thomas Tarball grunted his acknowledgment. He was a bald man of middle age, grizzly fringes of hair hung to his shoulders. His beard, too, seemed coarsely knotted even though he'd clipped it short. "Damned drunk Indian split Dickerson's skull with a tomahawk. Never seen anything like it."

"Dickerson? Runs the Penacook post?" Joseph asked. "The post Waldron owns?"

"Right. Waldron and Coffin, his partner. Ann sent me to get cloth that day."

"I got there later," Adam Blood said, dragging his hat off a thick brown mop of hair that fell to his shoulders. "Payne and Dickerson were both working. He said they sent some Indians to Waldron's post at Piscataqua for guns, ammunition and a bit of cloth. You know the court licensed Waldron to sell arms to Indians last year."

"Right," Uncle John said. "Another commonwealth crony! He profits, we pay.

Joseph clapped his hand on his knee. "No lie there. We had it right thirty years ago; no one sells guns to Indians. But at least he pays the province a cut for any gun or ammunition he sells. The tax goes to our common good, doesn't it?"

Uncle John coughed conspicuously. "What good? The Indians turn those guns on us. Think the tariff will pay for our militia? Our ammunition?"

"Not happening here," Adam Blood bragged. "Menfolk trained, four garrisons now."

Thomas Tarball steered them back. "Well, the Indians didn't bring any guns back. Just rum. And Dickerson sold it all, against the law!" He grimaced. "Payne said there must have been a hundred Indians drinking all day, all night and into the next day. I got there after they'd gone home. Left a mess!"

Uncle John wiped his mouth. "Not the first time Waldron ignored the law. He's been to court for selling rum to the Indians."

Adam Blood shook his head. "But they acquitted him."

John Morse nodded. "No justice when he *is* the law in these parts." He turned to Thomas Tarball. "You said the Sagamore came to break it up."

Tarball nodded. "Tahanto's asked those traders not to trade firewater before; he wanted Dickerson and Payne to empty the jugs on the ground. Said it made his people Devils."

"Tahanto a Christian?" Joseph asked.

"That's the word." Tarball pulled a draft from his mug. "Tahanto came, but too late. An Indian heard the argument: the drunk claimed Dickerson charged too much. I heard the scream, but the first I see of it, Dickerson is lying on the floor in a pool of blood. Payne called for help, and the constable sent to Groton for witnesses."

Suzanne, who listened intently, her spoon arrested over a serving bowl, couldn't stay quiet any longer. "Did they catch him?" She hadn't seen Dancing Light in more than a week; she wondered what her friend would know. Apprehensive as she was, Suzanne knew that there'd been no eruptions between whites and natives since the incident. *Surely, that's a good sign.*

Tarball said, "When help came from Groton, it was all over. Seems the Indian that saw the whole killin' went after the drunk and brought him back. Tahanto got his full confession."

Blood swallowed, leaning forward. "Payne said the drunk pleaded he didn't know what he was doing, he drank too much, but Tahanto said it was no excuse. He'd murdered a white man, and they had to avoid conflict. They condemned him to die right there."

Tarball added: "He'd sobered up by then, said he was sorry, and begged them to shoot him." He paused for effect: "They obliged on the spot, as they should. Shot one of their own through with an arrow."

Adam Blood shifted on the bench, reaching for seconds from the savory platter. "I won't compare the Penacooks with our own Nashaway. Our neighbors aren't given to drink. But I have to admire the Penacooks' sense of justice."

"We go to court now," Tarball said.

"Wait! Slow down. You're going to Boston?" Joseph had lost track. "You said justice was done."

"Courts looking into the rum sale." Tarball wiped his hands on the towel Suzanne passed to him.

"Did Tahanto make demands?" Uncle John asked.

"I don't know, but the magistrates will examine it," Tarball answered. "A hundred Indians gathered for two days, drunk? Only God knows what prevents them rising against us."

Joseph glanced at Suzanne, who began to gather serving platters from the table. "You would do well to find out more from Dancing Light."

Suzanne nodded, keeping her head down, wishing that he'd not said anything in front of Thomas Tarball. Ann Tarball had made his censure of her friendship with the Nashaway medicine woman clear. At least Joseph didn't insist that she break with her friend.

Tarball stared at Suzanne to get her attention. "You're dancing with the devil. The Nashaway are Abenaki, same as Penacooks. You think they won't retaliate?"

Suzanne stood in place, shaking her head. "Tahanto has spoken. He's Christian, as are his followers. They'll not be revolting against him. And Indian justice is different from our own at any rate."

"You don't know that," Tarball said.

Joseph interceded for his wife. "It's what we hear, and Suzanne has a point. Their view is they fight for justice when they raid neighbors to replace the loss of a tribe member. We judge that as kidnapping. In this case, doesn't matter the Indian kills a white man. Murder is murder, and they punished the killer. If it was the other way around, white man kills an Indian? Would we punish the killer?"

Adam Blood settled it. "Justice will be done. The Constable has summoned John Page, Thomas, and me to testify."

Suzanne, who had nothing to add, cleared away their plates as they rose to leave, her gut registering an odd combination of fear and annoyance.

At the end of the month, word came from Boston the investigation ended with fining Payne and Waldron's partner Coffin for selling rum. Boston meted out punishment for the traders, which justified the Sagamore Tahanto, but again, the trading post owner, Waldron, escaped without censure.

Chapter Twelve

NEWCOMER

Groton, July 1669

Greeting the pair at her door, Suzanne had thought it before about the Coopers: opposites attract. Her husband's younger sister, Sarah, was like her brother: tall, thin, and dark haired; in fact, her hair was a bush of tight curls that were as unruly as Joseph's. Sarah's second husband, Timothy Cooper, was the same height, but there all likeness ended. He was a blond clear through: yellow straight hair hung to his shoulders and a thick beard cupped chin and cheeks on a ruddy, round face. Of a stocky build, he had wrist bones easily double the size of his wife's. Sarah cradled her five-month-old infant in her arms.

Suzanne smiled broadly, "I'm so happy you've come." She was never happier than when people surrounded her, which made her buzz with energy. The couple entered and advanced to the hall.

"Suzanne, I've brought maple sugar from Watertown." Sarah turned to her husband. "Timothy?"

Timothy fumbled with the package that he'd carried in a pouch, producing the block of sugar he'd wrapped in a cloth. "I have it."

Suzanne took it, weighing the heft of the package in her hand with pleasure. "Perfect. It'll sweeten our strawberries!" She'd picked the strawberry patch that morning, and the ones not as ripe would be tart and need sugar.

Her girls, now five and seven, ran to greet her. "Aunt Sarah, can we see the baby?" Suzy was so eager she jiggled on her tiptoes to see him.

"You may. This is Johnny." Sarah knelt to show them the infant, who sucked his fist, eyes blinking at his eagerly staring cousins.

Suzy expelled an exclamation of delight, treading on the edges of her aunt's puffed skirt to get close. She voiced a "peep" to get his attention but succeeded only in drawing her aunt Sarah's indulgent smile.

"He's too little to play peekaboo."

Suzanne followed Sarah. "If you'd like, you can put him in the cradle. My son's outgrown it, and the girls would love to rock him." She turned, bending to address Suzie. "Wouldn't you?"

Suzie jumped with excitement. "I'll do it. I'll do it."

As Sarah was settling the baby in the cradle, they heard Reverend Willard calling at the front door. Samuel and Abigail Willard had agreed to the supper to meet Joseph's sister, a newcomer to Groton.

Although Suzanne had moved to Groton before Joseph's sister had married the first time, her mother had written of Sarah's husband's accidental death, a tragedy that left her a pregnant widow. Then, four months after she'd borne her son, their uncle John had risen to the occasion of finding a good marriage for his widowed niece. Timothy, a Groton selectman since the town was founded, had stepped up to marry her, adopting the baby. Suzanne had been happy to pitch in to help her sister-in-law settle in Groton. Their new house sat on a one-acre land grant between the town and the Nashua River; it was right next door to the burial grounds and across the road from the meetinghouse. Since Joseph's land was adjacent to their plot, he'd invited them to use a corner of the fallow flooding meadow for their own until they could buy farmland. "I can't plant it now, anyway," he'd explained to Suzanne. "He can clear it."

Suzanne hurried to the door, where Abigail and Samuel Willard stood. "Where's Abby?" she asked, noting that no one carried the baby, who would be about one year old now.

"We left her with our help," Abigail said.

"Too bad. The girls would have loved seeing her. Was she ill?"

"She's a little feverish, teething again. I thought she was too fussy to move. You know how they are."

Suzanne pulled Sarah near. "Sarah, I want you to meet Mistress Abigail Willard. She is our minister's wife. Abigail, I want you to meet Joseph's sister, Goody Sarah Cooper." She motioned to the Reverend, who stood talking with Joseph and Timothy. "Reverend Willard, this is Goody Sarah Cooper."

When they finished introductions, Abigail nodded toward Suzy who, at seven, was already one of her pupils. "They seem busy." She walked to the cradle the girl attentively rocked and bent over it. "Who is this, Suzy?"

"Johnny."

"Well, hello Johnny." Abigail turned to Suzy's sister. "Hester, I hear you'll be coming to our house for school with your sister this fall. Are you excited?"

Hester nodded her head so vigorously that Abigail mused she might dislocate it. Hester announced, proudly. "Yes, Mistress Willard. I'm five years old."

"That's old enough." Abigail smiled and stood. "You'll be reading in no time."

Suzanne sidled up to Abigail and took her hand, "Come. I have something to show you." She led her to the corner where she concocted her medicines. "I have plants for you to take home. Daisies."

"Daisies? They're medicine?"

"Yes." Suzanne had wrapped a rag around a large bouquet of the yellow-eyed blossoms still rooted in a tangled dirt-clotted mass. "Boil these—blooms, leaves, stems and roots—to make a strong tea. Not long. Until the water's yellow. Rub it on your skin to keep mosquitoes away. It's good for cuts and scratches, too."

"Thank you, Suzanne. You amaze me."

"It's an old Indian remedy." Pesky mosquitoes were just one of the wonders of their new world, and few could claim they had no allergic reactions to them. Dancing Light had let her know many ways for repelling them or treating the bites. While not as effective as bear grease salves, the daisies had the advantage of smelling better. "Let's join the others. I think we're nearly ready to eat."

Abigail grasped Suzanne's arm to stop her and leaned to whisper in her ear. "I'm with child again! I didn't want another so soon."

Suzanne studied her friend's concerned face. "We must talk. Can you come next week? I would like to help."

Abigail nodded. "Thursday?"

Suzanne squeezed her hand and turned back to the table.

The last guest to arrive was Joseph's uncle, John Morse, who entered without knocking, as usual, announcing himself loudly. "Better late than never."

Joseph led him to the table. "When were you ever late for a meal?"

"A barb there, I wager. You imply I'm a—"

"Leech?" Joseph laughed at his own joke.

Uncle John joined in, eyes squinting, and retorted, "Takes one to know one." It was Uncle John's turn to laugh, though it was a stretch. Bachelors were notoriously fond of home cooking when they could get it.

"You've got me there. Sit. Sit. We are just about to eat."

With much scraping and bustle, they pulled the benches up to the table boards. The children, who'd eaten before guests arrived, continued to play with their cousin. It was usual in the colonies to feed children separately, though in East Anglian households they were fed last. The adults joined hands and bowed their heads while Reverend Willard thanked God for the summer's bounteous food.

Suzanne had made sure to seat Abigail nearby; the two women had business to discuss. Abigail had been a great help and eagerly shared the information Suzanne learned from Dancing Light, who'd showed her sources for four more plants native to Massachusetts. She'd learned of bloodroot and stinging nettle in the spring, black cohosh and golden seal in the summer. What's more, she related that her friend had found new wild sources for yarrow and wild raspberry, which both healers used in childbirth.

Suzanne had seated the Coopers next to the Reverend Willard, where he could acquaint himself with the newly married young couple. Joseph and Uncle John sat at one corner of the boards, discussing the recent meeting of the Groton town council. Since the council had elected Uncle John as Town Clerk in the November election, he never missed an opportunity to delegate tasks to the board. He could easily enlist his nephew Joseph, now that he aspired to become a freeman.

John Morse tapped his spoon on the boards to get everyone's attention and announced with ceremony, "We need to congratulate Reverend Samuel Willard. The council has seen fit to deed the church house and land to him. And …" (he paused for effect), "he's now a 'freeman.'"

The minister, who rarely smiled, dipped his head modestly, trying to suppress the lift of his cheeks and the twinkle in his eyes, and nodded his thanks. He suffered no pride, not in others, nor in himself. The council hadn't just granted him the house for his time as their minister but in perpetuity. They'd deeded both house and land to him and his heirs. The time was an occasion for his sincerest gratitude, not pride. "Thank you, John. The town has honored me, indeed, and I think I can speak for Abigail as well."

Abigail nodded vigorously and spoke for herself. "We are so blessed."

"You must understand it's a token of our gratitude." Uncle John spoke with unaccustomed gravity. "God has seen fit to grant on us your wisdom and guidance."

"God willing," the minister answered humbly.

Suzanne was suddenly struck by the realization Reverend Willard was now a freeman. "Now you are freeman, will you certify my practice?"

Reverend Willard stiffened, not answering immediately. "I must speak with you before I do."

She'd expected a resounding 'yes,' and glanced at Abigail to see if she knew what he reacted to but found no enlightenment. Abigail looked mystified, and Suzanne determined her friend had heard no reproval before now.

"I am aware that you have formed an alliance, a friendship ... I don't know what you call it ... with the Nashaway's medicine woman, the witch."

"She's no witch. I know she's not Christian, but her medicine is no different from my own. She's a healer who works for the good."

The minister was clearly uncomfortable with continuing the conversation, and he looked left and right. Settling on moving forward as necessary, even in the present company, he continued. "A healer who worships a heathen God? Who wears a wolf's head, a beast, in ceremony? Who practices magic?"

"Are her customs and tokens more magical? Do we not nail wolves' heads to our church walls? Doesn't God speak to those who make covenants?" The minute she said it, she wished she hadn't. She tried desperately to cover up her suggestion that a Puritan's conversion bespoke magic. She immediately brought her argument back to the personal. "She calls on a higher power as I do. No one has suffered from her medicine. What's more, her knowledge of herbs that grow here exceeds my own, medicines that are new to us. And she's found wild sources for herbs that I used to have to cultivate."

"I've heard this from Abigail, who shares your excitement about the new remedies. I'm not talking of that. Rather, you are drawing criticism from the congregation."

Abigail tried to get Suzanne's attention, suddenly concerned that Suzanne would think she had complained to her husband. She reached for Suzanne's hand. "It wasn't I," she whispered.

Suzanne granted her friend's denial. "I'd never suspect you." However, even as she said it, she thought, *he has come between us. She must obey her husband, and I must guard my actions with her.*

The minister continued, "You've been seen at the Indian camp. I don't need to tell you that many in our community distrust natives. Can you imagine they'd be happy you use a witch's medicine or prescribe it to their children?"

There's that word again, she thought. *He believes in witches.* Suzanne had little trouble finding the source of gossip that might inform Reverend Willard. The Tarballs', near neighbors, were first on the list. Martha's mother was second. She must admit she had critics if not actual enemies, but she'd never expected this rebuke from the Reverend Willard, the enlightened minister who had defended their Indian neighbors. *Indeed!* She thought. *It was he who told me of Dancing Light to begin and now he denounces her?*

"I do not personally believe in witches. Rest easy there. But you must know that doesn't rule out the Devil and evil malice. I'm concerned because this adventure may come between you and your faith. I feel you may be slipping away from the one true path."

What must they think? she agonized. Suzanne scanned the faces at the table for telltale signs of scorn. Most disturbing, Sarah and Timothy looked ill at ease, embarrassed. They weren't used to such confrontations outside prophesy circles in Watertown. Suzanne's first anger at the injustice of his public rebuke oddly mixed with gratitude. He'd confronted her publicly, but she realized it could have been worse if he'd taken this up in front of the congregation. *He's sparing me, keeping it in the family,* she thought. *It's a warning.*

"I'm devoted to God and work only through his blessings, Reverend. Of that you may be sure. A healer *never* takes the Lord's name in vain." She knew in her heart that prayer was many times the last resort for any healer.

Suzanne could see Martha hovering behind Joseph, her forehead knotted in concern. *At least I know I have Martha's support,* she thought. *What would I do without Martha?* She nodded to her and mouthed "thank you."

Reverend Willard sat back and regarded her for a moment and then leaned in, his words scorching her conscience. "Can you swear on the Bible the heathen woman's Great Spirit is the same as our Holy Father? Can she, like you, who have received the Holy word through our Bible, claim that her God has healed the sick and comforted the dying?"

Suzanne's cheeks blushed red in answer. *She recognizes the white God. If Dancing Light respects my God, mustn't I respect her God?* She knew, though, the Puritan minister could never extend that respect to the neighboring tribe. He thought of them as heathens, condemned and excluded unless they converted to the Puritan faith. Publicly, too.

He continued. "I must certify your practice and assure the congregation that you are firmly one of us. Can I do that if you persist in this friendship? I don't know."

"I see." Suzanne exchanged glances with her husband, who looked sympathetically concerned. He too had warned her. "Reverend Willard, I promise that I will be vigilant in my dealing with Dancing Light, but I cannot denounce her. Isn't befriending her our way to show Christ's teachings?"

Reverend Willard spoke slowly. "I am gratified to hear your testament. So, to answer you, yes. I can certify your midwifery but ask your vigilance against sinning; you are working with a heathen. Beware! Is it the Puritan way to leave it so?"

Uncle John interrupted the conversation with a jovial prod. "Suzanne hasn't claimed her wolf headdress yet, though we cured it for her."

Even Suzanne couldn't help but join in the titters that followed this outrageous suggestion. She was grateful Uncle John had once again stepped into a fray and lightened their hearts. But she'd understood the veiled suggestion of the minister. He wasn't asking her to denounce her friend, but to convert her. For him, it was Suzanne's Puritan duty.

The lengthy supper ended long before sunset; the long summer days gave them leisure. Everyone left Suzanne and Martha to clean up. Late, when the sun began to set, the Sabbath began. Suzanne opened the back door and walked to the makeshift bench she'd placed in the garden. She still stung with her minister's rebuke because she realized that he was right. She didn't want to admit that she was wandering from the true faith. She had kept the protective pouch at her child's bedside, dismissing the thought that it stood for magic. No such talisman was needed to secure protection from the Lord God she worshiped. In her mind, she used Joseph's Indian name, Standing Heron, as a nickname to distinguish her son's name from her husband's. Now, she examined her conscience. *Was not the Christian name he's been christened preferable for God?* Enlightened suddenly, she understood the baby blessing ceremony had been a pagan christening. *Must allowing a great spirit mean I have abandoned my God?*

Chapter Thirteen

WARNINGS

Watertown, July 1669

Later, lying in bed, Suzanne could not free her mind of the burning question, *Must allowing a great spirit mean I have abandoned my God?* She'd lived with Joanna Morton, an apprentice to Joanna who had only a shallow connection to the Puritan religion. Joanna taught her that while Puritans understand the cause of all disease and suffering is sin, a midwife must separate matters of faith from the physical nature. 'For us,' she'd taught, 'the proper herbal cure takes precedence over our patient's conscience and penitence.'

As for legitimizing her practice, Joanne had explained that too. She'd said, 'Ministers typically approve midwife practices so our patients don't confuse what might seem miraculous healing with magic and works of the Devil. Our patients believe God must forgive their sins to heal. If they single us out as pawns of the devil, witches who work magic, it's much to be feared.' Suzanne learned that, while religious leaders must lean toward the spiritual and faith, she must lean toward the science of healing. *I need Reverend Willard's certification,* she thought. *No one can accuse me of witchcraft then, even if someone dies.*

Suzanne had to admit that she was only shallowly educated in the Puritan faith. She'd never experienced conversion such as many confessed in the church. Because she'd never experienced a numinous moment, she thought these confessed conversions were fiction. T*hey make it up to gain membership in the church; it's not real,* she thought. *Isn't* *it the same for Dancing Light when she talks to plants?* She had kept her head down when it came to religion.

Moving to Groton had changed everything. Now the Reverend Willard had rebuked her relationship with what he called a 'witch,' she paid heed. Joanna had taught her that she must never allow this to happen. However, her unenlightened relations to the great mystery now bled into her workings with Dancing Light. It was clear to Suzanne by now that every move in her Indian friends' practices sprung from some spiritual core of which she knew nothing. The effect did not open her to Dancing Light's mystic reality, although it mightily whetted her curiosity; she *was* drawn to the mystical rituals of her neighbors. Instead, she sought a religious equivalence from Samuel Willard, whose sermons drew on her upbringing as a professing Puritan. The young Reverend Willard gave well-conceived, reasoned sermons that lit up Puritan beliefs with great clarity.

Early the next day, the heat preceded the sunrise. Parishioners shuffled into the stuffy meetinghouse with the usual murmur of voices punctuated by the shrill screeches of children and stern hushes from their parents. Once the windows were opened, clothing rustling and shoes scraping the wooden floor faded to a backdrop for birds calling outside. Fluttering air testified to breezes flipping leaves on the surrounding trees. It was a peaceful day, full of God's providence and joy. Once they'd all settled, the Reverend climbed to his podium.

Suzanne, who sat at the front of the church in the Morse gallery, still smarted with the disapproval Reverend Willard had expressed at supper the day before. She was especially attentive to the sermon that began with a reading from a Bible passage that spoke of day and night in symbolic terms, which the minister clarified for his parish.

The first part of the sermon brought up the subject that he often returned to. In times of prosperity, when the congregation feels secure, their attention to God's words and commands begins to wane. Growing degeneracy is visible in the full light of day. Then he pointed out that in the scriptures, the Watchman, a prophet, tells us it is already night. "Known sinners may enjoy prosperity; that season may even continue. In the end, though, they should be assured that day will end, and night will come," he preached. "Learn hence, that outward prosperity is no sure token of Gods special favor, Ecclesiastics 9:2."

Suzanne registered this sermon as she had others about sinning; he didn't speak to her. *Am I not a good person who works to heal, to erase people's pain, to lighten their loads?* But this changed when he began to characterize night. "Night," he preached "is a time of calamity."

When he spent nearly thirty minutes describing it, she naturally began to compare his commentary to her state of mind when she had defended her friend Dancing Light.

"First," he said, "night obscures everything and we can no longer judge right from wrong, good from bad". She felt uneasy remembering the native's baby blessing that she had compared to a christening. She'd made no distinction between the two. *Does this mean I'm passing into night?*

He continued. "The dark is joyless; the dark hides from us objects of joy and mirth just as, in times of calamity, all objects of joy are removed." He dismissed the idea of night as sacred and a source of joy in that "we find our joy in the stars and moon: the light, not dark." She couldn't argue with his logic. A family blessed a christening with the approval, with laughter and feasting. She fidgeted, trying to find comfort on the hardwood of the pew. The baby blessing had taken place in utter dark of the sweat lodge and was attended by strangers.

"What's more," he argued, "in the light we know whom to trust, but the darkness has an influence on our fantasies, which can possess us with fears and fearful expectation of sudden miseries. Last, the night is a solitary time that breaks up and scatters societies. Alone, we feed upon our melancholic thoughts and fears."

Suzanne, who was never comfortable alone, could only agree; she'd felt it at Dancing Light's baby blessing. She didn't know their language and knew even less about the women who attended.

After he had set out this connection of sin and grievous trouble to night, he admonished his congregation. Suzanne now felt he was talking directly to her. She must prevent a day of calamity by shunning sin, because if she continued to provoke God's judgment, she would know the night in full measure. The Minister, now in his stride, roared out the conditions of darkness, the shadow of death.

"Joyless," he boomed. "we shall see the difference between joy and sorrow experimentally when God shall have removed our comforts away from us, our peace, our outward supplies, all our precious things. We shall then feel what it is to be benighted.

"*Terrible.*" He struck the podium with his fist. "Full of amazement. Ah! Little do we know what the terror of this *night* means: To be oppressed with pining hunger, with pinching penury. To hear the cries of children following us for bread and none to give them. To hear the sound of the trumpet and alarm to war. To hear the cries of the wounded and see the slain in our gates. To see the raging of famine and pestilence, and natural affection changed into a tiger-like cruelty, tender-hearted mothers shutting up their bowels of pity and laying violent hands on the children they have born. To go into captivity and serve an enemy whose tender mercies are cruelty. To live in fear of every sight, every noise, lest it should be some messenger of death, or that which is worse."

He itemized God's apocalypse; the Bible he assured them did not seek to amuse them; history gave testimony to God's wrath.

With this resounding finale, the congregation broke up for lunch, and the afternoon was spent in discussion of his moving sermon. Suzanne, having entertained Reverend Willard's vision in her head, decided that she must work to bring her friend Dancing Light into the Puritan fold lest they both fall into this "night."

Chapter Fourteen

CHANGING MINDS

Groton, September 1670

In the intervening year, Suzanne increased her practice. Of the fifty families now resident in Groton, most households had women of childbearing age. Her friend Abigail gave birth to Samuel junior in February, but made it clear she didn't want to follow her mother's example in the future. "If I have my way," she'd told Suzanne, "I'll have no more than six children."

Suzanne kept on gathering herbs from the wilderness surrounding Groton both with and without Dancing Light. While she complied with Reverend Willard's request that she be discrete, she knew he couldn't know that some of those herbs were Abigail's salvation.

In the first week of September, Dancing Light came with her digging stone and collecting sack to ask for company. "Time good to dig roots," she said.

"Wah-dub?" [roots]

"Yes, wah dub. Wa-ni-ke wah-dub. *Dig* roots."

Suzanne pulled her notebook from the mantel and added the new word. Bound to practicing her medical arts in dark, cramped domiciles most of her days, Suzanne longed for these forays into nature. She appreciated the open air, where she viewed nature without the limiting frames of doors and windows, the confining press of smoke clouded ceilings. She only hesitated long enough to consider her condition. She was seven months into her fourth pregnancy, but the baby had turned, which let her breathe easier.

"A moment!" She tied up her skirts and put on her moccasins, then strode to the yard, where Martha harvested summer squash and beans. Her helpers now, Suzie and Hester worked beside her, paying scant attention to their little brother Joseph, who was nearly three now.

"Martha, I'm going to be gathering herbs this morning. I'll return this afternoon."

Martha had come to enjoy the days both her master and mistress were gone. With the house to herself, she imagined she was herself a householder and ruled the children with a firm hand, extracting their obedience with zeal. "It's no trouble," she answered. At that moment, little Joseph headed for the woods at full speed on his long legs. "Joseph, you come back here."

The boy didn't stop, but Suzie took after him as was proper for the oldest child. She'd learned she was responsible for her younger siblings. She grabbed him around his middle and lifted him kicking and screaming. "You aren't going anywhere!" she said.

Suzanne smiled, feeling more confidence at Standing Heron's capture. "Joseph, you mind your sisters."

The two women made their way through the forest along a familiar path, this one following the contour of the Nashau River. 'Wa-ni-ke wah-dub' she knew meant digging cohosh and goldenseal. Each fall they made their way to dig up the new year's supply. These medicinal roots treated ailments more prevalent in winter, and they ran out before the spring. She would be restocking the tinctures and salves she'd mix from these roots. 'Cohosh' was Algonquin for "rough," which described the rough black roots of the plant used to treat the aged for stomach disorders, rheumatism, and swollen joints. It also helped women with painful courses and change-of-life discomfort. Dancing Light told Suzanne that Abenaki braves would sometimes ask for cohosh before battle because it made them fierce warriors; some called it 'battleroot.' Suzanne named it 'black cohosh' in her journal and had noted its efficacy for two winters now. She only wished she could see Joanna again, to let her know about it.

The cohosh patch rested on the bank of a shallow valley. As the trail rounded the top of a hill, she could see the telltale white spikes of the flowers across the dell. They were nearly six feet tall, well established in the wild though mostly wilted and drooping by September.

"Baby come soon?" Dancing Light pointed at Suzanne's bulging waist as they crossed the valley and climbed the slope to the cohosh.

"Two months. I'm thinking it's a boy. Boys sit differently than my girls did." Suzanne smoothed her skirt, revealing her belly's contour.

"True. We say girl is here." Dancing Light patted the top of her belly, then lowered her hand. "Boy low." She nodded. "Two moons. Good. Time before winter camp. I give baby blessing."

Suzanne rolled up her sleeves and knelt before the plants, pawing through the rustling foliage to decide where to start digging in the loam. She wanted only the most mature plants. The cool leaves caressed her bare arms and she turned to Dancing Light. "I thank you forever for blessing my Standing Heron. He is loved by the Red God and the White God. But for my next baby, I can't come to your blessing. Reverend Willard forbids me, and I must have his approval.

"Why he say no?" Dancing Light shook her head. "Great spirit not same God?"

"Well, there's trouble. The Reverend tells us that white God is the only God. A just God. He'll punish me for listening to red spirit God."

"Did your God come to you? God tell you?"

"No," Suzanne laughed nervously. "Nothing like that. My God speaks to prophets and ministers, not to me. I would sin if I thought he talked to the likes of me."

"Then how you know he punish?" Dancing Light took another position on the bank and began to dig the roots, taking care to bury the flower for each plant she removed to reseed the patch. *Pa-gid-din-nahn*("plant a seed"), she'd explained to Suzanne; they must replace the cohosh they removed, which could not grow back after they'd removed the roots. "Great Spirit send me dream. Then I know."

"White God's words are the Bible. In the good book, God tells us he doesn't want his people to worship any God but Him. It is written as He has spoken. The words are written forever. He will not change." She snipped off the flower and placed it in the cavity left by the cohosh she'd removed.

"Do words speak here?" Dancing Light asked, pressing her heart.

Suzanne stared at the plant she'd pulled roots and all, then added it to her sack. "No. But He speaks clearly. I know that He wants me to have a christening so He can protect my baby."

"Christening?" Dancing Light pronounced the three syllables slowly.

"Making my child Christ's child. Christ-en-ning. A second birth. We bathe the baby in Holy water to clean his sins. God will protect him then."

Dancing Light sat back on her heels, pondering. "Born two times. Yes. My baby blessing same. Ask Great Spirit take birth cord, become sky mother, protect him."

"Very like, but the white God is our father, not our mother." Suzanne didn't say it aloud, but the idea popped into her head: she wanted to invite Dancing Light to her baby's christening. It spurred her on to ask: "Have you ever thought of becoming Christian?"

"When I am girl, Reverend Elliott come to speak of white God. Jesus. He not come again. We are too far."

"Jesus. Yes. He is Christ. Did our Reverend Willard talk to your people?"

"Yes. He is good man." Dancing Light nodded and smoothed the soil with her hand.

"But you do not pray with him?"

"Trouble. White man want adopt red man in his tribe. Red man know this." She stopped to hack at the earth, then continued her complaint with a story about a red man who'd become a Puritan. "Man move to Christian town: Nashoba. Indian town. Near Groton."

"I've heard Reverend Willard talk of Nashoba. Only a few Indian families live there."

"No matter. Man take wife, children. All move away. Leave Nashaway camp empty. Live in English House. Wear English clothes. Eliot steal Indian spirit."

"Yes, I can see that is a problem."

"Red man loses brother or sister, son or daughter, great spirit helps us heal heart." Dancing Light patted her bosom. "We ask great spirit for one we lose. We take captive. Worthy one, we adopt, teach our ways, teach our tongue. White man, same. White man want adopt red man. Same."

"But prisoners are forced!" Suzanne stopped to face her friend; her forehead creased. She found her friend's acceptance of abduction repugnant.

"Yes. They fight, but soon see Great Spirit way is good."

"But Christian Indians *choose* to come to a Christian town."

Dancing Light turned to her frowning and grabbed her wrist to stress her words. "Christian Indian make Red tribe weak, make white tribe strong."

"I see." Her friend was so adamant that Suzanne gave up pushing her argument farther. Dancing Light's objection to Christian conversion surprised her. She hadn't realized that the *pau wau* saw the capture and kidnapping of souls as allowable in her faith. Nor had she realized that her friend considered the act of converting tribal people to the Puritan faith comparable to these abductions. She needed another approach before she could speak to her friend again on the subject.

Dancing Light turned back to her digging, accenting her words with jabs of her digging stick. "Some Christian *squa* ("woman") leave praying town. Come back. Bible tell woman, 'Obey man. Woman not worthy. Woman smaller than man.'"

Suzanne couldn't deny this, nor did she see this would be objectionable. She listened as her friend's voice rose vehemently. "Woman say Minister tell men: 'Beat woman she not obey husband. Man own land, own woman.'"

"It's true. But isn't it the same for you?"

"No. Sister is planter. She is *squa-sachem*, woman sagamore. Woman chief marry she still chief. Land is hers. Not husbands. Her husband *sachem*, chief, then he has his land. Land not hers."

At this revelation, Suzanne saw that the women of Dancing Light's camp had powers she could never dream of in Groton. She had filled half her sack, saving room for the next stop. "Finished?" Suzanne rose.

"Yes. Plenty now." Dancing Light performed her ritual to thank the cohosh for its sacrifice and stood.

The two women descended the bank to reconnect with the trail and followed it another mile to a low patch of golden seal. This plant received its name from its bright yellow rhizome, which when broken, appeared very like a wax seal. Dancing Light had explained to Suzanne the Indian used these roots for a yellow dye as well as for a tea and a salve. She'd shown Suzanne how to mix golden seal with bear fat to keep bugs off in summer. That was responsible for the colonist's insistence the Indians smelled bad, though the Indians bathed daily, and the settlers rarely did. In winter, she'd used it for respiratory and digestive problems. Again, gathering the roots, they had no way to avoid killing the host plants. However, Dancing Light had shown her that she could replace these precious herbs by planting one rhizome for every one she removed. They were easily divided, but the new plantings would not mature for seven years. That made replanting necessary and conservation doubly important.

Dancing Light knelt and plied her digging stick and lifted a plant. She turned to Suzanne. "Bible say red spirit not bless baby? Pastor say too?"

"Yes," Suzanne confessed. She plopped to her knees near the patch. "That's the other reason I can't attend the blessing. My pastor tells me that my neighbors are talking about me. They say I am practicing magic."

"Magic. All medicine magic." Dancing Light gave an extra shake to remove the dirt from a root and placed the plant in her bag.

"No! If my neighbors think that, they will say I do the devil's work, call me a witch. Only God can heal people."

Dancing Light tapped her chest. "Some call me 'witch'?"

"True. That's why my neighbors complain. If they call *me* 'witch,' the magistrates in Boston can hang me dead."

Dancing Light sat back on her heels in shock. "Will they hang me?"

"No," Suzanne reassured her. "You are an Indian. If you were a Puritan, they could. They would."

"Then me not ever Christian." She drove her stone into the soil with vigor, jabbed in the rhizome, and patted earth over the root.

"But you do not practice magic. Cohosh and golden seal are not magic." She didn't want to give up on the possibility she could invite her friend to the christening.

Dancing Light again, doggedly, pronounced: "Medicine is spirit. Spirit magic." She reached into her sack and removed a tobacco pouch. Sprinkling tobacco on the new plantings, she murmured words to them in Algonquin. Suzanne knew that she was thanking the golden seals' spirits for their sacrifice. Perhaps she's right, she thought. In her world, every living thing is a spirit.

The following month, Suzanne gave birth to Samuel, shortly before the Nashua tribe left for their winter lands and added to the muffling silence of the early snows. In the next month, the family gathered for the christening at the meetinghouse. Joseph and Uncle John stood on Reverend Willard's right, and Suzanne on the left. Timothy and Sarah Cooper, who was showing the first sign of expecting her own child, completed the circle. "I christen thee Samuel," the minister pronounced. The baby squirmed, craning his head inaptly at the startling immersion.

That night, she and Joseph sat by the fire enjoying the warmth on a blustery November night. She propped her infant on a pillow to nurse; hearing his loud gulps and tiny grunts made her smile. A good weight at birth, Sammy radiated good health.

Joseph tamped the tobacco in his pipe. He used one of the wood shills he kept in a box on the hearth to light it. The flame crackled as he held the flame to the pipe bowl and drew. He relaxed as he exhaled a puff of smoke. Suzanne smelled the spicy scent.

"Uncle John says that he has put my name forward at the council meeting. I may be a freeman."

"That's wonderful. God has been good to us. When will you know?"

"The council meets again in March. Not soon enough for me. I'd like to vote on the mill. But you're right about providence. We'll have enough stored for the winter. I couldn't have done it without Timothy's help. He's worked tirelessly for all of us. We must share what we can."

Suzanne frowned. "Will there be enough for all of us?"

"If we're not greedy, there's enough. We cannot deny them anything. Timothy cleared the meadow for me. He worked by my side to harvest. The man is selflessly generous with his time. My sister couldn't have married a better man." He then drifted into his own thoughts.

In the last light of the coals, the pair stood above the cradle where they'd laid the sleeping Samuel before they retired to the bedstead. A barn owl hooted softly outside the window, and Suzanne noted a mourning tone she'd not heard before. Do birds know when they've lost their *own*? She wondered.

Chapter Fifteen

BEWITCHED OR BEDEVILED?

Groton, November 1671

Although Joseph was still too young to attend school, both Suzie and Hester walked more than a mile each day to Reverend Willard's house, where they learned to read the Bible, to write and figure. Massachusetts' law decreed towns must build schoolhouses and hire teachers if the populations exceeded the quota. However, growing Groton could not yet collect the town rates that would support a full-time teacher and schoolhouse. The Willards, thus, collected small fees from those parents who would send their children to learn the basics.

Suzanne had barely weaned Samuel when she again found herself with child. She was well along, in her fifth month when she was called away to deliver Goody Tainter's seventh baby, staying overnight and into the afternoon before she arrived home, exhausted. She dropped her bag in the medicine corner and joined young Martha Crisp in the great room, where she was preparing the evening meal.

"You look exhausted," Martha exclaimed, looking up from the vegetables she pared. The table boards were littered with the autumn harvest: Martha was preparing corn, acorn squash, carrots, and potatoes for supper. A small turkey hung from a rafter, ready to be dressed. Looking up from the vegetable she pared, she exclaimed, "Are you alright?"

"I'm just tired. The labor was longer than any I've attended."

"Have you slept?"

"I did have a nap early this morning, enough to get me through. Could you groom Black Lock? I have two hours before the girls come home, and I need to sleep."

"Yes ma'am." She walked to where Joseph played. "And maybe Joseph would like to help me curry our Black Lock?" Joseph didn't need encouragement. He loved horses best, though he had a way with every animal in the yard, down to the lowliest baby chick.

Suzanne pulled the bedstead curtains closed before she stripped off her outer clothes and slipped beneath the counterpane. From the moment she laid her head on the pillow, the world dimmed, and she felt the heavy wave of sleep course through her legs and then her chest. She closed her eyes and slept dreamlessly.

It seemed only minutes later, she woke with a start. Her oldest daughter was calling, "Mother, wake up." She groaned. The short nap had revived her mind, but her body was resisting all motion.

She heard Martha whisper loudly to Suzie, "Why are you home early? Shush. You leave your mother sleep!"

Awake now, Suzanne pulled the curtains aside to find Suzie standing next to the bed, with Hester behind her; both were nearly standing on tiptoes with excitement.

"Mother, Elizabeth Knapp had fits today," she said.

Suzanne didn't know James and Elizabeth Knapp, who lived on the west side of Main Street, at the southerly end of the village, not far from Uncle John. They came from Lancaster, and their daughter boarded with the Willards as help in exchange for education. Samuel and Abigail Willard freed the sixteen-year-old Elizabeth from her chores while classes were in session so she could attend, despite her advanced age.

Suzanne rolled to a sitting position and lowered her feet to the floor. "Elizabeth? Abigail's helper Elizabeth? What do you mean 'fits?'"

Hester shrieked, then covered her face with both hands. She shrieked again, and this time began to laugh crazily. Then Suzie joined in giggling at her sister's behavior. "Do it," she egged her sister. Hester fell to the floor, curling around the horrible laugh she pushed from her mouth then arching her back, stiffened, shrieking.

"All right girls, that's enough now," Suzanne reproved. "We do not make fun of people who cannot help it."

Suzie stood up for her sister. "We're not making fun. You wanted to know what's a fit."

Suzanne smiled wryly at her daughter, who had a moment before been laughing at her sister's antics. Her oldest daughter was so skilled in defensive excuses that she supposed even a merciful God might damn her.

"Oh, I suppose you were laughing at Hester, not Elizabeth then?"

Before her sister could stop her, Hester blurted out: "Reverend Willard says she's sick, and we mustn't laugh." Suzie blushed, staring down at her feet.

"I see. You *were* making fun of Elizabeth, in class, it seems."

"But she's not *sick*. She doesn't throw up. She isn't coughing." Suzie might be embarrassed but would never accept shame.

"Yeah," chimed Hester. "She screams and then laughs. Sometimes she starts crying and jumps around, acting spooky. Then she laughs."

"She laughs so hard she falls on the floor."

"Reverend asked her if she was all right, and she said she was."

Suzanne began to frown. The behaviors her children were describing went beyond any illness of which she was familiar. These actions were responses to pain or joy, not a physical ailment. In Groton, such actions might be thought supernatural. *Is the child bewitched? Are there witches?* The minute she thought it, she put it out of her mind. *Witches don't exist*, she thought.

"Well, the Reverend is right. You mustn't laugh at her if she is sick as he says. That wouldn't be right. I'll ask the Reverend about it at Sabbath."

"Reverend says we don't have to come back to school until he says." Suzie ran out the door, happy to have the last word before her mother took a notion to punish her.

At the Sabbath that week, Reverend Willard announced to the parish he'd restored order, and the children should come back to school again on Monday.

Still mystified about her children's stories, Suzanne sought Abigail when they paused for their noon meal. "Come sit with me." She patted the pew. "The children told me that Elizabeth Knapp had a fit. That's why he dismissed them."

"It's true."

"What happened?"

"It started the night before. We were sitting by the fire with the help as is our habit now the nights are cool; we join in prayer before we go to bed. Suddenly, she slapped her legs and cried out 'oh, my legs.' Then it was her chest. She clutched it crying 'my breast' and started coughing. She grabbed her throat. 'I'm strangling,' she chokes out. No one knew what to think. Was she acting or in earnest? We left it for make-believe, though she complained she couldn't breathe to our helper, Anna, when they went upstairs to bed. Of course, she *was* breathing."

"It does seem she might have been acting. How strange."

"Well, the next day she was in a stranger way. Your children saw it. We all did. Sometimes she was weeping, sometimes laughing. She was leaping about making foolish and apish gestures. Falling on the floor."

"And that's when you sent the children home from school?"

"We didn't know what else to do. Children are cruel and began to mimic her behavior, but that didn't stop her; Elizabeth disrupted all our lessons. We decided it was best. Until we can find what's causing this conduct, we'll have to separate her from the class."

"I'd do the same. Has she improved? Is that why Samuel invited back the children?"

"No. She's worse. That night, she went into the cellar and we heard her scream. When we rushed to find out what happened, she told us she'd seen two men there. We could see no one, but she turned her head to speak to someone we couldn't see. 'What cheer old man?' she says. Not an expression a young girl would use. So odd. Later, she woke the whole family when we'd gone to bed. Sarah, who shares a room with Elizabeth, said she was thrown violently to the floor and taken with a fit. It took three of us to keep her from destroying herself in the fire."

"Convulsions. It sounds like convulsions."

"From that night until today, the fits have continued. It takes three or four to restrain her; she's that strong! In these strange agitations, she roars and screams, like she's tortured. Sometimes, when she's able to speak, we hear her crying 'money, money, money,' and sometimes 'sin and misery,' or something like it."

"How terrible. What will you do?"

"Samuel feels great pity for her, you see. He believes that she's afflicted by some force and that God can intervene to cure her. For now, he will work with her as much as he can to find the cause, but I will take over teaching until Samuel can join us again."

"Oh, I see. Perhaps we can all pray for her."

"Yes, I think we must."

Abigail had no better news on the next Sabbath. Elizabeth Knapp's condition continued to grow worse despite the ministrations of Reverend Willard and the girl's abject remorse. Abigail spilled out the story.

"On Wednesday, the fits subsided enough for Samuel to talk with her. The girl accused our neighbor, Mary Parker, of afflicting her. Samuel thought it wasn't Goody Parker, but the devil in her likeness and habit (he wore the same riding hood). Elizabeth swore Mary had come down the chimney and struck her down. Of course, Samuel would not be happy without proof, so he sent for Mary and invited witnesses. Of course, Mary didn't know why he'd sent for her."

"You say Samuel brought in witnesses?"

"Yes. He must. What if the Devil does control her? If she be accused of being a witch? He'll need witnesses if he gives evidence."

"I see. Yes. He'd need evidence."

"In truth, even with her eyes bound shut, Elizabeth knew when Mary touched her. Mind you, Mary had not said a word. With evidence of such a bond, he made them both pray with him. Then, Elizabeth confessed Satan had deluded her. It wasn't Mary she'd seen. She's not complained about Mary since, even though her fits continue."

"Samuel dropped the matter?"

He swore, 'God has justified the innocent.' But that didn't stop it. The next day she confessed Satan had tried to win her. She said she'd first met Satan three years ago, before she began boarding with us. He had presented a covenant to her, promising her money, silks, fine clothes, ease from labor. He promised to show her the whole world. At first, he had rarely appeared, but lately, she says he comes more often. Most recently, he urged her to murder her parents, her neighbors, and our children. Suzanne, she was to murder the youngest! He told her to throw Beth into the fire, into the oven. One time he put a hook into her hand to murder my husband while he was asleep."

"Murder a minister of God?" Suzanne was aghast.

"Yes. And Samuel said he remembers meeting her on the stairs that time because she was in a strange mood and trying to hide something! Evil we could never imagine. She claims the Devil even persuaded her to drown herself in the well, and she had climbed up on the curb when God's providence prevented her from jumping."

"Then has she a contract with the Devil?"

"She denies it. She told Samuel she thinks God has ordered this temptation to make her stronger."

"I doubt that."

"I agree, but I can't tell you how abject she is when she repents: tears, self-condemnation. My Samuel must write all of it in case the matter goes to Boston. Elizabeth—she is so contrite when she is sensible—has asked for her own minister, Reverend Rowlandson, to come from Lancaster. He'll come on the next Sabbath."

The following Sunday, the visit from Reverend Rowlandson had no benefit for the ailing Elizabeth. Though he offered the comfort of familiarity, the prayers and counsel had no effect on her fits, which continued as before.

Abigail, still charged with running the school for her now absent husband, seemed overcome. "Suzanne, Elizabeth is now stricken with long lapses where she can hear us and understand but cannot respond. She can only babble 'money, money, sin and misery.' Samuel has gathered more witnesses because it can take as many as six to restrain her fits. I am worried about Samuel now. He's so obsessed with Elizabeth, I fear he's a captive of Satan too."

"Do you believe she's bargained with Satan? That she's a witch?" After a month of Abigail's descriptions, Suzanne was beginning to think she'd been wrong about unnatural forces.

"Suzanne, I don't know what to think. Samuel believes the Devil has infected our town. He's afraid and says he wants me to stop seeing you."

"Not see you! Does he think I have something to do with her possession?"

"He does. He claims your work with Dancing Light could be at the bottom of it. But I'm sure he's wrong. Suzanne, I don't know what to do."

Suzanne slumped. "Convulsions are well-known in medicine. People used to think the falling sickness was a sign of possession but now know it has a physical cause. He is right to ask the question."

"My husband will not give up. He prays that she has some physical illness. He told me he will send for Dr. Knox to rule out possession. He cannot imagine that she must be hanged as a witch; she's still a child."

Facing the need of declaring her a witch, with the terrible results, had frozen Reverend Willard's ability to decide at all. He doggedly continued to record her condition.

Chapter Sixteen

THE POSSESSED

Groton, December 1671

Although Suzanne missed her working relationship as well as friendship with Abigail Willard, she understood that it was better she had no contact with the Willards while Elizabeth was ailing. Joanna had taught her well that even the slimmest connection to imaginary sources of evil would end badly for a midwife. She could not deal with life and death matters so long as another could accuse her of malice and magic. She accepted their separation was for the best and bowed to the necessity of keeping the children home from school.

Soon after her last meeting with Abigail, Suzanne was surprised to find her younger brother standing at her door, his saddle satchel slung over one shoulder, a leather pouch in his hand. Dr. Philip Sherborn, now twenty-three, had completed his apprenticeship to Dr. Stone in Boston. A practicing physician, he'd married Deborah Barstow and moved to Cambridge. He'd never visited her before, even though Suzanne had been close to him before she was apprenticed to Joanna Morton because they played at being healers together. Of course, Philip was six years younger, and most often he played her willing patient.

"Philip, I don't believe it!"

Philip grinned from ear to ear, setting down his satchels, stretching out both hands to grip hers. "It's I, truly. I'm here."

"Joseph," she called to her husband, "Look who's here. Philip." She turned to him again. "What brings you? I'm assuming you didn't drop in without good reason. Come in. Come."

Philip followed Suzanne to the hall where Joseph stood up from his chore. He was sharpening harvest tools to store them for the winter months. "Philip! What a pleasure."

"I'm here on Reverend Willard's request, with my fellow, Dr. Richard Knox. I believe you know him."

"Dr. Knox, yes. He practices in Concord. But I didn't know you knew him."

"He was apprenticed to Dr. Stone when I was, but he became a Chirurgeon. Surgery suits his trade."

"And you?"

"I've followed the physic's path. We'll use our combined knowledge to treat Reverend Willard's help."

"That must be Elizabeth Knapp."

"Yes. That's her. But enough of that. I thought it a perfect time to visit you."

"You will stay with us then? Please, sit down. You can put your satchel there."

"I'd be grateful. I'm tired; it's a longer ride to Groton than I thought."

"Why has Reverend Willard called you?"

"He didn't. He called Richard Knox to examine the girl. Richard asked me to come with him because he knows I've done some reading on witchcraft and can provide a physician's view. Elizabeth might be possessed by an evil force, but he'd like a second pair of eyes at the examination before he prescribes any treatment.

"Witchcraft. You?"

"I don't believe in witches, but I do find the mental processes most interesting. She's suffering convulsions but confesses to working with the Devil if I've heard right. I am curious if both states are symptoms. Are the causes spiritual or a physical failing? It's the state that interests me."

That night at dinner, after the children had been fed and put to bed, they gathered around the table boards. Suzanne had many questions about the Watertown family, but Philip, who had moved to Cambridge, couldn't answer them. She knew that he and Deborah had only just buried their first child, a son who lived only eight days. When she'd offered her condolences, Philip had reacted with anger, snapping that he would not talk about it. She delicately avoided the subject thereafter. Suzanne helped Martha clear the table and filled a pot with water to boil cranberries for the next day.

Philip's line of inquiry led to questions about Reverend Willard, the man who had hired Elizabeth Knapp.

"He is a great speaker," Joseph ventured. "So great that the town has doubled his salary in the three years he has been our pastor."

"He makes twice as much?" Suzanne was astounded. She hadn't realized the man's salary was now the major expense of their town rate. She unfolded the cloth that held the berries she'd gathered, dumped them in the pot, and put more wood on the fire. Then she sat by the hearth to make sure they didn't boil over.

"I believe the council decided that because of his double duty as minister and schoolmaster."

"But Abigail is the teacher. Not Reverend Willard."

"No one hired her as such." Joseph lit his pipe and puffed on it, eyes narrowing with content.

"You would not pay compensation for a woman who works?"

"You are a midwife. Reverend Willard certifies you. That's different. Of course, the women pay you. But they've never appointed Abigail as teacher. They appointed Samuel Willard."

"Do you know the Reverend's views on witches?" Philip came back to his subject.

"I find him to be, from his sermons, an orthodox Puritan. He believes in the Devil and accepts possession, but he also has a strong faith that God's grace is generous. God is more powerful than Satan, who cannot destroy us. Wouldn't you agree, Suzanne?"

"Yes. He is not above threatening God's punishment for our sinful ways, but he doesn't condemn man as the

Devil's pawn, so lost he must be hanged or burned at the stake. He does show unusual compassion."

"I look forward to working with him then." Philip drank the last of his ale, pushed the mug aside, and gazed steadily at his older sister. "Dr. Knox tells me that you are the main source of healing in Groton now."

Suzanne reddened. "A compliment from Dr. Knox! He prefers to doctor his soldiers. Women tell me that before I came to Groton, he sent them to Lancaster for medicine."

"That sounds like him. He never took to common diseases, and hated women's problems. He wants to practice surgery, save lives."

"And you? Do you think Elizabeth's fits could be natural? Convulsions common in epilepsy?"

"It's possible, but we must observe her first. If so, the recommended cure is trepanning, surgery that Richard Knox is qualified to perform."

Suzanne shuddered, imagining Dr. Knox sawing a hole in Elizabeth's skull to release fluids. *Qualified, but hardly experienced to expose brains to the light of day,* she thought. *He's eager to perform such a procedure just for the experience.*

"But I still believe the Greeks have it right; balance the four humors is the path to health."

"Then you think digestion is all?"

"Not just diet. Cleansing poisons from the body is fundamental."

"You ignore her spirit. Isn't it God who sends all afflictions and God who can end them?" She could hear the pot of cranberries had come to a rolling boil.

"I know that's the basis of our Puritan faith, but I'm surprised to hear your question."

"I've had need to call on God in *my* practice." Suzanne sighed and sat back in her chair. "I am alone in my work and find even an unseen spirit supports me." She smiled. *I used Dancing Light's word for God,* she thought.

"Well, I believe in Satan, dark forces."

He said it with such force, his face scowling, that he alarmed Suzanne. "I thought you were a scientist."

"I am, sister. I follow Dr. Harvey and the rest. Have you heard of him?"

"I have not." The cranberries began to pop as they emptied gelatin flesh from the tough skins.

"He's published a work that proposes blood circulates through the body, a closed system. He's changed everything, gives an entirely new perspective on cupping and bleeding. Richard tells me his theory explains why these treatments have been so effective."

"But you play the Devil's advocate. Do you think that ill humors and poison fumes are Satan's manifestations?" She noted from the scent and sight of the now thick cherry-red sauce, the cranberries were done. She pulled the pot from the fire and scattered the wood.

"Do you have a better explanation? You see what I mean," he challenged, "if I give evil a name, a person? We'll do our best with Elizabeth tomorrow."

She caught his meaning. The sound of cooling embers popping in the hearth suddenly struck Suzanne with the likeness to exploding cranberries. Musing on the resemblance, she bid Philip goodnight and followed Joseph to her bed.

Philip left the next day before noon, explaining that Dr. Knox had ruled out epilepsy, and they were treating her for a physical affliction. They'd sent Elizabeth home to her parents with directions to purge all physical toxins. It wasn't until Philip returned to follow up on Elizabeth that she heard any more detail than what came to her from the pulpit on Sundays. He informed her that Dr. Knox had observed a fit and declared: "There's nothing we can do. It's up to the men of God now. Only they can reclaim her soul."

Reverend Willard continued to work with Elizabeth, relying on witnesses and onlookers during his sessions of prayer and confrontation of a demon who took over her body. By now, her case was famous throughout Massachusetts, and his sermons passed on what wisdom he could. He spoke to them of the only certainty he knew. He preached on Sunday: "There is a voice in it to the whole land, but in a more especial manner to poor Groton. It is not a judgment afar off, but it is near us, yea among us. God has in his wisdom singled out this poor town out of all others in this wilderness, to dispense such an amazing providence in. Therefore, let us make a closer, special use of it. Let us look upon ourselves to be set up as a *Beacon upon a Hill* by this providence. And let those that hear what hath been done among us, hear also of the good effects, a reformation it hath wrought among us."

Even though his words seared her soul, anger overcame her anxiety. She was too practical to analyze his religious superstitions; she dared not. Suzanne missed working with her friend Abigail, who she knew had to obey her husband as demanded by the scriptures. Suzanne rationalized. *Haven't the women in this town benefited from Dancing Light's herbs? Haven't I saved the lives of two?* Then she lapsed into blaming. *How am I worse than those who cheat the Indians, steal their land? Is God to punish me for good and reward them for evil? Wouldn't God be more likely to strike those who sell the Indians rum in cahoots with Waldron? What I do is for the glory of God, even saving an Indian.*

In the end, her arguments didn't quell her anxiety, and she prayed on her knees at her bedside for forgiveness.

Too busy with readying her life for her next and fifth child, Suzanne paid little attention to the notice she heard from a neighbor returning from Watertown. Her sister Rebecca was to marry. It was her mother's letter that alerted her to the wedding date and named the preposterous groom, Sam Church. Suzanne wouldn't be able to attend the wedding because her baby was due in just weeks. As it turned out, a nasty storm checked any travel in any event, but even the weather couldn't stop her giving birth to her third daughter, Mary Morse, at the end of January.

She'd not planned another child so soon; little Samuel wasn't even two yet, and she'd have to rearrange her life to make room for a nursing infant. What's more, her helper Martha would turn eighteen this year and would be eligible for marriage; she would need to replace her. This was especially imminent because Martha had a suitor, Jimmy Roberts, a neighbor's son. While her sister-in-law Sarah had been a great help, she had her own family to support now.

Then, Elizabeth Knapp took a turn for the better and by March, all her symptoms disappeared. The congregation believed that God had healed her through Reverend Willard's patient intent. The girl had so many times repented for her sins, that no one could doubt it. Samuel Willard had documented the entire ordeal with such detail, that his report cleared Elizabeth Knapp of all suspicion of witchcraft. He sent it to the Reverend Cotton Mather in Boston for precedents in other cases of witchcraft and possession. Believing the threat was now gone, he invited Suzanne's children back to school.

Chapter Seventeen

HEART STRINGS

Groton, March 1672

Suzanne did have passing thoughts about the rumored wedding of her sister; Watertown's Sam Church had a terrible reputation and was twice as old as Rebecca, who, at fifteen, wasn't even close to her majority. *Well sixteen in February,* she thought. She guessed that her father, such a righteous and devout Puritan, had only allowed such a union under duress. Nor would her mother have approved. Suzanne suspected that Rebecca was with child. The church could charge her with fornication. Ruined, even if she married, the town-born would suspect an early birth. *Poor Rebecca*, she thought. She couldn't wish the public shaming that came with it on even an enemy. *Samuel Church!* She was certain who to blame.

Then Joseph brought home news the Groton town council had granted five acres to Samuel Church, courting this sawyer for a skill needed in any frontier town. They'd granted acreage that was right across the road from Sarah and Timothy Cooper, just south of the Gilsons' and next to the church burial grounds.

Suzanne was mollified by the news; she'd missed family so much when she'd come to Groton. When Sarah and Timothy had moved in, she had welcomed the sense of a growing family, and the thought her sister and husband would join them excited her. She would have the family life she had missed. Moreover, she knew the whole town would welcome the newcomers, who would enlarge the town's potential. They would have no end of help to homestead on their acres; new residents were necessary to their survival on the Massachusetts frontier. And, as Joseph said, Samuel Church's reputation would not precede him, and if he joined the Groton church, he would have a fresh start on life. But Suzanne feared reputations were too often the result of character, and Rebecca alone couldn't hide the facts.

All midwives, and Suzanne was not an exception, held the Puritan church's charge of ensuring the morality of the Puritan community. If a woman had a child out of wedlock, and the father was already married, would not claim his child, or admit paternity, the mother-to-be often hid his identity. In these cases, the midwife must intercede. The townspeople couldn't afford to support fatherless children. Customs enforced the laws, which had the dual effect of deterring fornication as well as its results—dunning for the child's upkeep. Laws charged midwives with interrogating the laboring woman under duress to reveal the father's name, which midwives must then report to the clergy. Their certification as healers depended on this colluding support of church morals and civil laws.

Suzanne found the practice heartless because many midwives threatened God's punishment, even death, to extort the confession when a woman was at her most vulnerable—in the throes of labor. However, Joanna Morton had taught her, *that* trust also gave her a greater power—her testimony. If she believed her patient had broken a rule without malice or negative result, Suzanne's word could eliminate social stigma though it couldn't absolve the sin. She could bear witness that a full-term birth was early, with no one the wiser.

Suzanne had assumed this power with her mentor's blessing, taking full responsibility that she was not only breaking civic law but also her covenant in the church. While she only exercised it when she was sure her actions demonstrated compassion—a Christian impulse, not false pride in her power—she sometimes felt doubt. She could only add this transgression to the growing list of those she committed in her friendship with Dancing Light. In this matter, she would surely exercise her power to protect her sister if so needed.

At the end of March, with Mary rocked to sleep in the cradle, Suzanne enlisted Martha's help in getting the loft ready for the newlyweds. They would stay for two weeks while the town's men finished roofing the Church couple's house they had raised on Monday.

Around supper time, Suzanne heard the commotion in the yard as Sam and Becky arrived in their creaking cart, which grumbled beneath the load of their household goods. Joseph hailed them, and the two men led the mule to the barn, where they unharnessed him for the night. Suzanne knew instantly when Becky crossed her threshold why she'd married Sam Church. Her sister's pallor, even more obvious on a red-haired girl with fair, but freckled skin, made her case clear. Green at the gills, greasy hair escaping from her cap, she was in the early months of a pregnancy.

She held Becky's hands, inspecting her sister as she greeted her. "You look exhausted. Are you ill?"

Becky nodded. "I thought I'd die. The road was so rough the swaying of the cart made me sick. I had to walk part of the way. Three days! When I saw smoke rising over the trees, I could have kissed the mule. I'm frozen to the bones."

Suzanne hugged her sister close. "I'm sorry. It's a rough journey even in summer; I remember it well. Come. Sit down." Suzanne led her to the high-backed settee that faced the fire. "Warm yourself here. You can have supper and take your rest after." She turned to Martha, who worked at preparing supper. "Martha, come and meet my sister."

Martha stood to acknowledge Becky. "Pleased to meet you, Goody Church."

Becky, not one for formalities, objected to the title. "Please call me Rebecca." She turned to Suzanne, "I prefer Rebecca to Becky. It's more proper; I'm a married woman now." She tittered.

"That's certainly the case!" Suzanne laughed to herself; this self-puffing was so like the colorful sister she remembered. Fondly, she excused her pride: *She's still a silly girl.* "Rebecca, then."

Suzie rushed her aunt. "Aunt Rebecca, I have a dolly. Would you like to see?"

Suzanne frowned. "No Suzie. We grown-ups want to talk now. Your aunt will talk to you later." Rebecca's face fell. Disappointed but obedient, Suzie returned to Martha's side.

When Suzanne tried to take her cloak, Rebecca motioned her away. "I'm too cold. Maybe when I've warmed up?" She dropped into the closest chair, pulling her wrap close. She began to talk, haltingly at first. Then, as though her words had been frozen in a great block of ice that was now thawing, her words poured out a nonstop and rambling stream from memory. Suzanne only caught the drift in snatches when Rebecca's voice raised above a hoarse whisper.

Lost in the string of unrelated details, Suzanne tried to slow her down. "Becky, you have so many stories, but I can't listen to all of them at once." Suzanne laughed, good-humoredly standing, hands on hips. "We'll have plenty of time to catch up. Joseph tells me that your house will not be ready for another week. Will you take some food?"

Samuel, so tall that he had to stoop as he entered the house, preceded Joseph, who slammed the door behind them. Suzanne's first impression of Samuel Church was a receding hairline and graying hair framing a face with even but indistinct features. He was not without appeal, though she reacted to a slump that took off two inches from his height. *Is he trying to shrink himself?* she thought, but remembered he was a sawyer. Working all day at one end of a saw under the dogs might disadvantage a tall man.

Joseph rubbed his hands together briskly to warm them. "Tonight's a good one for some hot rum. These folks are frozen." Suzanne pulled her sister from the chair and they made their way to the great room, where Martha worked to set out their meal. Rebecca fell silent through the entire meal.

Later, sitting around the table, Samuel accepted Joseph's offer of a pipe. He tamped the tobacco in it and lit the bowl, drawing deeply, and sighing as the smoke curled from his nostrils and mouth, and continued his story. "We would have been a day earlier if Rebecca hadn't gotten sick. She insisted on walking, which even slowed down the mule."

Suzanne bristled at this remark, looking askance at Rebecca to see how she'd react. *He complains when a pregnant woman cannot ride?* she thought.

Rebecca responded by turning from him. She focused on Suzanne, as though to enlist her as an ally. "I couldn't drink or eat for puking. I'm so sorry."

Samuel scoffed. "It's all in your head. You're fine now."

Rebecca grimaced and pulled her arms around her belly. "Thank God, I am."

Suzanne could only go along with her sister's public compliance. She would speak to her in private, but couldn't help reproving Samuel. "She's a healthy and strong young woman, but also pregnant. It's part of what women must endure with a pregnancy."

Martha began to stir from the kitchen, stacking the cutlery and bowls from the table.

Samuel puffed at his pipe with an ease only the entitled exhibit. "Well, I don't know much about that." It was unspoken among the family seated at the table that, as a man, his wife's problems were not his concern. It was her duty to obey his commands.

Suzanne struggled with the thought that she had begun to dislike this new family member before she learned anything about him. This grew over the next week, after

Timothy joined Joseph and Samuel to unload the cart at their new house.

As the summer wore on, Suzanne came to regret her own aversion to coming between them on the day that she saw bruises on Rebecca's arms. Samuel, she was sure, was a wife beater. While wife beating wasn't unlawful in the Puritan church, such punishments had to be deserved. As far as she could tell, in the church's eyes, Rebecca was innocent of everything except the fornication that led to her pregnancy.

In August, Suzanne was surprised by yet another visit from her Watertown family. Will Sherborn junior was Suzanne's third out of five brothers, the one who had followed their father to learn the weaving trade. Suzanne was shocked to see her little brother standing at her door in the morning; the last time she'd seen him six years ago, when she'd moved from Watertown, they'd stood eye to eye. Now he was nineteen, she had to crane her head to greet him. However, still wiry and lithe, he had changed little, and she could never mistake the narrow face, complete with close-set blue eyes and brown forelock flowing from a widow's peak.

"Will! I can't believe you're here." Her baby, only six months old and still nursing, voiced a welcoming screech. Suzanne had strapped baby Mary to her back in a shawl, and the infant peered over her shoulder.

Will Junior bent to catch her eyes, his face glum. "I have news," he said. "It's father." He reached out to take her hands.

"Father! What?" she stammered. The last time she'd seen him her father was a healthy man in his forties.

"He's gravely ill," he explained. "Philip says it's apoplexy. He believes he hasn't much time left before his end. Father wants to give us our blessings and has asked that you come."

Suzanne, a practicing midwife used to emergencies, regained her equilibrium quickly. She knew what this heart trouble could do. "Is he still of sound mind?"

"Yes. He can talk and reason. Philip says he was lucky."

"Indeed. Then we must leave immediately. His condition could change fast. Have you told Rebecca yet?"

"No, it took some time to find *you*. I don't know where she lives."

"We'll go now." She turned and walked swiftly to the great room. "Martha," she called. "I will leave now. You have charge of the children. I'm leaving Mary with you. She'll be good for an hour. I'll be back for her feeding."

When she returned to the hall, she said, "Rebecca's house isn't far; we can walk. You know John leases some of his land to them?" Suzanne led him out the door; he walked stiffly, and she guessed, painfully after his long ride.

He grimaced and spoke. "I recall that was the plan when they married."

"Do you see John much?"

"I did. We both joined Captain Beere's company. But father wasn't happy about it. He said I should be in cavalry, not infantry, so I switched. He even bought a new horse for me to train. And you know him. He thinks John's a bad influence in any event."

"He still hasn't forgiven John for leaving the church?" Suzanne, now sweating with their exertion, fanned herself.

"Not likely. Father's a covenanted churchman, won't change. We mustn't forget his faith brought him to Massachusetts."

"That's not the way John sees it. When he stayed here, he said father left to avoid conscription in the civil war."

"I've heard it, too. He thinks father's a coward. But it's just his way to justify his own choice. And he would. He's Captain Beere's convert."

"He's wrong! Cowards don't cross an ocean to live in a wilderness."

"No argument from me. Father's no fool. He knows John well."

"And isn't above bribing you with a horse, either." Suzanne smiled wryly at this brother's innocence.

Rebecca, though gravid with her pregnancy, insisted on joining the Morses' travels to Watertown. Her husband declined, giving the excuse that he'd be needed on Captain Parker's parade ground. They left Groton with the cart and mule for the youngest three children and cargo, the rest intermittently riding Black Lock or walking. No weather events interrupted their progress on the main thoroughfare to Boston, and they reached Watertown and the Sherborn homestead in due time.

Once they'd checked in, the Morse's four children were surrounded by the Sherborn cousins, absorbed in recalibrating their loyalties and identities. Residents in the sleeping loft had nearly doubled on their arrival. Suzanne and Rebecca, now reunited with their mother and siblings, glowed as they bustled through the common room, helping to prepare meals in an atmosphere that belied the occasion—a man dying on his sickbed.

During these last days, their father suffered from a deep exhaustion. He drifted in and out of a restless sleep, with barely the energy to speak. Suzanne carefully regulated the visits with his grandchildren as he slid in and out of consciousness.

When she at last stood with her own children clustered around her, she knew he had not long on earth. Little Suzie dared to hold his hand. Suzanne smiled, sniffing back the tears that rolled down her cheeks; it was hard for her to see him like this. Her children stared wide-eyed, not knowing what to make of their grandfather's labored breathing and pale face. "Say good-bye to your grandfather now. You may kiss him."

She introduced them one by one, and they kissed him. William closed his eyes and exhaled a "thank you." As the children filed out of his room, he raised his head to watch them go before he relaxed, staring up at Suzanne, who carried baby Mary. "I know that you named this one after your sister Mary." He lifted a finger from the bed to indicate her baby's head nestled in her arms.

Suzanne nodded. He continued, "Tell your sister. She doesn't know how you feel and needs you more than you can know."

"Yes Father. I will." She was mystified by his last words, his asking her to take care of Mary. She might have expected him to say the same about Rebecca since she was now living in Groton. But Mary?

She bent to kiss him and, realizing he had spent all his energy, left the room.

He died the next day and Suzanne pitched in to prepare for the procession to his burial place. Suzanne didn't know what she felt about her father after his death; she suffered no acute grief, though she was certainly sad. She'd been apprenticed when but a girl and so, had not been close to him after that. What is more, it was always clear to her at get togethers that he treated her very differently from her sister Mary. He favored Mary, claiming that she was clairvoyant, as their grandmother had been. Suzanne hadn't minded. She had ever been one to strike out on her own, which required a level of acceptance rare for anyone whose feet were less firmly planted in the here and now like her sister's. *Mary*, she'd often mused, *was ever never present.*

Following the reading of her father's will the day after the funeral, they packed the cart and the family made their way back to Groton. Two weeks after they arrived Rebecca gave birth to a daughter. Suzanne had insisted that she come to the Morse house to give birth, assuring her of privacy. She alone would see the child born; she couldn't risk a helper knowing the child was carried full term. She intended to put out the word that Rebecca's child was premature to protect her from any punishments for getting herself with child out of wedlock. *Rebecca can deal with Sarah. She'll know the baby isn't premature, but they're friends,* she thought.

Chapter Eighteen

THE DARKENING SKY

Groton, March 1673

Once the threat to the stricken Elizabeth Knapp had passed, Reverend Willard relaxed his control on his wife's friendship with Suzanne. By spring, he even allowed Abigail to help deliver the twice-bereaved Sarah Cooper. Suzanne had delivered Sarah's second child in her sixth month. Though the infant could breathe on her own, she was unable to nurse despite all their efforts and died in her first week

In March, when the winter ice melt released swelling river tides and scents of fertile earth, Suzanna's sister-in-law went into labor. The two women delivered Sarah's first daughter, a round and red-faced, full-term cherub who cried lustily and latched properly on her mother's breast. After she and Abigail had cleaned up, they left the new mother nursing her newborn to prepare a small meal for themselves in the great room.

Suzanne felt a gratitude that lifted her hopes for both Sarah and her baby. She had suffered as much as Sarah on her last delivery of the infant born too soon. Abigail too, rejoiced. "She will thrive, this one." Abigail rummaged through the carpetbag she'd brought with her. "I have bread and cheese. Do you think Sarah has some ale?"

"I agree. She has a lusty cry, a sure sign she's strong. She'll survive." Suzanne searched the hearthside for the fermenting crock that graced everyone's home. "Here it is." She found clean mugs on a shelf. The ladle for the brew hung beside the crock, and she lifted the wooden cover and dipped enough ale to fill two mugs. The two women relaxed on the fireside table benches after the long labor.

"Has Dancing Light come back?" Abigail sliced the cheese and pulled a hunk of bread from the loaf. While Samuel Willard had forbidden her to visit Suzanne when he'd thought the powwow had something to do with their servant's affliction, he'd relented after Elizabeth had recovered. If the powwow had bewitched her, his Godly presence and his subject's penitence had dispelled the demon. Abigail was always curious about the Nashaway' s, even though she squinted at Suzanne's easy adoption of moccasins, wampum, medicine bags, and cradle boards. "We've heard the drums."

"Yes. We too, but she hasn't visited yet. She will, of course. We gather skunk cabbage this month." She passed a mug to Abigail. "Do you have news from your father of Watertown?"

"Nothing particular. Samuel says he's heard rumors the Indians in Plymouth are arming themselves against the English. The Boston magistrates are mediating conflicts now." Abigail chewed thoughtfully.

"Joseph has heard that too. Have you heard news from the Major?" Major Simon Willard, who had moved to Groton the year before, was the Reverend Willard's father.

"He hasn't talked about an uprising. But I believe Boston is firming up the militia. The general court has promoted our James Parker to Captain. He'll command a colonial company. Mary Parker is a little too proud of her husband's appointment to my way of thinking."

Suzanne sliced the cheese. "Pride is a failing, but she's probably happy he's paid, some advantage over our local militia. I heard it from Sam Church. Joseph's drilling with the militia on the commons, too. He says that William Larkin and Nathaniel Lawrence are to be Captain Parker's ensigns."

"It's sounding serious." Abigail sipped the ale. "The Major has insisted that we build a garrison wing and palisades around our house. He's sent for riflemen to defend it.

"Joseph says the plan is to have four garrisons. Nutting and Parker, your closest neighbors, are putting up palisades, too. And Sawtell's place, down the road, the fourth.

"Oh, Suzanne, I'll be living in a fort. I married a learned man, a minister, not a soldier. It's all because of Samuel's father. What will become of us?"

"But you'll be safe if there's trouble. Your husband's father is in command of colonial troops for all of Middlesex. Isn't that comforting?"

"The Major brings small comfort. Even he admits our neighbors have never been hostile; so, why are we arming ourselves?" Abigail rose to clear the table. "I worry more about the likes of Tarball. You've heard that he was caught selling spirits to the Indians."

"I have but found it hard to believe. I've heard him rail against the 'savages' and their drinking. He sees no good in our neighbors across the river. He's a church elder. Who'd ever suspect he was complicit with the worst of them all along?"

"Sachem Tahanto—he doesn't tolerate liquor in his camp—complained, but no one believed him. Tarball denied his charge, said Tahanto was lying. They believed Tarball, him being a selectman and all."

"Tarball being a hypocrite, you mean."

Abigail laughed, stacking the bowls. "No shortage of those in our poor town. What do you make of it? He accuses you of siding with Satan because you work with Dancing Light. But he sells spirits to the natives, breaking our laws at the same time he is corrupting them. Is it hatred?"

"I think he sees only the profit. He isn't thinking of souls, neither theirs or his own." Suzanne prepared pallets for sleeping.

"He might have gotten away with it, but Goodman Daniels marked a bottle to test the chief's accusation. Even after he was caught, Tarball still denied it, all the way to court. I want you to be careful of Ann and Thomas Tarball, Suzanne. There's no telling what they may do."

After looking in on the mother and baby, now both asleep, the two women settled for the night, lying on pallets, listening to the pop and crackle of dying embers, which lulled them to sleep.

That Sunday, Reverend Willard announced to the parish the council's plan to build four barricaded garrisons. They would also impose a plan assigning each resident family to one of them should Indians attack. "We who live on the edges of civilization must prepare for the worst, if history can teach us."

Joseph Morse had trained for combat in the Watertown militia like all males over sixteen in the Massachusetts colony. The military alliance in Boston drew from these militia to man the colonial troops. In Groton, Joseph continued to drill with the town's men under the newly commissioned Captain Parker; he was ready if conscription began. Cleaning his guns for these drills, he'd set six-year-old Joseph to work. He removed two rifles from their pegs above the hearth.

He'd explained to Suzanne the smoothbore barrel muskets that Boston required weren't as good as his rifles, whether they were matchlock or the newer, superior flintlocks. While a musket could be reloaded faster—good in battle—his rifles had a greater range and were more accurate. They were great for hunting. And for defense in any emergency. He wanted her to know how to load and fire both of them. Suzanne had put off the lesson when they lived in more-populated Watertown, but in Groton she'd reconsidered.

Today, Joseph bent close to his son, demonstrating the proper angle at which to sharpen the flint for the firing mechanism of his flint-lock rifle.

"You just need hard surface. An antler tine, a nail, a stone." Joseph held the flint and pushed the antler across the edge, chipping off a bit of flint that left a sharp edge. "This will do. See? Now, you try it."

While Joseph junior worked at duplicating his father's work, Joseph continued. "It must be kept sharp. Three or four shots, you need to clean the power pan and change the flints. If you do it right, the gun will never fail you."

"Is that it?" Joseph stopped to ask for his father's approval.

Suzanne nodded at the pair. "You mind what he says now. Your father knows."

Joseph stopped to stare at her. "I think your husband needs you to take this lesson more seriously."

Suzanne smiled. "Sadly, I must agree."

Dancing Light appeared at her door the following week, and they made their way to the swamps to gather the blooming skunk cabbage. Suzanne was grateful her friend didn't mention she'd heard of the settlers plans to palisade houses but wondered if her tribe's removal for the winter had cut her off from the rumors spreading now. It also occurred to her that Dancing Light might be concealing news, a thought that left her unsettled. It appeared that both might have reason to avoid any discussion of rumored conflicts. *I can wait*, she thought.

The year sped on: crops sowed; summer rains that brought the seedlings unfurled row on row of leaves. In June, Abigail brought Suzanne a letter from Watertown. She gathered the family around her to read it aloud when they returned from the Sunday sabbath meeting. She began:

Dear Suzanne, Rebecca, and family,

I don't know how to send you this news. I am barely able to put pen to the page with this, but there's no help for it or softening the blow. Your sister Joanne has passed on.

Rebecca cried out, "No! Not Jo!" Rebecca had been close to her sister, six years older, who was charged with her care from infancy. Suzanne reached for her hand to comfort her and continued to read.

I grieve so. She died so young, only twenty-three, never married, never to have the love of a man or children. This is a sad end, indeed, coming only six months after your father's death.

I didn't write to let you know about the burial because I knew that you both have families of your own and travel is perilous. We had a small wake for her here at the house, with a few church members who brought her coffin to the graveyard.

Rebecca appeared to hold her breath to hear her words more clearly. Suzanne's brows wrinkled as she read on, wishing with all her heart that her mother could have spared them the details.

I wish I could say that her death was easy, and that she drifted into a long sleep, but that is not the case. She had a hunting injury that brought on a rare condition. Philip called it "lockjaw," and she suffered more than a week. Nothing he could do to ease her pain did any good. At the end, she could not open her mouth to eat or swallow and twisted and turned with muscle spasms. She couldn't breathe. I hope I never see the likes of such a malady again. I felt more relief than grief when she finally passed and ended that pain. What Philip has taught us? We must clean any wound, or cut, or opening in the skin with water right away. But perhaps Aunt Joanna has taught you that?

"What a horrible death," she said to Rebecca. "Mother's right. Joanna taught me to treat lockjaw because sometimes mothers give it to their babies. It's thought the disease passes to the baby through the umbilical cord."

Rebecca stared at her sister as though she'd just heard the Devil speak. "What are you talking about? Jo … Joanna, our sister … is dead."

Suzanne kept on reading relentlessly until she'd finished.

I hope this letter finds you and the family well. Do write when you can, though I know you must be busy midwifing.

Is Rebecca still living with you? Give her my love as well. I wish that I could see you both. Without Jo, Abigail is left to care for the boys, and I fear Ben and Sam are a regular case of Cain and Abel, sworn enemies.

Now Will has moved into the old homestead, we see less of him. I do miss my children; the house seems empty without all of you. Please write to me soon.

Give my love to my grandbabies. And to all of you! Mother.

The tears poured from Rebecca's eyes, flooding her cheeks. She threw herself onto the settee, covering her head with her arms and sobbing. Alarmed, Suzanne rose and strode to her side. She sat and held her sobbing sister, wishing that she could release the sadness in her own heart and cry. But her emotions remained elusive. She'd moved away from home when her little sister–named for her own mentor, the midwife Joanna Morton–was only two. At ten, she'd been the older sister who took care of little Jo when she was a baby. These memories of her sister, who learned to walk and talk during her time with her, were faint.

In the week after Suzanne learned of her sister's death, Rebecca retreated into a private grief. She became forgetful and neglected the children. She would stop in the middle of tasks and stare into space, fixed, for long minutes without cause. Impatient with her, trying to step in to fill the gap and still fulfill the demands of the town's women, Suzanne, in frustration, called her to task.

"Rebecca, please change that child's nappy. She stinks."

"I'm her mother. I'll change her when I decide to."

"Don't you think little Becky would feel better if you cleaned her bottom?" Suzanne tried to appeal to her mothering instincts.

"Becky is fine just as she is. And since when do you know how people feel? Even your best friend knows better."

"What do you mean?"

"Mother writes that your sister died a terrible death, and all you can think is that babies can get lockjaw too. I heard you say that."

"That doesn't mean I don't feel. I was in shock. People act differently."

"People, grieve. They are sad. They are hurt. But not you."

"I'm a midwife. I can't let my feelings rule. I have to think how I fix the problem."

"You can't fix dying. So, what then?"

"Well, then, there's the burial. Feeding the children, feeding the animals, binding wounds. Life doesn't stop for death."

"For me it does. Why can't you feel that? You don't understand anything! All the women talk behind your back. They all say you are in the thrall of the devil medicine woman. You have no heart. I don't want to be seen with you anymore because they'll point at me, too"

"I don't think you're in a place to talk about *my* reputation Rebecca. You have their respect only because I covered up for you. Don't forget *that*!

"How can I ever forget that? My guardian angel who lied to the Groton citizens so I could hold up my head. I, a married woman."

"Rebecca, I know life hasn't worked out as you wished—"

"No more. I'll not hear another word. I love Samuel, and I'm moving back in with him. He'll love little Becky in time."

"Rebecca, please think again. I need you here."

"Yes, you do. You aren't going to find another helper in Groton. None of the women are going to let their daughters work here. And it serves you right."

Rebecca moved out the next day, and Suzanne put out the word that she needed a new helper. In the meantime, Abigail pitched in to help, eventually finding another girl who could move in and provide support. In September, Suzanne found she was to have yet another child; this would be her sixth baby. Months went by before the rift between Suzanne and Rebecca had eased, and gradually, with Abigail and Sarah's intervention, they were able to mend their relationship.

Suzanne delivered Abigail's third child, named Elizabeth, in February. Abigail, who had lived with the fear she'd end up like her mother with eighteen children, had been able to postpone this birth for four years thanks to Suzanne. But they both thanked Dancing Light for her knowledge of herbal remedies. The winter sped by, and Suzanne gave birth to her daughter Hannah in June.

Chapter Nineteen

WORDS ON THE WIND

Groton, June 1675

Congregants filled every pew in the church. The chatter filling the room was punctuated with loud exclamations. When Reverend Willard climbed the stairs to his podium, parents signed to their children, 'quiet.' When their shushing ended, an intense quiet, one filled with expectation, even silenced the sounds of birds and breezes filtering through open windows.

The minister began, "You've all heard word of the Indian uprising at Seekonk. These aren't rumors. Wampanoags and Pokanets have joined forces to attack the settlement there. Last week, a messenger brought news to Plymouth that Indians plundered Job Winslow's house in Swansea, and the next day, burned several houses to the ground while people were attending worship. The Allied Forces have sent Captain Benjamin Church to quell the uprising, and he'll join a force of horsemen at Swansea. We must pray for his success."

His audience couldn't repress their commentary and, for minutes, their murmurs rose in response. When they'd quieted, he continued. "I will not waste time on details; you may read the news posted on the door. But I can give you this: Major Willard has assurance from Boston that order will be restored quickly. The natives are no match for our allied military. However, they also recommend every town in Massachusetts prepare for worse. In this, we'll reap the rewards of the faithful. Thank the Lord that on the Major's advice, we have already prepared four barricaded garrisons for our protection, and we have called for help from the allied forces. Our men stand ready to defend our Groton. God is our savior; with his providence, we will prevail. Now, we must plan our defense in case of attack. For our prophesying today, I am asking that Captain Parker, Goodman Nutting, and Goodman Sawtell join me to assign each family to a garrison."

That afternoon, Goodman Nutting stood before the congregation and read the names of families who lived nearest his barracks, the garrison closest to the Nashua River and the Indian encampment on the far bank. Suzanne could see that Rebecca and Sarah, who were neighbors, were happy he'd called their names; close friends, they'd be together. When Nutting had finished his list, and Captain Parker stood to read his, Rebecca made her way to Suzanne, her face grim with anxiety.

"Suzanne, I thought we'd be together. Can you ask them to change your garrison?"

"Rebecca, you didn't know, but I've already spoken with Abigail Willard. The Willards have invited us to stay with them. I can't change that. Is there a problem? You and Sarah will be together."

"But the family should be together. Your nanny is with us too. Who will help you with the children?"

"I won't be called out overnight if we're sheltering in garrisons, so it's not likely a hardship. I'm sorry, but my preference is to stay with my friend, Abigail."

Captain Parker's garrison was only a few yards from Goodman Nutting's house. Like his, the Parker house faced the main road to Boston, so close the Parkers could yell across the side yard to talk to the Nuttings. The Captain read from his list, all the names of those closest to his house. He called the Tarballs, the Roberts, the Lawrences and the Greenes. At the end, he read "the Morses."

Suzanne, startled that this had not been resolved before the meeting, gripped Rebecca's hand. "There's been a mistake."

Rebecca postured, hip thrust to the side, hands on her hips. "I agree. You belong with us."

Suzanne sought out Abigail, who had rejoined her family in the Willard pew at the front of the church. By then, though, Reverend Willard had taken Captain Parker's place to read the names on his list. There'd been no mistake. No one in the Morse family, not even the most venerable town clerk, Uncle John, would stay with the Willards. In fact, Uncle John, who lived the farthest from the river, would join Goodman Sawtell's garrison. His place was just southeast of Mill Highway branch from the Bay Highway, a full mile from the center of town and the other three garrisons.

Suzanne realized the family would be broken up, scattered end-to-end across the four garrisons.

When the meeting ended, just before sunset, Abigail made her way to Suzanne.

"Suzanne, I'm so sorry. I argued with Samuel and told him how important it was we be able to work together. But he wouldn't hear it. He used the excuse the Parker's garrison is closer to you than our house. But the real reason is his fear of Dancing Light. He thinks you are too close to the Nashua Abenakis. Now he's worried they are spies and using you. The Major tells him we must suspect even those Indians who declare they are friends as possible spies."

"That doesn't sound like Major Willard. He was ever friends to our neighbors."

"This conflict is confounding all of our loyalties, Suzanne. You must be careful. The hostiles are treacherous."

Suzanne could only accept her friend's explanation. For now, she couldn't fix the problem. "I understand. Abigail, don't think I'd ever hold that against you."

The next time that Dancing Light stood at her door, she didn't smile or nod. Suzanne, sensitive to her friend's unaccustomed gravity, quickly motioned for her to enter. Aware now of the minister's new suspicion of spies, Suzanne hadn't considered that Dancing Light might be facing the same charges from her tribe. They'd have to be doubly discreet.

Suzanne looked to both sides. Fortunately, her helper was in the garden with the children. They hadn't seen her. "Meegwich," Suzanne said. "Come in, quickly."

Dancing Light nodded and slid through the door. "I come to talk." Dancing Light motioned toward the table boards, raising her eyebrows in question.

Suzanne caught her meaning. "Yes. Please. Sit. Let's talk. What have you heard?" Suzanne took her place at the table across from her. "Can I get you drink? Food?"

Dancing Light waved her hand. "No. I come to say our Sagamore is friend of English. Our tribe not fight with English. Some Nashua join Metacom. Monoco leads them. But our camp always friend of English. Wampanoag enemy to us. Monoco enemy to us."

Suzanne understood the urgency with which her friend stated this. "I'm happy to hear it."

"You tell pastor. You tell Groton. Our people want no trouble with English."

"Has anyone in Groton threatened you?"

"No. Monoco, in Lancaster. He say English start war with Indians. Englishman kill Indian, now Indians must fight. We not fight. Not listen to Monoco."

Suzanne was uncertain at first, wondering if this exchange couldn't be construed as spying. In the end, she reasoned that she must trust her friend first. "Monoco. Is that One-Eyed John?"

"Yes."

"Major Willard knows him. Captain Parker, too. They say he can't be trusted." Suzanne had heard the Indians *did* start the war. King Philip (she knew Metacom by his Christian name) executed a Christian Indian he'd employed as his counselor for spying, a betrayal that bordered on treason. This provoked the governor of Plymouth to seek justice for the murder of the Christian Indian. When the militia found the two murderers and brought them to Plymouth, the magistrates tried Philip's men in court and found them guilty. They hanged. That's how Indians came to harass towns near Seekonk, burning houses and killing cattle in retaliation.

"Nashua have saying. If we kill someone and start war, we lose war." Dancing Light held her attention, not blinking once. She insisted. "Indians not start war. Not Indian way. Indians raid. Indians burn. Indian not kill."

Suzanne was puzzled. Dancing Light seemed to be talking about a different event than the Governor's just punishment of two killers. "Indians raiding? When?"

"In Seekonk. Indians burn field. Steal cows. White man and son come. Father tell boy don't shoot. Boy afraid. Not listen to father. He shoot and kill Indian." Dancing Light shook her head, saddened by what anyone could see was an accident. She would not hold a child responsible for such a rash act.

"And the war begins." Suzanne whispered the words, now wondering if anyone could step outside blame. Before shooting the Indian in the field … before justly hanging the guilty Indians … before assassinating the Christian Indian and alleged spy … before that, which innocent killed an innocent? Set free, certain that they'd not begun the war, the Indians could unleash their just fury, count coup, even the score. The raiding and marauding Indians had now attacked three towns in Plymouth and Rhode Island, killing randomly as they raided.

"Our Sagamore, our people friend to English," Dancing Light reassured her. "Not fight English. Wampanoag fight English, Metacom's friend fight."

Now that Dancing Light had brought up the subject of King Philip's friends, she wanted to know more. "The Christian Indians don't fight the English. Can you ask for help from Christian Indians in Nashoba?"

"English send Noshaba Indian to Concord, but the people say Indians are enemy. Send them to Deer Island."

"Deer Island? They have nothing there."

"We not go. English say Christian Indians join Metacom. They say true."

"What? They will fight the English?" Suzanne couldn't believe what she was hearing.

"Some Christian Indian fight English because Wampanoag kill Christian Indian not fight. Yes. Some not fight English. But Indians have law, must protect kin. You tell pastor, our Nashua not fight. Penacook Sachem Wanalancet not fight. He lead his people north."

Suzanne agreed, assuring Dancing Light that she would get the word to the town council. When her guest stood to make her way to the door, she turned at the last and said, "I not see you, maybe long time. Like Penacook Sachem, we follow trail north. Safe there."

"Will you come back? These conflicts will end."

"We must see."

Suzanne nodded, realizing it might not ever be safe again. Before she stepped from the door, Suzanne took her hands and held them. "My friend, go safely."

Dancing Light nodded and made her way unseen into the woods.

That night, Joseph brought Uncle John, Timothy Cooper, and Sam Church home with him to make plans for the family. The men sorted out their certain conscription and could talk only of the coming conflicts.

Suzanne, who heard them from the bedroom, hastily pulled her apron from the hook and after putting it on, tied on her cap. Entering the room, she saw Joseph stride into the great room. He piled the weapons he'd been carrying on one end of the table. He nodded to Suzanne. "We're hungry. Do we have enough?"

"What a question," she exclaimed. "When have we turned away guests?"

Satisfied, he turned to help Sam Church, who followed him in after stamping the mud from his boots. Joseph pulled a stool over and helped him put aside his guns and ammunition. He bristled like a porcupine with the ammunition strapped to his body: the musket, the sword, the powder bags strung on straps across his chest and the bag of lead bullets. He leaned his pike against the wall, continuing their previous conversation. "You aren't going to wait for the captain to conscript you, are you? If the colony needs men, who could refuse?"

Unburdened, Sam flexed his arms, shaking out the stiffness in his shoulders. "It's not that; I'll fight with the best of them. I just resent going to battle with the Indians when it's the magistrates in Boston who brought this on us. They're stupid. Who taught the Indians to use guns? Who sold them the guns? Who invited them to all the musters and trained them to fight? So how do they expect a peaceful result?"

Uncle John and Timothy Cooper stamped their feet at the threshold, then crossed the hall to pile their gear next to the pile beside Sam Church. Suzanne nodded to each man.

Uncle John commented. "You'll be happy those Indians mustered with us when you go to battle against warriors counting coup on your scalp. The only mistake I see the English making is underestimating them. I hear some poor sheep bugger bragging the English infantry is so superior to naked painted warriors, I gotta' laugh." Uncle John pulled up the settee and plopped down, twisting his hips into a comfortable position.

"I agree with you, Uncle John." Joseph turned to help Suzanne ladle ale into the mugs. "If it weren't for the friendly Indians at Seekonk, there'd been more casualties."

"Rightly said, son. I know it's not a popular view, but we'd do best to keep them on our side if we can. Suzanne, you heard from Dancing Light? Here, sit down." He cleared a space for her on the settee.

Suzanne pulled her skirts tight and sat next to him. "She told me that Monoco, One-eyed John, is leading a band of warriors against the English, but wanted me to tell Reverend Willard that the Nashua on the river are our friends. They will not join Monoco."

"She know why he's rising against the English?"

"Monoco's telling everyone the English started the war, and they feel they have no choice but to fight back."

"Started the war?" Sam Church swore. "That's a lie."

Suzanne ignored him and continued. "She told me it's a rule with Indians. They believe that if they start a war by killing someone, they are destined to lose that war."

Uncle John snorted. "Probably true. So, they harassed the settlers, burning houses down, killing cattle to get a rise out of them. So, when the boy who doesn't know better shoots and kills a warrior, that clears them. Then it's outright war. Sounds about right."

"They've killed eighteen!" Sam exploded.

Uncle John winked at Timothy, who had frowned at Samuel's outburst, then turned to Samuel. "You're right. The Indians killed first. Metacom sent his warriors to kill the Plymouth spy."

Timothy's sympathies compelled him to speak. "He was Metacom's adviser, a Christian Indian, not a white man. Metacom must have thought the man treasonous. The Governor would do the same if the man betrayed him."

Uncle John ignored Timothy's remarks. "A Christian Indian is as good as a white man. Plymouth didn't want war, just justice. The governor tried the culprits who killed his Christian friend. Hanged them. For the governor, that was the end of it. Justice done. Might have worked, too, but he demanded Metacom's guns."

Timothy tried to reason with him. "Justice! One Indian executed and two Indians hanged. And you say they killed the first man to start a war?"

Uncle John smirked. "Well, you have a point there."

Timothy continued. "The English assume the natives are going to behave like Englishmen. Suzanne, would you make that assumption? Do you think Dancing Light is going to follow our laws, has our sense of justice?"

Timothy was getting too close for comfort, and Suzanne side-stepped his question. "All right!" Suzanne rose, smoothing her skirts and turned to the hearth. "If you want to eat, you'll have to put your mouths to better use."

"I'm for eating," Uncle John laughed. He stood and followed Suzanne to the table boards. As he passed Sam, he couldn't help ribbing him. "Sam Church, you going to use that pike in the woods? You think the Indians are going to be riding horseback on an open field? *Pshaw*."

His teasing started humorously enough, but the teasing didn't let up and took a more menacing tone. Suzanne knew Uncle John didn't much like Samuel, and Samuel's self-defense wouldn't help.

"I'm a pikesman! Any Indian comes in range, I'll have his gizzard. Captain Parker will know where to use me."

"Well, get ready. Maybe you can use that pike like a hatchet when you need to hack through thickets. Or a cane when your clambering over treefall. Or not. Long as that pike doesn't tangle in the branches. Long as it stops you sinking up to your knees when you slip off a log and slog through the swamp. How many open battlefields you see in Massachusetts?"

Joseph came to his defense. "Uncle John, I know you fought the Pequot. But settlements have grown and fields around towns are commonplace. Captain Parker is training pikesmen in our troop for a reason."

Sam Church was not a town council member, nor even a freeman, and he needed defending. He looked gratefully at Joseph. "If it comes to that, like you say, I still have my musket and sword. Nothing stopping me from tossing the pike. I'm infantry."

"As I am," Timothy cut in. He sent Uncle John a reproving look as he climbed over the bench, taking his seat at the table.

Suzanne, who'd already eaten with her children, passed steaming trenchers of stew to the men and strode to the back door. There, she took in the last sun rays, listening to the screeches and laughter of the children playing in the yard. She had the unsettled feeling that their merriment couldn't last. *What will become of us?* she thought.

Chapter Twenty

WAR PATH

Groton, July 1675

In July, the Indians destroyed Middleboro and Dartmouth, attacking Rehoboth, Providence, and Mendon. While Captain Parker and Major Willard were building up their militias, they argued that Groton's needs were not the same as other towns. Groton's location on the frontier made it crucial to have home defenses. The Major insisted that they reserve their forces, setting them to patrolling the surrounding woods for hostiles. For that reason, Joseph and Timothy stayed at home, while Sam Church marched with Captain Parker's company to support defenses elsewhere.

In late July, the Nashua suddenly abandoned their encampment across the river from Groton, stealing into the night. Uncle John and Joseph, who had surveyed the grounds with a small party, explained to Suzanne that every wickiup was empty, and the Indians camped across the river had even abandoned their planted fields.

It was dusk when they gathered in her kitchen. Her nose prickled with the metallic scent as Joseph cleaned his gun.

Uncle John picked through a bowl of strawberries Suzanne had set on the table. "This looks bad, Suzanne. Major Willard and Captain Parker both think they may have joined One-Eyed John in Lancaster."

Suzanne frowned when Joseph set his ramrod down and asked, "Have you met with Dancing Light recently? Did she say anything?"

"I haven't seen her in a month. The last time I saw her, she insisted that her tribe would never harm the English here. I believe her. She asked me to tell Reverend Willard that they will not fight the English."

"If what you say is true, it doesn't prove they haven't joined with King Philip's allies. Metacom has attacked Christian Indians who wouldn't join him? Why not the Nashaway?" Uncle John pushed the bowl toward Joseph.

Joseph picked a strawberry and bit into it, mouth pursing with the tart sweet berry. "It's not as though they have a choice."

Suzanne leaned toward him. "Would they choose to become a marauding murdering people? No. I won't believe it. And anyone who does will do them great injury. They are our friends."

Uncle John granted her defense. "Major Willard will not act rashly; he has traded with both the Nashua and Pennacook for years. He's leaving with a troop of fifty men and some friendly Indians to scour the woods hereabouts. He'll follow any trail to Lancaster. Until we know for certain, I don't want you to have anything to do with Dancing Light."

"You need not worry then," Suzanne said, stuffing a napkin into her apron. "Dancing Light told me that I'd not be seeing her for a long time. I think her people are as suspicious of her as some in Groton are of me." Suzanne avoided looking at Uncle John.

He noticed her gesture. "It isn't I, Suzanne. You mustn't think it."

Joseph stood and walked to the hearth, where he placed his gun in its rack above the mantel. "Uncle John, what did the council do on the new rates? We paying for Plymouth?"

"We are. Cost of the uprising. Twenty-three pounds besides the usual rate."

Two days later, Reverend Willard climbed to his podium and announced the whole colony was called to a day of fasting and humiliation. In his sermon, he asked them to consider every act in every part of their lives to ferret out sins that had angered their God. He spared no facet of their lives. Had the church failed? Had the governor or magistrates? Did a tradesman cheat his fellow citizens? Examine the ways of your family. Are your children taught to obey you? Are your ways just with them? And last, he asked them to look into their own hearts, their thoughts. Do you lie? Blaspheme? Take the Lord's name in vain? Know that God has sent the Indian Devils to punish us. We must repent.

Oddly, Suzanne heard this sermon with relief. The minister gave so many reasons for God's displeasure that he absolved her of her chief failing. *Walks in the woods with Dancing Light could never be the sole cause of what's brought us to a war*, she thought. He never mentioned their Nashaway neighbors' disappearing, but it came up in prophesying after the service.

Abigail didn't waste time in calling Suzanne away. "Suzanne!" She motioned for Suzanne to follow her outside. "Suzanne, you must be careful. The Tarballs are spreading the word the Nashua have joined with King Philip's forces. They say they've seen their sagamore with One-Eyed John. And they've attacked you as a spy. They are saying that you are telling them the locations of our militia, our ammunition stores. It's vile!"

"They're lying! Of course, I'm not a spy. Nor is Dancing Light our enemy. Nor their sagamore."

"But people don't know that. Did you notice that Samuel didn't bring up the matter in his sermon? He's still harboring suspicions even though he knows Tarball is the worst hypocrite. He may be a selectman on the council, but we have no respect for politics. Only now, Samuel doesn't care whether Dancing Light is in league with the Devil. Samuel's new Devil, King Philip, is real. He's entertaining the idea that Dancing Light is using you, that her tribe has allied with the hostiles. I know it. He'll not act on it, but I know him."

"Abigail, what defense do I have? I don't know myself if Dancing Light is our friend. I too have doubts. I will defend her as I must believe. But ... she did explain to me that Indian customs demand that they shelter their relations, even those who are hostile. It's not a black and white world."

"Do you take that as fact? The Christian Indians are victims of Metacom's people. No one has found that to be true."

"I think she was talking about King Alexander's widow, Weetamoo. The Narragansetts have told Plymouth they are neutral, but they had to take her in and shelter her. She's family. It's not a case of friend or enemy."

"I agree we mustn't generalize. You must stand by your convictions. That is all any of us can do. And pray."

"Yes, and pray."

"I'll try to reason with Samuel, but the distance between the spirit world and the material world is narrow. I know you are no spy."

Within weeks of the Nashua camp's disappearance, One-eyed John attacked Lancaster, fired buildings, and killed seven settlers. While Boston responded, sending Lancaster fourteen soldiers and the arms for two garrisons, Groton's citizens, discouraged and fearful, reacted immediately with growing concern. Lancaster was nearby, only seven miles away by footpath, little more by river.

Major General Denison of Boston had insisted that Moseley send twelve men to Groton in August, but necessary as they were to Groton's defenses, the added mouths to feed taxed the community. Fortunately, Major Willard had prepared their shelters when he'd ordered the town to palisade garrisons many months earlier.

With the conflicts escalated into a full war involving every new England colony, Boston declared war on King Philip and his allies in September. Simultaneously, Suzanne learned of her brother John's drowning. He'd survived an ambush only to succumb to high wind and waves crossing the Charles River on his way to report to Boston officials.

Sadly, he left his widow Ruth with four children under eight years old. Captain Prentice had given Will junior leave to ride to Groton to let his family know. For Suzanne and her family, travel to Watertown through enemy territories in wartime was not an alternative. Caught in the critical need to get the crops in before winter, she had little time to reflect on her brother John's death or grieve.

Major Willard was scouting the countryside for hostile Indians with forty-eight troopers when the Marlboro garrison sent him word that a force of five hundred or more Indians had attacked Brookfield in the Connecticut valley on their western front. They were holding Ayer's garrison under siege. He left Lancaster immediately, riding with purpose to drive back the enemy.

Captain Parker again wrote to Governor Leverette with a more urgent appeal. Thanking him for the received relief, he pleaded that Groton was "weak against insolence and potency of enemy if they appear in number and violence as they appeared at Brookfield." He begged Leverette "to do for your new England Israel at such time," asking for ammunition and twenty good musketeers for their pikemen. A week later, Major Willard sent twenty men to Groton from his troops. The court also impressed William Hawkins, a butcher by trade, as surgeon to attend soldiers at Groton.

Chapter Twenty One

ALLIANCES BROKEN

Groton, September 1675

When townspeople had secured the harvests and tree trunks showed bare through the last fall leaves, the Morses took advantage of the shortening days to visit. Abigail Willard greeted Joseph and Suzanne at the front door; she'd promised them a tour of their now-converted garrison. After they had moved the school into the meetinghouse, Suzanne had no reason to visit Abigail's house. Thus, she found the changes the palisades had wrought to the Willard home interesting.

Abigail led them through the back door into a second great room nearly double the size of their home. A clay and stone-lined hearth stretched across the back wall, great timbers framing the box.

"The main room is for cooking, Abigail said. "I insisted on keeping our own kitchen separate from the garrison." She pointed to the stairs. "Our soldiers live upstairs."

Suzanne noted the militia had strewn ammunition and other trappings about the yard. "How many soldiers are staying?"

"Every garrison received five infantrymen."

"Are you feeding them as well?"

"The Major sees that we are repaid. But yes."

Abigail continued, leading them across the room, exiting into the yard beyond it. Ten-foot-high palisades now surrounded a wide expanse of gated yard, marked by a square tower and ramparts for guards. "We're able to keep horses here."

Joseph, impressed with the tower, remarked, "the Major has built a fort for you."

Abigail laughed. "Yes. Only our garrison has a rampart and tower. Samuel is embarrassed at his father's insistence."

Suzanne surveyed the large wood watering trough, noting that having a Major for a father-in-law wasn't the worse that could happen to a woman. The Major had thought of everything.

"At first, I was dismayed we must live in a garrison. I'm a minister's daughter and married one, too. You remember my complaint, Suzanne."

Suzanne recognized their conversation with a nod. "You have changed your mind?"

"How not? With what is going on in Plymouth—and Lancaster—well, I am grateful. We'll be safe here."

Suzanne followed Abigail back into the house, Joseph at her heels. He asked, "Have you heard more of the Brookfield attack?"

"Ah, yes. I didn't tell you. The Major will join us today, and you may ask him yourself. He will only stay the day to rest. Then gone again. I understand that many troops are moving the Christian Indians this month, emptying their towns. The coalition wants to make sure that Christian Indians are in no danger that the hostile tribes will massacre them."

Abigail invited them to sit at the table. Joseph asked, "Where will they move the Christian Indians? Our present danger extends for the entire colony, I'd say."

"He said they'll gather in Cambridge. From there, they'll ship praying Indians to Deer Island."

"Deer Island!" Joseph barked. "It's a rocky, treeless place. Surely, not in winter. Have they prepared shelters for them?"

"I don't know more than that, I fear. I only know that we have the Christians' best interest at heart." Abigail turned to see her husband and his father, the Major, enter the room. "Perhaps the Major can enlighten us."

"Father," the Reverend boomed, "I want you to meet the Morses. Joseph is our town clerk's nephew. I think you know John well. And Suzanne, Joseph's wife, is our midwife."

Joseph stood to shake the Major's hand. "Major, I am honored to make your acquaintance.

"I've heard much to recommend you and your uncle. I fear I am gone so much that I am amiss when it comes to knowing my new neighbors."

The Major, who despite his obvious years showed a spritely energy, swung his leg over the bench to sit at the table across from Joseph. "I understand from Samuel that you have just enlisted with Captain Parker?"

"That's right," Joseph answered. "And you have just recently returned from Brookfield? Word is that you routed the Indians, Sir."

The Reverend poured himself a tankard of ale and filled one for his father. Shoving it toward him, he asked, "Do you have a story to tell us? We're eager for news." Abigail bustled about the hearth, directing her helper to pour ale while she prepared their supper.

The Major thanked his son and drank heartily, setting the mug down and not heeding the ale splashing on the table. "I and Captain Parker ranged west of Groton and Lancaster with a small troop—only forty-six and some Mohawk scouts. We were looking for any Indians that might be a threat after the Lancaster attack. The messenger rode after me to say the Nipmuc attack on Brookfield was bad, wasn't sure anyone survived the attack. It's a small settlement near on the Quabaug River, not far from a Nipmuk camp."

Joseph nodded. "Brookfield's just south of Mount Wachusett, isn't it?"

"Right, maybe fourteen or fifteen families, only incorporated fifteen years ago. I headed there immediately. We didn't have provisions with us and hadn't slept much, but he assured us their defense was urgent. We straightway marched for Brookfield and got there an hour after nightfall.

Their garrison isn't palisaded; Akers place is a tavern, but the largest building and built of stone. We made it through Muttawmp's ambush with only two men wounded." He nodded to Reverend Willard.

"Who was leading the attack? How many?" Joseph asked.

"Muttawmp led over two hundred Indians. We fought the night through but couldn't drive them off."

Suzanne exchanged glances with Abigail, who stood at her elbow, holding a serving platter. She took it and placed it on the table as the Major continued. "Captain Wheeler and Hutchinson were at the fort, both injured. They'd come when the General Court had charged them with negotiating peace with the Nipmuk. They brought Ephraim Curtis to interpret and three praying Indians to guide them, not knowing that Muttawmp had already laid siege to Mendon. But Muttawmp was treacherous; he ambushed them, killed five men and even more horses. Captain Wheeler told me the Brookfield selectmen swore the Sachem David Tanewases, Christian, was loyal. They'd headed to his village unarmed." He shook his head at the foolishness.

"Wheeler didn't make it. Tried to move him to the garrison after the battle, but he was too far gone. The town held them off for three days before we got there. Day before, Muttawmp's warriors tried to fire the garrison, tried firebrands, battering ram set afire. Kept the men busy putting out fires, but at its worst, a storm came up, soaked the Indian's fuel. That ended the fires."

Suzanne saw Samuel Willard frown at his father. "You mean the good Lord sent rain. It was providence." Abigail reached for her husband's hand to deter him.

Simon Willard laughed good humoredly and drank another swig of ale. "Have it your way. Providence didn't stop Muttawmp. He was still blocking eighty people at Akers when we got there, and they were out of ammunition. Not much providence there. Forty-eight troopers I brought. We got there after dark, and fought half the night, but we couldn't stop the siege. The Indians kept going. Wasn't until we got reinforcements that Muttawmp changed his mind."

"Word got out?" Joseph asked.

"Captain Hutchinson told me Ephraim Curtis must have made it to Marlboro. They ran the word out. I ended with 350 men when reinforcements came, several Mohegans. Guess Muttawmp decided he had what he wanted. They had already looted every house in Brookfield and torched them. By morning they were gone."

Suzanne, who'd listened intently, was filled with questions. *Is Muttawmp a Nashua?* She asked herself, then shuddered. *Was he from Dancing Light's tribe?* She leaned forward and asked the Major, "Is Muttawmp a Nashua?"

"No. He's Nipmuk. Allied with Metacom now."

Joseph snorted. "The Indians are treacherous."

"But think on it," the Major leaned in. "Boston sent Captain Hutchinson and Captain Wheeler for reinforcements and Muttawmp ambushed them. He might have routed them, but our men had Natick guides. What's more, when both captains were injured and their troops scattered in confusion, the Naticks took command and led them to Brookfield, Muttawmp in pursuit all the way. We'd be fools to think every Indian is a savage enemy."

Reverend Willard leaned forward. "I know that you worked with Elliott to write the covenant for the praying Indians in Concord. We know your mind on the matter. But how do you explain the treachery of the sachem, Dave? What's his name, the sworn Christian? You said he led them to the ambush?"

Simon Willard took a long draft and harrumphed. "Hutchinson confessed his guides had warned them the minute they found an empty village, but he didn't take their advice. I'd stake my life on it the enemies were all gathered on Mt. Wachusett."

Joseph broke into a paroxysm of coughing, and Suzanne noticed the discomfort of the Willards, who said nothing but exchanged glances. Reverend Willard bent toward Joseph, "Is this a case of the shoemakers children going barefoot? Has Suzanne no cure for that cough?"

Joseph cleared his throat, smiling lamely. "It's a cold. No cure for that! Right Suzanne?" Suzanne nodded with a wry look signaling she had a lot to say on the subject but wouldn't in present company.

Once Reverend Samuel had led them in their grace, the conversation dwindled to requests to pass a dish, thanks to the cooks, or grunts of satisfaction.

By November, the English alliance, which had honored the Rhode Island Narragansett tribe's treaty of neutrality when the conflicts began, turned on them. The English claimed the Narragansett had broken their treaty when they harbored King Philip's sister-in-law, the widow, Weetamoo. She'd married a Narragansett sachem, but she was a Wampanoag sachem in her own right. Now both were considered enemies for harboring Wampanoag relatives. In December, the colonial alliance assembled a fighting force of one thousand from all three colonies to attack the large Narragansett fort. It promised the Massachusetts soldiers—the largest of the three colonial forces—thirty-acre land lots to pay for their service. Suzanne's brother Will rode with Captain Prentice's cavalry and took part in the battle, as did Sam Church and Timothy Cooper, pikeman and musketeer in Captain Parker's troops. Joseph, who was still recovering from what Suzanne thought was a bout of influenza, took his place in the local militia, rangers who scouted the Groton forests for Indians.

Unlike men with military discipline, trained to make distinctions between combatants and civilians, most of the men fighting were armed settlers trained in local militias. Full of fear, believing themselves entitled to their land holdings, they were brutal in warfare. The combined New England troops had burned the Indian fort to the ground with all the residents and winter food stores in it.

When news of the slaughter of more than five hundred Narragansetts, most of them old men, women, and children, reached the congregation, Reverend Willard asked his followers to fast and pray for days of contrition. Puritan believers prayed for God's forgiveness and redemption for this extreme aggression against the Narragansetts, who had tried fruitlessly to remain neutral. However, the news of Indian attacks on towns, both south and north, appeased their guilt. The Indians were gaining ground despite the setback in the Great Swamp battle. The settlers lost their ability to discriminate between tribes. Any Indian was a threat.

Chapter Twenty Two

HELL TO PAY

Groton, March 3, 1676

Suzanne wouldn't have reacted to the rider so quickly if she'd not first heard news of a second attack on Lancaster. Just a week before, news had come that Indians had sacked Lancaster, brutally murdering many, and taking captives, even Reverend Rowlandson's wife Mary and their three children. In the following week, Suzanne couldn't help staring towards Dancing Light's camp. Once, she'd even walked to the river to see for herself they were gone. She missed her friend, and despite the town gossips, couldn't believe Dancing Light had joined King Philip's band. Her friend could have reassured her as to why they had gone, where they had gone. The town's accusations eroded her trust, leaving her on edge.

The garrison militia had patrolled the area for days but had found no Indians. Nevertheless, at Sunday meeting, the congregation again went through their evacuation plans. Groton had four palisaded garrisons, enough to supply shelter for the town. Each family knew their assignment, and each had prepared their emergency supplies of food and clothes. Suzanne and Joseph gathered food and clothing in packs and stored them by the door for a getaway. Joseph cleaned his guns and packed ammunition. His guns were loaded and ready to shoot. She had the children memorize the shortest route to Parker's garrison, going over it twice at their sides. Together, they found every hiding place on the way, not an easy feat in winter when the foliage was gone.

On edge for days, on Wednesday, she heard Joseph Gilson's galloping horse and guessed his alarm before she'd grasped the meaning of his shouts.

"Indians!" he shouted. "Take cover. They've slain Timothy Cooper. Take shelter."

Joseph Gilson wheeled his horse around the yard and left for the next house on a wild ride to warn their neighbors. She sprang to action immediately, her heart pumping adrenalin through her veins. *Where are the children?* She thought. Then she ran through her heart list. *Joseph … in the barn, he's heard. Timothy Cooper dead! Sarah widowed again. Poor Sarah! Suzie … and Hester … they're in charge of Sam, Mary, Hannah. Where's young Joseph?* At nine years old, a boy, Joseph didn't fit into either group of his siblings, so he often was left to entertain himself. She ran to the house and found the girls dressing the younger ones. *All here! Except Joseph!*

"Indians! Go to Captain Parker's house! Now!" she said. "Take your packs and run. You know the way." Mostly, they'd avoid the roads. If they could cross Parker's forest and field direct—just a few yards down the road—they'd run a mile. Unfortunately, they must cross James Brook, which had marsh on both sides of it. On horseback, it made sense. On foot, they'd need to veer left to John Nutting's garrison. Once there, they could take the highway bridge west across the brook to Captain Parkers. It added time and exposure to their escape. Fortunately, Nutting's garrison was less than forty yards away from Parker's garrison.

"Where's Joseph?"

"He was going to go fishing," Suzie said.

Timothy Cooper's fields are close to the river. If he went that way … the Indians, she thought. Suzanne's heart stopped, stung by the news.

"I'll get him," Suzanne said. "You stay together. Go. I'll see you there."

She nearly collided with her husband as she headed for the door. He'd slung his rifle and sack of ammunition over his shoulder. "Joseph went fishing," Suzanne nearly cried.

"No," Joseph said. "He was with me. He's bringing the horse."

Suzanne ran to open the door. There, Joseph stood, bridling the mare. She clapped her hand over her heart. "Thank God."

"The children?" Joseph asked.

"I told the girls to flee, but it'll be slow going with the little ones. Follow them; we can put Samuel and Mary on the horse. I'll get the bags."

She reached for the bags piled in the hallway, ready for an evacuation. When he joined her, she yelled, "Go. Leave this."

"I already have them!" Joseph exclaimed. The pair hauled the bags to the yard and tied them to the horse. "Pick up Samuel and Mary," he said to Joseph. "I'll get Hannah."

Young Joseph sprang into the saddle and dug his heels into the mare's side. "Git!" he cried. The horse erupted in a gallop, and Joseph and Suzanne followed, running hard through forests and fields. When they overtook Suzie and Hester with Hannah, Joseph stooped to take the two-year-old piggyback, and the four, thus sped up, reached the gated garrison safely.

The Parker's palisaded yard was barely large enough for the horses. Suzanne inspected the interior of the garrison. The log building had been daubed with mud. The main entrance room had plank floors but had not been finished. An enormous stone hearth crossed one wall, which had doors to the Parker quarters on each side. Suzanne could see the design of the Parker's garrison had followed Major Willard's instructions. The Willard's garrison, more fort-like than Parker's, had the same layout. Although James Parker's house was the largest and his wealth second only to Richard Blood's, arrivals already crowded it. The great room walls were lined with bedrolls. Settlers had stacked foodstuff and supplies, casks of ale, and trunks by the hearth.

James Robert's wife, Adelaide, sat on a cask by the section of wall she'd claimed. Her children sat in a circle nearby, playing what looked like a game of pickup sticks. Suzanne knew her well, not only because she was her closest neighbor, but also because she'd delivered three of her babies in the past nine years. Two-year-old Hannah let out a screech of recognition, tugging at Suzanne's hand to run to Martha Roberts, Suzanne's former nanny, who sat next to Adelaide. Jimmy and Martha now lived with his parents.

"Martha," Suzanne exclaimed. "I worried about you. I thought your family was to go to John Nutting's garrison."

"My family did," Martha said. "But my husband's family needs me."

"And your mother agreed?" Suzanne said. "She won't worry?"

"She said I'd be safer here than so close to the river," Martha said. "And Hannah would miss me!" She reached for the two-year-old, pulling her into her lap, nuzzling the back of Hannah's neck.

"I must thank the Lord," Suzanne said. "The children always counted on you, and in times like these, you will give them comfort."

Adelaide, who followed the exchange with interest, interrupted. "We heard about Timothy. We're so sorry. Sarah Cooper is your husband's sister, isn't she?"

"Yes," Suzanne said. "Terrible to lose Timothy. Widowed! A second time! And three not yet five years old! What have you heard about his murder?"

"Only that Timothy was gathering hay from the field," Adelaide said. "Joseph Gilson saw it from his house. Two Indians slayed him where he stood. Timothy mustn't 've suspected they were hostiles. Cut him up close, took his scalp. His body lays where he fell. Sarah may have seen it too; their house is so close to the Gilson's. They're right across from the meetinghouse. But I've not heard more."

"God have mercy," Suzanne said. "My sister Rebecca is also to shelter at Nutting's garrison. She's Sarah's closest friend. We can pray they've made it to safety and can comfort each other."

"God willing," Adelaide said.

At that moment, Joseph Parker's wife, Mary, joined them from the Parkers quarters. "Adelaide, Suzanne," Mary said. "I'm relieved to see you here, all safe."

"We are as well," Suzanne said. "Are you staying with your father-in-law?"

"Yes," she said. "There's little room once everyone has come. Have you seen the Tarballs, Greenes, and Lawrences yet?"

"Not yet," Suzanne said. "I can only imagine they've been waylaid! We must pray."

The soldiers garrisoned at Parker's were militia from the 181st Infantry. Boston had spared soldiers to Groton before the Narragansett battle, and they already filled the loft on the second floor. Joseph and the rest of the town's men would join them. He climbed the stairs and claimed his space on a wall farthest from any window. The icy March winds still held them in the grip of winter.

Within the hour, their missing neighbors had arrived, and they reorganized their dwindling space to house them.

Suzanne was in the odd position of knowing every woman at the garrison. As the only midwife, she had the intimate knowledge of any neighbor who'd given birth in the past nine years. What's more, she'd also treated their children. However, some of the women she'd treated were critical of her relations with the Nashua healer, and Ann Tarball was their leader. With the Tarballs occupying the garrison, Suzanne knew tensions could arise.

Later, over their evening meal, Joseph reported the soldiers had ranged the woods surrounding Groton all week. They'd seen no one and now decided the attacking Indians could only have come from across the river, from the camp there.

"I can't believe that," Suzanne said. "They have proven our friends in the past. I have Dancing Light's assurances on that point."

"But they did disappear suddenly," Joseph said. "How can you be sure?"

"Only in my heart," Suzanne said. "I believe her. She told me they went north to avoid the war. They are not enemies. Dancing Light will clear the matter if they come back."

The following day, a messenger rode through the garrisons to carry news. Suzanne was happy to hear that Rebecca and little Becky were safe. Joseph Gilson and James Allen had been able to recover Timothy Cooper's body from the field, and they buried him in the churchyard across from the meetinghouse.

On the messenger's return from his rounds to the four garrisons, they had good news from the other end of town. Joseph's Uncle John, who lived in east Groton, had made it safely to Richard Sawtell's Garrison. The Groton council would have need for John Morse after the conflict; he'd served five years as head of the Council.

As the week wore on, the town's men returned to their homes to tend livestock or get supplies. However, each time someone would stir, they would hear news the Indians had raided the outlying houses and looted barns. So far, the Indians had harassed and vandalized them but not carried through a full attack as they had in Lancaster.

Joseph could no longer sit still. He loaded his rifle and announced to Suzanne; "We need cornmeal and ale. I'm going to take the mare and check out the house."

Suzanne instantly reacted. "You've heard that Indians are about. I think it foolish to dare it."

"May be," Joseph said. "But that won't stop me from going. Others have gone and come back."

"And Timothy is in his grave! I cannot bear to lose you."

In the end, she had to resign herself to his decision and let him go in peace. When he returned two hours later, he had much to report. He had loosed Tarball's and Roberts' cattle, and their own cow, to common pasture so they'd not be slain. He said that Indians had not touched their home.

He handed her a sack filled with the last of the cornmeal. "Careful. There are eggs." Then he threw down a second sack.

Suzanne peered into the first bag; he'd nestled more than a dozen eggs into the cornmeal to prevent their breaking. Suzanne was grateful for the added food supplies as the siege lengthened. This attack in March, when food stores were always sparse, even in peacetime, was so cruel.

The second sack brought mixed feelings; Joseph had brought the books and her precious life's work, her notebooks. Her gratitude mixed oddly with the fear this elicited; Joseph acted as though their belongings weren't safe.

So far, the settlers could discount the Indian's actions as harassment and not full out attack. But knowing the fate of Lancaster and other towns kept the townsmen on edge. Indians had attacked these with numbers in the hundreds, not the marauding few they'd seen so far. *Where are they hiding?* Suzanne thought. *Where did Dancing Light go?*

Sunday brought no relief with reports that a parcel of Indians had taken possession of three houses on the outskirts and were feasting on corn, swine, and poultry they had seized. But the soldiers went out regularly, combing the forests for signs of Indians and found none. Still, the colonists were so much on edge, they would not risk gathering in the meetinghouse on Sunday; families held the Sabbath at their respective garrisons. Reverend Willard visited each of the garrisons, speaking at each and leading the faithful in penitent prayer. God had spared them so far, but they were in mortal peril. Only the most fearless ventured out to their homes for supplies after Sunday.

Before dawn on Wednesday, March 9, Suzanne woke when she heard a neighbor stirring at the hearth. She stared in confusion for a moment, thinking it was Joseph lighting the fire. She raised up on her elbows, reached out and felt around her in the dark, her memory flooding in. Joseph and Mary spooned her front, and Hester and Joseph curled into her back, as if a mother's body contact alone could spell safety in the threatening circumstances. She had no life experience that she could recollect to match their own. She counted the lumps in the dim light, *six, they're all here. I'll let Suzie sleep a little longer,* she thought. She could see motion where Martha slept. *She's up.*

Suzanne slipped from between them to dress, pulling on her skirt, lacing her bodice, and thrusting her arms into her jacket. Mary stirred, and fearing she would wake, Suzanne bent to smooth her hair until she slept soundly again.

It had become a routine day after a week. She walked to the hearth and greeted Adelaide Roberts, who already worked there. Suzanne hauled water from the yard to the hearth and filled a cast iron cauldron. She twisted the legs until it sat squarely over hot coals, then threw in scoops of oats from her own larder. Each morning she made enough porridge for her neighbors and any soldiers staying at the garrison. Rationing what the six families brought—by March, no one had much—stretched out the supplies longer. No one knew how much longer the soldiers would need to stay or the settlers need refuge. Though the county and town rates paid for their board, the new occupants of the garrison were expected to supplement their militia with the food they brought. So, the settlers fed the five soldiers bivouacked at Parker's garrison. Adelaide had filled a pot to boil dozens of eggs, and Ann sliced the last of a ham into thin sheets. Others began to stir.

"Suzie," Suzanne called to her oldest daughter, "you and Martha get everybody washed up now."

Martha and Suzie gathered the children together and marched them out the door to the yard. The water trough, a vat used for watering horses and livestock, served for human utilities as well. Martha broke through the thin ice that had frozen on the tank's surface overnight and ladled water into a pail as Suzie lined up her five siblings to splash water on faces and hands. The cold water left them gasping and wide awake.

When they returned to the hall, the line of people had grown longer.

Just before noon, Thomas Tarball opened the garrison's gates to Goodmen Woods and Green, who shouted outside. He braced himself for bad news; they were from Willard's garrison. On foot, out of breath, they stumbled into the yard.

"We got away," Sam Woods panted.

"They took us in the field behind Willard's." Will Green's sleeve was slick with fresh blood, and he held his arm close.

Thomas Tarball trussed the gate again. "Slowly. What happened?"

Sam Woods took up the story. "No reports of Indians in the woods for days. Sentinels tell us all's clear. Four of us take carts out to gather hay, and a parcel of Indians ambush us."

Will Green interrupted. "They split Ong's head with a tomahawk. One tethered James Fiske and took him off."

"And wounded you, seems like," Tarball added.

Goodman Green continued as if he hadn't heard, weaving on shaky legs. "They stripped Lewis naked, mangled his body. Cut him all up. Savages!" His voice rose with anguish. "Left him lying in the highway."

Thomas Tarball grunted. "We know it. Savages."

Sam Woods stared at his feet. "We don't know what they'll do with James."

Suzanne knew from Dancing Light Indians had only two fates for captives; they adopted them into their tribes, or they tortured and killed them. It was hearsay that the Indians might even eat a captive's flesh, if that prisoner was exceptionally brave. She feared that Goodman Fiske would be slated for the latter. He was old, a man who wouldn't accept Indian ways, neither a candidate for adoption, nor afraid to speak out. "I fear for him," she said. "Here, let me bind that wound."

Thomas Tarball looked at her sharply. "You fear? You know what they're up to? Indian lover!"

Suzanne's stomach jolted at this assault. The Tarballs' were unanimous and relentless slanderers. A selectman on the Groton council, Thomas Tarball was an untouchable foe; Uncle John her only defense. As she led the man to her quarter, she heard some commotion from the soldiers. They leaped up checking their guns, slinging ammunition belts on their shoulders.

"What is it?" Suzanne asked.

"Captain Nutting's man saw two Indians on the hill behind his garrison. We're backing them." Thomas Tarball pulled the bar and let them out.

Chapter Twenty Three

DEVIL'S NIGHT

Groton, March 9, 1676

When Suzanne had bound the man's wound—a shallow cut from a tomahawk—she followed some of her neighbors, who had climbed the stairs for a better look down the Bay Highway. Nutting's garrison was just rods away from Parker's, and they had a partial view of its palisades. Beyond the garrison, they could see a hill through trees showing only the faintest thickening plush of early spring. They crammed into a small space behind Elder Roberts where he knelt at the open window.

"What can you see?" his wife asked. Adelaide elbowed her way closer.

"I can't see anything on the hill, just the soldiers on the road."

At that point, all could hear the guns. Then Elder Roberts saw the Indians crest the hill whooping and shrieking. Two Indians had become many pouring down the hill. "It's an ambush!" Roberts cried. Several men, plainly those who'd volunteered to check out the sighted Indians, became visible just as the Indians discharged a volley of shot. He saw one fall, and the others retreat.

Then again, Elder Roberts yelled. "There's another parcel. I can hear them. Closer, behind Nutting's garrison." He stood, his head weaving to see through the trees. "No! The palisades are down."

"They've breached Nutting's garrison?" "Are they in?" "Is it on fire?" Everyone talked at once, asking the Elder what he couldn't possibly know. In the chaotic chilling moment, their hearts pounded with fear. More gun shots and the screams of women and children rose from the walled garrison as did the tendrils of smoke from the fired rifles. The smell of gunpowder drifted in the window, but not of fire.

Suzanne knew immediately the difference of this war cry from the loud singing she'd heard across the Nashua. The warriors were terrifying. They brought chills down her back and a gripping stomach.

Suzanne had never been one to stand by and watch; she knew she'd have wounded to tend. Then her thoughts reeled to her sister and three-year-old niece. *Rebecca? Sarah?* She ran down the stairs. The pounding on the gate proved she'd been right.

When Tarball opened the gate, the soldiers who'd gone to back up Nutting's search party rushed in with the news. As Tarball barred the gate behind them, they spoke breathlessly. "We couldn't get to Captain Nutting. Another bunch of Indians drove us back."

"They stormed his garrison. Tore down the rear palisades. Drove us out."

Suzanne nearly screamed it. "And the women? The children?" Ann Tarball and Adelaide Roberts came running to her side.

"They were alive."

Ann's face was livid. "You left them there?"

Adelaide's eyes popped open when realization hit. "Without the men?"

One of the soldiers moved forward, motioning them to stay calm. "Someone covered them. The women escaped. They're behind us."

Thomas Tarball immediately ran to open the gates. A ragtag stream of women and children headed to safety. Women carrying infants tripped on long skirts as they ran; mere children carried toddlers piggyback, weaving beneath their loads. The Skinners, Allens, Gilsons, Kemps, Bloods, Lakins and, last, Sarah Cooper stumbled through the gates, faces twisted in fear and grimy with shed tears.

Suzanne, who stood to one side to scan the crowd for injuries, cried out when she saw her sister-in-law, who carried thirteen-month-old Timothy in her arms. "Sarah, thank God."

Sarah didn't answer but turned, arm flailing in panic as she searched the line of families. "Where's Johnny? Sarah?"

Johnny, at seven, was bowed with the weight of his three-year-old sister who rode piggyback. "Let me down," she complained. He stooped while she slid down, then stepped forward to tug his mother's skirt. "We're here, mother."

Sarah slumped in relief, setting down Timothy, who stood wobbling but stamping his feet, happy to be standing on solid ground. "All here, then."

Suzanne, unable to relax, pushed closer. "Have you seen Rebecca?"

Sarah shook her head, but Goody Gilson overheard and stopped to give her witness. "We lagged behind. Indians too close. Her girl tripped and fell. Rebecca tried to protect her, threw herself over her. He had a tomahawk, I heard gunshots. Oh, Suzanne, Sarah, I didn't stop. I'm so sorry."

Suzanne took the stairs to the second floor two steps at a time. She pleaded with Elder Roberts. "My sister is out there. I need to see."

Despite the trees blocking their views, she could make out a pile of skirts. She thought she saw the bodies of two, fallen where they'd veered from the Boston Road with Indians in pursuit—there was no movement. There was nothing she could do in daylight to recover them. She'd ask Joseph to go under cover of night. *Becky was only three! John and Joanna and now Rebecca, too?* Her face twisted in pain. When Sarah learned of their fate, stricken with grief for two husbands, a child, and now her best friend, she uttered a wrenching wail.

Mercifully, at Sarah's wail, Suzanne's pain dulled, and numbed.Thus, she had only the need to work. Suzanne took her hands. "Are you alright? The children?"

"Yes," she wept. "Please, tend to the others."

Men who'd escaped the ambushes straggled into the yard. Walter Skinner, who'd escaped the ambush on the hill with Timothy Allen and Joseph Gilson, had three gunshot wounds and was bleeding heavily. Timothy and Joseph had been shot as well; the Indians had nearly succeeded in scalping Joseph but had left him with just a flesh wound. They were fortunate the surgeon had survived uninjured. He removed the bullets and stitched up the head wound. Suzanne, moved to act, could provide her services at cleaning the wounds and tying on poultices. Samuel Kemp, Richard Blood, John Lakin, and Joseph Lawrence had held off the Indians while the women escaped. They in turn escaped the fort before the marauding Indians squatted there. They lamented they'd not been able to rescue food and belongings; the Indians had them now.

That day, the Indians plundered empty houses and torched the meetinghouse. All that day, they feasted, raising voices in celebration. The townspeople crowded into Parker's garrison had no defense. Angry, fearful, and despairing, they passed the day in hushed reassurances.

Suzanne busied herself tending the men injured in the ambush, but late, before starting up those tasks she had come to share with her neighbors, she rested by the hearth. Ann Tarball passed by her kicking her foot. "Indian lover!"

Suzanne reviled the woman; she'd tried to reason with her but had finally given it up. The worst of it was that her neighbors, Adelaide Roberts and Mary Parker, said nothing. They too looked uneasy. *Has Ann poisoned their minds?* She wondered.

That night One-Eyed John, the captain of the ambushing Indians, called out to Captain Parker. They all heard it and crowded into the yard to hear better. He harangued Parker at length, and no one slept that night. What's more, neither Joseph nor Suzanne dared to venture out to recover Rebecca and her daughter's bodies.

"*Captain* Parker" he sneered. "Willard was my neighbor in Lancaster! No more Lancaster now. Burned. Me owe English nothing. Nothing!"

Suzanne woke when the voice rang out clear in the eerily silent night. Sitting up, she saw Captain Parker, half dressed, make his way from his quarters up the stairs to the outlook. Some rose from their beds to join him. Fully alert now, Suzanne heard the rest.

"I burn church. Where your God now? Your God abandon you. Why you pray to him? You make peace with *me. Monoco.*"

More residents woke and sat at attention.

"You can't win. Me have four hundred and fourscore warriors. Me take corn. Me take cattle. No trade for English goods. Me now. English owe me."

The haranguing continued almost without end. "Maybe you make peace? No peace. Me burn Medfield. Me burn Lancaster. Next me burn Groton. You no army. Me have four hundred warriors. What me will, me do." He continued to brag as other warriors had done: Sagamore Sam, old Jethro, and the Sagamore of Quaboag.

Elder Roberts stood behind Captain Parker at the window, but they could see nothing in the dense dark. "He brags like the proud Assyrians do threatening Jerusalem," he exclaimed. "Let's pray God repays these savages the same as he did them."

The Indian ranted on, "Next time, me burn Chelmsford, Concord, Watertown, Cambridge, Charlestown, Roxbury, Boston. What me will, me do. Your God not stop me."

The dark was just lifting when the Indian went silent.

The next day, Thursday, March 10, Thomas Tarball received a signal from the watch at the gate. He saw an old Indian carrying plunder down the road. He was staggering under the weight of a black sheep on his back, plainly old and decrepit, not a threat. Prompted, soldiers shot several times, but missed him. Then, James Roberts motioned to several of the soldiers to come forward. He decided that together they could take the Indian alive. Maybe they could learn what One-Eyed John planned next. Suzanne saw them leave, but quickly they returned. The Watchman had spied an ambush waiting behind the house and called them back. They narrowly avoided an attack that might have broken into Parker's garrison, but on the defensive, they felt keenly the threat surrounding them.

Shortly after this, the Indians in the garrison next door ended their noisy revelry, and the war party removed to a valley nearby. They could hear them even at the distance throughout the day and night.

The next day, Elder Roberts called them together for prayer, leading them in a Bible study. Under siege, the townspeople banded together to beg their God for deliverance and read the Bible for His instruction. Elder Roberts rose and began with a prayer. "We do not have our Reverend here to speak for us this day, but after the long night, we might take a lesson in our prophesying from 2 Kings, Chapter 18." He turned to Richard Parker and nodded. "You heard it." He turned to the silent parishioners. "We heard it, One-Eyed John blaspheming God. He spoke like the Devil himself, trying to destroy our faith in God."

A murmur arose, and many nodded their heads. "He's the Devil alright," "That's right," and "We heard it!" The response bubbled up from their shared consent.

"The Bible tells us of another people under siege and what happened to those who kept their faith and those who did not. It may assure us God will not abandon us in our trial. It lets us know that we are not abandoned. The Assyrians laid siege to the cities of Judah and divided the northern from the southern kingdoms. First, they destroyed the Israelite's faith, then made them promises. Once the Israelites had strayed, the Assyrian King moved them to Assyria and enslaved them.

"But in the south, Israelite's King, Hezekiah, was faithful to the Lord and kept the commandments. Only twenty-five when he became king, he lived through the aggressions of the king of Assyria that continued for fourteen more years. The King of Assyria took all the fenced cities of Judah.

"To save Jerusalem, Hezekiah agreed to pay the tribute demanded by the king. He stripped the silver and gold from the temple and paid tribute. But still the king sent his agent, Rabshakeh to turn them against their God. He shouted to the people, 'Don't let Hezekiah deceive you, for he can't deliver you. Don't listen if he tells you your God will deliver you. Where are the gods of Hamath and Arpad? Where are the gods of Sepharvaim, Hena, and Ivah? Have they delivered Samaria out of mine hand? Who are they among all the gods of these countries have delivered their country out of mine hand, that the Lord should deliver Jerusalem out of mine hand?'

"Rabshakeh delivered the Assyrian King's promises, but Hezekiah's people held their peace. They obeyed Hezekiah's commandment: 'Answer him not.'"

The Elder pounded the Bible. "We've heard the same from the savage, Monoco. The Bible gives us an example of Satan's word to warn us. Like good King Hezekiah's people, let us answer him not."

Suzanne felt uneasy with the passage, which was not an exact fit. The King of Assyria had tricked the Israelites with promises after he destroyed their faith. Monoco had tried to destroy their faith, but Groton townspeople knew they'd perish or be taken for slaves if they left their garrisons. Monoco had no way to deceive them with peace or a land of milk and honey.

The Elder ended their meeting with the Bible's lesson, drawn from Hezekiah's story. Hezekiah, through penitent prayer, wins Gods reward. Elder Roberts continued, "When Assyrians lay siege to Jerusalem, '… it came to pass that night, the angel of the Lord went out and smote a hundred fourscore and five thousand in the Assyrian camp. When they arose early in the morning, behold, they were all dead corpses.' Our faith is being tested, and we must trust in God to deliver us from this present evil. But we must remember that we may not suffer evil in our midst and expect God to relent. Suzanne Morse, will you please stand."

The townspeople looked at each other, shocked, although Goody Tarball sat back, smugly lifting her chin. Suzanne, face drawn, stood, unable to look at her neighbors.

He turned to address her. "We know you spend many hours with the Nashua witch doctor. We ask if you've forsaken our Lord and Master and waywardly seek the savages' way? Only Lord may grant life and good health. I denounce the Nashua witch and ask that all here do denounce her so our congregation may receive the Lord's deliverance and bounty. Do you denounce Dancing Light?"

The women, especially the women, stirred uneasily in their places, keeping their silence as decreed by the scriptures, but signaling their fright in glances. Suzanne had delivered their babies, cared for their children, set bones, sewn up wounds, tended the aches and failures of their elders. Suzanne had saved lives. But her best friends weren't present. Adelaide and Reverend Willard were staying at the Willard garrison. Suzanne's and Joseph's uncle, who had clout as head of the town council, wasn't there. Uncle John Morse was staying at Sawtell's garrison. Who among them would speak for her?

Suzanne grimaced at this accusation, and Joseph scowled at Thomas Tarball as he leaped to his feet. The Tarballs had denounced Suzanne's commerce with the Nashua from the beginning. "The Nashua joined One-Eyed John when they suddenly disappeared this spring. We know this, but I've heard her defend them. She is aiding the enemy, brought them down on us."

Joseph stood to confront him. "Why would my wife bring the Indians to Groton, to rob us, to attack us? Do we not stand to lose as much as you?"

"She needs no reason; Satan has entered her heart. The witch doctor has bewitched her, and she now holds malice for the Groton townspeople."

Captain Parker interrupted, raising his voice. "I beg to differ with you. Mary and I have seen no evidence of this malice of which you speak. In fact, the women of Groton have one and all received the benefit of her care. Malice! The idea!"

"I have proof by word from my wife Ann. She's told me of the midwife saving foul bits of flesh—for satanic rituals, I say."

Suzanne blanched. He was speaking of the umbilical cord she'd snipped for the Nashua baby blessing. Only Ann Tarball and Adelaide Roberts, the Elder's wife, knew of that. *It was years ago,* she thought. *Surely, they can't hold that as evidence for our present danger. Oh, where is Abigail?* But she knew Abigail could not defend her now.

"We don't believe it." Captain Parker had little respect for Tarball since the Boston trial where he'd testified on the Waldron Post murder. He was sure that Tarball had testified on behalf of Waldron, in exchange for goods. Waldron had paid him. He even believed that Tarball had continued selling contraband liquor to the Indians.

Suzanne's friends nodded vigorously agreeing with the Captain. They knew Suzanne spent time with the Nashua shaman, but Suzanne brought them remedies only the Indians knew. Useful remedies. But many more looked puzzled or dismissed the Captain's remarks with a frown or shrug.

"Suzanne and Joseph Morse have been outstanding members of our church and have brought positive changes to this community," the Captain continued. "I, for one, will hear no more of this Elder Roberts."

While Suzanne was happy to have the Captain as her defender, the reactions on the faces of her neighbors caused her some worry. Clearly, some were of the mind that she'd brought the Devil into their midst.

Ann Tarball glared at her with malice and Adelaide Roberts turned her face away in shame.

Chapter Twenty Four

GOD'S WRATH

Groton, Sunday, March 13, 1676

On the third day, before the sun set on Saturday, the evacuated settlers prepared for the Sabbath. Attempts to order the common room were defeated almost before they began. More than a dozen families had held out in the garrison for ten days under One-Eyed John's siege, counting the families who fled Nutting's garrison when Indians breached the palisades. And the upper story now held the men and older sons as well as the ten military men Boston appointed. Captain Parker had sent a messenger to Concord asking for backup, but it could be days before relief arrived.

Suzanne had exhausted her supply of herbal remedies to calm the terrorized congregation; no help remained for the cowed and fearful women, the whining children. To remove a two-week clutter, grime, and decay to make their quarters suitable for Sunday meeting was impossible.

Suzanne pitched in to clean up despite the general demoralization she felt. Lugging the pail of potable water, collected from a cold spring rain, she weltered through mud and horse manure past the makeshift benches and tables where men worked to clean their guns and sharpen tools. Their labor transformed the random piles into a neat array of arms ready for use. The few horses stabled within the garrison dozed on their feet in dirty straw. They hadn't been able to empty the stinking slop pots or discard the animal waste outside the gates in days. The vat of water that had served animals and humans alike, was no longer usable, even boiled. Clouds of an unnamed slime swirled on the surface. Before One-Eyed John's Indians had breached Nutting's garrison, the older children had been able to gather water in the nearby creek, hauling back containers in a horse cart. Afterwards, they were reduced to collecting rainwater, not daring to leave the shelter, even at night. Pails and cisterns now lined one side of the yard; the water rationed for drinking only. Still, outside in the yard, she could breathe comparatively fresh air. Once she'd entered the great room, the close air was best sampled in shallow breaths.

The dozen families sheltering had lined every wall in the large room with rolls of bedding and sacks of supplies. Those who'd escaped from Nutting's garrison brought nothing but the clothes on their backs; nevertheless, conditions had declined to a chaotic jumble. Settlers had walled one corner with blankets for privacy and filled it with the necessary chamber pots. Twice a day, they'd filled to the brim; the older children drew straws for the job of emptying them. Oddly, though an onerous task, the children felt gratified because they could walk outside the palisades for a short time after dark. That had ended with the Indian occupation next door and men had dug a covered cesspool within the compound.

The only relief from odorous unwashed bodies was preparing food at the open hearth. The aromas of cooking food could overcome any stench. To keep the children from underfoot, the women had set up "schools" and appointed caretakers. One Elder and two girls took over a "nursery," surrounded it with boxes and bags to keep toddlers from wandering. Across the room, away from the hearth where the appointed cooks worked, those children learning to read and write circled Adelaide Roberts, making their marks on slates and repeating the rhymes they read. Any child over twelve worked beside an adult to keep the area in some orderly fashion.

Adelaide Roberts spoke with Suzanne about their quarters.

"It's hopeless. We can't hold our meeting here."

"Then what do you propose?" Suzanne asked.

At that moment, Mary Parker opened the door from the Parker quarters and strode to their side. "Suzanne, Adelaide, my mother wants you to tell the congregation that Elder Roberts wants to hold our Sunday meeting in our great room."

Suzanne stared at Adelaide. Their prayers had been answered even before they'd put them in words. *What was it Reverend Willard said?* She reflected. *Intention. Yes, God knows our intents.*

Adelaide and Suzanne spread the news to the settlers, who fitfully tried to muster attention to their appearances for the Sabbath. Here and there, women combed each other's hair, pulled locks into buns and braids, plaited braids for their daughters. One woman washed the faces of her infants with spit, others boiled clothes in contaminated water from the vat to clean clothes. A few men brushed their breeches and waistcoats free of dust, trimmed and combed their beards, keeping their posts in the garrison the while. All were cocked like the hammers on their rifles.

At sundown, the beginning of the Sabbath, the Indians next door went silent. All sounds of their presence came to them on the wind from a distant place. When lookouts reported they had left for a bordering valley, the refugees' apprehension eased, though no one would venture to check if the Indians had abandoned Nutting's breached garrison. Some dared hope that God had heard their pleas, and the Indians were leaving.

When Elder Roberts expressed this view, though, Thomas Tarball challenged him. "Why would they leave now? If One-Eyed John had the numbers he bragged about, they have an unbeatable advantage."

Captain Parker agreed with him. "He said he had five hundred warriors. We have fifty households in our town and ten men sent from Boston. We've lost Nutting's garrison, and it's not certain we can hold the three garrisons we have left. It's a miracle we hold them off, but we must fight to the end. God willing, backup will come from Concord before they attack."

Joseph Morse, ever an optimist, voiced his argument. "But they stand to gain little here. It's March. We've nothing left of our winter stores. They have no use for our cattle. They slaughter them indiscriminately."

"Sheep. Chickens. Goats. That's what they want. Anything they can carry on their backs." Thomas Tarball spat out his disgust.

Adam Blood, who had narrowly escaped from the garrison next door when Indians breached the palisades, offered his eyewitness. "They're foot soldiers. They carry weapons. Nothing else, most, not even clothes. They eat what's in front of them."

Everyone in hearing range shuddered. Green spoke up: "We must thank God that most don't carry guns. Arrows and tomahawks are no match for our rifles."

Suzanne couldn't bear to hear more. She left the circle and found her way to Goodmen Skinner, Allen, and Gilson, who were still healing from their gun wounds. She checked their bandages and talked to the girls she'd assigned to nurse them.

At sundown, when the Sabbath began in earnest, a humbled group gathered around the hearth for prophesying. No one could keep their minds on the scriptures; their hold on life was too uncertain.

Overnight, no one could rest; the children sucked their thumbs and buried their heads in blankets. Villagers sat up late into the night, alert to every sound. Suzanne could hear scuttering. *Is it a wild animal or an Indian?* Suzanne thought. Then she heard scuffles, whispering, a branch scraping the palisade walls. *It's the wind*, she decided, but could see nothing. The night was moonless and black. The children whimpered. *It's a night like the one Reverend Willard told us about.* He had warned them, and now it was all coming to pass. The children were hungry; not enough to feed them; they'd heard the voices of the enemy, seen the wounded, witnessed the slayings. On the brink of disaster, she feared for her children. *It has come. God has forsaken us.*"

Before the Sunday sunrise, they heard the first volley of shots ring out; a full body of the armed enemy surrounded them. Sentinels posted at the upper story yelled as hundreds of savages made themselves known. Under cover of dark, Indians had scattered throughout Groton, hiding near abandoned houses, strategically surrounding the three remaining garrisons. On the first volley of shots, on cue, they rushed from hiding, lighting torches. They dressed to raid, nearly naked, with nothing to impede movements. Painted faces and burnished red bodies flashed across the still barren spring land. A hellish shrieking rose from the multitude of Indians brandishing firebrands and tomahawks. Arrows rained in the yard amid ratcheting gunshots fired from both sides.

Chaos descended on the groggy townspeople at first shock, but the men found their way to their posts. Captain Parker dispatched yet another messenger to Concord with a plea for military backup. Then the two dozen men held the palisades, with orders to waste no gunpowder. Boys helped their fathers load the matchlocks; few men owned flintlocks. Good marksmen, they fired on the marauders and held the walls, but the Indians were to manifest their worst fears. Once the Indians had lit their firebrands, they torched every standing building: houses, barns, cribs, and stables.

Suzanne and the residents all choked on the fumes; the thick clouds of smoke rose to blot out the sun. She reluctantly turned away from her children; swept up in tending those wounded in the assault, she couldn't help them. Martha and Sarah joined forces to give the children comfort in the terrifying attack. Suzanne worked tirelessly beside the doctor to bandage and patch the men injured by arrows and gunshot through the long day. Fortunately for her, his supply of medicines was enough; her own had dwindled.

Neither Suzanne nor Joseph could see their homestead from the palisaded garrison, but thick smoke in that direction was telling. With heavy heart, Suzanne battled the desperation she felt at this wanton destruction of the work of ten years. Her apothecary, ingredients carefully gathered and prepared for her medical needs, all lost. Homesteading had been fiercely difficult, and their hold on the land weak. *At least Joseph let the cows out. Bessie and her calf might survive,* she thought. Humbled before God and man, they'd only the horse, the clothes they'd brought, what remained of their food. *And my journals, my medical books, thank the Lord, thank Joseph! I can rebuild.*

The fires burned all day; and that night, they could again hear Indians who occupied Nutting's breached palisades. Most of them, however, camped in the valley, where they danced to war drums and feasted on what they'd looted. The villagers could hear the drums, and the voices carried loudly through the bare trees and echoed against the surrounding hills. By morning, the buildings were gone, blackened squares marked where they had stood, the still warm embers. The scorched fields stretched clear to the forests, not a tree or shrub left. Only the three garrisons still stood, strung along the main road to Boston, now dotted with patches the fire skipped, trees and shrubs still thick with an early spring blush.

Again, no one slept that night. Early the next morning, the Indians surrounded Captain Parker's, Major Willard's and Goodman Sawtell's garrisons. The townspeople waited in dread; they were so badly outnumbered that their defenses wouldn't hold.

Then, the surrounding bands issued three volleys of gunshot. The Sachem, Monoco, who had heard that reinforcements were coming from Concord, stood with his men outside Parker's garrison and announced to the Captain they were leaving.

They vanished as suddenly as they had come, slipping into the woods and terrain like ghosts. Hardly breathing, the besieged townsmen waited in silence. They were too rattled, too fearful to rejoice or even realize God had sent them what they'd prayed for, begged for—deliverance. That afternoon, the column of militia arrived to rescue the settlers and take them to Concord. They led a train of carts that would carry the injured, young children, and any salvaged goods or livestock the Indians had spared.

Chapter Twenty Five

WARNING FRIENDS

Groton, Monday, March 14, 1676

When the column of militia arrived to take the settlers to Concord, Joseph joined the volunteers to aid the militia in scouring the town for salvage. Suzanne, who had sealed off all thoughts of her sister and niece during the siege, now begged him to look for any signs of them.

"Goody Gilson saw them fall and heard screams. She thought she saw the Indians raise his tomahawk to scalp her. She left them for dead. I last saw them where they'd fallen, lying on the path, a few yards from Nutting's garrison."

"How long were they there?" Joseph asked.

"I don't know. I wanted to get you to help recover their bodies, but it wasn't safe with the Indians still at Nutting's. The next morning, they were gone." Suzanne's voice rose and she stared intently at him.

"It's possible they were alive, then."

"No. The Indian was on her. Mary Gilson heard their screams. A mother hears pain. Oh Joseph." Suzanne laid her hand on Joseph's arm. "The Indians! Please be careful."

Joseph left with the small troop of volunteers, supported by the militia.

Suzanne, still tending to those injured in the attack, checked the wounded and their wounds. She stooped beside Goodman Green; she'd helped extract an arrow from his thigh, cauterize the wound, and apply a poultice to keep it from festering as it healed.

"The bandage is soaked with blood. You've been walking!" She tightened the new bandage with a jerk, which made him wince.

He laughed to cover it up. "You need to get it tighter. I can't sit. Got to get the family to Concord."

"You can. And you must. You'll be riding a cart, too. Your children are fit and can walk."

At that moment, Martha appeared, pushing a reluctant Hannah, her youngest daughter before her. "Show your mother," she demanded.

Hannah stood staring at her feet, clasping her hands in back of her. "Yes, ma'am," she said, not moving.

"Can I see?" Suzanne turned her and pried her hands apart. Hannah winced when she spread the fingers she had protected so fiercely. Now blistering burns covered the skin of both her index and middle fingers. "What happened?"

Martha knelt by the pair. "I told her to keep away from the fire, but she doesn't listen. I think she caught a spark or hunk of ember."

"And she held it in place, looks like." Suzie kissed her hand. "Does it hurt?"

Hannah sucked her lower lip and nodded. "Are you mad at me?"

Martha expelled her breath and gathered her close. "No! Just worried, you silly."

Suzanne, never one to coddle her patients, stood looking down at her cowering daughter, hands on hips. She shook her head, as if to rebuke her with *what am I going to do with you?* But she didn't. "Bad fire! Bad fire! Let's make that burn go away."

While Suzanne rummaged in her medicine bag for the right salve for burns, Adelaide Roberts, accompanied by Ann Tarball, interrupted her. "My husband wants to talk with you when you're done."

Suzanne felt a sudden chill. After the prophesying, her request could only mean trouble. Suzanne glanced sidelong at Ann Tarball, nodded, and having found the salve, returned to her ministrations of her daughter's burns.

Joseph and the men returned before nightfall. Concerned he had no good news, he didn't notice Suzanne's crestfallen posture. She bent, chest hollowed out, over her efforts to arrange their sleeping ground. He reported that they hadn't seen any Indians, but every farmstead was burned to the ground and their stores with them. They'd found some cows still alive, but Indians had slaughtered cattle and left the bodies rotting in the fields where they'd fallen. Their cow and calf had met that fate. He found some of the glass bottles from her apothecary and salvaged any that remained in any usable shape.

"I saw no sign of Rebecca. Nothing."

Suzanne's face wrenched with the grief at his announcement. "Oh, Rebecca, Rebecca," she whispered. Joseph held her tightly.

When she'd recovered from the news, she spoke. "Joseph, We have a problem. Elder Roberts spoke to me. He brought up my friendship with the Indians again and told me the congregation has decided that I am responsible for the Nashua's attack. They have no proof, but they all feel that we shouldn't join the convoy. He was so cruel!" Suzanne's voice broke in anger. "He said we weren't welcome in Concord. We should go back where we came from. I tried to reason with him, but he said I could talk to my Indian friends, see if they'd protect me."

"Does Uncle John know of this?"

"Oh, Joseph," she cried. "Your Uncle was kidnapped. The Indians took him. No one knows where he may be. They may torture him!"

"We have no one to speak for us then? Perhaps Reverend Willard? Abigail Willard?"

Her answer cut with bitterness. "We must try."

At dusk, the garrison occupants busied themselves packing the carts, mostly happy to leave the confines of their prison. Others balked, clinging to the garrison as a sailor might cling to a raft in heavy seas. They were still uncertain the Indians were gone.

Suzanne, not satisfied with Joseph's report, decided to explore the exact place where Rebecca had fallen. She wrapped herself in her shawl and, under Thomas Tarball's nose, slid unnoticed through the gates, opened for returning scouts. She had little light before nightfall, when he'd lock them, though many scouts ranged out and about.

She ran down the path quickly, reaching the small hillock where they'd fallen. On her hands and knees, she patted the ground, searching with palms and fingers for any sign of their clothing, any object they might have dropped. Then she froze; she heard the footsteps of someone creeping toward her.

"Boo shoo!"

Relief rushed through her with recognition of the familiar voice. "Dancing Light?"

Dancing Light grabbed Suzanne by the arm and pulled her behind the trees. "We no safe. No sound." Amazed, Suzanne heeded her warning.

"What are you doing here?" she whispered. "Willard thinks your people have joined Monoco and King Philip."

"No. I tell you we no fight English. We go north, with friends. Hide there."

"I tried to tell him, but he doesn't believe you. Now, here you are."

"You don't believe me?"

"You cannot have gone far!"

"We are running—day north of Concord. We hear Chelmsford soldiers attack Wamesit, Nashoba Christian town. Kill boy, injure children."

"I'm so sorry, Dancing Light."

"I come from north to warn you, my kin." Dancing Light tapped her heart. "Monoco take revenge. Run two days."

"You come too late. He destroyed Groton."

"No. More danger. No go with wagons. Monoco will attack."

Suzanne held her friend's hands. But you are in danger too. You must go."

Dancing Light pulled her closer. “What you search? Here. Tonight.”

“My sister and her daughter. They were running from Monoco’s raiders when they captured Nutting’s garrison. Rebecca fell. A neighbor tells me an Indian brave killed them, scalped the little one. But her body disappeared. I thought if I could find something, any sign.”

“I find out. You let me. Great Spirit willing. I no see you again. In morning, you no go to Concord, no go with soldiers. Monoco ambush English. His men hide on road to Concord. You take family south through woods. No Indians in south. Go to Marlboro, then Watertown.”

Suzanne was shocked. “Are you sure? I must warn the people.”

“No. No warn. Danger for me. Danger for Nashua. We friends English.” Dancing Light held Suzanne’s hands tightly. “Promise me. I talk to Monaco. I try to stop Monaco.”

“I promise.”

“Good. Take nothing. Go in morning. No stop. I have this for you.” Dancing Light thrust a bulky deerskin sack into her hands. “For journey. No stopping to Watertown. You go now.”

As suddenly as she had appeared, Dancing Light disappeared into the dark. Suzanne ran back to the gate, still open for the returning soldiers, and made her way to Joseph’s side.

She was torn between protecting her friend or her neighbors, even though the community had turned against her. She sought no revenge, but Suzanne wanted to trust and protect her friend more than she wanted to save them. She decided that she must keep her promise, but she had to tell Joseph.

Chapter Twenty Six

FLIGHT

Groton, Tuesday, March 15, 1676

Joseph Morse was still angry at the parishioners for abandoning them to the hostile Indians. He'd been unable to reason with Elder Roberts, and their protectors, Uncle John and Reverend Willard, were not available. So bitter was he that he wouldn't have betrayed Dancing Light's warning except that his sister Sarah told him she was joining the caravan. She had cried, wanting him to know that she in no way shared the Groton township condemnation of Suzanne's commerce with the Nashua. She wanted only to save her children.

Now, if he kept silent, he was abandoning her to a possible Indian attack in the open. He argued with Suzanne. "We cannot let them fall to an ambush. My conscience will not let me"

"But I can't betray Dancing Light. Joseph, as long as they suspect the Nashua have joined Monoco, Elder Roberts will think she is the enemy. He won't believe any warning from *her*. You *know* that."

"I agree, but I must convince Sarah."

"Dancing Light is going to try to stop the ambush. You must trust providence on this."

"You have faith in *her*, not in *God*. Sorry, I can't share it. The Nashua haven't declared their friendship openly."

"They can't. Joseph, the English have sent all the Christian Indians, our 'friends' to Deer Island to keep them safe from hostiles. But it's a terrible fate. The Indians have no food or shelter there; they die in scores. Where can her people go? Please don't say anything. But know that God is with us when it seems that all the world is punishing us for crimes we didn't commit. *Her* word restores my faith in the Lord."

Suzanne didn't believe her own words, which she felt condemned her. She felt such guilt after telling Joseph that Dancing Light would be able to halt the ambush that she couldn't ask whether he'd warned his sister. She preferred to assume he had but suspected he hadn't because Sarah didn't join their flight to Watertown.

Later that night, after they'd had supper to say good-bye to young Martha and Jimmy Roberts, Sarah and her children, she looked in the sack. Dancing Light had given her moccasins for the family, already stuffed with straw to keep their feet warm and dry. She had packed pemmican to eat on the trail. Suzanne's eyes stung with tears. She knew how little food the small band of Nashua must have at winter's end. Her friend's generosity overwhelmed her; Suzanne's tears were as much grief as gratitude. She let the tears flow, stifling sobs. Grief was a luxury in their besieged lives. She must be a parent for her frightened children. The whites of their eyes showed as they gathered their blankets and donned layers of clothing.

At dawn, Suzanne worked with Joseph to saddle and pack their belongings on their horse. She would not open the bag of moccasins yet, as she thought the children would resist. To wear them, so symbolic of their enemies, when they'd just survived a terrible siege on their behalf was unthinkable. She would tempt them after their feet had tired or blistered. Once she had them gathered, she began.

"Suzie, Hester, and Joseph. You are the oldest, and I will need you to take turns riding the horse. You'll be riding triple with Samuel and Mary. Your father and I will switch off carrying Hannah. Everyone else walks. Do you have that?"

Joseph was proud to be lumped with his two older sisters. "We can draw straws," he said eagerly.

"Indeed!" Suzanne nodded. "That's a good beginning, Joseph." But she thought, *Standing Heron, I think you're still attached to that spirit in the sky.* His nature was distinctly different from his brothers and sisters, always eagerly helpful.

She continued. "We won't be stopping at night, so you might get sleepy riding, but you mustn't nod off. You are responsible to make sure Sam and Mary stay on the horse. Now we don't know what weather we'll meet, but we have blankets if it turns cold. All you have to do is ask."

Young Joseph held out straws to his sisters. Hester was the first to ride horseback. He helped lift his brother and sister, five-year-old Mary sitting in front of her, the older Samuel in back because he could hold onto Hester better.

His father stooped to scoop up Hannah, not yet two. She climbed up to awkwardly ride piggyback as she avoided the use of her bandaged hand. Suzanne had lathered salve on her burns and hoped that would prevent her from whimpering. She shouldered the deerskin pouch gift of footwear and pemmican, and they set out.

Thomas Tarball opened the gate, and they left on what felt like a trail of shame under an overcast March sky of moderate temperature.

"Can we go by our house?" Suzie asked.

"Yes, mother! Can we?" the rest chimed in.

"Joseph, what do you think?" Suzanne wasn't sure she wanted to see it.

"It's on our way," Joseph said. They turned from the main road to Boston at the juncture of the road to Lancaster, sometimes called Farmers Row, and headed south. To their left, the charred ashes of the meetinghouse had gone cold, and across the road they could see the mound of the new grave dug for Uncle Timothy. Suzanne stared at the churchyard. *I can't believe that was just two weeks ago*, she thought. The weeks under siege had ruined her sense of time.

"We should pay our respects to Timothy," Joseph said. He spoke to the children. "Come. Let's say good-bye to your Uncle." He led them into the churchyard but nearing the grave he suddenly stopped. "Stay where you are! Don't come further." However, Suzanne had followed close after him. She too stopped, stunned at the sight before her. She was speechless.

One-Eyed John's men had dug up the body, dug a Christian's body from his resting place. And cut him up. They had mutilated him. She caught sight of an arm with his hand still attached. Scattered about the grave. His head? A torso without ... they'd unwound the burial shroud, and she could look no further. She was shaking from her core. "How? How could they?"

Joseph spat out, "Savages. It's what we've been trying to tell you."

"This wasn't our neighbors. Not Dancing Light's people. Monoco is an evil man. You *heard* him."

Still, Suzanne felt the same revulsion for these senseless acts of desecration as her husband did. *Owl magic*, she reflected. *This is what Dancing Light was telling me. Was it her people?*

Joseph feared Indians might still be present. He called out, telling the children to turn around. They obeyed without argument. They rode past Timothy and Sarah's place, where smoke still rose from charred remains of their buildings, and their field where slaughtered cows lay festering with bloat. Rebecca Church's house had fared no better. Suzanne felt eerie, walking through a town denuded of its houses. The roads led them through lots that, abandoned, fallow with winter frosts yet, felt like an old ruin. Signs of previous occupation were already shabbily scattered in empty fields. When they reached the Morse lots, little Suzie gasped when she saw their home. Where barns and sheds had stood, little was left to show. Without buildings, the plots appeared shrunken. She started to run toward the charred shadow where the house had stood, but Suzanne caught her hand as she passed.

"Stop. Don't look back Suzie."

Suzie began to cry, and young Joseph and Hester looked away. Their neighbors' houses had burned to the ground: the Roberts, the Parkers, the Crisps, and the Bloods. No one could live in Groton now. The devastation weighed like a hundred stones on their hearts. Suzanne was grateful when they entered woods just south of Groton and followed the Nashua River south, away from what they'd known as civilization.

By then, Hannah fussed, struggling to get down. They set her down for a time, and Suzanne and Joseph traded their loads. For a while, Hannah was content when her mother carried her.

Samuel, riding behind Hester, held on tightly and asked "Where is Aunt Becky? Didn't she want to come?" He could still remember the trip to Watertown when his grandfather had died. Rebecca had been pregnant with Becky that year, and her baby was a playmate for Samuel at every family gathering. They'd gone by cart on the main road to Boston that time.

Suzanne, who walked beside the horse, afraid the two younger ones could easily fall off, answered. "Becky had to go with her mother. She and Aunt Sarah are going to Concord with the soldiers."

"Why aren't we going to Concord?" little Joseph asked.

"Because we have a place to live in Watertown," Suzanne explained. She didn't want him to know what had led to their present lot, walking forty miles to Watertown with one horse between them, their cart having burned with their house and barns. She could hardly admit the reason to herself: the censure of the Groton congregation. When they had walked half the day and Suzanne could see Suzie and Joseph lagged behind the horse, their steps heavy, she called for a rest. It was also time for them to eat and shed heavy shoes.

"We'll be passing near Lancaster soon." Suzanne caught Mary and Sam as Hester handed them down.

"Will we go?" Hester asked, dismounting from the horse.

Her big sister scoffed. "No silly, Lancaster was burned down, just like we were. There *is* no Lancaster now." Suzanne saddened to hear her daughter so hardened, so young.

Chastened by her older sister, Hester sulked, but soon rallied when her mother began handing round cornbread and thin slivers of cheese.

"Let's not think about that right now. We can't look back. Come, I have a treat for you. Sit." Suzanne pointed at a log that stretched a good length where it had fallen to the ground. "All of you, sit. You too, husband."

Her husband, who had not an ounce of pep left after their dismal passage through what felt like Hell, sat without a word.

"Take off your shoes," she demanded. "Everyone."

Joseph junior shrugged when his sister looked at him mystified and unlaced his shoes, which were still wet after the last stream they had leaped across. Suzanne threw balls of wool to them that turned out to be socks. "Dry socks. Before your feet blister. I'll take your shoes now. She emptied the deerskin pouch on the ground, spilling moccasins everywhere, and gathered their shoes. "You'll wear these now. Mary and Sam? These are your size. Leave the straw inside. That's to keep your feet warm and dry." She handed out the rest.

While no one in the family resisted her demands, they handled the Indian footwear as though it could bite them. Only little Joseph smiled broadly. He'd harbored an envy for his mother's moccasins, which he'd seen her wear many times. Suzanne encouraged them. "Try them out. See what you think."

Once they had begun to move about in these featherlight shoes, they began to understand the advantage. Suzanne smiled when she heard exclamations from them that echoed those she'd made herself when she'd first walked in Dancing Light's gifts. "Everyone like the new shoes?"

Joseph stood, bouncing and lifting on his toes. "These will help. We have a long way to go before we reach Marlboro. We'll be walking all night."

"At least we have the moonlight," Suzanne said. "We'll be able to find our way."

Suzanne then lifted Hannah onto her lap. "Let's check that burn, shall we?" She needed to see it in the light of day. As she'd suspected, the honey-based salve had prevented any infection. The blisters had held. As long as they didn't break and weep, they'd heal. She lathered on more of the salve and rewrapped the bandage, wincing when Hannah cried out in pain.

When they started out again, this time, Joseph junior riding horseback, they passed by the road that crossed the Nashua River to Lancaster. The temperature began to fall, to a notably stinging low as night fell. The road at that point narrowed to a horse trail through the woods and fields, poorly kept. Unlike those roads that carried both passengers and goods on carts, these narrow roads were barely wide enough for two abreast, or rather, two abreast if one of them was a horse.

"We have ten miles of this before we reach Marlboro."

"Is the trail marked the whole way?"

"I don't know. We'll find out."

Suzanne breathed deeply, appreciating the wonderful fresh air, associating the narrow road with those paths she'd spent days combing with Dancing Light. She relaxed for the first time in weeks, but prematurely.

They were passing through a clearing just at dusk when Joseph asked his son to halt. "I want to point out Mount Wachusett, there." He pointed to the distant steep slopes of a hill that rose from the plain on their right. "That's an Indian stronghold. They say Philip took his men there last winter."

The children froze. It was too close for comfort.

"We want to get by this as fast as we can," he ended. "Quiet now. Not even whispers. Walk fast."

As night fell, they heard voices in the distance. Suzanne couldn't judge how far they were; voices carried further at night and might be far away. They might or might not be traveling on the road. But she knew their speech pattern was Abenaki. "Joseph," she whispered, "They're Indians."

Joseph didn't answer but signaled to the children to follow him. He led the horse through the darkening forest to a large outcropping of rocks a few yards from the road. "God willing, we can keep out of sight," he whispered. "Not a peep from anyone." He handed Hannah to Suzanne. "Keep her quiet."

He needn't have warned them. Young Joseph looked terrified as he handed down his little brother and sister to his father and dismounted. Suzanne rummaged in the saddlebags for a sweet potato, Hannah's food.

"Get down." He pulled the horse to its knees. A four-legged animal might attract attention if these men were hunting.

When the Indians' voices went silent, they strained, not breathing, to hear where they might be. Suzanne's heart was beating so hard that she thought anyone might hear it. As the group came nearer and again spoke, they guessed the Indians were following the road. They could hear footsteps; there must have been four or five, running. Suzanne squeezed Joseph's hand, with the thought they must be warriors on the move. At the first grunt from Hannah, Suzanne was ready; she mashed the potato with her fingers and filled her mouth with the bits. It worked.

They lay behind the rocks as night settled in and froze as much from the cold as from fear. As the runner's footsteps receded, their heartbeats returned to more normal rhythms. But an hour passed before their fear subsided enough to allow them to move. Now, at moonrise, they felt how exposed they were, alone in the forest. The moon was still bright, and the leafless trees provided no barrier to the flooding light.

Suzanne handed out pemmican, hoping it would provide some comfort for their growling stomachs. She pulled out blankets, and each one of her children accepted them gratefully. Suzie took her turn to ride with the youngest. Joseph had taken over the task of carrying Hannah, who was now able to nod off, her belly full, sleepy from the swaying rhythm of her father's stride. They didn't stop to eat because they'd lost an hour, which would delay their arrival in Marlboro to the following day.

The road—narrowed to the width of a man on horseback—was clearly visible in moonlight. Joseph called for them to stop around midnight. He'd noted that Mary could sleep because young Joseph could hold her upright in front of him. But Samuel nearly fell from the horse as he repeatedly nodded off.

"Time for some changes," he announced. "Hester. You are riding next. Mary, do you think you can hold onto Hester if I put you in back? That way your brother can get some sleep."

Mary nodded yes. When everyone had dismounted, Joseph, who stood steadying the horse, turned and cried, "Hush. Listen."

They stopped and heard the clear sounds of branches breaking underfoot. "Too much noise for Indians," he whispered. "Might be an animal." When the sounds disappeared, he signaled them to wait. He quickly unlashed his rifle from the saddle and walked ahead to investigate. In minutes they saw the huge brown bear loping toward them on the road. The horse was the first to catch sight and reared, huffing, whites of his eyes showing. Flight was his natural instinct, but Suzanne was close enough to catch the rein. She was no match for the horse's mass; he knocked her from her feet and dragged her a few feet before Hester could rein him in from the saddle. Screaming, her brother and sister held tightly.

Instantly, the children on foot began whooping and hollering. Their father had trained them from early childhood what to do when facing a bear. He'd taught them to "Scare it away. If that doesn't work, then play dead. Roll up; protect your head." In other circumstances, Joseph would have shot his rifle to scare a bear, but he feared Indians might be near. So, he waved his arms to make himself larger, brandished the rifle above his head and yelled with the rest. The bear stopped, crouching, his large head weaving left and right. Then he reared, and coming down on all fours, decided to leave them. He trotted into the woods.

Suzanne was shaking as she struggled to her feet. "Mother are you hurt?" young Joseph asked, grabbing her arm.

"My pride." Suzanne's dress was littered with pine needles, dried leaves, and dirt, and had ripped at the shoulders. She'd scraped her hands when she fell. "I've a few bruises, but nothing worse, thank the Lord."

Once the bear's bumbling, crashing flight had trailed off, they began again. Hester rode the horse, and Mary sat back of the saddle holding onto Hester's waist; Sam sat in the front where Hester could keep him from falling if he fell asleep. The family, now collected, began their walk in earnest.

"It's only a short way now. We'll soon be there. Just a little bit farther." Joseph kept encouraging his exhausted family. After two hours of this, his manipulations of their expectations began to wear thin. At one creek where they stopped to drink, Suzie sat down and announced she could no longer walk. Only with much pressure did her father convince her that she had no choice. "We're almost there, but you can take Hester's place."

Hester reluctantly dismounted from the horse, now so stiffened walking was at first painful.

They all heard the Assabet River before they saw it. Water tumbling over fishing weirs created a series of shallow falls that could be heard at a distance. Also, before they had crossed the river, they sighted the Indian village to their left. "It's a Christian settlement. Okommakemesit," Joseph said. "Captain Parker told me it was abandoned after trouble started with King Philip last year. His men carried away the praying Indians, willing or unwilling, stripped the town as they left."

"Praying town looks like it's been vacant for a year!" Suzanne could hear no sign of life in the abandoned houses. The fields still had unharvested crops that had turned brown after winter frosts. Where the wind had stripped the bark from many wickiups, they saw bared domes. "I think we should stop here for the rest of the night. We can start again in the morning." She knew the children were long past what their constitutions could take.

"There are Indians about. What is to keep hostiles from occupying these huts?" asked young Joseph.

"Nothing. You're right. But right now, there's no sign of life here. No fires. No sound. No dogs. No animals."

Suzanne was too exhausted to pass without at least trying. She crossed into the village yard and stood at the door of the largest close wickiup. "Boo shoo," she called loudly. Receiving no answer, she repeated the greeting. She looked around to see if anyone stirred from the other wickiups. But the crystal cold wind continued to whip up leaves and flap coverings. When she was sure no one remained, she cautiously pulled aside the hide covering the doorway. It was empty. No stores remained but the sleeping shelves that buttressed the walls looked inviting. They could even build a fire in the circle, though the interior was degrees warmer than the air bitten by the cold winds outside. They'd not counted on the falling temperatures and needed shelter.

"God works in mysterious ways," she told her children, who balked at the idea of spending a night in an Indian wickiup. "He's providing shelter for you. You can sleep. An hour, two hours. We'll be gone at dawn."

After much argument, Suzanne pushed them through the door, where they settled on sleeping platforms gratefully.

At the break of dawn, Suzanne shook the children to wake them.

Joseph junior woke with a start, his face in fear as if waking from a bad dream. "What? Are they here?"

"Calm yourself. No one is here but us. But we must leave early to make it to the Marlboro garrison. Sleepy, they pulled their blankets around them like shawls in the chilled morning. They munched on pemmican and washed it down with water.

It wasn't far to Marlboro on the widening road.

Chapter Twenty Seven

WOMEN'S WORK

Marlboro, Wednesday, March 16, 1676

When they left at dawn, they walked into heavy fog. The clouded sky had lowered; clouds spilled blustery across forests and fields. To the left a canyon of visibility let them see features of the terrain whereas, walking straight ahead, they journeyed into a wall of mist. Suzanne felt safer, as though she could pull it around her like a cape that rendered her invisible to the threatening natives. Land veiled by the dense fog that dispelled all sense of distance alternately receded or sped toward them. Viewing the thick fog swirl in phantasmagorical shapes around her as she walked destroyed this false security; the fog could conceal more danger than it deflected. Unlike the river's aura, where the moist air calmed their spirits, the fog cloud's moist scent was tinged with metallic accents, as though great lightning strikes had imprinted them in an ancient past.

They'd slept two hours in the shelter and, refreshed, made better progress on the widening road. When the trees thinned, and the forest opened to cultivated fields, they saw the few outlying houses appeared to be unoccupied. Suzanne eagerly searched the road before her. Soon enough, the dark shape of William Ward's palisaded garrison at Marlboro broke through the fog.

Suzanne felt relief when the gate swung open and two soldiers, who brashly looked them up and down, at last signaled them to enter.

"I don't recognize you." The taller soldier, looking not a day above sixteen, pulled the children into the yard so he could close the gate. "Name's Willy Gant. Where are you coming from?"

"I'm Joseph Morse. We come from Groton."

"Groton!" The other soldier barked. He revealed broken teeth when he spoke, a homely man with a patchy beard and pocked skin. "We heard the Indians routed the town."

"You heard right. We were under siege for weeks. One-Eyed John had hundreds of warriors. Burned us out."

As they spoke, people began to gather in the yard, circling to hear more. Willy Gant swept the crowd with his eyes and turned back to Joseph. "A spy told us two days ago that hostiles are near. Spotted a band on the run. We sounded the alarm. Folks have been coming to shelter for two days now. Thought you might be some latecomers. Good you came in the fog. Almost thought you was Indians, though. You dress like 'em." The soldier laughed.

Joseph looked at Suzanne sharply. She didn't flinch. The moccasins and blankets may have saved their lives. More concerned about the mention of spies, she thought, *the Indians who passed us may have been the ones they saw. We were in grave danger. God was with us.*

Joseph chose to ignore the quip. "We saw Indians pass on the road yesterday."

"Lucky they didn't see you first. I'm George Frost. Stationed here to protect these good people." He stepped forward and took the horse's reins from him, smoothing the horse's neck. "I imagine your young'uns will be wanting to stand on their feet again."

Joseph nodded and reached up to his son, who needed no prompting. As he handed Mary and Samuel to his father, the men continued.

"You must have passed by Lancaster. What else you see?"

"Just the band that passed. Didn't see anybody in the praying town by the Assabet, either."

"Okommakemesit? Whole lot of them left last year. Around October," Willy said.

"Don't the hostiles use it?" Joseph asked.

"They stripped anything useful from that town two weeks after it was abandoned," George said. "Just wind living there now."

Willy shuffled impatiently. "You expect any more coming from Groton?"

"No. Far as I know, they joined a cavalcade bound for Concord. We're on our way to Watertown, to stay with family. Thought the Boston Road was too dangerous."

A man came forward from the group milling around them and approached Joseph. "Name's John Fay. My sister lives in Watertown. Do you know Martha Granger?"

"I don't, but Suzanne might." Joseph pushed the dazed children toward their mother, who pulled them close, hands resting on their shoulders.

Suzanne nodded. "I do. Joanna Morton introduced me. Joanna was her midwife."

"I wouldn't know much about that." John Fay smiled at Suzanne, dismissing her. "But my missus would." He pulled his wife forward.

His wife's eyelids drooped, her dress bodice was stained, her skirts, too. Suzanne wondered how long she'd stayed at the garrison. Dark circles under her eyes spelled sleepless nights. *When was the last time she combed her hair?* Suzanne thought, but immediately felt hypocritical. *Who am I to criticize?* I must look a sight myself.

The woman spoke. "I'm Mary Fay. Was Goody Morton your midwife, too?"

"No. I was her apprentice for ten years. I've met your sister-in-law. I helped deliver her baby."

"Oh! Are you a midwife then?"

Joseph spoke for her, proudly. "She's the best midwife in Groton, Goody Fay."

Suzanne smiled. "He means I was the only midwife in Groton." Any jollity seemed impossible in their circumstances. In all, she felt so weak that she thought she might never laugh again.

John Fay picked up the thread. "Welcome Goody Morse. We're crowded here, but there's space near us. Follow me. If there's anything we can do, just ask."

About six families had crowded into the garrison for protection at the warnings from Captain Thomas Rice. Suzanne was grateful to feel the reassuring presence of people surrounding her, which raised her spirits. When the children threw down their blankets to mark their space near one corner of the great room, she busied herself folding them neatly. She knew that after they'd eaten, they needed to catch up on their sleep. They still had another twenty-mile walk before they reached Watertown.

Suzanne heard the cries of Mary Fay's infant before she heard the angry voice of one citizen."Can you shut that baby up?"

Mary picked up the infant and tried to calm her, walking and jiggling her up and down, but the child wouldn't stop. Suzanne recognized the angry cries of a hungry infant. She wondered why Mary didn't nurse her immediately. Not wanting to offend, she decided to take a tack. She strode to her side and peeked at the red face of the squalling infant.

"Look at this precious one. Born recently I'd say!"

"She's a month old, but she hasn't grown. I fear she has some terrible malady."

"I'm a midwife. Would you let me help?"

"Yes. I was going to ask. Oh, yes."

Suzanne waited as Mary paused, looking to each side. She wondered who Mary feared, maybe an angry neighbor?

When Mary began to talk, she couldn't stop. "She's been like this since birth. She never seems to get enough milk but cries day and night. I nurse her, but she's not like the others. She only sucks on my nipples. They're so sore I can barely stand to nurse her anymore. I rest only when she sleeps, but she doesn't sleep. Not true. She sometimes sleeps a whole day; I think she's exhausted from crying. It goes on day and night. My first two were never difficult. Two boys, and now I have Elizabeth! Have you seen infants like this? Now we're at the garrison, it's worse because our neighbors hear her. It's bad enough the Indians out there want to take our scalps, but my neighbors want my baby's. I don't know what to do."

Mary began to cry, still trying to comfort her wailing baby.

Suzanne had heard enough to know what might be wrong. First, she was right about the baby crying from hunger if she was nursing Mary's nipple. No child could take in enough milk to thrive that way. It narrowed the problem to a few possibilities. "Can I see her?"

Suzanne reached out to take the bundled infant from Mary and began her examination. *It's a nursing problem. Not likely Mary couldn't show this baby how to latch. She's nursed two babies successfully. It could be physical, her frenulum*, she thought. She positioned the baby in a sitting position on her lap facing out and probed her mother for more information. "You said that she only sucks on your nipple? Have you tried to get her to latch on your breast?"

"Of course. I have two boys, never a problem. It seems like she can't open her mouth wide enough, but she can, until she nurses, that is."

Suzanne stuck her baby finger in one corner of the infant's mouth and pushed it along her gums. *Ah, there it is*, she thought. *The frenulum. She's tongue-tied.* The two v-shaped flaps of skin that bridged gums to lip were enlarged. She knew these children typically couldn't nurse because they couldn't stretch their lips and tongue around the breast's areola. Relieved because the solution was simple and had few possibilities for complications, she hugged the infant. "I see we have a tongue-tied girl here." She bounced her up and down. "A very hungry little girl. Well, we're going to fix that right now."

Mary's eyes widened. "You say you can heal her? What do you mean tongue-tied?"

Suzanne took on her midwife teaching role instantly. "A frenulum attaches our lips to our gums. You have one. Run your finger along your outer gum."

"Yes, I can feel it. Right in the middle."

"That's a frenulum. You have two: one above and one below. Now, come and see *her* frenulum. Run your little finger across."

"Oh, my heavens. It's huge."

"Yes, both top and bottom are too tight. It's no wonder to me why she hasn't been able to nurse. She can't extend her lips enough to latch your breast.

"But how can you fix it?"

"A simple process. I can cut the frenulum and free her lips, so she can latch properly. Once she has her belly full, she'll be happy." She again hugged the crying infant, stroking her cheek with her index finger. "You don't know what happy is yet, do you? But you will."

Suzanne gave the infant back to her mother. Then she found her medicine bag and rummaged it for the razor-sharp knife she used for simple surgical procedures her profession allowed her to perform. With the help of two neighboring women, who were eager to help, Mary and Suzanne cleaned a space to work. In minutes, the infant howled in pain and not hunger. A mouth wound, the cuts bled profusely, which alarmed Mary. But when the bleeding stopped, and the baby's cry returned to normal, she rested. Suzanne assured her that even with the unhealed cuts, her baby could now nurse.

Suzanne watched Mary apply all the techniques she'd used with her other children to teach her infant to latch. After one failure, the infant greedily latched and sucked noisily until she fell sound asleep. Silence. Bliss. Mary's helpers murmured their congratulations to Mary, their thanks to Suzanne.

She finished her teaching. "Mary, check the cuts to see if they are healing. They should heal in two days. If you see any redness or if they begin bleeding again, apply this salve. And if you hear even a whimper from her, nurse her immediately."

"You don't need to tell me *that*," Mary laughed. "We've lived with 'little hungry' too long. I'm anxious to meet my daughter Elizabeth."

That night, families gathered to share an abundance of food Suzanne had not seen in weeks. They'd only subsisted at Parker's garrison during the long siege after One-Eyed John had breached Nutting's Garrison.

John Fay, whose neatly trimmed mustache and beard bespoke a high status, had liked Joseph from first sight. When his wife told him of Suzanne's work, he now studied her as well.

"Goody Morse," he said, "we can't thank you enough for your curing Elizabeth. Joseph here said you were the best midwife in Groton, and you've proved it."

"You're welcome, Goodman Fay, but no thanks are necessary. It's what I do. It's my responsibility."

"I've never thought much about midwifing before. I mean, midwives help my wife deliver babies. But it seems I should know more."

Suzanne laughed. It wouldn't be the first time a man had been ignorant of her work. "I can assure you that I receive as much training for my work as a doctor. More. My apprenticeship lasted ten years. And didn't end there. I've been working with a native—"

"She had an entire apothecary in the corner of our house," Joseph interrupted, "mixed all the salves and potions herself."

"I'm impressed. I will have to revise my ways of thinking."

One of Mary's neighbors, a blond woman who'd helped position the baby for the operation, laughed outright. "I'd say it's about time. You agree, Mary?"

This raised more laughter from the women, and Mary suppressed a grin in deference to her husband.

"I put together something to pay you for your troubles. We are so grateful. You've brought peace to our house." He handed her a deerskin pouch. "It's just a bit of jerky to eat on the trail. Joseph told me you had severe rationing in Groton."

Suzanne's eyes opened wide. "You couldn't have found a better payment. Thank you!"

Talk moved to the latest news from scouts visiting nearby towns and those who chose to stay at their homesteads. Joseph, in turn, answered all their questions regarding the siege at Groton. The evening ended with the men huddling in the yard while the women cleaned up.

Later, Joseph made his way to Suzanne, stepping over sleeping bodies he could see only by the light of two guttering candles. He shook her shoulder and whispered. "Wake up."

Suzanne moaned. The long-withheld sleep had swept over her after the meal, and she had entrusted the care of her children to her new neighbors, who encouraged her to sleep. "What's wrong?"

"We need to talk," he whispered.

Groggily, she sat up, seeing only his silhouette against the candles by the doorway. "I'm listening. Should we go outside?"

"We might wake them. Whisper."

"Yes." She waited through a long pause while he gathered his thoughts.

"The captain has orders no one is to leave the fort tomorrow. I told him we planned to leave early, but he said we take great risk. One-Eyed John's threats have spread through the colony. Marlboro and Sudbury are both on high alert. And word has come that a large force of Indians is massed to attack. He said if we stay two days, he can provide an escort for us."

"The Indians that passed us were running north," Suzanne said."I doubt Marlboro is One-Eyed John's next target; too far south. We may stay ahead of them if we leave sooner."

"Good. It's what I'm thinking, too."

"So, we leave in the morning?"

"When the cock crows. I'll see to packing the horse."

Chapter Twenty Eight

CLOSE CALLS

Marlboro, Wednesday, March 17, 1676

Suzanne woke the children on the first rooster crow. Already dressed, they had only to slip on their moccasins. Warned not to wake anyone, they dutifully managed exiting to the yard before they spoke.

"We'll eat on the way," Suzanne told her son Joseph. "We have twenty-five miles to go, and we won't be able to stop again."

"Why are we going?" he asked. "Dad and I heard Indians are about. They'll attack."

"They may be. But they'll strike the garrison, not us." Suzanne and her husband agreed that the attacks did appear aimed at destroying property more than the slaughter of residents in past conflicts. When they did kill, they mutilated their victims shockingly. Suzanne was left with the question, *What are they after?*

Joseph added, "The Indians don't know where we are, or care. We saw Indians before. Did they see us?"

"No. But if they did—"

"They won't, son. Trust me." His father had heard enough.

Once on the road, now a wide and cleared route running from the western interior to Boston, they made good time. As before, much of the route took them through forests. But the boy had told his sisters about the massing Indians the scouts had sighted, and every one of the children kept looking over their shoulders fearfully.

Suzanne tried to bolster their courage and ease their shock. "Don't look back. Life, our life, is before us. God will provide."

When they'd left the Marlboro garrison, she'd put off all thoughts of Indians. Her denial was absolute. If her attention to their journey could be likened to climbing a mountain, she'd taken every step to the peak looking back. The walk to Marlboro was heavy with grief and terror. But once she'd topped the peak, she thought only of the future. She wanted no more of Indians and scalping and fires, no more of beheaded bodies or boasting Devils. She wanted no more of herself than this dogged march to somewhere else, anywhere else. She began to see the faces of Watertown.

As she walked, she began to think of her sister Mary, who she was sure waited for them. Mary, the clairvoyant one. Then, an idea took hold of her. *Does she know? If she knew, would she send help?* These questions challenged her usual ways of thinking. She never was a woman who believed in the supernatural. Her world, she could see and hear; it didn't include messages that passed through the atmosphere like smoke in a wind. *Or did it?* she asked. Of the spirit world, Dancing Light had tutored her, but she'd only observed, had never participated.

In the end, she couldn't dispel the thoughts of her sister. *Isn't it blasphemy to think I can call Mary? Isn't a prayer always to God? God's providence? I should be asking God for help.* The questions nagged her, made her feel deeply disloyal to her God. But she couldn't erase Mary's face, and she called on her. *Mary, we need help. Send help.* She said it with every step: a prayer, a chant, a misguided belief, blasphemy?

Suzie had seemingly decided that she was no longer a girl and didn't need to ride horseback. She thenceforward walked with her parents, helping them carry Hannah. They made such good time that they reached the crossing at the

Sudbury River just as night fell. Knowing that Sudbury, only a day's walk from Marlboro, was one of the targets on Monoco's long list, they decided they couldn't stop for help on the way. It was best to hurry through cover of the deepening dusk, which had emptied the road and sent the townsmen to their homes. They kept their heads down as they made their way through town, past the garrison, and across the bridge. They walked doggedly onward, again leaving civilization behind. But when the sun set, the temperature plummeted, and a freezing rain covered the road and forest with ice.

After dark, walking on slick ice, they could make little progress. They were forced off the wide road to the sides, where twigs and leaf cover could provide traction for their moccasins. Under the cloud cover, they had no moonlight, so the dark was dense. Joseph would not allow them to light a lantern. The dark was safer while Indians threatened. Though they had no danger of getting lost, they still stumbled, tripped, and fell without vision. The worst came when their clothes soaked through. Their wool clothing kept some warmth, but the children's teeth were chattering. Suzanne, too, was half frozen in the rain. Her soggy skirt clung to her over the wool petticoats that twisted between her legs, impeding her stride. Her great coat was stiff with ice. Every nerve in her body felt like it was in a permanent retreat from her skin. She drew her arms close to stifle little Hannah's shivers. She knew they were in danger.

"Joseph, stop. Children, stop." She emptied the packs and made them strip and put on every piece of dry wool clothing before they wrung out the wet. The heavy wool blankets, draped into hooded shawls, could help keep the worst of the rain from soaking them further.

"Joseph," she called. "Hannah needs body contact. She's too little to store warmth. Here, I can help you." While Joseph tented them with a blanket, Suzanne untied his great coat and vests, baring his chest. After baring Hannah's skin, she bound her daughter to him with a scarf, then pulled his dry clothes over them. His body heat could boost her daughter's.

It was hours, though Suzanne was no longer counting them, that they doggedly walked that way, not daring to stop should they lose more body heat. As long as they moved, they had body warmth. But the children wove unsteadily and stumbled with exhaustion. She could hear the broken branch from a tumble and a whimper from Samuel. Then, Joseph heard a sound in the distance. He pulled the rein to stop the horse in place. "Shhh."

Everyone stopped. Suzanne strained to hear what he'd heard. A long way off, but, yes, someone was coming. Terrified, the children needed no prompting. They scattered in the dark, beating their way to trees, embracing them frantically to find a trunk wide enough to hide behind, hunkering down. Joseph led the horse to the side, not bothering to hide. No one could see them in the pitch-dark woods.

As the sounds neared, Suzanne could make out the steps of an animal. It might have comforted her, but the animal could be an Indian riding a horse. Closer yet, she made out the creak of a wheeled cart. No Indian would be driving horse and cart, she reasoned. We'll have help.

Joseph shared her realization. Filled with hope, he called out, "Halloo. Halloo. Who's there?"

It was minutes before the answer came. "Is someone out here?"

"Yes. We're English. We're here."

Again, a long silence grew while the cart neared. It nearly unnerved Suzanne, who began to second guess her first thoughts. *Out on a night like this? When Indians are about? Might be up to Devil's work!* Her first relief fled and left a pounding heart behind. Then she heard, "Who are you?"

Joseph spoke for them. "Joseph Morse," he answered.

"Joseph? I've found you?"

"Who is this?"

"I'm Will, Suzanne's brother. Mary sent me to get you. Suzanne, are you there?"

Suzanne jumped from her hiding place and made her way to the road. "Will? Is that really you? We're here. All of us. You've answered my prayers."

Joseph reached out and touched the head of the mule that hauled the cart. "Stop."

Will halted the mule and strained his eyes; he had good night vision, which allowed him to see Joseph in the dark. "Joseph, I see you now. Everyone," he called. "Speak so I know where you are."

The answers rained down. "Uncle Will, I'm here" and "Suzie here."

"You can all hear me. Just a minute and you'll see me." Will lit a lantern, which spread a dim light fading into the surrounding dark. "You can come out now."

The children made their way to the cart, teeth chattering. Suzanne could see that he'd mounded the cart with straw, which he'd covered with blankets. Only two months before, Will served in a cavalry move against the Narragansetts where scores of soldiers froze on a long march. He knew well what to do for exposure. Dry them. Warm them from the core out. For soldiers exposed too long, doctors first warmed their torsos, but not too quickly. The heart might fail with shock. He barked out orders the children should remove all wet clothing even if it was wool.

"Wear it only if it's dry. I want you to lie down in the cart. Spoon. You need to warm one another. Skin to skin. Boys with boys, girls with girls."

Suzanne helped the children undress, sorting wool and linen into separate piles. She took Hannah from Joseph and turned her over to Suzie and Hester. "She rides in the cart with you. Put her between you, bare skin to skin."

"Mother," Suzie complained. "I can't. I always wear my shift."

Suzanne groped her shift. "It's linen and wet through. You need to take it off. Do as Will says." She turned to Will. "Will, can you move the lantern away."

As the children followed orders, Suzanne caught Will's arm. "How did you know where we'd be? Mary?"

Will nodded. "She's a seer. Father told me when I started school, but now I've seen it firsthand."

"How did she see the road?" Suzanne held up Will's lantern as he covered the children with straw. Their body heat would fill the hollow stems, providing warmth.

"She'd seen you, heard you, but didn't know where. Then she remembered she'd heard water flowing. Footsteps on a bridge. I've ranged with Captain Prentice on both the roads to Watertown. Once she'd described a wide road, I figured it was the bridge at Sudbury."

Suzanne marveled. To her mind, neither Mary nor Will had known what they knew. *They guessed*, she thought. *Guessed right*. She didn't know she'd just given the materialist's definition of "intuition."

Once they were in place, Will topped this insulation with every blanket and even the wet clothing.

"You too, Joseph. Suzanne."

Suzanne could understand why her daughter had been reluctant to take off her shift. She felt quite the same. She couldn't remember a time that she and her husband had ever laid together naked. She might have experienced his naked body spooning against her as sinfully delicious if it had not been for the shivers that raked her body and chattered her teeth.

"We have a long ride ahead. Might as well get some sleep." Will extinguished the lantern and they set out, rumbling through the dark woods. Warmth crept through her arms and legs, thawing the icy fear and grief. A dark wave swept through her chest and lodged in her throat, which tightened painfully. Tears flowed involuntarily. Joseph tightened his arms around her and held her until the pangs of anguish subsided.

The rain mercifully ended. At the first stirring of the light, Joseph asked Will to stop. He dressed in his still-wet wools under cover of a blanket and mounted their horse. One by one, as the family woke, they dressed.

The day warmed as the sun rose in the sky, drying their clothes, warming them. That was not to last long, though. They watched the clouds build in the sky as the afternoon wore on, and by the time they arrived at Will's house in Watertown at dusk, they were again, soaked through from a capricious March thunderstorm.

Chapter Twenty Nine

REFUGE FROM THE STORM

Watertown, Thursday, March 18, 1676

"Hurry. Get out of the rain. It's freezing." Her sister, Mary, stood on the stoop waving them in.

The children jumped from the cart and ran, shouting. "Come on. Get inside," said Suzanne. They needed no prompting, but Suzanne stood where she'd stepped down, overcome by strong emotion. She'd been ten when she'd left this house and her family for her apprenticeship to Joanna Morton. The sight of it spelled a dual sense of security and an aching loneliness. She took a deep breath, steadied her emotions, and walked toward Mary. Joseph and William turned the mule and horse to the barn.

Suzanne stopped when Mary held her by the shoulders to take in her drawn and severe face, the layers of grime from weeks at the Parker's garrison in Groton. "Suzanne, what happened?" Mary, true to her nature, intuited the deep anguish that Suzanne had successfully repressed in her flight.

Suzanne, shocked by her own vulnerability, suddenly buried her head in her sister's shoulder. "Rebecca's gone. Her girl. Uncle John too."

"What do you mean, 'gone', Suzanne?" Mary pulled back, looking her straight in the eyes.

"I can … I ccca …" Suzanne was stricken. Suddenly, what had occurred was unthinkable and therefore unspeakable. Her tongue seized. The reserve that had carried her, allowed her to lead her family bravely through the ordeal suddenly melted away. In response, she could feel her strength ebbing, leaving her trembling and weak.

"Take a deep breath. Start at the beginning." Suzanne let Mary unwrap her wet cloak, shake water from it, hang it on hooks by the door. Let her take her bonnet. "Here, let's get you dry. Come." Mary led her by the hand to the fireside and sat her in the high-backed settee for warmth. She chafed her hands, until Suzanne felt the itching burn turn her stiff, white fingers red.

"The Indians attacked, burned everything, on Sunday." Her voice rose sharply on the word 'Sunday.'

"Everything?"

"All gone. Groton. House. Barn. Cows." Her voice broke into a strangled wail.

"And Rebecca?"

Suzanne, whose capacity to cope had fled, felt her sister's unrelenting questions were inhuman. She stared wildly at Mary, reacting in anger. "Dead!" She stared, incredulous. "Her daughter, too."

Stung by her blunt answer, Mary gasped, and apprehensively pressed for clarification of her sister's first words.

"Joseph's uncle?"

"Captured."

Four-year-old Samuel wailed "Mama," when he wandered into the room. He buried his head in his mother's lap. He was followed by three older children whose wide eyes registered their fright and exhaustion at once.

"We walked for two days and nights before Will found us. God in his mercy, brought us the cart. We couldn't walk another step. The rain soaked through, turned to ice. Will said you sent him. How did you know? Mary, did God send you a vision?" Suzanne clutched Mary's arm, not ready yet to move from the warmth of the fire. She clung to Mary as she clung to the shred of hope that God had not abandoned them, that he'd forgiven her.

"He did. I saw you in a forest, moving on foot. And a horrible sight, a girl's scalp." She shuddered.

Suzanne turned white and whispered, "A girl's. Little Becky. Our neighbor saw, but the children didn't. Merciful God."

"Missus Hastings had heard that One-Eyed John attacked Lancaster and threatened to destroy other towns. All I could think is that Groton is right down the river from Lancaster. I just knew you were in danger. I could feel the dread."

"We're hungry, Aunt Mary." Suzanne's oldest girl, who was the same age as Benjamin, approached her mother's chair.

"I think we can find something to eat. Let's go see." Mary led the children to the hearth, and Suzanne could hear her clear instructions to someone in the kitchen, "Dry them off and feed them." Still struggling with the pain she'd controlled so long, she focused on the fire before her, where flames threw out a feeble light. She absorbed the warmth, appreciating the solid feel of the stationary bench beneath her. The walls, the hearth, and the furnishings, all familiar to her as a child, might have given her comfort but for the creeping decline. The house was dirty and neglected now. She bent to strip off her wet moccasins, peeling the soaked straw from the boots and throwing it on the fire.

Mary returned to her side. "They'll dry if you put them on the hearth. You can wear my slippers. We're the same size."

"I brought some for all of us. Joseph will bring them from the stable."

Mary sat across from her sister. "Suzie told me that you have an Indian friend who gave you moccasins. Did Boston send militia to escort you to Concord? Why didn't you go with them?"

"Boston did send a caravan from Concord. We wanted to go. But I worked with a Nashua midwife. She was my friend, Mary, but the town thought that I was colluding with the enemy; they didn't believe that any Indian could be a friend, once the conflict started." Suzanne smoothed out the moccasins and set them at the edge of the hearth where the heat could dry them. She noted that her sister's face held doubt, which pained her. "They banished us. Turned us away." She shut her eyes and shrunk into her shame.

"How could they?" Mary was incensed, her face now registering anger.

"Please understand. They thought that I'd given information to the tribe across the river, a peaceful tribe. They thought our Nashua neighbors attacked. It didn't matter in the end. Dancing Light came to tell me she'd heard that One-Eyed John planned to ambush the caravan and didn't know if she could stop him. So, she told us to take Farmer's Row south on foot and loop back on the Old Boston Road. We couldn't take a cart, but we had the horse, thank the Lord. We took turns riding, to rest, you know."

"Were they? Ambushed?"

Suzanne saw the shock on her sister's face and quickly tried to set her account straight. "It wasn't like that. I didn't take revenge. I told them before we left, but they wouldn't listen." She knew that telling Joseph wasn't exactly warning them but couldn't admit any complicity to her sister.

"Of course, you warned them. What an ordeal. I suppose we'll hear about the ambush now." Mary held out a blanket for her sister. "Wrap this around you, and we'll go get food."

Suzanne complied, but now felt compelled to talk. "The neighbors saw them take John Morse, Joseph's Uncle. Him and another. John was our council leader, and we're hoping they'll not torture and kill him. They are ransoming some, Mary Rowlandson, the minister's wife. She was taken from Lancaster."

"We heard about Mistress Rowlandson. And her children, too."

Suzanne followed Mary to the great room, where the rest of the household sat at the table boards. Again, the scene haunted her. *The table setting is the same,* she thought, staring at the fragrant stacked bread loaves. Then she reasoned. *Well, it's Mary's doing, and she learned from mother*. Her children were scooping spoons of stew into their mouths faster than the youth, a stranger, could fill their trenchers. She realized he must be her little brother Benjamin. *He's Suzie's age, that's right.*

When Joseph and William had finished unloading and bedding the horse and mule for the night, they came in stamping mud off their feet, dropping bundles of clothing by the door. Suzanne, who could eat little, immediately jumped up to go to the packs. She rummaged through, pulling out wet clothing and the sheepskin slippers. She was so relieved to find something familiar from her present-day that it arrested her for a minute; she hugged them to her breast with gratitude. No sign of normalcy was insignificant to her now. Though she'd always been an adventurous soul, never one to cling to the past or to traditional ways of doing things, she suddenly craved a life of simple routine.

For Suzanne, pulling into the yard at Will's house had been a true homecoming. Her brother had inherited half of their parents' first homestead and farm, the only home that Suzanne, as the oldest, remembered. She'd spent her first ten years in the two-room house with a loft, her father's weaving workshop in the lean-to attached to the great room. Her parents had moved to their large house on the hilltop when her father bought it from Goodman Sanderson. That was two years after Suzanne had moved in with Joanna Morton to start her ten-year apprenticeship. The gap in time made the homestead's following neglect more shocking. Mary had explained the reasons.

When their father died and left Will the old homestead and looms, their mother remarried. She and Richard Norcross now occupied the house on the hill, now home to both the Norcross and Sherborn children. However, because the older Benjamin was prone to bullying the youngest, Samuel, Richard Norcross and their mother Susanna decided to separate the boys by sending each to live with a different brother. They were at the right age to enter apprenticeships. Thus, she sent ten-year-old Benjamin to live with Will. It was given the brothers might have inadequate skills in homesteading. However, the Boston military alliance had conscripted Will to fight the Narragansetts in early winter, and he'd left the now thirteen-year-old Benjamin to keep the farm going for four months.

"Benjamin is good with animals," Mary said. "You'll see the barn's cleaner than the house." She laughed. "But now your family is here, you can make this a proper home."

In the following week, Suzanne and the family reintegrated with life in Watertown. Her first Sunday at the meetinghouse, they sat in the Morse family pews, which were rather empty because Joseph's brother Jonathan had never married. Suzanne felt some state of belonging as Reverend Sherman was familiar to her. At the same time, the meeting brought Suzanne a sense of dissonance when she saw her mother sitting in the Norcross pews with her former teacher's children.

The Watertown siblings had made sure that Suzanne's and Joseph's family had enough food; indeed, made sure they wanted for nothing. For now, they were cramped: the two adults slept downstairs with Will and Benjamin, the six children, in the loft.

Suzanne would never have predicted it, but Benjamin took such a liking to Joseph that he began to mimic his brother-in-law. He took up smoking a pipe, and Joseph encouraged him, giving him a pipe of his own that he no longer used. The two shared a love of philosophical conversation, and Suzanne began to wonder if Benjamin might begin dabbling in poetry as well. She'd heard only reports of his bad and bullying behavior. *Had anyone ever known Ben?* She began to wonder if his success with animals was related to this person no one had ever known. Of course, Joseph had instantly become friends with Benjamin's yellow tabby, which spurred Ben's fawning.

Chapter Thirty

BEGINNING AGAIN

Watertown, March 1676

For Suzanne, who had discovered the natural world in her forays with Dancing Light, the small overcrowded house became a prison. She fought the feelings that rose, that her household duties cut off her being herself, but with the necessary cleanup, she seldom had the time to reflect on it long.

Richard Norcross came to visit them at mealtime, assuring Suzanne that he'd reserved places for the children in school and they should begin immediately. She agreed to send Suzie, Hester, Joseph junior, and Mary.

Then, Joanna Morton sought her out. Suzanne, who had not seen her mentor in ten years, noted the changes time had wrought. The once handsome dark-haired woman had turned gray, and her face had begun to sag at the jowls; she'd become stout. Suzanne searched for that likeness to Joanna she'd found in her friend Dancing Light.

Mercifully, Suzanne could bridge the gap when Joanna spoke. Joanna sounded the same. She spoke with authority: "With each attack, people are arriving in Watertown. That alone would make it impossible to keep up, but we have people with a new disease. I've not seen it before. It starts like the ague, with fever but affects the lungs. They can't breathe. So many die. If one child in the family falls ill, within a week, others in the family get sick. It's spreading. I need your help, Suzanne. Watertown needs us."

Suzanne took Joanna's hands in her own, gratefully responding to her request. "It would mean much to me. The older children are attending school, but I don't have help for Hannah and Sammy. And I can't rely on Benjamin."

"Your sister Abigail is available. Could you ask her to help with your children? To free you? Between you and me, I think she'd like the change."

"If mother will agree." Suzanne felt hopeful throwing herself into work might improve her sentiments. She could shed feelings of entrapment if she could leave the house.

Their ordeal—the Groton attack and their subsequent flight—had taxed them. Joseph now became tired with little exertion and had developed a cough. More than the crowded conditions, his health made him withdraw. They had suspended any intimacies, though Suzanne had attributed that to their close quarters instead of his fatigue. Suzanne felt good, but had trouble sleeping through the night. Any sound—Joseph coughing, an animal outside, a creaking floorboard—could wake her in a panic. She'd freeze, holding her breath to hear better. Then, screwing up her courage, she'd rise and check every door and window to make sure they were secured. Her oldest daughter, Suzie, who slept in the loft with her little brothers and sisters, reported to her that they were having nightmares. They missed their Martha and cried for her. While the changes didn't spell a loss in completing tasks, changes certainly affected their enjoyment of life. She was spurred to act, however, by the thought that she could restore her apothecary, destroyed when her house had burnt down. Joanna had a large collection of herbals.

The next week, the school-age children began school on Schoolhouse Hill, leaving Hannah and Sammy under Benjamin's watch. She walked part of the way with them that first morning, reveling nostalgically in the rare spring morning air and the high-flying clouds in a brilliant blue sky. She sent them on with the neighbor's children when she reached the crossroad to reservoir hill, which she took to her mother's hilltop home. She was relieved that it had not changed much from her last visit at her father's burial. She clung to any consistency in her new state of mind, which mystified her. She'd never lived in the past; in fact, she'd chided Rebecca for it. She was all about solving problems as they arose, her path always forward. She had no use for tradition and had even thought her parents backward for their slow responses to immediate concerns.

Abigail and her mother were the only ones at home, and she found them in the great room spinning yarn to meet their household quota to avoid the fines, still levied despite the war. Abigail, now twenty, had lost the girlish slightness she'd carried past her time and was now a pretty, young woman with an ample bosom and small waist. She had coiled her brown hair neatly beneath the white cap, which framed a round face with a high brow and wide-set blue eyes. *She takes after mother's side of the family,* Suzanne thought. *She's like me.* Her mother, however, looked younger. *Is it her hair?* she wondered. Her mother's hair had faded to a mouse brown, but it wasn't gray as her friend Joanna's hair was. She was wearing it differently too, braided in coils at the side like Abigail's. Her mother, always unselfconsciously unadorned, now looked composed, even stylish.

"Where is everyone?" Suzanne knew that Richard Norcross had five children. She'd expected to find them at home.

"Mary, Nate, and your brother Sam are in school. Where did you think they'd be?"

"Of course. They've grown. I lose track of time."

"It certainly goes fast. Richard junior enlisted the day he turned sixteen and Jeremiah joined when Boston conscripted men for the Narragansett campaign. Sarah married in seventy-four. You wouldn't have heard."

Suzanne realized how out of touch she'd been since her father's death. Their correspondence had dwindled. She had supposed her mother's grief was the reason she'd stopped writing. "Sarah! She's younger than Abigail, isn't she?"

Abigail grimaced. "She *is* younger than me. But she was wise, married the year before the war started. Not like I have a chance now all the men are gone to war."

Suzanne was surprised when her sister sounded jealous of her new stepsister; in the past, her mother would have scolded Abigail but now remained silent. Suzanne had never stopped to think how the war would affect her unmarried sister. For married women, especially those with mouths to feed, the absence of their menfolk was unarguably a heavy challenge. But the marriageable men, whether landowners like Will or dependent bachelors like Ben, were all perfect fodder to wartime conscription. *Poor Abigail*, she thought.

"Abigail," her mother reproved, "you don't find a man to marry on a schedule. Who cares how old you are? A good man of property, one you can love, is more important."

"Yes, mother. You're right."

Susanna took her daughter's sassy reply without comment, but stopped her work, hanging the skein on the hook. "What brings you this morning? Do you need anything, Dear? We have venison that will spoil now the weather is warming. It shouldn't go to waste."

"Mother, you've given us so much already, more than we're used to having, in fact. But I do come about a need. Aunt Joanna came to me at church and asked me if I'd work with her. Influenza is sweeping the town, and she needs me."

"That's wonderful! She has missed you so much."

"Yes, and I, her. But Hannah and Samuel are home, and midwifing can take me away overnight, even days. Benjamin has helped with them, but he resists, and I can't rely on him. I need a nanny to live with us. Joanna thought that Abigail could help out."

"Abigail! Joanna didn't tell me *that*. Wouldn't dare."

Suzanne braced herself at her mother's last comment but turned to test Abigail's feelings. "What do you think? Would you like to come and live with us?"

Abigail smiled broadly. "I'd love to. Mother, you don't need me here. And I miss Ben and Will. Well, I miss everyone." Her smile faded to a pensive wistful shadow.

Her brothers and sisters had been replaced by the new stepbrothers and sisters, the Norcross family.

"What do you mean, I don't need you here? Are you the only one who misses them? What will I do if you, my last child, leaves me? How can you be so selfish?"

Suzanne didn't want to come between her mother and sister; they'd have to work it out between them. She rose, smoothed her skirts, and prepared to leave. "Well, I can see that you need to discuss this between you. I have an errand to run, and I will check back later." She left them with the impasse unsettled.

That week, they learned from soldiers relieved from duty that, while Groton had been under siege, bands of Wampanoag had laid waste to colonial settlements to their south. Fires burned in Plymouth from Casco Bay in the north to Stonington in the south. That Sunday, Reverend Sherman announced the Nipmuc Indians, who had banded with the Penacook sachem, One-Eyed John, had attacked Marlboro. They'd taken advantage of the townspeople while they gathered for the Sunday meeting to burn down empty houses and barns. What's more, the latest blow on the southern front burned down the Providence Plantation on March 27. At prayer, Suzanne thanked the Lord that he'd let them pass through Marlboro safely on their way to Watertown.

At the break before prophesying began, Suzanne recognized her sister, who made her way to the Morse's pew. Abigail took her hand, smiling broadly. "Yes. I'd like to stay with you. And, thank you."

"Is mother alright with it?"

"Joanna intervened. She encouraged mother to join the women's auxiliary. They meet every Sunday. Exclusive women. Mary's in the group. Mother just needs people to care about now that we're all gone."

"It's understandable. None of us can take this much change at once. But I'm excited. We've a lot to talk about."

"I know. Me too."

"When will you come?"

"Tomorrow? I'll bring my clothes. We're so close to mother's, I can stop by if I need more and see mother while I'm about."

Suzanne waved to her mother, who sat with Mary and another woman, who dressed in fine clothing that bespoke a higher class. Though she was curious, she wouldn't be able to stay through the prophesying as she planned to meet Joanna at her house. Just as she was leaving, Suzanne saw a face that looked familiar. The man of medium height with thick brown wavy hair worn loose had a distinctively trimmed mustache and beard. *Where have I seen him before?* She wondered, matching the face she viewed with places she might have met him: Groton, Watertown. When she knew, she was surprised. She recognized him as the husband of the woman whose infant she'd treated in Marlboro when they'd fled from Groton. *He did say his sister was here*, she thought. *Yes. Martha Granger. Before I left Watertown, Joanna and I delivered her baby.* She craned her head to see where Mary Fay might be, but she couldn't find her. She made her way to John Fay to ask him.

Chapter Thirty One

REFUGEES

Watertown, March 1676

"John Fay?" Suzanne stood before him, looking at him quizzically.

For a moment she knew he didn't recognize her. "Oh, yes, Goody Morse is it?"

"It is. I was so surprised to see you! I'm sorry to hear about Marlboro. Since you are here, I imagine you had losses."

His round face had laugh lines around a thin mouth, that curved in a frown. Sad blue eyes that narrowed to squint lines mirrored what she guessed were the facts. "Worse than I could imagine. Indians burned the farm, animals slaughtered, all gone."

"And Mary? I don't see her here."

He slumped, eyes peering at the ground for some moments. "She didn't come. I mean, she couldn't," and he began to stammer. Impatient with himself, he forced the words that wouldn't come, the only words he could say. "She's gone."

"I'm sorry. I don't mean to pry." Despite feeling as though she'd intruded in a room wherein she had no title to be, she felt his answer raised more questions. 'Gone' could mean she was kidnapped, could mean she'd died, could mean she'd left him, though the latter seemed absurd the moment she thought it. The Fays, she'd thought, were well matched, though he annoyingly belittled women's work. She'd not forgotten his slight when she'd healed their tongue-tied newborn.

"You aren't prying. No. It's hard for me to talk about it." His face wrenched in a spasm. "It's just that I don't know why God spared me and not her."

He'd assumed that she knew what he'd intended by that word 'gone.' Suzanne now knew Mary had died.

"Elizabeth—my sister—she's promised to take the children. I'll stay until I can rebuild."

Suzanne still did not speak, seeing from his face he'd not finished.

"Indians murdered her." His bitterness oozed through his more obvious grief and shock.

"Horrible! So sorry!" She paused, making eye contact. "I have no words that can comfort you."

He stared at her, noncommittally, saying nothing. Suzanne could not help but read in his silence his agreement with her. He could take no comfort from words. "My sister tells me it helps to talk of it. But you suffered as I now do, and my heart couldn't understand your losses when you told me. Was it just two week ago? And now, I do."

"We've shared similar fates, it's true. I don't know that talking helps, but if you'd like, Joseph and I would like you to have supper with us. We can share our meal and perhaps our grief. We haven't gotten over my sister's death and the attack in Groton."

"After prophesying?"

"Yes. See, Joseph is just there." Suzanne pointed to where Joseph sat with the men. "Why don't you join him. He can show you the way."

He craned his neck and nodded, "I will. And thank you."

Suzanne turned to hail Joanna, and the two made their way from the church for the afternoon.

At sundown, Suzanne lit the lanterns and the family gathered to break bread at the Sabbath's end. It was soon dark, and Abigail had little trouble coaxing the sleepy children to retire in the loft.

Joseph and Will were filled with questions about the attack on Marlboro, but aware of John Fay's loss, they approached the subject with care. Benjamin listened intently, absentmindedly stroking his cat, which covered the boy's lap and spilled off, the cat's front legs hanging down. Suzanne could hear the loud purr across the room.

When Joseph took up his pipe and lit it, Benjamin found his own and puffed on it in synchrony with Joseph, now, his idol.

Joseph began. "When we left Ward's Garrison, you were safe behind walls because you thought the Indians were going to attack any minute. Yet, Reverend Sherman said you were at the meetinghouse for Sunday service when the attack came. I'm confused. What happened?"

"After that day you left, the scouts didn't find a single Indian in the area. A week went by with no signs. So, Captain gave us an 'all clear' and we returned to our farms."

Will nodded knowingly, familiar with the patterns of Indian warfare. "Indians were planning an ambush?"

"That's it. We found out later, after help came from Sudbury, that hundreds had camped north of us, not far from the praying village on the other side of the river."

Suzanne shuddered. They'd stayed at that village in their flight from Groton.

"We didn't know; the scouts hadn't ranged that far north. So, that Sunday we went to meeting. The minister—Reverend William Brimsmead—saw them first and warned us."

Joseph drew on his pipe. "How far was the garrison?"

"Ward's garrison wasn't half a mile. We had stayed there before. But she …" He stopped to quell the spasm that passed across his mouth. "She fell. Shot. A neighbor promised to take the children, and I went back." Here he stopped, overcome by anguish. He whispered hoarsely. "She was gone."

Suzanne intervened. "You don't need to speak of it. Be still now."

He was silent for a long pause, then shook his head. "I couldn't leave her, but I had baby Elizabeth. The children."

Joseph put down his pipe. "I cannot imagine. You did the right thing, but it must have been horrible to leave your wife."

"Most of us made it to Ward's garrison."

Suzanne's chest caved in remembering the two weeks they'd sheltered in Parker's garrison in Groton, not knowing their fate minute to minute. It had felt more prison than haven. "Were you under siege?"

"No volleys of gunshot. Nothing like that, but if we dared to leave the garrison, Indians shot us down."

Abigail, the children safely asleep, joined them. She stopped short in her tracks at these words. Suzanne motioned for her to sit beside her on the bench.

Will stared at Benjamin. "You listen, Ben. Before you go enlisting." He turned back to John Fay. "That when they started firing the town?"

"Right. They took advantage. They fired burning brands at the houses; they slaughtered cattle; they cut down fruit trees, too. They want us to leave."

Suzanne noted this last remark, which stood out from the speeches she'd heard from colonists since the war began. He made her think. Unlike their ministers who preached from pulpits, John Fay spoke as though Indians had wills of their own. As though Indians were not the instruments of God, his puppet devils sent to punish sinners. Instead, he casually remarked they fought with purpose. *Dancing Light would have said the same*, she thought but dismissed the question that followed: *Can penitence end this war?*

"You said help came from Sudbury?" Will sat forward in his seat, leaning elbows on the table. He ignored the gory descriptions and focused on the maneuvers. He'd seen enough in his own battles.

"We sent a runner, and he made it that far. The people of Sudbury came up at dawn next day and killed about forty of them. They got Netus, who was the one destroyed Thomas Eames's house, close neighbor. The Indians left then."

Will shook his head. "Doesn't sound like Sudbury has any troops left to secure the town if they are securing Marlboro."

Suzanne felt a chill. "Monoco boasted all night what he was going to do next. Burn Marlboro and Sudbury, too."

Abigail leaned closer and took Suzanne's hand in both of her own, as though to warm them. She was concerned for her sister's mind-set now. She hadn't missed her sister's edginess and vigilance, which consumed her.

Will stood and raked coals in the firebox. A few meager flames licked the last bits of partly burned logs. "Boston will send support. They must know by now."

Suzanne didn't have the heart to ask about Elizabeth, the six-week-old infant she'd treated. "Where are you living now?"

"We're at my sister's house. She's promised to take in the children."

"Yes, I remember that you had three? Is that right?"

"Yes. The baby you know. Elizabeth. And I have Johnny, who's seven now. And a girl, three."

"Johnny's age is right between our sons' Joseph and Samuel. Are you sending him to Norcross's school?"

"Yes."

"Good. We'll have Johnny over." Suzanne was already entertaining the thought in the back of her mind. *He will need a wife, and Abigail needs a husband.* By caring for his son, Abigail would have a way of ingratiating herself to John Fay.

John Fay turned to Will. "I heard you are part of Captain Prentice's cavalry. Will he call you back?"

Will set down the poker. "We head out next week. Are you wanting to volunteer?"

"Not the cavalry, but as infantry."

"Brother-in-law's a rifleman in Captain Tyng's Fifth. Jonathan Brown. I'll let Jonathan know."

"Appreciate it. I feel like I have to do something."

"We all must."

John Fay left long after the time the Morses usually ended their Sabbath. Suzanne felt that in some elemental way, hearing his plight, a man who'd suffered the same fate, comforted her.

For all Joseph's optimism on news that Mohegan warriors had captured the fiercest warrior, Cononchet, Suzanne didn't see any end in sight, especially after he joined Jonathan Brown and John Fay in the fourth regiment. Fortunately, they assigned him to a small cadre of armed settlers who patrolled the Watertown surroundings for Indians breaking curfews. As she treated more refugees from surrounding villages, she thought the war was ramping up, not down. The attacks came like waves rolling onto shore on several fronts. On April 9, Thursday, Wampanoags entered the village of Bridgewater, south of Plymouth, where they set fire to fourteen houses before help came. On Wednesday, the following week, she heard of another attack, in the north this time. One-Eyed John's warriors had attacked Chelmsford, a town just northeast of Groton, and left it a smoking desolation. Displaced settlers streamed into Concord. Then, two days after that, the Nipmuk bands began gathering to the north of Marlboro and Sudbury, unknown to the colonists.

That Sunday, April 19, Reverend Sherman announced the Wampanoag Indians on the southern front had traveled from Bridgewater to enter Weymouth and then Hingham, burning houses as they traveled northeast. They were closing in on Boston, which was only twenty-five miles north of their last attack.

By now, settlers had abandoned towns north of Watertown: Groton, Billerica, Lancaster, Chelmsford, and Marlboro. Every town west of Sudbury followed suit, and Sudbury became the temporary western border of Massachusetts. It was only twenty miles from Boston, and Watertown and Cambridge were all that stood between.

Wooded Indian lands the Nipmuks had reclaimed surrounded them.

The Boston magistrates, now worrying the closing ring of battles gave them little room to defend the center, issued orders to Cambridge, Watertown, and other of Boston's closest towns to protect themselves by stockades. On April 20, they sent seventy men under Captain Samuel Wadsworth to Marlboro by way of Sudbury to secure the borders. At the same time, eighteen mounted men under command of Mr. Cowell, formerly of Brookfield, abandoned the previous year, also entered the fray from a different route.

While Joseph was now a regular in the colonial troops, they'd assigned him to serve with the local rangers. So, at the end of April, as the reports of attacks rolled in, all the men remaining in Watertown were either armed rangers to protect the home front or called to serve the colonial troops in the fields.

Chapter Thirty Two

NO END IN SIGHT

Watertown, April 1676

Suzanne threw herself into her work with Joanna, which deflected the steady stream of war news so she could attend to more immediate concerns. The epidemic spread through the communities surrounding Boston, a trial she faced daily. The speed in which the infection swept through whole families astounded her, and too many patients died despite every measure she took. Between the two midwives, they had the standard aids for ague. They prescribed analgesics and a mentholated salve for the chest, cough syrup to soothe the throat, and extracts to bring down fevers. Comforts, not cures. Only the heartiest survived if the illness moved to their lungs, the afflicted struggling to breathe. If they began spitting up blood, a life-and-death struggle followed to the end.

When Hester began to sniffle and cough, Suzanne realized it was spreading through Richard Norcross's school. She kept the children home the next day and sent Suzie on horseback for her uncle, Suzanne's brother Philip, who now lived in Waltham. *A doctor, he may know other treatments,* she reasoned.

That afternoon, her brother Philip and Suzie arrived. He dismounted his bay gingerly, tying reins loosely on a yard tree. Pounding the dust off his hat, he followed his niece into the house he'd not seen since his boyhood. Suzanne ran to him when she heard Suzie at the door, so happy to see him that she grabbed his arm and pulled him into the great room with an exclamation. "Philip, thank God you've come. How are you? And Deborah?"

"I came as soon as I could," Philip said. He couldn't help himself from stopping midstream, to peer at the house, his face showing his marvel at how little it had changed. "We are all well, but Suzie tells me someone is ill."

Suzie had joined her brothers and sisters in a corner of the room where Abigail was teaching them arithmetic. "Hester's sick," they called to Philip.

Suzanne silenced them. "You let us talk now." She turned to Philip again. "Their father is coughing, too, but it's chronic. I don't think it's related to this epidemic."

"Maybe not. But you mustn't ignore it. Is he sickly as well? Coughing is symptomatic of more serious diseases. Consumption, for one. Well, enough of that. I'm here to see Hester!"

"She's in the loft. I've separated her. Put her in a corner."

"Let's go." Philip tied a cloth over his mouth and nose. "Wear something over your face. The disease may spread through coughing."

Suzanne pulled a napkin from the table, holding it over her nose and mouth, and led him up the stairs to the loft, squinting in the gloom, split by one ray of light from a single window. Philip knelt beside Hester's pallet, smoothing her forehead with his hand. "She has no fever that I can tell."

"Right," Suzanne said. "She complains of aches and chills, but I don't think she is feverish. That's good isn't it? I mean, most of the cases I've treated, have fevers. High fevers."

Philip grunted. "Hester, can you cough for me?"

Hester coughed. "Uncle Philip, do I have the ague? Mother says I do, and I can spread it to everyone."

Philip gave her a thump on the chest and asked her, "Can you sit up for me?" He thumped her back and listened, ear to her back. Then asked her to take a deep breath, again listening. "You can lie down now."

Hester lay back in her bed and let Philip tuck her in again. "Hester," he said, "I think you have a bad cold, not ague, but you can spread a cold, too. So, I agree with your mother. You stay here for a few days. Get lots of rest."

When they returned to the great room, Philip sat at the table. "I'll fix us some tea," Suzanne said. She poured hot water into a pot and pulled two mugs from the shelves beside the hearthstone.

"In this epidemic, one symptom I've noted is the lungs fill. It's most like pneumonia. You can hear it if you have them take a breath. You'll hear the gurgle."

"I thank you for that."

"I'm glad that you called me. I've thought of you often. You and Joanna must be overwhelmed, as are all with this epidemic. I have news from Boston. Dr. Knox, you remember him? He told me that so many have died there, they cannot bury them fast enough. Hundreds. To stop it spreading, he's separating the infected from the rest. It's like a plague, though thank God, not as lethal. And I don't have to say, you and I are carriers because we treat them."

"Aunt Joanna, too. What are you saying, Philip? We can infect our families?"

"Yes. I've moved from home. I'm staying at an inn and keep my distance. I don't want to infect Deborah and the boys, the baby. You should be living with Joanna right now. Check on the family every day but don't live with them."

"That's possible now I have Abigail and Ben to help. I'm also concerned with treatment. Joanna and I have only palliative remedies. How are you treating these people?"

Philip sipped his tea thoughtfully. "I doubt we do more than you. We doctors choose between two alternatives. We either treat a systemic disease, those that travel in the blood and lymph, or we treat putrid disease, those that inflame the bowels."

Suzanne leaned forward, "so if it's in the blood, then you bleed the patient?"

"That's right."

"And the putrid disease?"

"These we treat with purgatives. We must cleanse the bowels. With the ague, our bodies instinctively purge through vomiting and diarrhea. Medicine can only help where the body fails its task or cannot overcome the illness."

"And fever? Which one?"

"We dispute cures for fever. Some say the heart causes fever, and so, we must bleed the patient. Others believe fever needs purging because a fevered body is one naturally purging through sweat."

"And you? What have you found in treating this ague?"

"I think you would approve. I'm letting nature lead; the body purges itself."

"Do you not think that sweating is more than purging? Isn't sweating the natural way a body cools?"

"There, I agree with midwives, too. Though I'm criticized for it, I don't bleed the feverish."

"Joanna and I use sweat to cool the fevers before they kill the patients."

"Continue. Meanwhile, keep distance from your patients as you treat them. Wear gloves. You must have a supply from funerals?"

"I don't, but mother will."

"Good. Coughing too may spread it. Cover your nose and mouth when you treat the ague. It's wonderful to see you again. But I must go."

When news came the deadly endemic had killed Major Simon Willard, their most loved commander of the Middlesex troops, just when Indian attacks intensified, the military establishment was rocked. Hastily, they put together a military escort to take his body from Cambridge back to his home in the town he had founded: Concord. Will junior joined Captain Prentice, who led his cavalry on the march. Another two hundred fighting men joined the solemn rendezvous to escort the Major to his grave. The church elders and many military men felt God had punished them in this Divine tit-for-tat, Major Willard for the warrior Canonchet.

Goodman Garfield, a younger member of the rangers scouting the woods about Watertown, heard his wife and two-year-old son were stricken with the ague and rushed home to be with his family. Suzanne and Joanna were already at their bedside and tried their best to comfort him as well as their patients.

Soon after he arrived, they were arrested by pounding on the door. Suzanne strained her ears to hear the words spilled out by a man in extreme excitement. She heard snatches of the words. "They didn't know … Five hundred warriors camped out north of Sudbury … Burning … We're called." She ran to the door, anxiously peppering the man with questions. "What is it? Who is called?"

"Any man over sixteen in Watertown, Ma'am. Things in Sudbury have turned for the worst."

"You are going to Sudbury? They have Sudbury?"

"That's it."

Panic suddenly seized Suzanne; unable to breathe, her heart racing, she sank to a bench, white-faced. Goodman Garfield ran to her side. "Are you alright? Mistress?" He ran for the bedroom. "Mistress Morton," he called.

Joanna left the bedside of her patients and made her way to Suzanne. She'd never seen Suzanne in such a state; her live-in assistant, from childhood on, had been remarkably capable handling emergencies. Usually calm and calculating, now, her hands were shaking, and she didn't blink, but showed the whites of her eyes. "Suzanne, what is it?"

"They're in Sudbury. Getting closer. Watertown is next. He'll come. Don't you see?"

"Who?"

"One-eyed John. He's coming."

Joanna worked alone because Suzanne couldn't leave the bench but cowered there. She sent her home when she'd secured their patient but decided that she needed to escort her because she was too disturbed.

Matters turned for the worse when Abigail told her that Joseph's rangers had left to aid the Sudbury colonists who were battling, it was said, a force of one thousand or more allied Nipmuks and Wampanoags. Aghast, Suzanne sunk under the weight of her sister's news.

Chapter Thirty Three

IMMINENT DANGERS

Watertown, Late April 1676

Joseph had been gone for nearly a week, and reports alarmed everyone. Witnesses reported some of the worst damages, and what passed took place in Watertown's backyard. The conflict had begun on April seventeenth in nearby Marlboro when Indians began to burn down any buildings left standing after their first attack in March. Those who'd sped to rescue trapped settlers had been ambushed and trapped in turn. Only a few eyewitnesses survived, and they reported the Indians had destroyed what remained of Marlboro. Indians had quickly gathered in Sudbury. Four days passed before the combined troops from Watertown, Joseph among them, could defend the town. Sudbury had become a strategic target for the desperate and, by now, starving Indian bands, who badly needed to renew both food and ammunition. On Tuesday, five hundred warriors attacked the town, killing seventy-four Englishmen.

Joseph had returned from the battle ill with fever. Suzanne wrapped him in a blanket when she saw he was shaking with cold, and prepared a hot rum for him. The mug steamed in his hands as he blew on the rim, slouching forward in his chair. He looked up with haunted eyes and coughed that wearying cough she now suspected was consumption. She sat near on the settee. In the kitchen, she could hear Abigail scolding her two youngest children.

Joseph talked eagerly, sometimes so rapidly that he bit off his words. To Suzanne, he spoke as though he needed to confess.

"We headed for Hayne's garrison. The Indians had surrounded the fort, trapping the families there; our orders were to hold them back long enough to rescue them." He paused to sip his brew, taking a moment to savor the heat that tracked to his stomach, then rattled on.

"A river divides Sudbury, and we marched into the east town. The Indians had already fired houses there, but we routed them, drove them across the bridge. We had to save the ammunition depot, the meetinghouse east of the bridge. We did that much."

"What do you mean?" Suzanne asked. "You sound as though you think it wasn't enough."

"It wasn't. Hayne's garrison was west of the river. In west Sudbury, Indians were five-hundred strong! They'd surrounded Hayne's garrison. We never got to the fort. They ambushed us, and we had to retreat."

"And you?"

"I was with them. They had guns, not bow and arrows. We lost so many. A miracle anyone escaped. We heard later that night that Captain Wadsworth's company tried to rescue them the day before. Indians ambushed them, too. When the company retreated up Green Hill, the Indians set fire to the grasses. Wadsworth's men fled the fire right into their firing range." Joseph gripped the mug, grimacing. "Only a dozen survived. It was slaughter."

"But you say you were successful."

"Not us. We couldn't make it to the garrison. We retreated, did what we could, held the ammunition depot. Those savages burned any house west of the river until Captain Hunting got there. His squad of troopers from Charlestown drove off the Indians long enough to rescue those trapped. He and a company of Christian Indians, survivors they recruited from Deer Island. Without them, we'd have lost."

Suzanne held his hand and, raising it to her lips, kissed it. "You are back, and I too thank God." The empty space in her midriff sent its familiar edge of fear trembling. *He could have died in battle. What would I do without him? He's my life. My goodness.*

Joseph safely at home, Suzanne's mood improved, but not for long. After he'd finished telling of his troop's defense of Sudbury, she wrung her hands, her heart racing. She felt the same malice she'd felt in Groton, barricaded in the garrison for two weeks, not knowing from day-to-day when their enemies would strike.

That Sudbury was only twelve miles from Watertown didn't stop the dispossessed from pouring into town. The refugees came, and the colonists opened their doors. The militia called Will Sherborn, Jonathan Brown, and John Fay to battle again though some men, Suzanne's own Joseph, took on the job of ranging. Once his fever had subsided, he joined those stationed to comb the forests near Watertown. It was next best to building palisades in a line from Boston to Sudbury as some magistrates had recommended.

Townspeople, who were supporting their relatives and friends from destroyed villages, were stretched thin to feed and clothe them. Some, recovering from injuries and the epidemic illness were unable to work, though many were immediately conscripted to the local militia. The women's auxiliary, which had spearheaded the organization of women to harvest the previous year, was disintegrating as the war casualties affected their ranks.

At the town council meetings, selectmen complained the new refugees, not being citizens or owning land, didn't pay into the town rate. "We're a charitable people, but how will we feed the extra mouths when Boston has raised our town rates to support the war?"

Reverend Sherman's sermons often began to speak of the golden rule. But such a sermon couldn't change the numbers. The selectmen argued, "How can the town absorb the two hundred twenty-five residents of Sudbury, or even half of them?"

Suzanne's one relief came from a visitor from Concord.

The visitor, a farmer from Groton, told the story at prophesy one Sunday. After the Groton attack, One-eyed John's men were lying in wait for the rescue carts, a line two miles long by his account. The Groton survivors had no defense with ox carts strung out single file on the road like that. Two men on the first cart were killed and others injured. Then, a miracle of God he thought, the Indians had disappeared into the woods. They'd been able to pass to Concord otherwise unharmed.

Suzanne, on hearing this news, secretly thanked Dancing Light. *It worked* she thought. *She got through to One-eyed John.* She couldn't imagine what the shaman must have promised Monoco in return for ignoring the train of carts and the plunder that would have given the warriors what they wanted. But perhaps what remained of the food supplies after they'd torched the town wasn't worth their energy. It would remain a mystery because the man reported that neither Indians nor settlers remained in Lancaster, Groton, Billerica, or Scituate. Colonial troops had even emptied garrisons. Reverend and Abigail Willard had moved to Boston, and he became pastor of the First Boston church.

As the weather warmed, the families infected with the ague waned. Joanna had insisted that Suzanne take time to rest, and Suzanne had moved back in with her family. Rest, however, wasn't an alternative. She took on new projects with fervor because it kept her mind off the battles to maintain safe borders.

News filtered into Reverend Sherman's sermons in May that the sachem, Shoshanim, had met with Boston representatives to propose a preliminary peace after sachem Monaco's defeat in Sudbury. The minister explained that Christian Indians, acting as interpreters, negotiated the release of several prisoners, including Mistress Rowlandson, the Lancaster minister's wife. The

Nipmuks, meeting between Concord and their reclaimed territories in Groton, released four more prisoners a week later, that included John Morse, Joseph's uncle. They'd drafted petitions to Governor Leverette to release Indian prisoners in exchange. The draft of a treaty included allowing Indians to return to their plantations to sow their crops and to fish at their fishing camps in exchange for the same promises to the English planters. Spring brought hope to the beleaguered Watertown congregation.

When the air turned fragrant with budding foliage, Suzanne and Abigail could no longer tolerate the stale air and shoddy interior of their home. Throwing open doors and windows, the restless pair had put Benjamin in charge of making a space for the boys in the stable loft. Her nine and five-year-old sons would stay with Benjamin now.

When Mary had visited, they enlisted her help, and the three sisters cleaned out the house loft and organized space for the girls. Because Suzie and Hester were now old enough to take charge of their younger sisters, the four girls would occupy one half of the loft. Abigail would have her own room once they'd put up a divider.

Mary stood viewing their work and commented. "It's still too crowded. Suzanne, how would you and Joseph feel about sending Suzie or Hester out to apprentice? They're old enough."

"Like I was?" Suzanne couldn't help her wry response.

"Yes," Mary said. "You alone inspired us with your independence. Wouldn't you want that for them?"

"I don't think you understand what *that* costs. I don't think I could do that to them."

Mary stopped. "Do *that*? What do you mean?"

Abigail faced her sister. "Mary, when Suzanne left, didn't you feel terrible? I missed her so much I cried myself to sleep."

"And I was lonely," said Suzanne. "You can't imagine how separation affects a child."

"I'm sorry." Mary leaned forward and took Suzanne's

hand. "I always envied you. Joanna picked you and not me. And your work is important. Has meaning. I only brought it up because John's widow needs help now with four children. She has asked."

"Ruth Sherborn wants one of my daughters to help?"

"She could learn so much working with Ruth. You are midwifing and haven't much time to spend. Abigail has had to teach them everything."

Suzanne frowned, staring at her feet. "It's true. I haven't fulfilled my duty with the girls."

"Maybe it's time to talk to Joseph. And mother was thinking that—"

"Mother! What?"

"She's missing Rebecca, and she thought maybe Hester could apprentice to Goody Cooke to learn tailoring. Like Rebecca. She wants Hester to come and live with her and attend Goody Cooke's school."

"Oh Lord," Suzanne exclaimed. "She thinks she can replace any one of us?"

"She's missing us. Don't condemn her."

"I'll think about it. But enough of this dreaming. We need to get to work."

Suzanne and Abigail dragged Joseph and Samuel's bedding to the top of the stairs and threw it down. Mary corralled Suzie and Hester to take the bedding to the stable and climbed to the loft to join her sisters.

"Abigail, let's get these beds straightened out." Suzanne began to move the hay mattresses to one side of the room. "I figure we can hang a partition here for your bed."

"It's a wonderful space. Are you sure?"

"Of course. It's the least I can do. You've been such a help to me. I couldn't work without your help. You know that!"

"I can't thank you enough," replied Abigail.

"That's because it's we who need to thank you," continued Suzanne."While I've got your attention, I want to say that I've been thinking a lot about what we can do for you."

"What's that?"

"You're not married. I know I'm being blunt. You know me. I can't soften my words like you. But it's true. And the men have been off fighting. No suitors around."

"Yes, that's true. It's my lot in life. Sarah Norcross was smart; she got married before the war."

Mary shook out a blanket. "Mother said you were a little sensitive about that."

"It should have been me," said Abigail.

Suzanne said, "Yes, it should, but maybe the Lord meant you to have better opportunities."

Mary added, "Men are coming home now. You have your pick."

Suzanne nodded. "I know a rich widower whose son is the same age as Joe junior and Samuel. I've invited him to bring his son to play with them."

"Do you mean John Fay?" asked Abigail.

"Yes, he needs a wife for those children of his. And I saw he showed interest when he was here last."

"I know I have to marry, but I feel he's too old for me. He must be your age."

"Am I that old?"

"That's not what I said. I didn't mean that," continued Abigail. "Mother said you married Joseph for love. That's what I want, too."

"I did. She's right. But you're not in the same position. You must marry wealth, as Mary did. Mary, can you explain?"

Abigail cut her off. "You don't know me."

Mary chimed in. "I know that a woman must have income. I understand your feelings, but you have no income or way of earning it. So you will need a man who is sworn to take your interests. You must marry someone who can provide for you the life that you want."

"I'm not like you, Mary. I can't marry for money."

Mary harrumphed. "Even if you were rich as Moses, all your money would go to your husband. He owns your children, too. And that's true for Suzanne even though she's independent. Isn't that right Suzanne?"

Suzanne nodded. "It's true." She rolled up the blanket she held, caught up in memories of her mother's counsel. When she'd become so homesick that she'd begged to come home, her mother had brought up all the advantages midwifing would give her. A midwife, such as Joanna, had choices other women didn't have. Learning a trade would make her independent of money concerns when it came to finding a husband. She'd remember her mother's advice forever, "You won't have to look in his pockets for love." Suzanne realized later that her mother had always envied her best friend for that advantage of independence, one that any intelligent woman would covet but only an heiress achieved.

Abigail frowned and studied the floor, her mouth set in resentment.

Suzanne studied her and felt the need to point out she spoke from affection, a motive Mary and Abigail often thought she lacked. "I only mean well, Abigail."

Abigail stood to leave. "I know, but I'll have to think about it."

Chapter Thirty Four

THE CAPTIVES

Watertown, June 1676

Uncle John, praise God you're here; we feared we'd lost you." Suzanne hardly recognized Uncle John when he stood at her door with his other nephew (Joseph's younger brother, Jonathan Morse). Though John Morse had always been a tall thin man, he'd wasted to a grayed wraith with grizzled, patchy hair and beard. The jovial and hearty ring to his voice had faded in both volume and tone. His appearance testified to six weeks of torturous captivity among the Abenaki.

"Suzanne, Joseph," he nodded to his hosts, motioning to Jonathan to enter first.

Jonathan Morse, a middle-aged, never-married man with a full salt-and-pepper-gray beard, stepped into the doorway gingerly. Like his older brother Joseph, he was tall with thick, graying, tightly curled hair he tied back with a thong. A scar on his left cheek and pale gray eyes distinguished him. He intercepted the question his brother Joseph expressed with raised eyebrows. "My Captain insisted I take the day. Isn't every day we get our kin back from the dead." The tanned squint lines already lining his eyes testified to the many days he'd spent bivouacked with his troop.

Suzanne held the door wide for them. Uncle John, only a week since his release, entered, head bowed. The government had paid the ransom for this leader of Groton's council, and he'd temporarily taken up residence with his brother, Joseph's father, in Watertown. To Suzanne, it was plain six weeks of captivity had taken their toll in spirit as much as flesh. Uncle John was not his always hardy self.

The small house was already teaming with guests for the planned supper to welcome him back. John Fay sat in the parlor with Abigail Sherborn, where his son Johnny helped Suzanne's son Joseph, his best friend and sidekick now, stack wood at the hearth under their watch. Suzanne's children would not return to school until September, and the racket that came through the door from the yard testified to high spirits. The boys kept glancing at the door, keen to join their playmates when they finished their chore.

Ruth Sherborn, the widow of Suzanne's brother John, worked at the hearth to prepare food; her oldest son aided her. John, a grave boy of ten, hardly looked up from his chore of churning butter. He didn't dare, as Suzie, newly apprenticed to his mother, supervised him as she attentively basted the spit of lamb legs, the animal slaughtered and dressed that morning.

Benjamin pouted in the back, sore put to get his favorite cousin's attention now that Suzie had moved out, apprenticed to his sister-in-law, Ruth; he stamped through the back door.

In the months following the Indian attack on Sudbury the war continued, but the Indian presence had subsided. Only four towns were attacked after April, and it was said that the magistrates in Boston were negotiating an exchange of prisoners for captives. The Christian Indians were the main instruments of drawing up peace treaties that would allow them to return to their plantations to plant and fish unmolested. They in turn promised the same for English settlements. It might have worked, but one hundred Connecticut men under Captain Turner, who'd heard that the Nipmuks had gathered for traditional spring fishing at Great Falls, without any orders from Boston or Connecticut, attacked. In the predawn hours they aimed rifles into the wigwams of sleeping families. The slaughter of more than two hundred natives, three-quarters of them women and children, was perceived by the Boston magistrates as a sign of "divine approbation." Although Captain Turner was ambushed and killed, by contrast, English casualties from attacks on Bridgewater, Halifax, Scituate, and Hatfield were fewer than fifty.

For Joanna and Suzanne, life also took a new turn when women again began to ask for their services. Suzanne and Joseph had decided the oldest girl would do well in an apprenticeship with Ruth Sherborn, especially since Benjamin, thirteen, the same as Suzie, had taken to mooning over her. Grandmother Susanna was happy to take her grandchild, Hester, who was apprenticed to a dressmaker.

With these changes easing apprehensions, and the news that Uncle John had returned from captivity, their spirits lifted. With more men home, townspeople could return to farming.

Joseph moved a chair into the circle in the parlor and motioned for his Uncle John to sit. "Uncle John, we're eager to hear about your ordeal."

John Morse took his seat with dignity, barely settling in, leaning forward as though he might jump up any minute. Will and Benjamin crowded close. Ruth came forward and extended a mug of ale to him, and he held it in both hands, staring at it appreciatively but not drinking. "I have news for *you,* Suzanne. Jonathan tells me you thought Rebecca and her girl were slain. I asked him not to say anything before I could tell you. Rebecca is alive."

Suzanne gasped. "You saw Rebecca. When? Where?"

"They were captured, same as me. Monoco's men marched all of us for days. Then I lost track. Saw Mary Rowlandson, too. But that was much later."

Suzanne spun toward him with this news. He'd explained their disappearance, but she had questions. *Did Dancing Light find them? Did she help them? Did they want ransom money? Adopted? Where were they now?* Her mind exploded with a need to know every answer at once. Joseph caught her as she swayed. She calmed herself the only way she knew how. *Breathe*, she told herself, and straightened.

Will stood transfixed. Across the room, she saw John Fay nod toward her; a smile flitted across his mouth. She registered he was happy for her.

"You thought they were dead. Why?"

Suzanne, still speechless with the news, passed her hand across her forehead. "Uncle John, I last saw them lying in a heap where they fell. How can you ask? You were there!"

"I wouldn't know. That day, they took *me*. Horrible day."

"I didn't see it. They'd tried to escape Nutting's garrison when the Indians took it. Someone fleeing said she'd seen little Becky fall. She said Rebecca threw herself over her, but an Indian was following with a tomahawk. She thought he'd killed them. Later, I saw them from a window. They were lying beside the path."

Joseph pulled a log from the stack, upended it for a stool, and sat. "What happened? We heard they'd taken you, but nothing more."

"We had no mercy from them."

Will, who drew closer to Joseph, stood spellbound. "How? Joseph said you were in Sawtell's garrison. Did the Indians take it?"

"No. They were gone, left that morning. Abandoned the forts. After they'd gone, but before the rescue party came, I and Clements left for Parkers garrison. We had folks there. Joseph and Suzanne. Indians ambushed us on the way. They slew my mate where he stood, cut off his head, and mounted it on a pole looking at his own land. Spared me. For the ransom."

Suzanne shuddered, remembering what they'd done to Timothy, dug up from his grave. They mounted his head and a leg on poles, his corpse naked as an Indian where they'd undone his winding sheet. For all the shock she'd felt at his graveside, she could no longer harbor feelings of hatred against them. She'd since then heard stories from Will, who'd survived the Great Swamp battle; she couldn't forget the scenes he described. The horror. They'd fired an Indian fort and left the charred remains to the crows:

five hundred old men, women, and children, burned alive. She'd heard, too, of the bounty on Indian scalps, full pay for men, less for a woman, the least for an infant or child. "Redskins," they called them, as though human scalps were fox or beaver, to be traded. In war, separated from God as Reverend Willard had so often preached, there was only darkness, darkest night, the soul's despair. All was blackest night where fear and hatred raged.

Benjamin couldn't check himself. Only thirteen, his curiosity was nearly morbid. "Did they scalp children?"

"You want to know the worst of it? Well," he said, irritably, "know it was the dead baby. They cut her in pieces and threw her to the swine to eat. That serve your appetite?"

Suzanne gasped at Uncle John's cruelty. It wasn't like him at all. Benjamin choked and stood back.

Uncle John frowned. "Sorry, son; sorry. Didn't mean that. Not myself these days." He cleared his throat and continued reluctantly. "They drove me and two others on foot for a day and night before we stopped to eat. But it's not like they ate. They were starving, too. That's when I saw her. And Becky. She was so poorly, I doubt she made it."

"Were you together? Did you speak?"

"They separated us. I saw a brave lead them off. Probably paid a pretty price. That red hair, you know."

Rebecca's hair had fetched a price. Why not ransom? Suzanne thought. *But they might adopt her and Becky into their tribe.* It was a stretch to think she'd meet no harm, but Dancing Light's accounts of abduction left her some hope Rebecca and her daughter might thrive. More certainly, she might be able to find her whereabouts after the war ended.

"She's alive. That's what matters. Thank you, Uncle John. This is wonderful news."

"If you don't mind, I'd like to hear someone else's story." Half his mouth lifted in smile. "Mine bores me now."

Suzanne saw a spark of what John Morse had been in his face. *He hasn't lost the will to joke*, she thought. *Time to rescue him.* She banged on a pan. "Time to eat. Everyone, let's gather for our blessing." Suzanne gestured toward the table, now extended with extra boards to accommodate the guests.

Jonathan and Joseph flanked their Uncle's place at the table's head, with a place for Ruth next to Abigail and John Fay, seated on Jonathan's side and Suzanne, Will and Benjamin on Joseph's side. Since Ruth and Suzanne were the oldest, they served the meal. Suzanne made sure that Abigail didn't serve so she might spend time with John Fay, who it must be said, was in the beginning stages of courting her. A small village of children, minus the two sleeping infants and their sitter, Hester, crowded onto makeshift log stools at the temporary table set up at one end. When everyone sat down, Joseph stood to lead them in grace.

While Suzanne set down platters of meat, bread, and greens, Ruth passed around the pitcher of ale. She didn't overlook the men, who would not refuse her infusing rum from the jug she held in her other hand.

Still standing, Joseph Morse held up his cup for a toast. "Here's to Uncle John, returned to our midst." This toast was met with stamping feet and declarations, "To Uncle John."

"What will you do now?" Joseph asked, seating himself again. "Will you stay in Watertown?"

Uncle John speared a crisped lump of lamb from the passing trencher with his knife and stared at it as though he'd swallow it whole. "No. I'll be returning to Concord. We've a meeting set to talk about rebuilding Groton. Sooner the better, I say."

"The war's not ended. Isn't that foolhardy?"

"It'll be months before we have funds. But planning takes time."

"How long do you think?" Joseph asked. "We'd like to reclaim our land."

Uncle John grunted. "Rebuilding houses and barns? Assembling the materials alone is at least a year. Will you stay here until then?"

Joseph nodded toward Will. "Will's choice."

Will answered with a resounding voice. "As long as you need, you are welcome here. You know that."

"We're eager to get back to Groton," Joseph answered. Suzanne's stomach lurched; she didn't share his eagerness to return to their homestead.

Ruth, who came near with her jug of rum, stopped when he signaled her. As she poured rum in his cup, she spoke. "I've just met Goodman Lawrence, Sunday, who's here visiting. He tells me nothing stands in Groton."

"Is that Enoch Lawrence? Heard he was in town. Excellent man. He's right. One-Eyed John destroyed Groton. We can start from the garrisons still standing; it's not impossible. We built it once. We can do it again." He chuckled dryly as she passed. "You talking with Lawrence now? He's not attached, you know."

Ruth blushed. She'd been John Sherborn's widow for nine months, but it was too soon to think of remarrying. "He's a Groton man," she replied. "My home is Watertown."

Joseph was quick to intercede. "John owned land in Groton. Isn't it your and the children's land now?"

When Ruth didn't answer, Abigail spoke for her. "Everyone knows Ruth told John she'd never move to Groton."

Suzanne laughed. "That's so. John told me he'd have to take her in a poke sack. He was keeping the land for the boys."

Uncle John drank and set down his cup. "Well, just saying, you'll not find a better man. Lawrences! Pillars of Groton. You've got those three boys to raise. Your daughter."

Ruth poured rum in John Fay's cup and crossed to where Benjamin sat, and Suzanne was clearing a platter. She leaned close and mumbled in Suzanne's ear, "Not like John Morse ever married. Who is he to counsel me?"

John Morse, now chewing with gusto, elbowed his nephew Jonathan's side when he overheard. "Just is—some like the single life. Right Jonathan?"

Jonathan, who had ever claimed he'd never marry, guffawed. "Best decision I've made."

Abigail, hearing Jonathan's response, bristled. To her, the convention of marriage was most important for a woman, and she already felt the old maid, a state she feared. Before she'd thought it through, she blurted out, "To my mind it's not likely you'll either one have to change; no woman wants to marry an old man."

Suzanne coughed. "Abigail!" She was shocked because her sister was always so careful of people's feelings, in fact, always criticized her own bluntness. But clearly this virtue had its turnabout; knowing how people felt, Abigail could sting like a hornet.

When Ruth heard Suzie giggling from the children's table, she rebuked her apprentice, barely suppressing her own mirth: "Don't be rude now!".

John Fay, who was eighteen years older than Abigail, was suddenly rendered uneasy. Suzanne didn't miss his expression. She again reproved her sister. "You don't mean it Abigail."

Abigail, unaware John Fay had taken her remark personally, smiled and turned to Jonathan. "I was joking brother-in-law. I fear I've been rude."

He laughed. "No offense." Nodding toward his Uncle John, he quipped, "He's the only old man here."

With this, the tension eased, and even John Fay laughed. Jonathan, who was sixteen years older than Abigail and had never noticed her to this day, was party to a broad smile and twinkling blue eyes that smote him on the spot.

Suzanne worried because when Ruth had finished serving and taken her seat between Jonathan and Abigail, they were leaning together deep in conversation. When she took her own seat across from John Fay, she noted John Fay had turned from Abigail to talk with Will. She wanted to repair any damages between her sister and her match, John Fay, but couldn't get a word in edgewise. It wasn't the first time she'd noticed the bond developing between Will Junior and John Fay, who were both fascinated with Boston politics. Will had followed in his father's footsteps and joined the Watertown council. No longer party to

Marlboro affairs, John Fay found this younger man a serendipitous source for political and economic news. Suzanne had once suppressed the thought his visits were more to see Will than Abigail.

"Will, what can you tell me of the King's new envoy in Boston?"

"Lord Edward Randolph," he spit out. "Only heard he's been nosing about, asking questions. We already know what he'll report to the King."

"What's that? He asking about the war? The Indians?"

"Yes, that. But I hear the Magistrates are concerned he's keen on tariffs, taxes, and the like. He's asked them for a census of the population."

"I expect the rates will be raised then."

"Isn't it inevitable? Father always said the crown had one interest in Boston: profit. Only our charter keeps England from running our business."

"I agree. If we lose our independence, we'll end like Plymouth."

Suzanne, who'd lost interest in the conversation, drifted into thoughts of the small garden plot she'd started. Joseph's announcement that they might return to Groton in a year posed challenges to her more immediate plans. She'd wanted to restock her apothecary now that she'd moved back in with the family.

Chapter Thirty Five

WARS END

Watertown, October 1676

In October, Suzanne stooped over the dry stalks in her garden to cover them with leaves for the winter, when she felt her stomach wrench and the sting of the acrid fluid that overflowed into her nose. The sting and the sour stench. She didn't feel feverish or weak. *Morning sickness?* she asked herself. *It must be. I'm with child again! Is there a worse time?* They were all immersed in harvesting crops and preserving food for the winter, an intensive time any year that kept them working dawn to past dusk. Still, she calculated, counting the months, the baby will be born in May, weather warming but not too hot. She'd take any advantage she could get.

As the fall progressed, Joseph showed worsening symptoms of consumption, but she held the hope he had an advantage that could save him: her and Philip's care. No one in Massachusetts had a better chance than a man with two medical practitioners attending him. Joseph, though, was the worst possible patient. He couldn't bear watching the family add all his tasks to their own. Time and again, he ignored their prescriptions that he eat more and rest. The result was the telltale wasting away until his clothing hung on him and he stood like an empty scarecrow by the fire, too restless to sit.

Once winter arrived in earnest, Suzanne had to force him to eat. Meals lengthened into bouts of argument, and Philip was at last able to make him rest when Joseph lost strength daily with nature's prescription. By the solstice, with barely eight hours of light, he could stay in bed long hours. The boys had moved back into the house, taking the two beds left by their apprenticed sisters.

In her eighth month of pregnancy, Suzanne could barely cross the great room without getting out of breath. The skin on her legs and ankles felt so tight it would burst. It won't be long, she thought. This too shall pass. Repeating this phrase from the Bible made the tasks go by easier.

She could hear the rain, steadily beating on the cider barrel by the window. The damp doesn't help, she thought, stretching out one foot and viewing her plump, swollen ankle with dismay. Through the window, she could see the few blossoms that raised above the leaf mold bowed low under the pelting cold rain. *Snowdrops and spring beauties can survive any punishment*, she thought, watching the rain turn to large flakes of snow. At that moment, she heard the knock on her door.

Ruth Sherborn's blond hair was crushed inside a hooded cape and cap, her cape beaded with large drops of melted flakes. Her cheeks were bright red and her smile wide. She glowed with an easy contentment. Suzie, standing behind her, also caped, carried a basket with the contents wrapped in a piece of linen cloth. She laughed and started to speak, but Ruth turned and tapped her arm. "Let me tell her."

"Come in. What do you have there?"

Suzie crossed to the table and set the basket down. "We have scones. For a special tea." She mugged the word, laughing, and unwrapped a platter of scones.

"Frosted," Suzanne exclaimed. "Special indeed. In April? Where did you find sugar?"

Ruth didn't answer but grinned conspiratorially. "For the new mother."

"Thank you. Let me hang up your capes. They're dripping wet." Suzanne laid their capes across her arm and hung them on the door pegs.

"Let me make tea, mother. I can do it." Suzie busied herself at the hearth, gathering cups and the pot, dropping in dried herbs and rose hips, pouring hot water.

"What's this occasion?" Suzanne asked.

"I have good news." Ruth scooted down the table bench, making room for Suzie.

"It must be. You're blooming."

Noting Abigail where she sat with Hannah, Ruth called to her, "Abigail! Bring Hannah. You'll want to hear the news, too."

"Now, let's have those scones," Suzanne announced. Her mouth was watering at the idea of sugar, which suddenly felt like craving.

Suzie passed the scones and set out the cups, then poured a round, but Ruth couldn't wait until they all sat. "Enoch Lawrence and I have posted the bans. We're getting married."

Almost on cue, the back door opened, and Benjamin came in stamping his feet. He'd been in the barn when he saw his cousin Suzie at the door.

"Cousin, you smell the scones from the stable?" Suzie teased.

Ben blushed. It hadn't been the scones that enticed him. He tried in vain to hide his crush on Suzie. "You have scones?" he asked, lamely giving away his purpose.

"Here," Suzanne said. "Help yourself." She pushed the basket to his seat. "Ruth, that's wonderful. I'm so happy for you. Will he settle here, then?"

"No. We'll be moving to Groton. He has farmland. But John's land is better for a house; we'll build there. And best of all, Suzanne, he will let the children keep their names. They'll be Sherborns."

"Groton! No, you simply mustn't." Suzanne plopped down across from her.

"What do you mean? You and Joseph will return."

"I only said it to make him happy."

Abigail looked shocked. She too had thought Joseph and Suzanne would return to Groton. "Have you told that to Joseph, yet?"

Suzanne saddened, staring down at the scored and stained table board, her mother's first table. "There's no need."

Abigail frowned as she caught her meaning. “He won’t be returning, either. You’re saying …”

Suzanne nodded, simply, her eyes moist. “No more questions, Abigail. Ruth is here with wonderful news.” She was happy for her sister-in-law, and her nieces and nephews would be secure now. But if Ruth moved to Groton, it would disrupt Suzie. Suzie loved working with Ruth and should be for at least four more years to complete her apprenticeship. What would she do now if Ruth moved to Groton?

Ruth leaned forward. “Suzanne, I know that you had a terrible time when the attack came. But the Indians are gone. The tribe that lived across the river never came back. All of Monoco’s allies were killed or sold to the West Indies. It’s safe.”

“Safe for how long? You can’t imagine what it’s like starting a homestead from the beginning. And you may think the Indians have abandoned their land, but I knew one of them well. They have only gone north temporarily. They’ll be back. It’s their summer grounds.”

Suzie piped up, “But Dancing Light is your friend. Her tribe won’t bother anyone.”

Suzanne stared at Suzie. *Why was Suzie arguing on Ruth’s side?* She wondered. *Why does she want Ruth to go?* She turned to Ruth. “And I was thinking of Suzie. She’ll miss you if you go. Will you abandon her with four more years to apprentice?”

Suddenly, Suzie and Ruth looked at each other uncomfortably. They were silent for a moment, but when Suzie started to speak, Ruth signaled with her index finger to halt. “Let me tell her.”

Suzie sat frozen. Ruth began. “Suzie wants to come with us. She misses Groton. It was always her home. My children would be lost without her. And, as you say, she needs four more years with me.”

Suzanne suddenly filled with anger. Her thoughts rained down on her. They just spring this on me? They don’t ask. Suzie’s not of age, doesn’t get to decide! She stood, leaned forward, pushing her knuckles into the tabletop. "I absolutely forbid it! Ruth, you have never been attacked, never seen a day of war. You don't know what you are asking Suzie to do. Or me. I'll not allow my daughter to risk that terror again."

"But mother," Suzie pleaded. "I want to go back. My friends are there. I don't like Watertown. And Enoch says the Indians are really gone. Oh, please! I want to be Ruth's apprentice."

"You'll not go. You'll stay here with me."

"I won't. If I can't go with Ruth, I won't be back."

Suzanne was trembling with anger by now. "And just where do you think you'll live?"

"With grandma," Suzie said. She ran to the door, pulled on her cape, and ran weeping into the storm.

"Benjamin," Ruth said. "Can you make sure she gets to your mother?"

Benjamin needed no more coaching but put on his coat and left to go after her.

When it was clear that Suzanne had closed any discussion of moving to Groton, Ruth left.

Later, as Suzanne and Abigail cleared the dishes, Suzanne's anger subsided, and she began to second-guess her reactions. "Abigail," Suzanne asked. "Do you think I was too rough on her?"

Abigail cleared her throat. "I know how much you've suffered. I understand that. But Suzie's young. They recover from ordeals like that quickly. And, honestly, if she wants to go, I think you should let her."

"To be captured like Rebecca?"

Abigail, realizing that she had no way to reassure her sister, decided to drop the subject. "Maybe I can't understand what you've been through. Let's talk of this another time."

When Joseph awoke later that day, Suzanne told him of the coming wedding between Ruth and Enoch Lawrence. "Uncle John had it right," he commented. "I'm not surprised that he talked her into moving to Groton."

"You aren't? After all her protests when John asked her?"

"Isn't it Ruth's way to bury her past? To appease John's ghost?" He changed the subject: "What is Suzie going to do?"

"She's staying with my mother. Mother tried to convince me to let her go. What do you think?"

"I agree. We'll join her there, soon enough. And Ruth is so good for her. She'll be fine."

In the end, she agreed that Suzie could move to Groton, but Suzie had stopped speaking to Suzanne. She didn't even say good-bye when she left with Ruth and Enoch for Groton after they married in May. Soon after, Suzanne gave birth to her seventh baby. Joseph named their new son Jonathan, to honor his brother.

Chapter Thirty Six

JOSEPH'S BIRTHDAY

Watertown, June 1677

At the beginning of June, when the baby was only a month old, Joseph was stricken suddenly with a fever that flamed intermittently for two weeks. Bedridden, he began to cough up blood. 'He's so very sick,' she told Philip when he called to check on him.

After examining him, Philip prepared her for the worst. "It's not likely he can overcome consumption when it reaches this stage. His lungs are badly damaged. There was nothing you could have done about his tendency; consumption often strikes those of his physical build. Tall and too thin, built that way, such physiques in both men and women are prone to consumption. I've seen it before."

Suzanne wasn't sure about his idea, but she'd heard that consumption often infected members of the same family. The Morses were all the same stock: willowy in build. It would stand to reason they were frail and more likely to contract a life-threatening disease. Her own family was the opposite, with compact and sturdy frames, energetic and strong. No Sherborn she'd heard of had ever died of consumption.

Over the next months, Joseph recovered so fully between attacks, at times he didn't even cough. But intermittent bouts with fever made recovery impossible; each one took him down further. She enlisted everyone's help to attend to him because, between nursing baby Jonathan and tending to her husband, she was near collapse from lack of sleep. Benjamin became her rock, saving her hours as he took over nursing his friend. He managed Joseph's every need, even changing soiled linens, and held him upright to ease his coughing. He helped Suzanne move him when they bathed his emaciated body to cool the fever. He even spooned broth into Joseph's mouth when he could barely swallow.

When Joseph felt well enough, he asked Benjamin to read from Milton, and the two would talk at length about each passage. Suzanne was glad of it because she had no patience for analysis that led to no action. Though she'd loved to hear him read, she could offer no insights to her husband. She grew impatient with words spoken for what she felt to be an empty exercise. She couldn't share his joy in just thinking.

In August, on Joseph's fortieth birthday, he was still ill, but could sit up and talk in short spurts truncated by fits of coughing. Benjamin's big orange tabby had crawled onto the bed and offered his kind of medicine. He curled his body into Joseph's side, purring loudly and kneaded Joseph's chest while Benjamin read aloud. When Suzanne entered the room, she stared at them tenderly, then crossed to the bed when Joseph motioned for her.

"Benjamin, that's enough for today. I need to talk to Suzanne."

"Are you sure?" Suzanne smoothed a cover. "I don't want to interrupt your talk."

Joseph nudged Benjamin's cat with a bony hand and the animal leisurely stood, then reared in the air, stretched out his front paws and lightly leaped from the bed. Benjamin, too, stood, nodded, and made his way to the door after his cat, that led, looking over a shoulder to make sure Benjamin followed.

"Please sit for a minute." Joseph waved toward the chair.

Suzanne sat, moving it closer to the bedside. "What is it?"

"Philip has let me know I'm not likely to get better, and I need to get my affairs in order." His head listed to one side as he examined her face for effect.

"Philip! How? He knows what only God can know? You've gotten better many times before. Yet you believe him?"

"I'm tired of fighting. Three years, Suzanne. And I'm so sorry. I leave you and the children with nothing. Not even my clothes. I'm ashamed."

"Joseph, don't even think it! None of it was your fault. If anything, it was mine. We had a good life. We can build again."

"Not I. Not now. Suzanne, you must see consumption will end me." He stopped abruptly when a cough erupted in a barrage of choking gasping spasms. When he quieted, he spat the phlegm into a napkin. "It's time we talk about my will. You, only thirty-six, with seven children." He cleared his throat.

Suzanne stood, plumped his pillow so he could sit up. He continued, "I have nothing to give you but our land in Groton and the horse. But I can't join you, can't help you rebuild."

At first, Suzanne was going to say nothing, go along with him, but she reconsidered. He was her only love, and he deserved her honesty. "Joseph, I can't return to Groton. I let you think I could, but even the thought weighs me down."

"I've known it, since Suzie left with Ruth. I could see it in you."

"Forgive me for lying to you."

"There's no need. You wished to please me, a wifely desire."

"If I lose you, it is doubly so. I'll never look on Groton again."

"Or Dancing Light? You may never see her again?"

"Especially her. God has forbade it, Joseph. If I lose you, nothing else matters to me."

"I don't believe Dancing Light was the cause of our fall. Nor do I believe God is punishing you when all have suffered the same. A just God wouldn't punish every man for one man's sin." Joseph, who had spoken adamantly, slumped into his pillow, exhausted. He was silent as he gathered his strength and continued.

"I've thought about the will. I'd like you to write this down and have it witnessed."

"Yes, of course."

"The horse is yours, but not the land. You'd have no way to build again. If I leave it to young Joseph, the land will be fallow, without improvements; the Groton council would repeal our grant. So, I'm willing it to my brother Jonathan."

"But then the children have no …"

"Wait. I have a clause to deal with Joseph's inheritance. When Joseph junior comes of age, he has the right to acquire the land. His uncle may buy it for four hundred pounds or give it to Joseph."

"You've thought this through. How long have you known?"

"I've had time to think of nothing else. I've spoken with Will. He says you have a home here forever. There's more. I'd like to bequeath my clothes and all my books to brother-in-law Benjamin. He has outdone himself taking care of me. He's gifted, has a mind that can value my books."

Suzanne held his hand, unable to stop the flow of tears as they both now faced parting forever. She held his hand until he slept and spent the night at his bedside.

When the church drumbeat sounded forty times, one tap for each of Joseph's years, the townspeople knew he had passed to his eternal home. When they heeded the call and gathered at the house to remember him, Suzanne felt she was everywhere at once. She was woodenly greeting her neighbors on the hot summer day, of course, feeling the sweat dampen and wilt her only black dress. *Who can dress respectably in this heat?* she thought, longing to tie up her skirts to air her legs. Suzanne was embracing the sobbing Hester, wanting to hold her at arm's distance to cool them both. She stood behind the women who prepared Joseph's body for the viewing. She nursed her son Jonathan shrouded by the bedstead curtains in a bed she'd shared with Joseph only a day before. She drank with neighbors, feeling the sweat of a good drunk bead on her forehead though she'd not had a drop from the cup she carried. He lay on the bier, eyes closed, and hands folded lovingly over his Book of Psalms. Suzanne read the verses visitors left on the bier from a distance. At the same time, she was so not there, but somewhere with soft, white walls, no sharp corners or edges, where all sound was nulled, somewhere, she thought, felt distant. How carefully she was passed from arms to arms: her mother, her sister Mary, her sister Abigail.

I'm alright, she thought. I'll be just fine. I've made it through worse. But this last thought, the worst lie, pierced her heart and shattered her will. Her head flooded with the cry 'Joseph,' over and over, without end. His lingering illness, the long journey to this end, her expectation of his death, could not lessen her anguish. He was the love of her life, and there'd be no other. She wanted to die.

Not long after their friends and family had escorted Joseph's body to the graveyard, her milk dried up. Without even a chance to wean little Jonathan, she couldn't manage his wailing hunger. Her sister Abigail sought a wet nurse for him.

Suzanne began to lose handfuls of hair; the balding circle grew from the top of her head. Though no one ever saw her without her cap and couldn't know, *she* knew.

After the last shovel of dirt had sounded on his coffin, she could no longer tolerate the children's demands on her. Abigail counseled her. Her mother counseled her.

After a week, Joanna Morgan sought her out on their request.

Chapter Thirty Seven

HEARTBREAK

Watertown, August 1677

Joanna Morgan found Suzanne stooping over her tiny garden plot, pulling weeds from the lot where she grew the rarest of herbs. "Your sister Mary was expecting your visit today, but she told me you didn't show up. She had to come to my house for her checkup. She's in her eighth month. Are we to understand you will not attend her baby's birth? Can you explain yourself?"

Suzanne bunched the handful of stalks in a ball and tossed them into a sack near her foot and straightened. "I'm glad you came. I haven't known what to say." Suzanne watched Joanna set down her basket, eyebrows creased in question. "I can't explain."

"Say to whom?"

Suzanne was too exasperated to hold her tongue. Joanna knew exactly whom. "My patients! I can't help them. I'm no healer. God doesn't want me to be a midwife."

Joanna's stance changed, and she stepped forward, hands on hips. "What nonsense! Since when have you believed that God decides your fate?"

"Don't you see? If I believe or don't believe, He punishes me." Suzanne felt so beaten she hugged herself. The bitterness rose to stick in her throat. *Does no one understand?* she thought.

"Punished? For what?"

"It's like Reverend Willard said. I've sinned against Him. I let in the dark, Dancing Light. God sent the devil in her image to test my faith. I let her spirits touch me, and now, I am cursed."

"You make no sense Suzanne. This isn't like you. From what you told me, Dancing Light was a skillful healer, like yourself, dedicated to human good. She's no devil. If God sent her, he sent her as a blessing."

Suzanne offered her proof. "God has stripped me of my home, my husband, my sister, for a *reason*. I must do penance." She tore off her cap, exposing her balding pate. "He's taking my hair, Joanna!"

Joanna's forehead wrinkled with concern, but she pressed her point. "How many medicines have you brought me and other midwives who follow because of your so-called witch doctor?"

"That was God's providence."

"And Dancing Light had no agency in showing you?"

"God sent her." Suzanne knew she'd struck home when Joanna heard *this*; her mouth dropped open, momentarily speechless.

"Unbelievable!" she pronounced, shaking her head. "You think Dancing Light isn't a person in the flesh, like you, who acts on her own? She's no puppet, not God's or the Devil's, either. When did you start thinking like them?"

Suzanne put her cap back on and stepped back, needing to explain. "Reverend Willard spoke to us, made it so clear. Every event on Earth is God's plan. If you could have heard him, Joanna, you'd believe too."

Joanna nearly growled. "I'm a healer. In my experience, God's providence doesn't include man's actions! We have free wills. Dancing Light was kind to you, her *will*. Indians fight for *reasons*, their *own*. It's grief that drives you to think she's a Devil. Bereaved, we feel evil crush us, we feel all life as sinister. Your sister Mary could tell you some tales. I heal twice as well with her clairvoyance when I must treat the bereaved."

When Joanna held out her hands, Suzanne took them, her face twisting. "Mary will never understand. She's God's chosen one, never suffered, never will."

Joanna continued. "You are not the only one who's experienced loss. You may feel you are going mad, and you sound like you are. But, my dear, it's grief. And it will subside."

Suzanne sobbed and choked out. "I've grieved for others: father, Rebecca, John. What I feel is *not* the same! It's not grief. I can't live without him."

"Aye. There's no greater pain than to lose our dearest love. I know that. I lost my own. The years don't matter; grief can still catch us unaware, shake us afresh."

Suzanne had never heard her mentor speak of her husband or her grief. The thought struck her: *She does know.* "Joanna, how can I go on?"

"I know of no other with greater courage than you, Suzanne. Trust me. You can. For now, I'll explain to your patients, take over for you. Do what you must to make your peace."

Joanna left Suzanne shaken. Her confrontation had penetrated Suzanne's thoughts but hadn't changed her mind. She now attended church religiously but spoke to no one. Before long, Suzanne escaped from the confines of the house and her memories, making her way to deep woods, where she found some comfort. She had a good excuse for her walks. Even though she'd denounced her profession, she could still tell her family that she needed to find the proper herbs. They didn't question her. She began to range as far from her home as she had done with Dancing Light in Groton.

In the last August sunlight, she lay across great granite boulders. Sunlight warmed them like voluptuous bosoms, and she clung to this imagined mother when she stopped to rest. At other times, lying face up to intensely green transparent leaves backlit by sunrays, she searched the canopy with her eyes, following a single bird's song with wonder. Walking, she found paths that beckoned her onward, spilling their mysteries as she passed: the moss on the stone examined close was a miniature forest. The myriad lichen that laced branches of spruce could only be realized at nose length. She could only see the mushrooms nosing up through leaf mold just beyond the perimeter of her skirts. Home from her rambles one night, she couldn't stay in the house. She sat in reverie beneath a tree watching the fireflies dart in the foliage, letting the night breeze caress her the night through. When summer came to its end, Suzanne found great solace in the crisp air. It allowed her to breathe deeply and erased grief for hours on end. She could hardly wait for spring and the long succession of wildflowers raising their blooms to the sun. She sometimes mused that her fellow settlers felt the woods were the walls of their prisons, but not for her. The deep forests she'd discovered in her rambles with Dancing Light had been her escape.

In her rambles, not minding a torn skirt or scraped elbow, dried leaves caught in her hair, she took on a wild air. One day, her daughter started in fear when she saw her mother beating dead leaves from her cap and escaped hair, as though she'd seen a thing turned wild.

Once the children returned to school in September, she had complete relief from their demands. Only three-year-old Hannah and Jonathan remained at home, and Abigail was willing to take over. Suzanne came and went like a ghost, avoiding them to avoid the hurt in their eyes that accused her of even greater sins than those for which she atoned.

Suzanne was happy at the news her sister Mary had delivered a baby girl with no complications, but the news made her grieve for the woman she'd once been. She remembered being that competent healer who could withstand any threat, overcome any trauma, the brave woman who'd made friends with a shaman. She kept returning to thoughts of Dancing Light as her world slowly revolved from its soothing green to the maples' fired reds. The months passed quickly, the falling leaves, the bared trees opening vistas across the hills, the gray drizzle into November.

One morning, her mother stood at the door. Surprised, Suzanne nearly dropped the crock of lard she'd recovered from the cellar. With the onset of cold weather, once again more housebound, she'd come to realize simple household tasks gave her some peace. She'd told Abigail before she left that she'd make a pot pie for dinner. She set the crock aside.

"Aren't you going to invite me in?" her mother asked.

"Of course. I'm sorry. I forget myself."

Her mother let herself in and walked to the settee. "I've been wanting to stop by. I have a letter from Suzy. I know you two weren't speaking when she left, but I thought you might like to hear her news."

"Oh! I've so regretted our difference. Please, mother. Thank you so much for bringing it. Let's have tea." Suzanne, solitary for months, had lost her social graces. She stood rooted on the spot, momentarily forgetting what she needed to do next. She searched the room, as though a stranger to it.

"Yes. I'll just make myself at home." Her mother laid her muff on the seat and her cape on the back of a nearby chair. She took her seat by the fire. Suzanne, finally recognizing the kettle at the hearth, made her way there to heat water.

"Where's Abigail?" asked Susanna.

"She's taken Hannah and Jonathan to visit Mary. You know Mary has Samuel and Deliverance at home now. She's nursing Deliverance, and Samuel is my Hannah's age."

"Good. It gives you a break, and I know that you need one. I've heard, dear," said Susanna.

"Abigail?"

"No. Will told me. You haven't visited in so long, Suzanne."

"You were the same when father died," Suzanne said. "You wrote few letters after."

"It wasn't grief—I had the children, the farms. There was no time for grief." She opened the page with the broken red seal still attached. "Let's see now."

Suzanne pulled a kettle from the hearth and measured out spoonfuls of herbs in a large pot. She poured in the water.

"Dear Grandmother," her mother read. "I hope this letter finds you well and that everyone in Watertown is recovering from papa's death. I wanted to come, but Ruth couldn't spare the time. I cried so when I heard. We have a new minister now; Reverend Gibbs came last week. He told us that father will rest in God's kingdom for all eternity. I'd like to think it. I can't bring myself to write to mother and don't know what I could say to comfort her. I miss him more than I can say, and she must, all the more.

"In Groton, all the houses are new. Returning families are few, but those building houses improve on what was. We are living in our new house, just four rooms, for now. Uncle John's land is near our old house, close to the river. There's nothing left of the house or barns now. Even the charred places are thick with grasses and weeds. I loved playing near the river, catching frogs and growing pollywogs. We played in the woods, too. When I think of father, I go there to feel him near again. I love walking in the woods."

When Suzanne heard these words, she looked down at her tea, cupped it in her hands, and smiled. *Suzy's so like me,* she thought. *The woods give her comfort too. She had the gumption to face her fears, return to Groton.* This last thought stuck in her throat. *And so not like me—anymore.* She snapped back to attention as her mother continued reading.

"Of course, for my cousins, Groton's all new. And I enjoy showing them. I really like John, who is the best kind of boy. I never have to tell him to do something. He sees what needs doing and does it. He is a great help with William and Samuel, who tend to be lazy. I like my cousin Ruth too. We haven't a school here yet, but I can act as teacher, so far. No one here is ready for Greek or Latin. I'm even helping our nearest neighbors. The Roberts and Bloods are back, and I teach their kids, too. Oh, and tell mother that Martha sends her love. She has a little boy now.

"I feel bad about the argument I had with mother. I was terrible, and I wouldn't blame her if she never spoke to me again. She needs to know that Dancing Light's people never returned to the Nashua

camp. No one has ever seen them again. I think even the Roberts and the Bloods think that they were wrong about her people. Rumors say they followed Sachem Wannalancett to the north country to live at peace."

These last words opened a room dimly lit with hope for Suzanne, who raised her eyes to her mothers. Wannalancett was a Penacook who had a reputation as a fair and peaceful leader. Dancing Light's people had moved away from the conflict. Friends. She heard the words that followed with even more gratitude. Her mother continued reading.

"Though I'm glad I came back to Groton, I want mother to know that I miss her terribly. And Will and Benjamin, too. Could you please tell her I'm sorry. I need to tell her how much I love her.

"With all my love to you, grandmother, and to Hester, Joseph, Samuel, Mary and Hannah, your loving Suzy. And love to little Jonathan though we've never met."

Susanna Sherborn folded up the letter and put it in the purse attached to her belt. Patting it, she leaned forward to pick up her teacup. "Will you write to her? Forgive her?"

Suzanne shook her head. "Mother, I have nothing to forgive. I accuse myself."

Her mother nodded. "Yes, you've been wallowing in guilt since you came. If there was any lying about, you'd scoop it up, whether yours or another's."

"Mother! You aren't being fair."

"Well, what is this about you wandering around the woods, looking to the world like a wild woman witch."

"It's in my blood. I inherited it from Suzy."

Her mother laughed. "But you must write."

"I will."

Her mother paused and set down her cup. "I know you've had a hard time after Joseph died. But I'm wondering if you would consider remarrying."

"Mother! It's not been three months!"

"I know. The hurt is still very much with you. But it seems to me you have a good friend who could help."

"Oh? And who might that be?"

"Why, John Fay. You've seen him often, I'd say."

"Yes, he was Joseph's friend, and I encouraged a match with Abigail. He came to see her."

She set down her teacup, arranging the handle to the right. "That's not how I see it," she said. "I'd say that Abigail is entertaining Jonathan Morse, not John Fay. I've never once heard her speak of the latter. But she prattles on about Jonathan."

"John Fay hasn't come by lately, I confess. But Jonathan Morse? He's a dedicated bachelor. He brags he'll never marry."

"Not lately," her mother said, eyebrows raised. "It seems that while he hasn't exactly proposed, he can't get enough of Abigail's attentions. He may just need a push."

"Are you sure?"

"I see Abigail a lot more than you do. In fact, I've been seeing more of the children since Joseph died. You need to get ahold of yourself, dear."

"Mother, I'm not going to marry. I know you mean well. But I can't. I loved Joseph, and there'll never be another."

"But you have so much in common with John Fay."

"Isn't that a problem, mother? We'd be mirrors. We'd have no way to escape our nightmares." Suzanne was internally screaming, 'No.'

"I understand your pain. I couldn't bear it when your father died. But you'll see that can heal."

"I can't just marry someone when I cannot even bear to hold my children. Everyone says only time heals."

"You don't have time. You have seven children to care for. Will and Abigail are not responsible for them. Your children need you, their mother."

"So, I should just forget and remarry? Like you did, mother?"

"Richard Norcross and I are a different case altogether. Our love grew from an enduring friendship."

"I know, mother. I'm sorry."

"Well, for what it's worth, you can at least think about it. Why not ask Abigail what she thinks?"

Her mother left her soon afterwards, and Suzanne

couldn't stop the violent resistance to her mother's ideas, resentment of her accusations, denial of her suppositions. *They need me? And what about my needs?* She thought, shaking out the bedcover.

Chapter Thirty Eight

DANCING EAGLES

Watertown, Winter Solstice, 1677

As her mother had suspected, Suzanne found that Abigail was set on marrying Jonathan Morse. Though he hadn't officially proposed, she admitted they'd entertained making a home in Groton on the land Joseph had deeded to his brother. Jonathan had laid out plans on his trips there in the fall and intended to begin building in the spring. In the days that followed, Suzanne learned the reason John Fay had stopped coming after Joseph died; he'd returned to Marlboro, though his children remained in Watertown with his sister. She realized the Marlboro settlers, like the Groton settlers, were rebuilding their homesteads. She slowly regained her awareness of town life, the interest in events she'd once entertained.

Suzanne was thinking that she wanted to begin midwifing again, but she was afraid after Joanna's criticism. Could they continue working together when she'd finally revealed her beliefs? So, she continued to stay at home, reintroducing herself to her siblings and children, letting down her defensive shield slowly.

On the shortest and darkest day of the year, Suzanne woke from a nightmare gasping for breath. The curtains around her bed felt ominously claustrophobic, and her chest ached with a pain, as though the dream had been real.

Suzanne almost never dreamed and, if she did, never remembered them. This dream though, she could never forget. She was in the sweat lodge with Dancing Light, the one they'd shared for Joseph's (Standing Heron's) baby blessing. Sheets of steam clothed them from the sage water splashed on white-hot rocks, their skin streamed with it. She even smelled the soothing fragrance of sage.

She wasn't aware of the purpose for this lodge, but vaguely assumed it wasn't a baby blessing. She was grieving for Joseph and a drumbeat disguised her cries. Then, a pair of eagles flew in on flapping wings, and the female, flanked by the male, began to peck at her chest. She had recoiled, yelling 'No. Get away.' But the eagle persisted until it'd opened Suzanne's chest, exposed her heart. The bird savagely ripped at the meat. First, horrified at this murderous act, Suzanne tried to push away the bird, which resisted, talons tearing at her arms. At the struggle's peak, she began to *feel* the message as much as she understood it. *It's broken. My heart doesn't work anymore. It's no good.* She felt it was right and watched the pair catch a piece between them, tearing the meat in their beaks, shredding and devouring a dark red morsel before her. *I can't do anyone any good. They're telling me it's done.* So, she let go, let them tear out her heart. She could feel Dancing Light's hand on her own, reassuring her to no benefit.

Suzanne woke confused, remembering the dream in detail, half afraid it signaled her imminent death, half wishing that it might. That Dancing Light was present, what could it mean? At the same time, Suzanne feared God had warned her again but didn't know why. Hadn't she given up her Devil worshiping friend? Hadn't she stopped practicing medicine? She didn't know what else she might do to obey Him. What was clear; she could tell no one of such a diabolical vision. *Even Mary will reject me,* she thought. Still, unable to put this dream aside, by the next day, she had bundled up for a winter's walk. The light snows had melted, though the day was icy and, by any standards, invigorating. She made her way down Hill Street to the Brown's house and knocked at the door.

Suzanne was surprised when Mary's oldest daughter, Lydia, and a swarthy-skinned Indian girl stood at the open door. Lydia, now fifteen and showing signs she had her mother's beauty, held her finger to her lip and showed the Indian girl how to curtsy. Then she turned and called out, "Mother, Aunt Suzanne is here."

Suzanne heard Mary from the sitting room. "Well, bring her in!"

The Indian girl curtsied as she was bid, her shoulders hunched and frightened eyes searching Suzanne's face. Suzanne noted that her black hair was parted in the middle and fell in two braids. Her eyes were wide in a rounded face, graced by a mouth not accustomed to smiling. The effect was far too somber for a child of her age. *She must be about ten*, Suzanne thought. *She's a war victim, no doubt.*

She smiled. "Boo Shoo! I'm Mistress Brown's sister. What is your name?"

"Meegwitch," the girl said, surprised.

Lydia interrupted with a scowl. "That's not her name. She doesn't speak English so we discourage any Indian talk! We just got her and her brother yesterday."

"If she hears her language, she won't be so frightened. Where is she from?"

"Father bought them in town. They're from Natick, but not Massachusetts. They're Nipmuk. Orphans, we think." Lydia led the way to the sitting room, where Mary sat in a rocking chair, nursing her son Jonathan. The Indian girl followed at her heels.

"Hello Mary. I see you have new servants."

"Yes. I've named this one Alice. Excuse her appearance. We bathed her and found a shift for her to wear. But she needs a proper dress. She is still a wild thing, as you can see. She's afraid of her own shadow."

"How terrible for her, to lose her family, then be given to strangers."

Mary nodded. "You'd be the one to know."

"I would, except I never lost my family."

Mary turned to Lydia and pointed at Alice. "Lydia, you and Elizabeth were showing Alice her chores. Continue." Lydia tugged at Alice's sleeve and led her to the kitchen in the back. Alice looked back at Suzanne with one flash of hope in her eyes, then followed her mistress.

"You should tell Will he should consider buying some of these children for the farm. He needs help if he's to weave again. They are indentured until they are twenty-four, which will give us great service." Mary turned Jonathan around to let him nurse the other breast, settling him on a pillow.

"I'll let him know. Aren't you afraid that she'll run away? Indians, even children, know the woods so well."

"The indenture states that we can prosecute any Indian who helps them run. Not all these children are orphans, of course. Christian Indian parents are asked to give their children to English homes. But once they agree, they can't change their minds."

Suzanne felt saddened at this reality of the war. While she could understand the reasoning of the council leaders—children raised as English would no longer be a threat to the colonies—she couldn't still the thought it was wrong. *We are enslaving them, bidding they do our work for us. It's indefensible.* She pulled herself away from these thoughts and changed the subject.

"I apologize for changing the subject, but I haven't much time. I needed to talk with you about matters I think only you can help me with."

"I? What might that be."

"Mary, I know you are clairvoyant, and I thought you might be able to help me interpret a very disturbing dream."

"If I remember our childhood, you claimed you never dreamed."

"That's right. I never did. Until now."

"Was it about Joseph?"

"Not exactly, though I was grieving in the dream. He wasn't in it. Dancing Light was there; she was holding ceremony in a medicine lodge."

"Medicine. A dream about healing?"

"I guess that could be said, though it felt more like dying."

"What happened?"

"Two eagles came in, pecked out my heart, and ate it in front of me. I couldn't stop them, either."

Mary, arrested by her story, stared at her sister as at someone she'd never seen before. The baby released her nipple and his head lolled back. Mary pulled a towel over her breast and wrapped Jonathan tightly in his blanket, lying the sleeping baby in his cradle.

"I think your dream speaks of what you are suffering, Suzanne. And so violently. All of it together, the siege in Groton … the murders … taking care of Joseph all that time. It's what you feel."

Suzanne shuddered, remembering the ripping of flesh. "But I *felt* nothing, Mary. Not in my dream. It was more about the idea."

"Did you hear words spoken? Did Dancing Light say anything?"

"No. No sound. I could smell the sage, the healing sage. I did have a thought."

"What was it?"

"I thought my heart was broken, no good anymore. It was right they should eat it. But the eagles might be messengers of God, punishing me."

Mary again stopped and stared.

"What is it? What do you see?" asked Suzanne.

"I see inside, and you haven't a heart. Just an empty space. I don't have a sense that you will die, or that God is punishing you. Nothing like that. Maybe that's what the dream means. Letting go and opening a space for the new."

Suzanne sat back, feeling let down. Mary was telling her what her mother had told her. Nothing magic about that. Just a 'get on with life, Dear.' She sighed. "That's what mother says."

Mary smiled. "Life is life; sometimes we can't see the forest for the trees. I have no special powers beyond these small visions. Commonplaces."

"Still, Mary, I'm glad I came to talk. I was afraid you'd think I was the Devil himself with such a dream."

"You must take care to heal, sister. We love you."

When Suzanne let herself out and returned to her home, she let go of the anxiety that gripped her and reveled in the low winter sun.

In the days that followed her dream, she couldn't get Dancing Light out of her mind. Suzy's letter had added fuel to Joanna's diatribe on her conversion to Puritan beliefs that humans had no agency of their own in God's scheme. They must obey God, not anger him. His was a justice all must suffer. When Suzanne heard that even her Groton persecutors now believed the Nashua were friends, she wondered if she could have returned to Groton had Joseph lived. Probably, Suzy had brought it up because she wanted her mother to come back to Groton.

What was curious to her was Joanna's insistence that she owed Dancing Light, not God, thanks for providence. Her mentor, she knew, couldn't begin to understand what she'd learned from both her native friend and the Reverend Willard. To Joanna, Dancing Light was Suzanne's patron for the herbs she found; she couldn't accept a spiritual source. Suzanne's mind had shifted. For Dancing Light, the benefactor that must be thanked was the herb she harvested. She'd never taken any substance from her surroundings without thanking it. She thanked the cohosh when she dug it up. She thanked the "grandmother" rocks she'd heated in the lodge. She thanked the river that gave her water. She not only thanked them, but she left a gift in exchange. 'What we take, we must replace for the people who follow,' she'd insisted. What would Joanna think? Not given to philosophical inquiries of this nature, Suzanne's thoughts produced more questions than answers. She did begin, dimly at first, to understand the Puritan faith had little in common with Dancing Light's Great Spirit. The only common ground they shared stemmed from magic: both were powerful unseen entities, and both knew good and evil.

In the Puritan world, no beings, not even humans, existed outside God's creation, and a flawed mankind, born in sin, was a mere reflection of the divine. Still, God had given man reason and set them above his creation, in his own image.

In Dancing Light's world, Great Spirit inhabited every creature; every living being radiated this divinity. A divinity, not the base, crass stuff Puritans believed mankind were made of, a mud doll He imbued with spirit that reverted to dust. Dancing Light's great spirit was a frog, a firefly, a stone, a star in the sky, and a weeping widow. Their journey on the good red road didn't end when they died but continued in another dimension. When she thought of Joseph, she found that Dancing Light's beliefs were more comforting than the Puritan's creed.

On the first of January, she bundled up. She walked into a cold clear day in the woods in a direction she'd not explored before. That day, she ached, missing Joseph, his voice, the smell of his body, the lean curve in his back when she spooned against him in the dark. Remembering her dream, she wondered if it meant she was soon to join him. The thought discomfited her, for all that she missed him. *I couldn't leave my children, could I?*

In the crisp wind, she hunched her shoulders, hands wrapped in the cape, tight around her, and teeth clenched against the cold. She took a new direction, heading toward a forest. She had not walked two miles past the commons when she entered a hushed clearing that felt haunted. No. She didn't recognize ghosts in this place. More, it seemed holy. A creek stained yellow with minerals ran across great slabs of granite stone, burbling its way over black grizzled mosses that made it slippery for crossing. Reflections from the water's surface danced against the underside of a jutting rock shelf as the sun lowered. A beaver had cut down a tree so recently the still-yellow leaves were now shriveling, caught between life and death. She made out a deer feeding in a camouflage of dry fawn-colored grasses across the meadow, like a mirage of what was real. She watched the sun throw long shadows as it finished its journey low in the sky. A dark bird flew just out of sight over her left shoulder; she thought she might be mistaken but knew it was there because she could hear the wings beat in air.

For a moment, time stopped, and she only wanted to stand there in the golden moment, never draw another breath, but she walked and stumbled. Steadying herself on the rocks beside her, her hand was stung by the energy it emitted. The icy charge ripped through her arm, shocking her straight through her chest. Suzanne straightened, aware that she was experiencing events she could not put into words and continued the path.

She'd not walked twenty feet more when her imagination brought her two eagles. She accepted their flight and landing before her as she did the rest of the wonders nature had wrought in this place. One of them carried an object in one claw. He fluttered up to her and she, without thinking, put out her cupped hands to receive their gift. It was a heart. Small as a baby bird, new, beating in perfect time. The Eagles held their place, fluffing out their wings, hopping in a dance, staring at her, until she understood. *They've brought me a new heart*, she thought. She looked carefully at the beating heart nested in her hands: it was small but perfect. The eagles fluffed their wings and screeched but stood their ground. She again understood. *It's a baby heart, like an eaglet. They want me to take care of it.* The moment she thought it, she knew it was hers to keep. She didn't know how long she stood looking at the empty place on the path. They'd disappeared, but she knew they'd never been there at all. What was she to make of it? Despite herself, she longed at that moment for the wisdom of Dancing Light. She would know. Tears stung in the icy air. Dancing eagles. Dancing. Dancing light. For the first time, she thought she understood her mentor's name meant life, a larger life than she had ever imagined before but could now cherish.

Chapter Thirty Nine

THE ALEWIFE TIDES

Watertown, May 1678

Suzanne rose, dressed, and was about to fix herself some porridge when she heard a knock on the door. At first, she thought it was the boys, back from the River Charles with their catch, but dismissed the thought. *They wouldn't knock.*

Mystified, she opened the door to a happy surprise. John Fay and his nine-year-old son Johnny stood before her, dripping wet and grinning widely. Her heart lifted when she saw his familiar face, the meticulously barbered beard that was his trademark, and she barely noticed the wet sacks full of fish they'd left in the yard.

"Will told me to come on ahead, to surprise you."

"I am sufficiently surprised," Suzanne said. She wanted to add 'and delighted,' but she bit her tongue. She didn't want him to think her forward.

"We ran into Will and Benjamin and your boys at the Charles River. Will invited us for supper. I hope we don't inconvenience you."

"Of course not! You are always welcome here. We've not seen you in so long." Suzanne bent to address Johnny. "Joseph and Sam have sorely missed *you*, Johnny."

John pulled off his hat, twisting it awkwardly. "I'm sorry I didn't stop by to tell you I was going back to Marlboro. I was in a rush to address some bad news."

"I did wonder where you'd gone but knew you must have pressing matters. Ah! I forget myself. Come in. We'll talk after you get dry." They were soaked because the fishers waded into the river to net their catches, and May was still cool enough to warrant their catching chills as well as fish. John nodded gratefully and entered.

She could see her brothers and sons entering the yard with their catches. There'd be a fish fry tonight.

They were a wet and noisy crew, exclaiming about the huge catch this year. "We've never seen so many … every container is filled to the brim." Will herded the boys to their quarters in the barn to change and then outdoors to clean fish for supper, and Abigail ran to the Clinnerys house down the road to borrow butter for this dish. With help from Mary and Sam, Abigail filled the crocks with salt and water, preparing the brine to salt the fresh fish.

Suzanne cornered her son. "Joseph, I want you to take a bucket to your grandmother. Master Norcross may have fished at the weir today, but we don't know that for sure. She'll be disappointed if she doesn't have alewife to salt."

At supper, Suzanne fried the fish a golden brown, charred to chips on the edges. For this occasion, Will passed the rum. The company lined the table boards, passing the platters, wiping hands and mouths on napkins. They picked at the tender flesh, removing the tiny bones, and savored the buttery crisp tails and fins. Will couldn't help but drill John Fay about Marlboro, a town he'd helped defend in his days with Captain Prentice.

Suzanne, who felt uncomfortable with the joy she'd felt in seeing John Fay at the door, was deliberately trying to keep her distance. She avoided his eyes and kept busy. She couldn't think that her mother might be right because, after all, John Fay hadn't come to see *her*. Her brother Will had invited him. It was likely Will had talked to her mother about the matter of her remarrying. *No*, she thought, *I'll not be letting them pander me.*

Will took a swig of his rum and addressed John Fay. "Have many returned to Marlboro?"

"About half of us," he answered. "We want to rebuild, but it's slow because supplies are scarce. We've been able to salvage some of the hardware from the burned sites, but most of the time, I'm waiting for ships from England. At least there's lumber."

Abigail commented, nodding. "You remember Jonathan Morse—he's building in Groton. He tells me the same."

John Fay turned to her. "Will tells me that you and Jonathan will marry and move to Groton in the fall."

Abigail beamed. "Yes. He's in Groton now, building our home."

"I congratulate you."

Still curious, Will asked, "Do you have enough help?"

"Another problem," John exclaimed. "Help is available if you count the captive's children as servants. The Bay is selling Indians, but with the new laws that prohibit selling Indians older than twelve years, I don't need to tell you the levels of skill leave us wanting in the short term."

"Have you bought any?"

"I have. Two boys and a girl. They've been helpful in farming and hunting. They've learned these skills from their parents. But they're hopeless when it comes to building or English standards of order. And they don't speak English."

Benjamin, ever interested in animals asked, "Do you have livestock yet?"

"I have a cow and two sheep, but I think it too soon. I must keep them in the house this winter if I can't erect shelters for them. I'm hopeful I can finish my house so I can build sheds for them."

Suzanne couldn't curb her curiosity. "Will your children be joining you?"

"Johnny will be with me this summer. But the younger two will have to wait until the house is finished. I'm building much larger this time. I have four rooms on each story. It's taking more time than I wagered."

"How wonderful," Abigail tuned in.

Suzanne might have thought he was bragging, and half wondered if he was trying to make Abigail sorry that she'd rebuffed his courtship. However, John immediately steered the conversation in another direction.

He turned to Will. "I heard from my sister's husband that you are now serving on the Watertown council, Will. That is a great honor. Congratulations."

Will squared his shoulders, suppressing a spontaneous smile at his praise. "Thank you. My father served, though, and sometimes it's unnerving because we have the same name. I am not my father."

"That would be unnerving," John Fay agreed.

At sunset, when Abigail began to clear the table and the children scattered, John Fay approached Suzanne. "We haven't had a chance to continue our talk. Would you join me for a walk?"

Suzanne's heart again leaped with a girlish gratitude, which she immediately squelched. She was not going to be one of those widows who pursued mates. "I'd like that," she said nodding in a stately manner, hoping that she gave him no cause to think she was anyone but a friend and neighbor. She brought a shawl as the spring night was cool, though the air was filled with the scents of trees bursting with flowers that would spread seeds far and wide. A tender breeze flipped her skirt as she walked.

"I again want to apologize for leaving so abruptly without a goodbye. I value your friendship more than you can know."

"I thought it was due to Abigail's discouraging you."

"I did entertain the idea of pursuing her briefly. But neither she nor I was truly interested. You seemed keen on the match, though."

They had come to the Pequesset commons and finding a boulder at the edge, sat to enjoy the sunset that spread a marmalade at the edges of spring clouds.

"I was. It was only natural. You would have been a fine match for her. I was surprised that you didn't drop us when it was clear that there'd be no match."

"Suzanne, I can't explain to you the respect I hold for you, and have, since the day you healed my daughter. I am awed by your knowledge. I've always felt honored you consider me a friend. Do you see?"

"I wasn't aware."

"And after Joseph died, I felt you alone could understand any of my life. You see, I couldn't court Abigail because I was still in love with my wife." John Fay's face twisted in pain and tears welled from his eyes. "I couldn't, you see."

Suzanne stared at him, suddenly sharing his anguish. "You have good cause to believe I understand you." Choking on her last words, she cried openly, cleanly, reaching for his hands. "I feel the same about Joseph."

He grasped her hands, staring earnestly into her eyes. "That's why I think you are the only woman with who I could conceivably want to share my future. Do you understand that? I'm not sure I do, but I've not been able to put the thought aside that we belong together."

Suzanne heard his words with astonishment. "Wait. Think what you are saying."

"I am. I have. Suzanne, I want to marry you. I have built *you* a new house. I want *you* to be the mother of my children. With yours and my children, I know it would be a burden. Ten between us, but your daughters will be marrying soon. I would take in your children as my own, I swear it. And I have the means to support them, even to hire help so you can continue your work. I'll make sure you have the largest apothecary in Massachusetts."

She wiped her tears with her sleeve and shook her head. "I respect your desire, John, but I have no way to give you the love I hold for my Joseph. If I made such a promise, it would be a lie. And could you, who do not profess love for me, honor such a commitment beyond what is obsessing you now?"

"I feel such a kinship to you precisely because we share a grief we'll never assuage. Can you honor that connection? Suzanne, will you marry me?"

Suzanne, still stunned with his confession, overwhelmed by his conviction, couldn't stop the warm glowing light that began to creep across her heart, dispelling the clouding doubt. *Could I?* she asked herself, receiving a resounding answer. She composed her answer in a stilted manner.

"I want to answer you with a resounding 'yes.' I feel in my heart that this might be a perfect match for such as you and I. But I think that love must be considered; marriages arranged for other purposes have their place. But you and I are accustomed to love in our respective mates. If we wait, and can cultivate even a part of that love, I say yes to you."

John took her hands in his and kissed them. "I can wait." They walked back in the dark, watching the last blush of light on the horizon disappear.

EPILOGUE

John Fay courted Suzanne for three months. Over the months, he returned to Watertown to help her plant, always bringing all three children with him. In a month, she agreed to marry, and they posted their bans in June. In July 1678, she was a flurry of activity packing the few belongings the family had put together in Watertown. She brought seeds and roots from her apothecary, and Joanna gave her another book for a wedding present.

It had been fourteen months since Joseph Morse had died. Her husband-to-be and she had tackled their fear head on. Both had lost beloved spouses. Both had witnessed Indians burn their homes to the ground. To return to Marlboro was as unnerving for John Fay as returning to Groton would have been for Suzanne.

On the day that they loaded the cart with her children and belongings, she left her past for a new beginning. On the path to her new home, she found two eagle feathers lying aside it. She picked them up, looking to see who had left them, half expecting to see Dancing Light. She dismissed that thought, though not the memory of the eagles that had renewed her heart. She now had three Indian children in her charge, and she must honor her friend. She had already committed to preserving what customs she knew while learning more of their language. She looked forward to teaching her servants what she'd learned from her Indian shaman friend. Even more, she thought her helpers might provide the links through their kin to find out what had happened to her sister Rebecca.

AUTHOR'S WORD

Book Three of *The Watertown Chronicles* is based on the life of the oldest of William Shattuck's daughters, my ancestry now relived in the fictional Sherborn families. When I read that Susanna had moved to Groton, a small trading post at the northwestern edge of the Middlesex county in the Massachusetts Bay Colony, I found her character most challenging. What would lead the daughter of a successfully established and prosperous man to move from the comforts she'd grown to expect, to pioneer in Indian lands? Her marriage, of course. While Joseph Morse, the man she married, was the landless son of a Watertown Puritan family, his uncle John Morse was a prominent land holder in Groton. The young couple might have moved to Groton to advance their standing. Joseph Morse could only achieve "freeman" status and emancipation if he owned land, which was becoming scarce (and therefore expensive) in Watertown.

From such a match, my fiction began to grow. Two factors might advance it. First, my fictional Sherborn daughter would need to be financially independent to marry a landless farmer with genteel leanings. This gave birth to Suzanne Sherborn-Morse, the midwife. One occupation open to women in a Puritan community would have been midwifery, and in communities where births averaged ten per woman, midwifery could support her in comfort. That independence would allow her a luxury denied other women in her community, the second factor. She could marry for love. She may have been passionately in love with the landless Joseph, at least, enough to follow him to the Massachusetts northwestern frontier.

This occupation would also ensure she'd not been a sheltered child but had been put out to apprentice at a tender age. Sending children to live with near relatives or putting them in apprenticeships was standard practice for English kin of the time, even the middle classes, and with such large families, it made sense. Being fostered would account for a thin veneer of connection to both her religion and her family. For my fiction, it could establish her character: independent, adventurous, open-to-the-new, mercurial. And, most importantly, alienated, given to bouts of loneliness and self-doubt.

At the book's start, the fictional couple move with their first two children to Groton, Massachusetts in 1666, eleven years after The Plantation of Groton's incorporation. Originally a trading post at the confluence of Nod Creek and the Nashua River in 1655, where peaceful Nashaway Indians have a summer plantation west of the river, liberal land grants assured the town's fast growth. These facts are the foundations for a historical novel that shows the friction presented by colonial progression from trading post to annexed territory, the changes resisted by occupying tribes that led to war.

While I could access digitized texts of all the town council meetings in this period, that narrative source ends after the Indian attack in March 1676, not to be resumed until the town was rebuilt two years later. Because Joseph Morse's uncle was the council clerk and responsible for recording the minutes of the council's meetings, I had a source for information on the town business, taxes, garrisons and the like. However, my narrator and her clients, Puritan women bounded by the gendered restrictions of their time, are party to the town's business only secondhand from their husbands. The fictional Dancing Light, as the powerful shaman and *sauksqua* (woman leader) of the Nashua, is the only exception to the gendered distribution of news.

I modeled this fictional character on texts describing the sauksquaWeetamoo.

I was also fortunate to have original texts regarding four other people of the time. Reverend Samuel Willard, his father, Major Simon Willard, the minister's servant girl, Elizabeth Knapp, and Thomas Tarball all left tracks in recorded history. The minister also left texts for his sermons and an amazingly detailed account of Elizabeth's bewitchment. Assuming that in a town comprising fifty families at the peak of its prosperity, Suzanne would know all four, I found ways to involve her in their histories. I took liberties with making the Tarball family Suzanne's anathema. In history, Thomas Tarball, a Groton selectman, was convicted of selling alcohol to the Abenaki Indians near Groton and served as witness to a Penacook trading post murder (the guilty party was a drunken Indian). I thought he was a fitting enemy to the midwife and her friend Dancing Light. Ironically, in 1707, during the French and Indian War, when Indians again attack and burn Groton to the ground, Abenaki abduct three Tarball children and adopt them into the tribe. The Abenaki Indians have a branch that carries the last name Tarball.

Since Groton was one of the frontier towns that was obliterated in King Philip's war, Suzanne's story takes me to the heart of the Indian conflict. I, like most authors who write of this period of history, struggle to do justice to both sides in King Philip's war. As Jill Lepore states in her work, *In the Name of War,* history is written from the biased viewpoint of the victors. In the case of wars with Natives, who left few written accounts beyond those connected to land deeds, writers must search eyewitness accounts, transcribed oral histories, and read between the lines to find the truth. Fortunately, I've found several histories that provide views from "other" viewpoints than white European settlers, in this case, a history of indigenous peoples.

The Family Trees of

William, the Patriarch

John Sherborn
B. 1593 in
Stoghumber,
Somerset, England
D. 1639 in
Stoghumber
Somerset, England

Mary Granger
B. 1594 in
Stoghumber,
Somerset, England
D. 1650 in
Stoghumber
Somerset, England

Susanna Sherborn
B. 1643 in
Watertown,
Massachusetts,
D. 1716 in
Marlborough,
Massachusetts

Mary Sherborn
B. 1645 in
Watertown,
Massachusetts
D. 1732 in
Waltham,
Massachusetts

John Sherborn
B. 1647 in
Watertown,
Massachusetts
D. 1675
Charlestown,
Massachusetts

William Sherborn
B. 1653 in
Watertown,
Massachusetts
D. 1732 in
Watertown,
Massachusetts

Rebecca Sherborn
B. 1655 in
Watertown,
Massachusetts
D. 1689 in
Boston,
Massachusetts

Abigail Sherborn
B. 1657 in
Watertown,
Massachusetts
D. 1694
Groton,
Massachusetts

William, the Patriarch

and Susanna's Family

William Sherborn
B. 1622 in
Stoghumber,
Somerset, England
D. 14 Aug 1672 in
Watertown,
Massachusetts

Susanna Andrews
B. 03 Apr 1622 in
Plymouth,
Massachusetts
D. 13 Dec 1685 in
Watertown,
Massachusetts

Phillip Sherborn
B. 1648 in
Watertown,
Massachusetts
D. 1722 in
Waltham,
Massachusetts

Joanna Sherborn
B. 1650 in
Watertown,
Massachusetts,
D. 1673 in
Watertown,
Massachusetts

Benjamin Sherborn
B. 1662 in
Watertown,
Massachusetts,
D. 1682 in
Watertown,
Massachusetts

Samuel Sherborn
B. 1666 in
Watertown,
Massachusetts
D. 1729 in
Bohicket Creek,
South Carolina

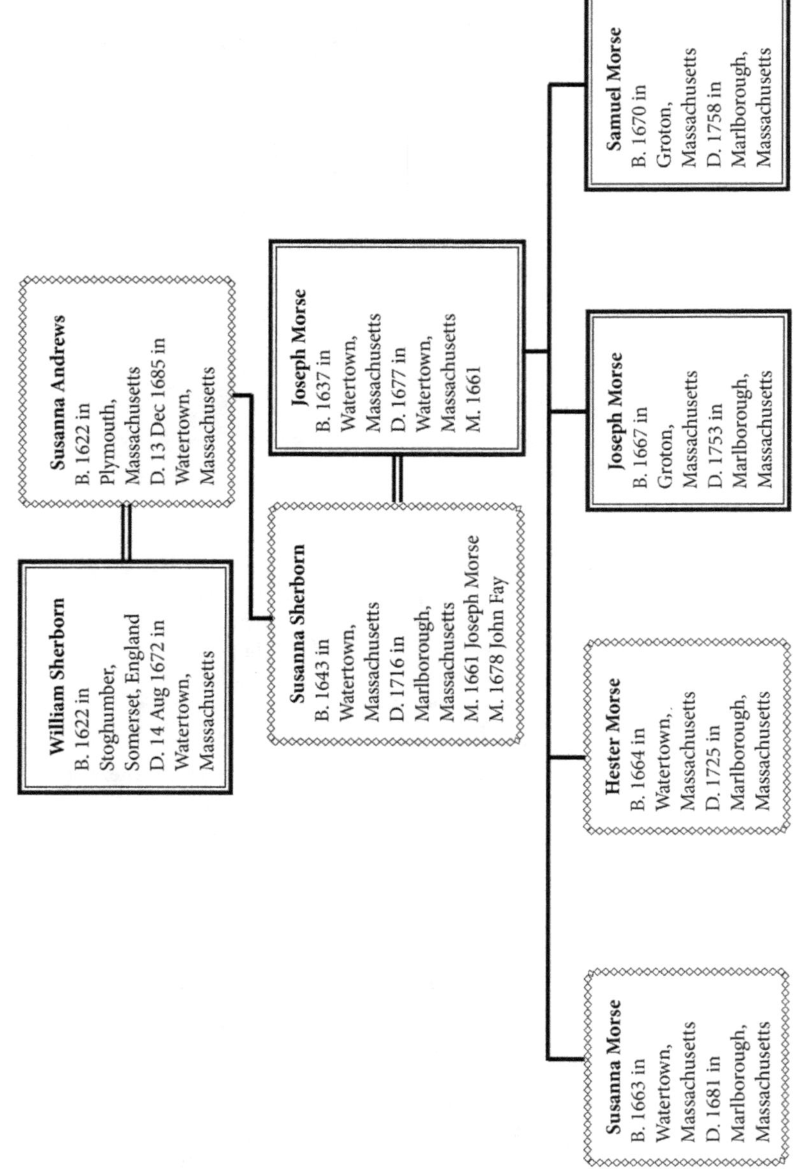
The Susanna and Joseph Morse Family - 1
William Sherborn
B. 1622 in Stoghumber, Somerset, England
D. 14 Aug 1672 in Watertown, Massachusetts
Susanna Andrews
B. 1622 in Plymouth, Massachusetts
D. 13 Dec 1685 in Watertown, Massachusetts
Susanna Sherborn
B. 1643 in Watertown, Massachusetts
D. 1716 in Marlborough, Massachusetts
M. 1661 Joseph Morse
M. 1678 John Fay
Joseph Morse
B. 1637 in Watertown, Massachusetts
D. 1677 in Watertown, Massachusetts
M. 1661
Susanna Morse
B. 1663 in Watertown, Massachusetts
D. 1681 in Marlborough, Massachusetts
Hester Morse
B. 1664 in Watertown, Massachusetts
D. 1725 in Marlborough, Massachusetts
Joseph Morse
B. 1667 in Groton, Massachusetts
D. 1753 in Marlborough, Massachusetts
Samuel Morse
B. 1670 in Groton, Massachusetts
D. 1758 in Marlborough, Massachusetts

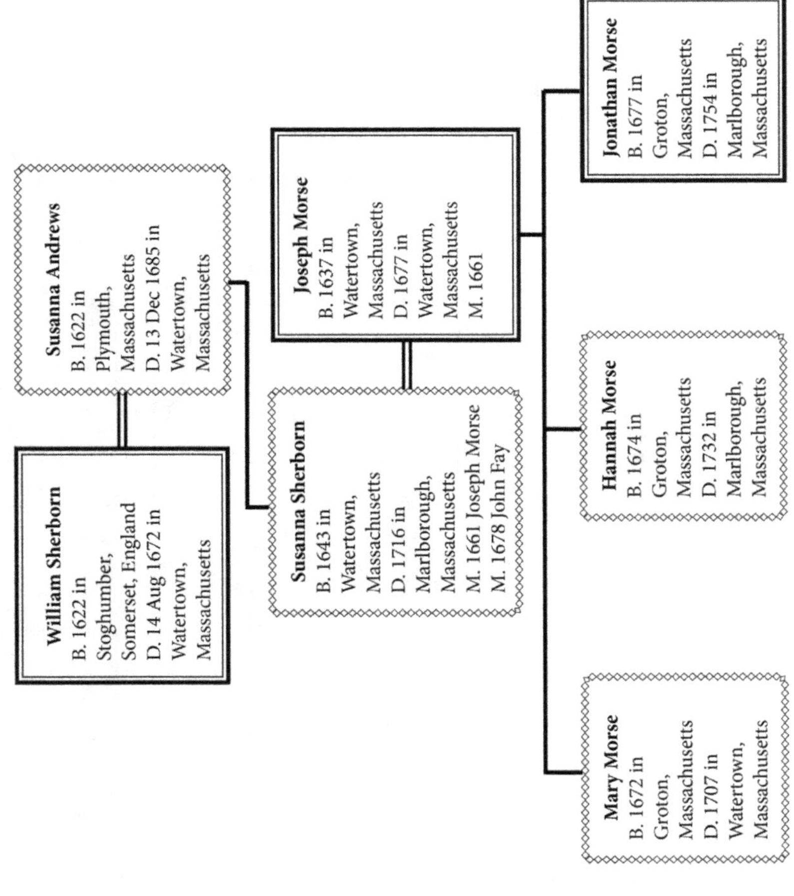
The Susanna and Joseph Morse Family - 2
William Sherborn
B. 1622 in
Stoghumber,
Somerset, England
D. 14 Aug 1672 in
Watertown,
Massachusetts
Susanna Andrews
B. 1622 in
Plymouth,
Massachusetts
D. 13 Dec 1685 in
Watertown,
Massachusetts
Susanna Sherborn
B. 1643 in
Watertown,
Massachusetts
D. 1716 in
Marlborough,
Massachusetts
M. 1661 Joseph Morse
M. 1678 John Fay
Joseph Morse
B. 1637 in
Watertown,
Massachusetts
D. 1677 in
Watertown,
Massachusetts
M. 1661
Mary Morse
B. 1672 in
Groton,
Massachusetts
D. 1707 in
Watertown,
Massachusetts
Hannah Morse
B. 1674 in
Groton,
Massachusetts
D. 1732 in
Marlborough,
Massachusetts
Jonathan Morse
B. 1677 in
Groton,
Massachusetts
D. 1754 in
Marlborough,
Massachusetts

The Susanna and John Fay Family - 1

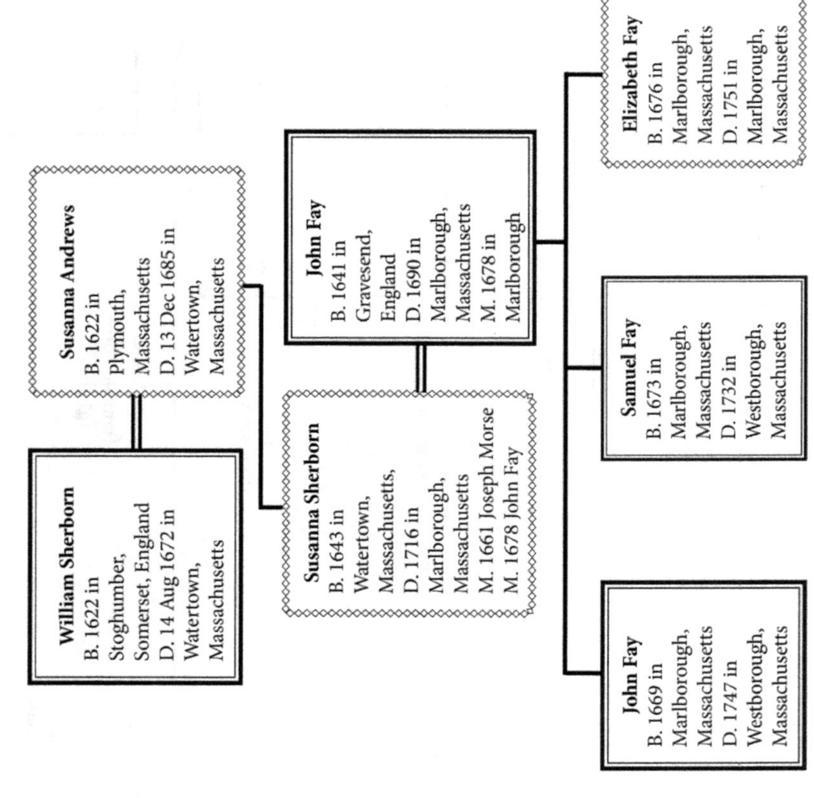

The Susanna and John Fay Family - 2

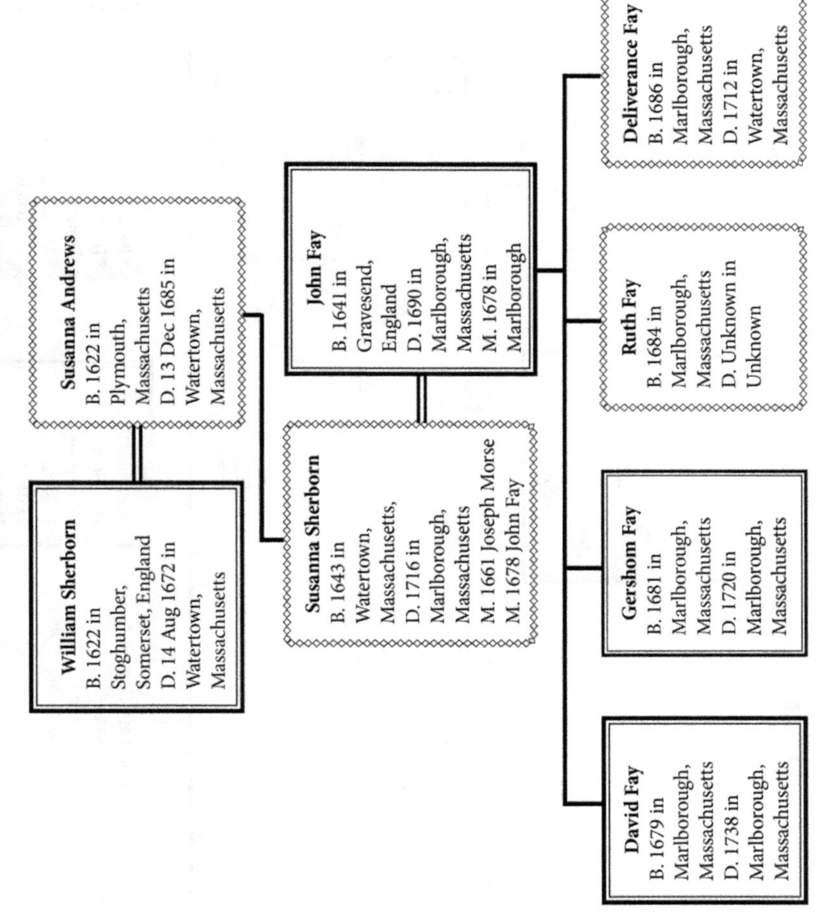

The Mary and Jonathan Brown Family - 1

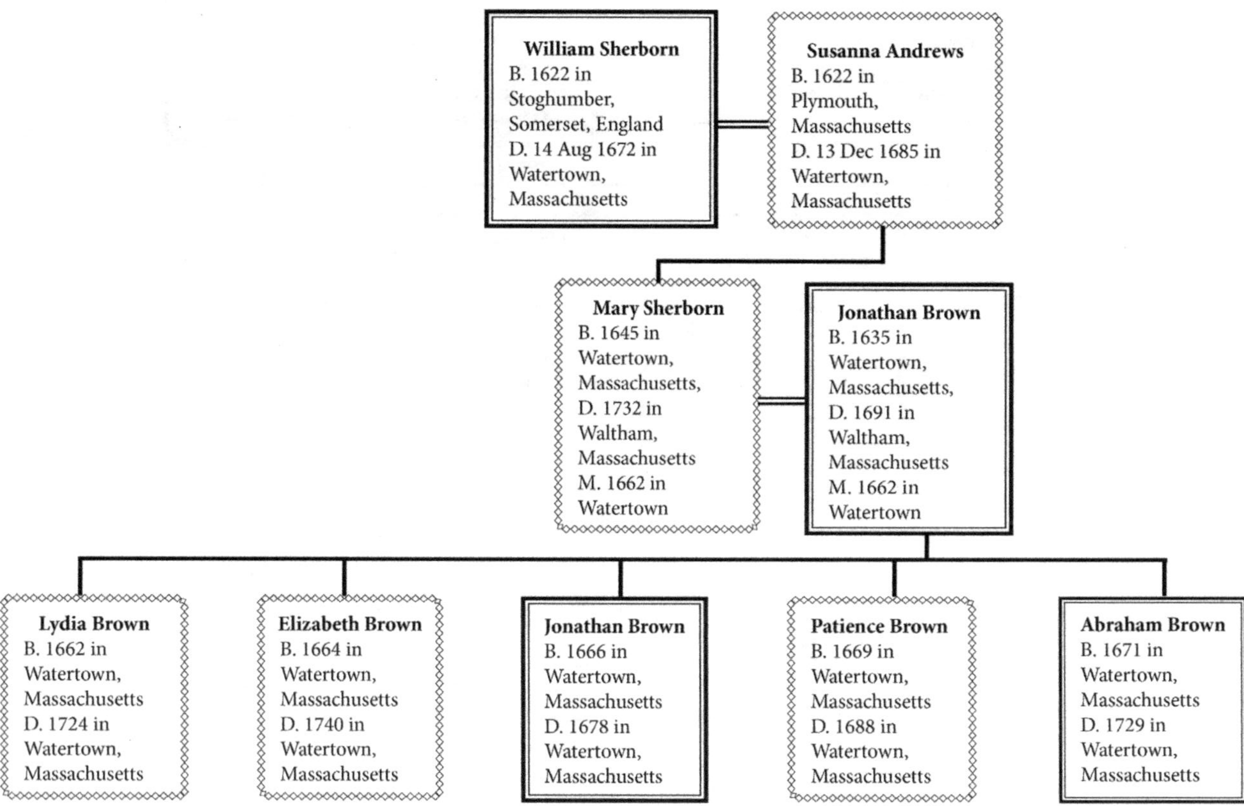

The Mary and Jonathan Brown Family - 2

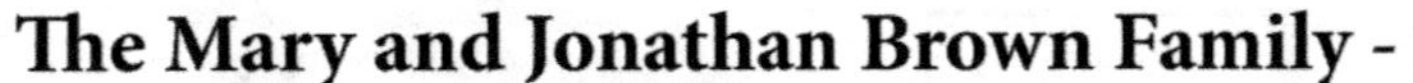

William Sherborn
B. 1622 in Stoghumber, Somerset, England
D. 14 Aug 1672 in Watertown, Massachusetts
Susanna Andrews
B. 1622 in Plymouth, Massachusetts
D. 13 Dec 1685 in Watertown, Massachusetts
Mary Sherborn
B. 1645 in Watertown, Massachusetts,
D. 1732 in Waltham, Massachusetts
M. 1662 in Watertown
Jonathan Brown
B. 1635 in Watertown, Massachusetts,
D. 1691 in Waltham, Massachusetts
M. 1662 in Watertown
Samuel Brown
B. 1674 in Watertown, Massachusetts
D. 1692 in Watertown, Massachusetts
Mary Brown
B. 1677 in Watertown, Massachusetts
D. 1711 in Lexington, Massachusetts
Ebenezer Brown
B. 1679 in Watertown, Massachusetts
D. 1694 in Watertown, Massachusetts
Benjamin Brown
B. 1682 in Watertown, Massachusetts
D. 1753 in Watertown, Massachusetts
William Brown
B. 1684 in Watertown, Massachusetts
D. 1718 in Watertown, Massachusetts

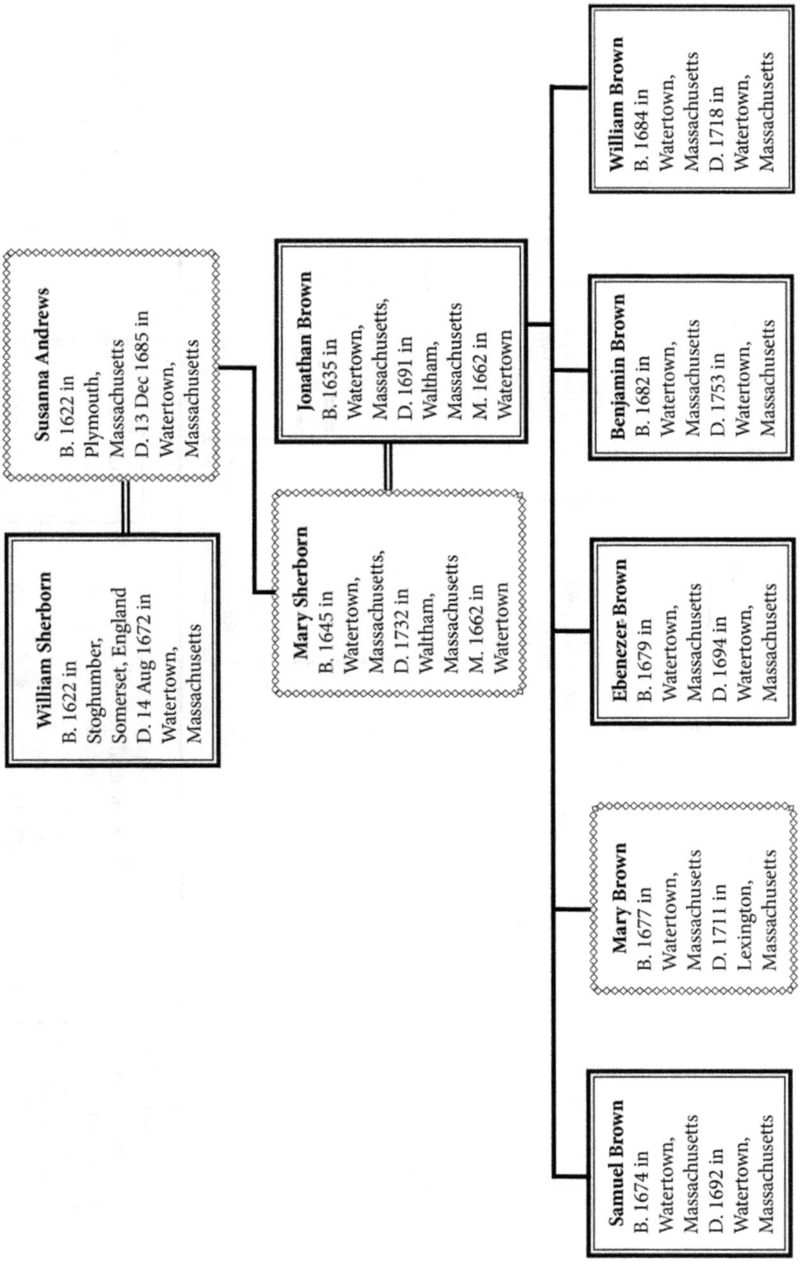

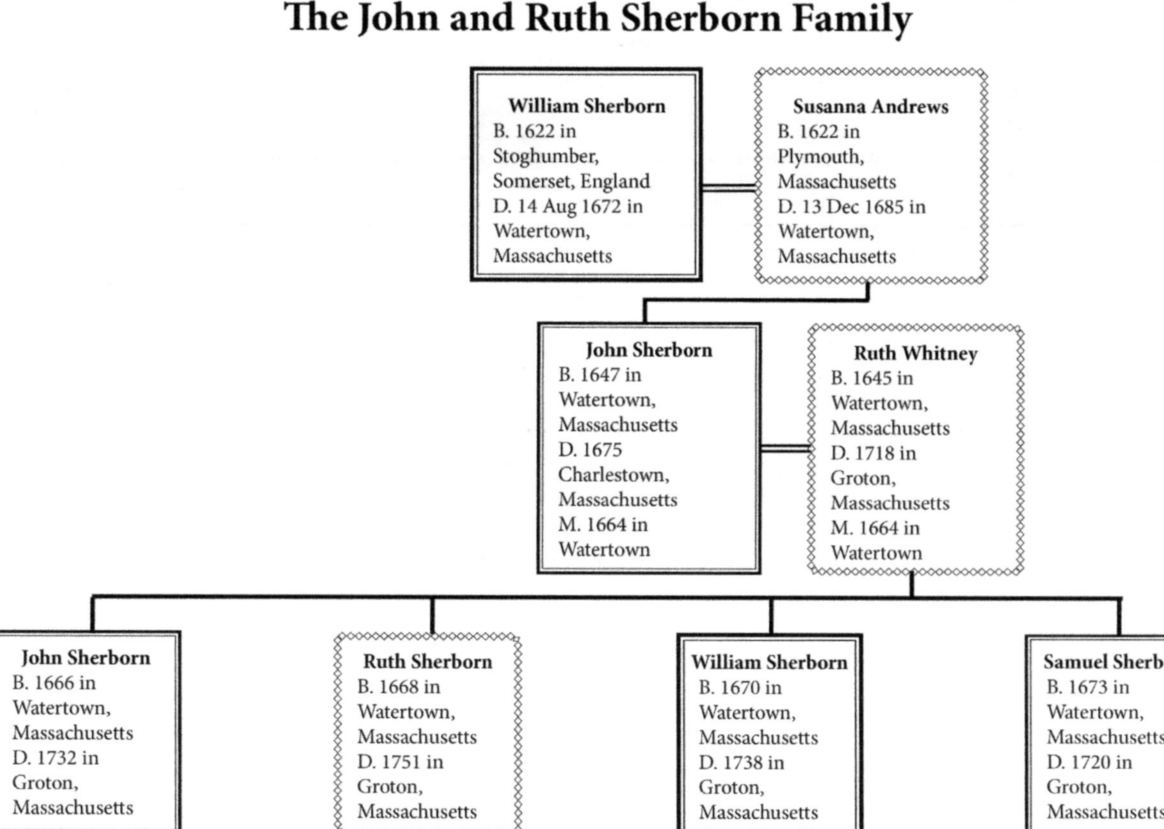
The John and Ruth Sherborn Family
William Sherborn
B. 1622 in
Stoghumber,
Somerset, England
D. 14 Aug 1672 in
Watertown,
Massachusetts
Susanna Andrews
B. 1622 in
Plymouth,
Massachusetts
D. 13 Dec 1685 in
Watertown,
Massachusetts
John Sherborn
B. 1647 in
Watertown,
Massachusetts
D. 1675
Charlestown,
Massachusetts
M. 1664 in
Watertown
Ruth Whitney
B. 1645 in
Watertown,
Massachusetts
D. 1718 in
Groton,
Massachusetts
M. 1664 in
Watertown
John Sherborn
B. 1666 in
Watertown,
Massachusetts
D. 1732 in
Groton,
Massachusetts
Ruth Sherborn
B. 1668 in
Watertown,
Massachusetts
D. 1751 in
Groton,
Massachusetts
William Sherborn
B. 1670 in
Watertown,
Massachusetts
D. 1738 in
Groton,
Massachusetts
Samuel Sherborn
B. 1673 in
Watertown,
Massachusetts
D. 1720 in
Groton,
Massachusetts

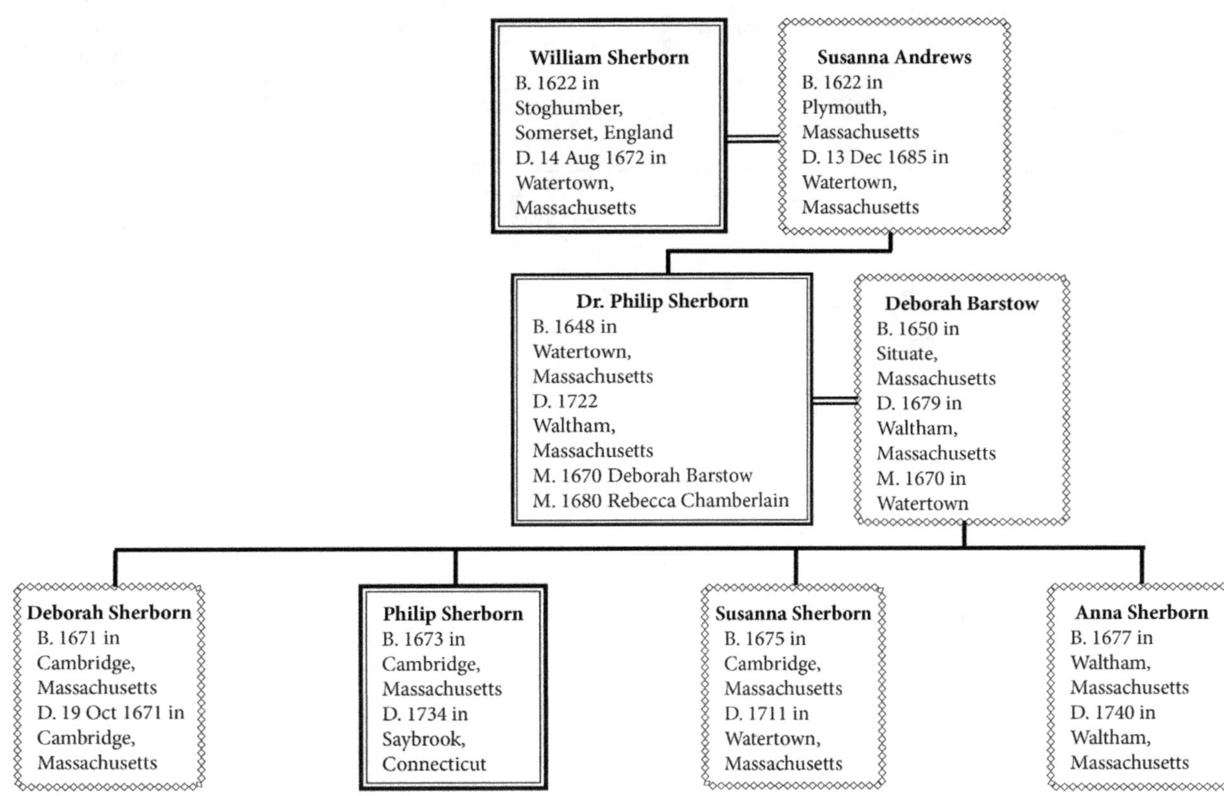
The Philip and Deborah Sherborn Family
William Sherborn
B. 1622 in
Stoghumber,
Somerset, England
D. 14 Aug 1672 in
Watertown,
Massachusetts
Susanna Andrews
B. 1622 in
Plymouth,
Massachusetts
D. 13 Dec 1685 in
Watertown,
Massachusetts
Dr. Philip Sherborn
B. 1648 in
Watertown,
Massachusetts
D. 1722
Waltham,
Massachusetts
M. 1670 Deborah Barstow
M. 1680 Rebecca Chamberlain
Deborah Barstow
B. 1650 in
Situate,
Massachusetts
D. 1679 in
Waltham,
Massachusetts
M. 1670 in
Watertown
Deborah Sherborn
B. 1671 in
Cambridge,
Massachusetts
D. 19 Oct 1671 in
Cambridge,
Massachusetts
Philip Sherborn
B. 1673 in
Cambridge,
Massachusetts
D. 1734 in
Saybrook,
Connecticut
Susanna Sherborn
B. 1675 in
Cambridge,
Massachusetts
D. 1711 in
Watertown,
Massachusetts
Anna Sherborn
B. 1677 in
Waltham,
Massachusetts
D. 1740 in
Waltham,
Massachusetts

The Philip and Rebecca Sherborn Family - 1

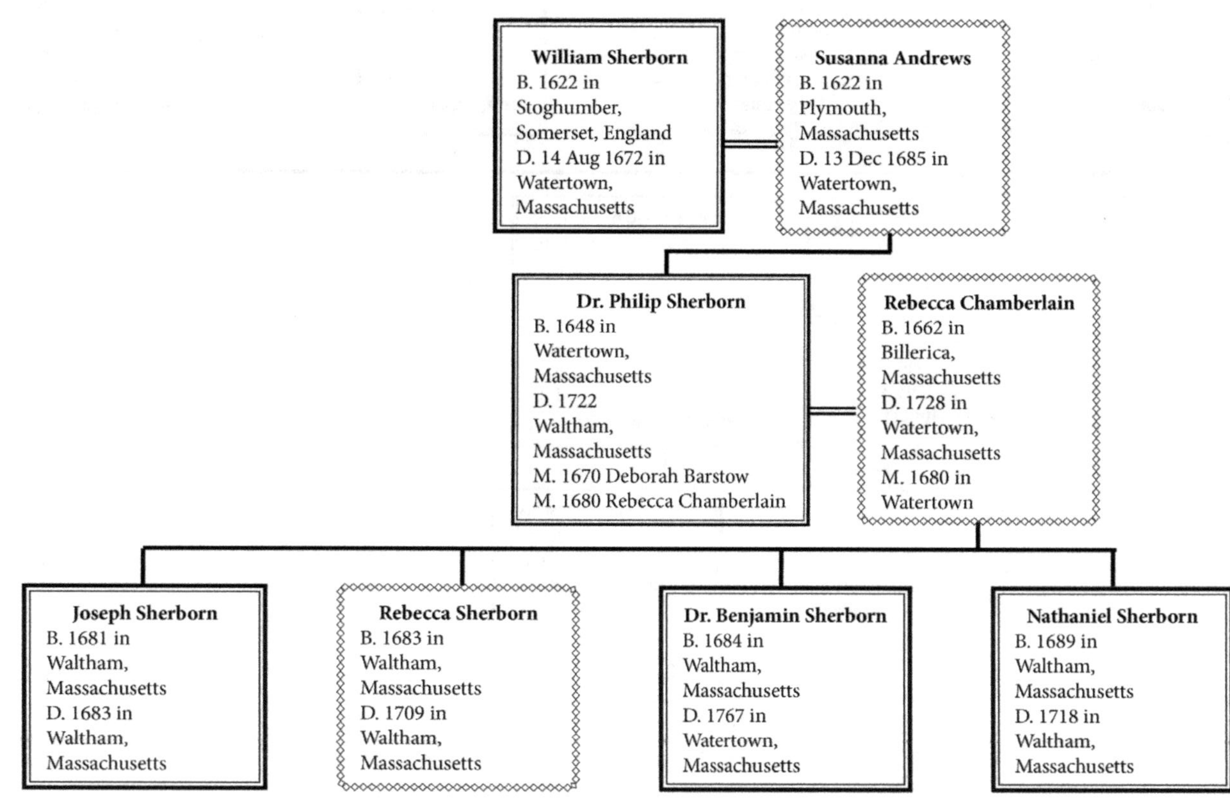

The Philip and Rebecca Sherborn Family - 2

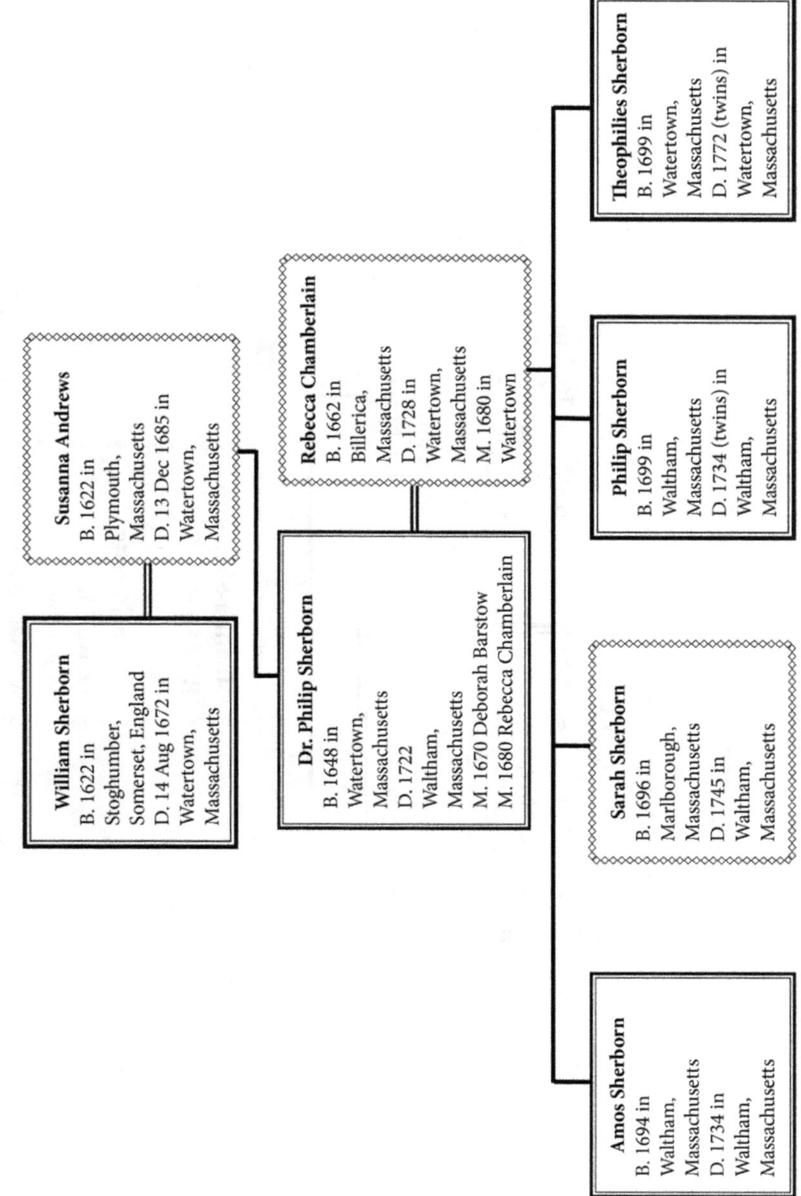

Joanna Sherborn's Family Tree

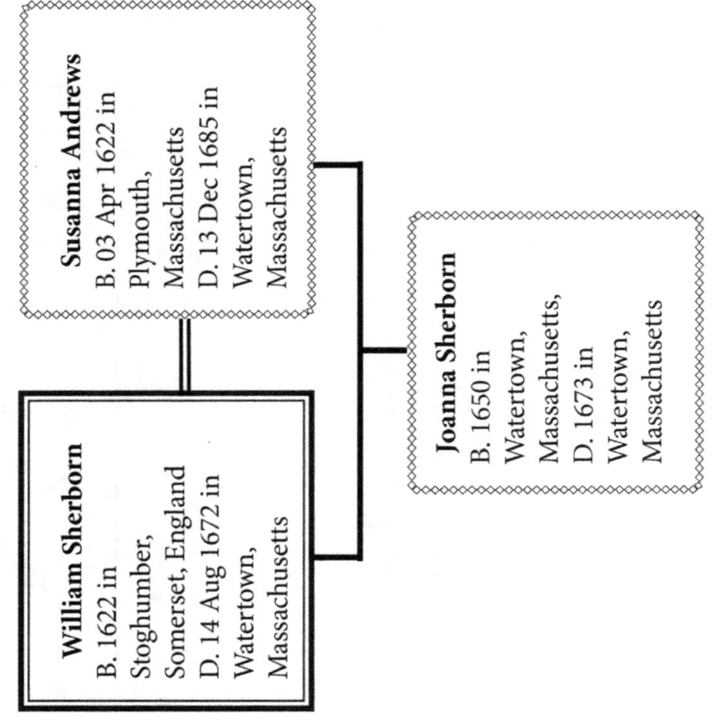

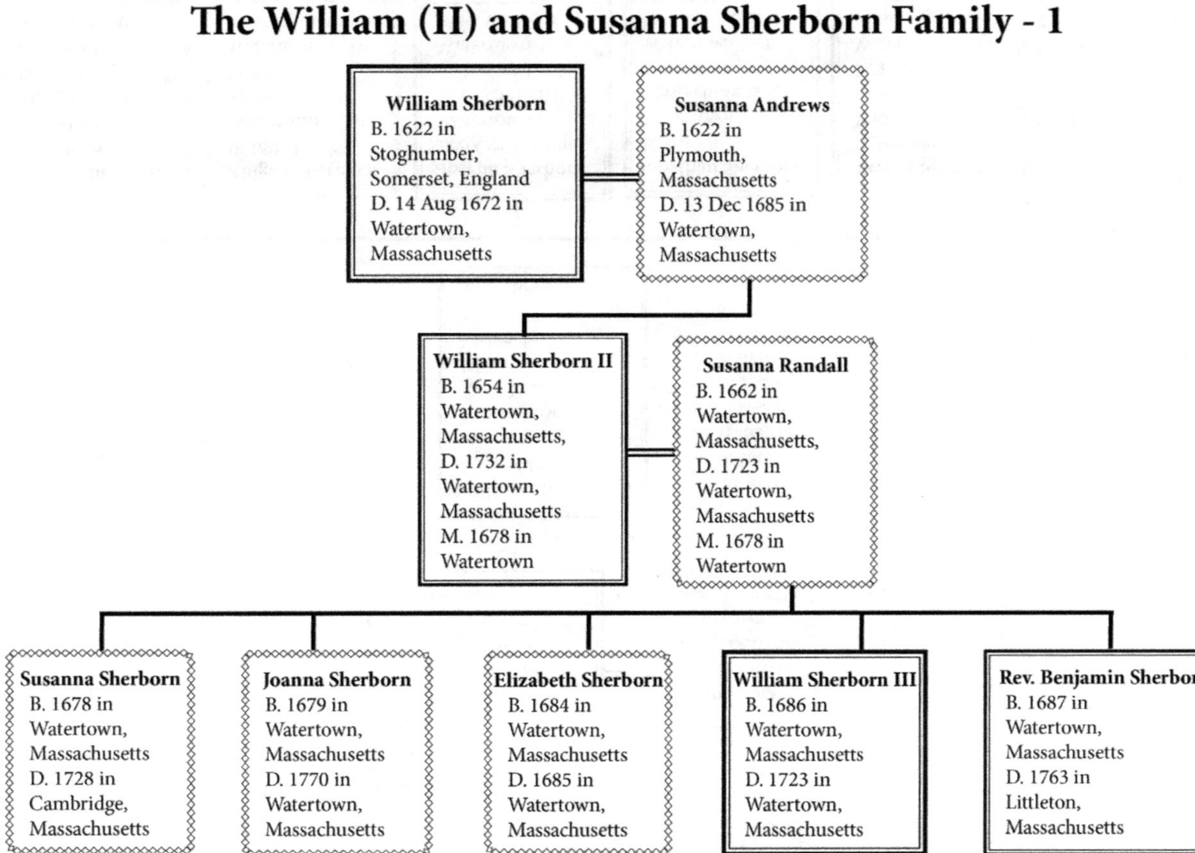
The William (II) and Susanna Sherborn Family - 1
William Sherborn
B. 1622 in Stoghumber, Somerset, England
D. 14 Aug 1672 in Watertown, Massachusetts
Susanna Andrews
B. 1622 in Plymouth, Massachusetts
D. 13 Dec 1685 in Watertown, Massachusetts
William Sherborn II
B. 1654 in Watertown, Massachusetts,
D. 1732 in Watertown, Massachusetts
M. 1678 in Watertown
Susanna Randall
B. 1662 in Watertown, Massachusetts,
D. 1723 in Watertown, Massachusetts
M. 1678 in Watertown
Susanna Sherborn
B. 1678 in Watertown, Massachusetts
D. 1728 in Cambridge, Massachusetts
Joanna Sherborn
B. 1679 in Watertown, Massachusetts
D. 1770 in Watertown, Massachusetts
Elizabeth Sherborn
B. 1684 in Watertown, Massachusetts
D. 1685 in Watertown, Massachusetts
William Sherborn III
B. 1686 in Watertown, Massachusetts
D. 1723 in Watertown, Massachusetts
Rev. Benjamin Sherborn
B. 1687 in Watertown, Massachusetts
D. 1763 in Littleton, Massachusetts

The William (II) and Susanna Sherborn Family - 2

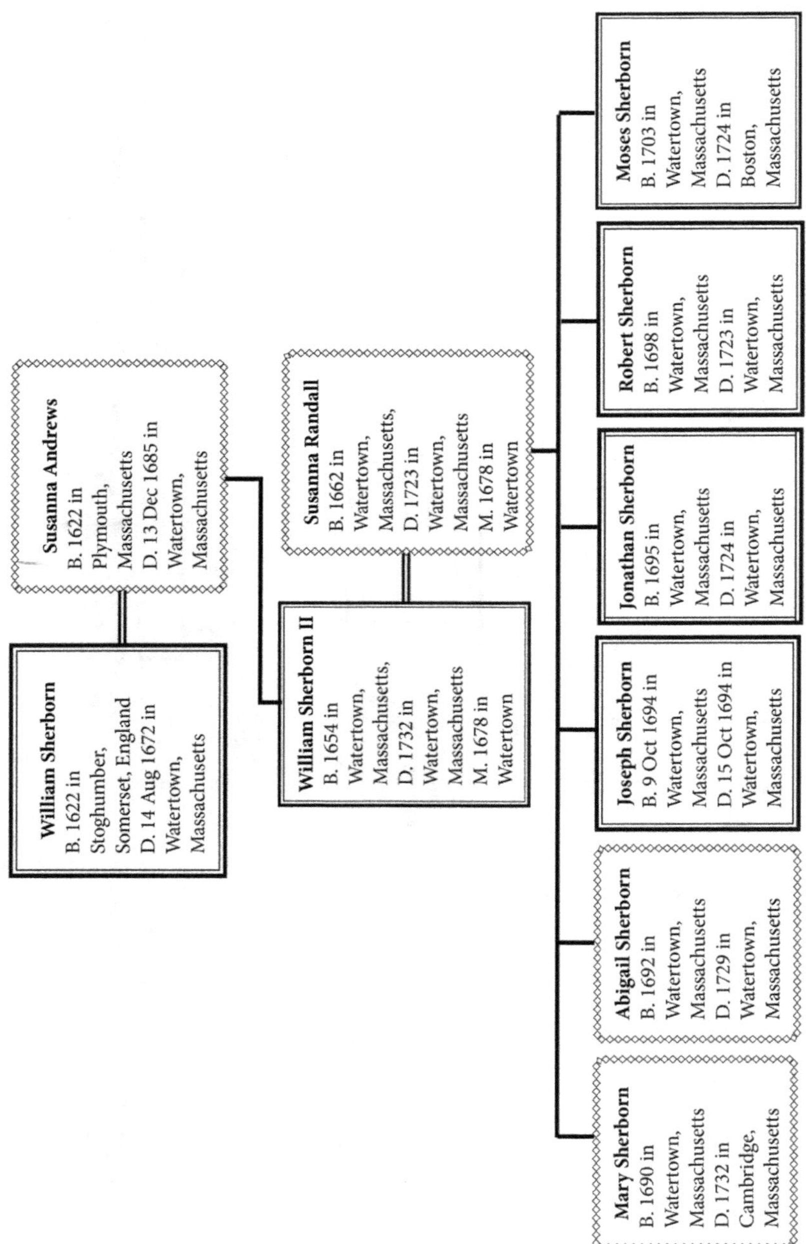

The Rebecca and Samuel Church/Abraham Davis Families

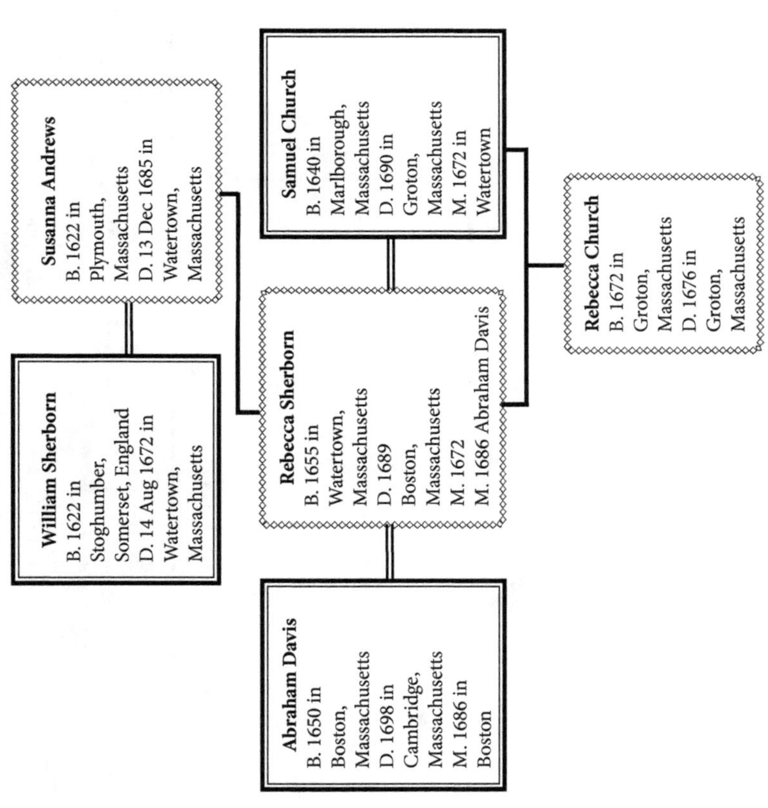

The Abigail and Jonathan Morse Family

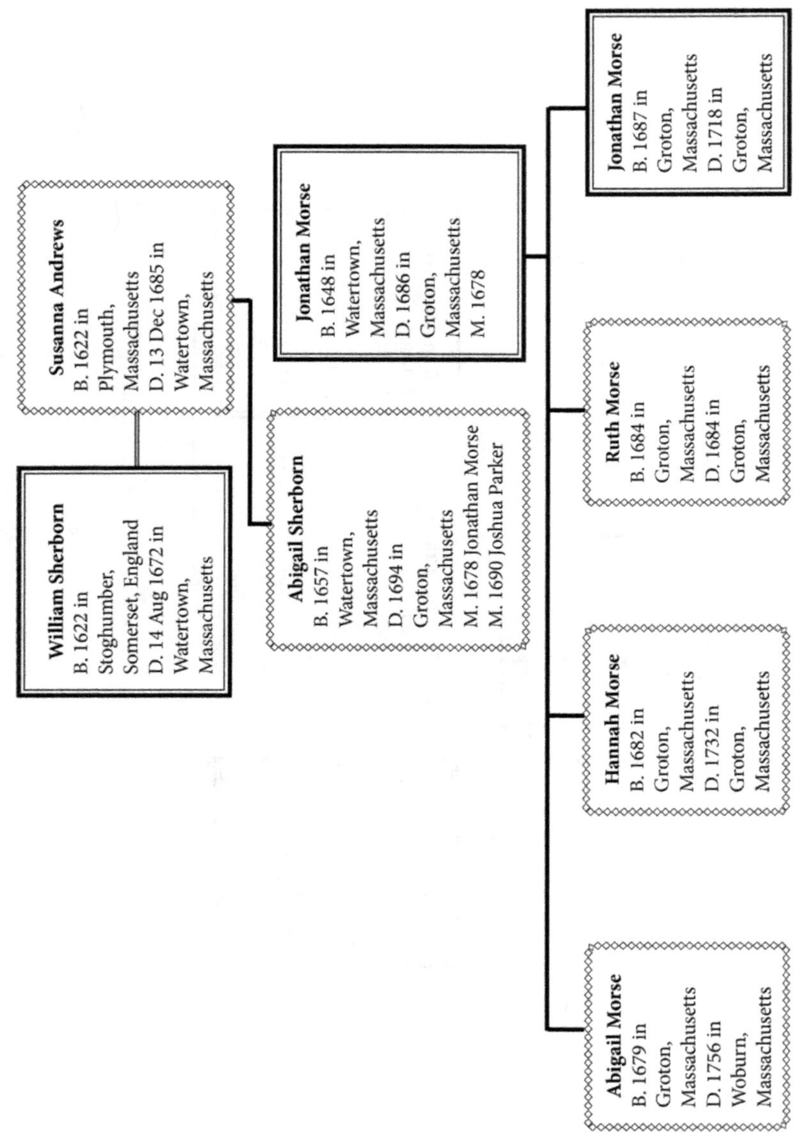

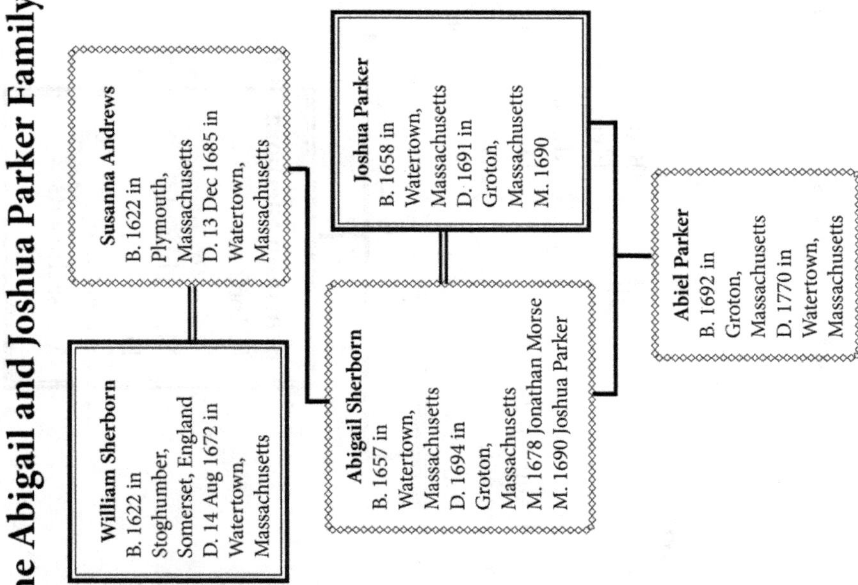
The Abigail and Joshua Parker Family
William Sherborn
B. 1622 in
Stoghumber,
Somerset, England
D. 14 Aug 1672 in
Watertown,
Massachusetts
Susanna Andrews
B. 1622 in
Plymouth,
Massachusetts
D. 13 Dec 1685 in
Watertown,
Massachusetts
Abigail Sherborn
B. 1657 in
Watertown,
Massachusetts
D. 1694 in
Groton,
Massachusetts
M. 1678 Jonathan Morse
M. 1690 Joshua Parker
Joshua Parker
B. 1658 in
Watertown,
Massachusetts
D. 1691 in
Groton,
Massachusetts
M. 1690
Abiel Parker
B. 1692 in
Groton,
Massachusetts
D. 1770 in
Watertown,
Massachusetts

Benjamin Sherborn's Family Tree

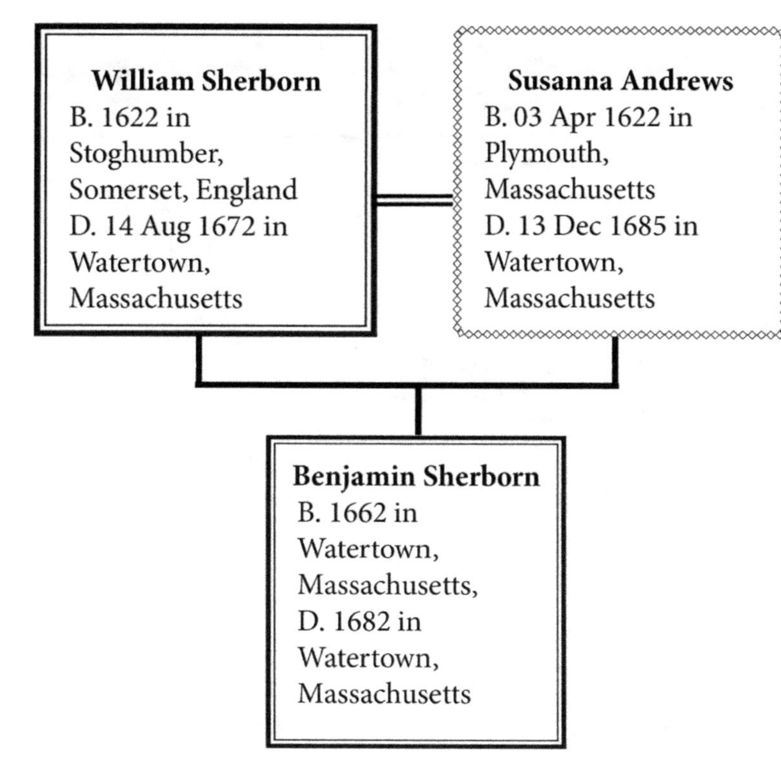

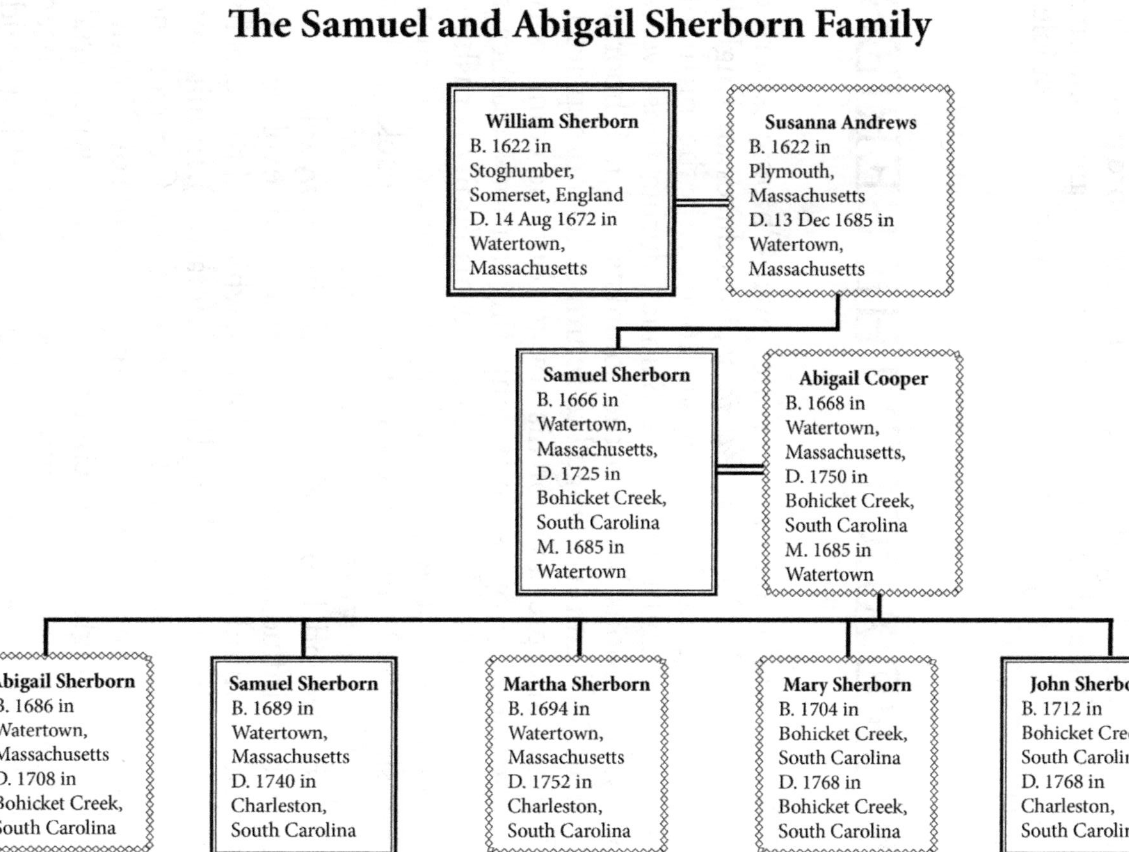
The Samuel and Abigail Sherborn Family
William Sherborn
B. 1622 in
Stoghumber,
Somerset, England
D. 14 Aug 1672 in
Watertown,
Massachusetts
Susanna Andrews
B. 1622 in
Plymouth,
Massachusetts
D. 13 Dec 1685 in
Watertown,
Massachusetts
Samuel Sherborn
B. 1666 in
Watertown,
Massachusetts,
D. 1725 in
Bohicket Creek,
South Carolina
M. 1685 in
Watertown
Abigail Cooper
B. 1668 in
Watertown,
Massachusetts,
D. 1750 in
Bohicket Creek,
South Carolina
M. 1685 in
Watertown
Abigail Sherborn
B. 1686 in
Watertown,
Massachusetts
D. 1708 in
Bohicket Creek,
South Carolina
Samuel Sherborn
B. 1689 in
Watertown,
Massachusetts
D. 1740 in
Charleston,
South Carolina
Martha Sherborn
B. 1694 in
Watertown,
Massachusetts
D. 1752 in
Charleston,
South Carolina
Mary Sherborn
B. 1704 in
Bohicket Creek,
South Carolina
D. 1768 in
Bohicket Creek,
South Carolina
John Sherborn
B. 1712 in
Bohicket Creek,
South Carolina
D. 1768 in
Charleston,
South Carolina

If you enjoyed this book, would you consider writing a review or even a short comment? Your responses help the aspiring author by getting the word out to more people. It's easy. Just link and comment at https://www.amazon.com/ Mary-Clairvoyant-Watertown-Chronicles-Chronicle/ dp/1721784322

MORE ABOUT THE SERIES

The first book in The Watertown Chronicles series, titled *William, the Patriarch*, introduces an English immigrant, beginning in 1666 with the birth of his youngest and tenth child, Samuel, during those years of rising tensions between the colonists and neighboring Indians. William has longed to return to his homeplace in England and prepares for his voyage, but the complexity of the allied peoples and competing nations reaches a dangerous pitch. History tells us that his family is rushing headlong into war with the Wampanoag uprising. Then all goes silent, and thinking it's safe to leave, he packs his bag to go. William must find his way home.

The second book, *Mary, The Clairvoyant*, relates the churches' influence on colonial rule and explores the suspicious mind-set of the colonists, which fed the ferocity of the Indian war with King Philip (Metacom). Immigrants to the Americas carried the legacy of the German and Swiss Protestant movement that split the atom of Christian religious thought: three centuries of wars and witch trials in Europe preceded the immigrations. Millions had been executed in these conflicts. Mary, the second oldest child, is psychic, and the seventeenth century is a difficult time for anyone who shows paranormal ability when such skills are considered witchcraft. Mary's position in the town is secure; she has married power and wealth, but can she claim that security given the conflicts between her gift and her religion?

Look for future releases in the Watertown series:
Book Four – *Susanna, The Matriarch*
Book Five – *John, Carpenter, Miller, Soldier*
Book Six – *Philip, The Doctor*
Book Seven – *Rebecca, The Dressmaker*
Book Eight – *William, The Weaver Warrior*
Book Nine – *Joanna, The Hunter*
Book Ten – *Abigail, The Pioneer*
Book Eleven – *Benjamin, The Farmer*
Book Twelve – *Samuel, The Prophet*

SERIES RETROSPECT

The fictional Sherborn family is modeled from the Shattucks of Watertown, Massachusetts. William Sherborn's prototype William Shattuck arrived at the Massachusetts Bay Colony around 1640. He originated in west Somerset, in and near the Tone Valley. The 130-square-mile area in Southwest England was the home of all the Shattocke family, Celts who migrated from the foothills of the Alps north of Italy. Ever wanderers, from England, they scattered to English colonies on three continents: Europe, Australia and North America, even New Zealand in Oceania. William's progeny account for more than half (around 8,000 out of a total 14,000-to-15,000) of all Shattocke's alive worldwide today. See www.shaddock.ca/ for an account of the Shaddock, Shattuck, Shattocke diaspora.

William Shattuck Senior emigrated from Stogumber, Somerset, England, that area of England where Samuel Coleridge wrote his well-known work, *The Rime of the Ancient Mariner* and visitors can now walk a forty-mile Coleridge Trail. Although we have no records of his crossing, William was around eighteen years old and a weaver. The Watertown Council meeting minutes dating back to 1630 record his land grant from 1640. He was successful, becoming a full member of the Puritan church and voting freeman; he was a selectman several years, acting as both highway assessor and hog greave. He eventually amassed the property of three neighbors and a farm near present-day Waltham. He died at fifty in Watertown, and the will he filed in 1672 was published.

Susanna Norcross, Widow of William Shattuck, gave birth to ten children by William before he died in his fiftieth year. She married a widower, Watertown's teacher RICHARD NORCROSS and occupied the Shattuck main home until her death. When she remarried, she became mother to her six children still at home and Norcross's seven children. She is known to have written the first prenuptial agreement in Massachusetts when she married the widower, who survived Susanna by five years. Her son William Shattuck Junior bought title to the homestead bequeathed to Benjamin and Samuel when they came of age.

Susanna Morse, Nee Shattuck, William's oldest daughter was widowed twice, and left with 14 children: seven with Joseph Morse, five with John Fay, and three from John Fays' first marriage. She and her first husband settled in Groton, but Indians burned it to the ground in King Philip's war in 1676. Refugees who'd lost everything, the pair returned to Watertown, where her husband died a year later. Another refugee who had fled to Watertown from Marlborough, which Indians also destroyed the same month, married her, and the pair returned to Marlborough. The seven Morse children and the Fay children became prominent in Marlborough. She remarried a third time to Brigham, also from Marlborough.

Mary Brown, Nee Shattuck, lived a long and venerable life with one husband. When her husband of 55 years died, she never remarried, living 87 years in the Waltham area of Watertown. She bore ten children.

John Shattuck Senior, the author's direct ancestor, is William Shattuck's firstborn son, who also has the distinction of siring the most Shattucks from William senior's branch. Though John was drowned in a ferry accident during King Philip's War, he left a widow, three sons, and a daughter.

We also note that John's father, William, slights him in the will; John never joined the church. John's name and the names of his issue show in colonial archives and histories, but the stories leave questions regarding their character. In one story, John accused a neighbor of improper behavior with a young woman. The case ended up in the Boston court, where Reverend Sherman, the minister, advised the court 'don't trust his word.' Another story of John Shattuck's descendants in Groton paints them as bullies. When the residents of the new subdivision, Pepperell, are trying to decide where to build the new meetinghouse, the Shattucks pressure the community to build the church close to their landholdings, which are extensive. Justice prevails, and the townspeople move the half-built structure to land that is more centrally located—the lumber, too—while a two-person-deep line of Shattucks lines the road in protest.

John Shattuck's name turns up in Captain Daniel Gookin's defense of the Christian Indians in King Philip's war as a story of retribution. Gookin's defense of Christian Indians shows a clear bias: he opposed the war and those engaged in it. Unlike many colonists who thought Christianized Indians had joined King Philip, he insisted they were loyal to the English.

Daniel Gookin was the official Superintendent of Praying Indians in The Massachusetts Bay colony. As such, he was the counsel for fifteen Marlboro Indians then on trial in Boston. He was critical of anyone who spoke against them, though two were eventually convicted.

Gookin records John Shattuck's response during that meeting and judges his character in his history of the ferry accident following it. Gookin omits from his story that John Shattuck had been sent to rescue the very settlers the fifteen Indians allegedly attacked. Seeing his fellow soldier's heads on spikes and the charred countryside on the chilling ride to Boston must have fueled John Shattuck's response. Gookin wrote:

> About this time a person named Shattuck, of Watertown, that was a sergeant under Capt. Beers, when the said Beers was slain near Squakeage, had escaped

> very narrowly but a few days before; and being newly returned home, this man being at Charlestown, in Mr. Long's porch, at the sign of the Three Cranes, divers persons of quality being present, particularly Capt. Lawrence Hammond, the Captain of the town, and others, this Shattuck was heard to say to this effect: "I hear the Marlborough Indians, in Boston in prison, and upon trial for their lives, are likely to be cleared by the court; for my part," said he [Shattuck], 'I have been lately abroad in the country's service, and have ventured my life for them, and escaped very narrowly; but if they clear these Indians, they shall hang me up by the neck before I ever serve them again.' Within a quarter of an hour after these words were spoken, this man was passing the ferry between Charlestown and Boston; the ferry boat being loaded with horses and the wind high, the boat sunk; and though there were several other men in the boat and several horses, yet all escaped with life, but this man only. I might mention several other things of remark here that happened to other persons, that were filled with displeasure and animosity against the poor Christian Indians but shall forbear lest any be offended.

That Daniel Gookin attributes the accident to God's punishment is not disguised by the stated forbearance "lest any be offended."

John Shattuck's widow, Ruth, married Enoch Lawrence, of a prominent Groton family and occupied the land that John had received as grants and bought from John Morse in 1666. (John Morse was the uncle of the two Morse men that Susanna and Abigail Shattuck married.) Enoch Lawrence didn't adopt Ruth's children; the three boys kept the name Shattuck.

Ruth's firstborn son JOHN SHATTUCK JR., also lived in Groton, married Mary Blood, and had children. When Indians again burned down the town of Groton, the Shattuck brothers decided to abandon it. However,

John Shattuck changed his mind and stayed. (The Bloods were the largest property owner, with acreage equivalent to half the town.) Then, on May 8, 1709, John Shattuck Jr and his oldest son, John, a young man of nineteen years, were killed by the Indians while returning from fields on the west side of the Nashua River. A suitable stone placed by the site bears the inscription: "Near this site John Shattuck a Selectman of Groton (MA) and his son John were killed by the Indians May 8, 1709 while crossing the stony ford way just below the present dam." (Stone erected 1882)

These deaths at river crossings that eerily reflect John Shattuck Senior's drowning while crossing the Charles River, might call up Gookin's inference of divine retribution. At the very least, they suggest self-fulfilling prophecies. Consider the following report:

> A remarkable fatality seems to have followed Mrs. Mary Blood-Shattuck's kindred. Her husband and eldest son [mentioned above] were killed by Indians. Her father, James Blood, was killed by Indians Sept. l3, l692. Her uncle, William Longley [was] also killed by Indians; so was his wife and five of their children - on July 27, l694. The remaining three were carried off as captives. A relative, James Parker, Jr and his wife were killed in this assault and their children taken prisoner. Her stepfather, Enoch Lawrence received a wound by the Indians probably [in] the same attack, July 27, l694, which almost wholly disabled him. The three Tarball children carried off to Canada June 20, l707 were cousins of Ruth Shattuck. John Ames the father-in-law of her niece, Ruth (Shattuck) Ames was shot by the savages at the gate of their own garrison July 9, l724. Lastly, her son-in-law Isaac Lakin the husband of her daughter Elizabeth, was wounded in Lovewell's fight at Pigwacket, May 8, l725. These calamities covered a period of only one generation extending from l692 to l725.

Source: *Epitaphs of the Old Burial Ground, Groton, MA.* by Dr. Samuel A. Green

While we might err to speculate on divine retribution or self-fulling prophecies for this family, we can agree it's an uncanny history

Dr. Philip Shattuck became a doctor in Waltham, and he and his wife fostered his younger brother, Samuel, from age seven. (Samuel's mother had married Richard Norcross and the pair apprenticed Samuel to Philip to learn a trade.) His first wife, Deborah, died after nine years, leaving him with four children and his brother Samuel, then thirteen. Oddly, he married his second wife seven weeks later. His second wife bore ten children. He was prominent in Waltham, serving as assessor, treasurer, and other offices of public trust and responsibility. He might have become the head of a long line of doctors if his son, Dr. BenjaminShattuck (the second) had seen his issue follow his lead.

William Shattuck Junior survived his service to Captain Prentice's cavalry during the Great Swamp Battle and the Hungry March of King Philip's War and lived to be 79. He is buried in the Waltham cemetery along with his sister Mary and his brother Philip. He sired eleven children by Susanna Randall, who died ten years before William. Oddly, William's son became the first in the line of Boston doctors, once referred to as "Boston Brahmins," and Shattuck Avenue, a Harvard Medical school address, is named after one of William's line. William served the Watertown council in many positions of public trust and lived at the family homestead on the road to the pond, now known as Washington Street.

The Massachusetts Bay Colony had promised land grants in payment for the attack on the Narragansett fort (Great Swamp Battle) but didn't give out the land until 1725, the year before he died. The thirty-acre Narragansett

2 (later named Westminster) grant to William Shattuck was in northwestern Massachusetts. Because there wasn't enough land to fill the grant, new land was granted in Amhurst, New Hampshire. Descendants who settled there are ancestors of Aron Draper Shattuck, known for his Hudson-River-style landscape paintings.

Rebecca Church, Nee Shattuck, was sixteen when she married Samuel Church, a man of thirty-two years, in January 1672. She bore one child in 1672, after which the family disappears from all records; however, a Samuel Church land grant is recorded in Groton.

Benjamin Shattuck died in his 20th year, leaving no issue or history. We know he suffered from a long disabling illness because his brother Philip petitioned the court for money from his inheritance to pay the medical costs. Benjamin was apprenticed to his brother William junior, who had just turned twenty when his mother married Richard Norcross, and his trades might have been weaving and farming if he had survived.

Joanna Shattuck never married and died the year she turned twenty-three, eight months after her father's death in 1672 and seven months before her widow mother married Richard Norcross in 1673.

Abigail Morse, Nee Shattuck, married her brother-in-law, Joseph Morse's brother, Jonathan Morse after the war. The pair moved to Groton two years after Indians had sacked the town. Abigail outlived Jonathan Morse after bearing four children (the first cousins of Ruth Shattuck-Lawrence's four children), and a second husband, Joshua Parker, after bearing one child. She died at thirty-seven, two years after her second husband died. She was survived by five children, ages five to sixteen.

Samuel Shattuck: We have no record of where Samuel went after the Indian wars of 1694-95. We know that when his mother married Richard Norcross, she sent seven-year-old Samuel to his brother Philip to learn a trade. He lived with Philip for eleven years before he married at eighteen, but we don't know if he became a doctor or used his brother's skills. Samuel, who was the youngest of William's children, married Abigail in Watertown, but after three children are recorded in the church records—Abigail, Samuel, and Martha are the issue—the family disappears.

Abigail was a covenanted member of the church in Watertown. We have no records of Samuel, Abigail and the three children being involved in King William's war, and it's more likely he sought land grant opportunities that were opening up in the south. There is a record in 1709 that a Samuel Shaddock and his wife Abigail bought land in Bohicket Creek, South Carolina, and DNA research also reveals that the South Carolina Shaddocks are genetically linked to the patriarch, William Shattuck instead of other, later arrivals from England. It is certain that this Samuel Shaddock was William Shattuck's son. Philip Shaddock, who has been tracing family lines genetically, proposes that Samuel may have changed the spelling of his name to be consistent with the southern pronunciation when he moved south.

ABOUT THE AUTHOR

Nancy Shattuck was inspired to write this series when she discovered her direct ancestors had lived through King Philip's War in 1675-76. Exploring their history, she was so impressed by the complexity of the colonial experience that each family member began to tell a different story. No longer a novel, the "chronicles" were born. Nancy earned a master's degree in Comparative and Japanese Literature at Washington University (WU) in St. Louis and completed the classwork for two separate doctorates, in Comparative Literature at WU and American Literature at Wayne State University. Previous publications include Book One of The Watertown Chronicles series, ***William, The Patriarch***, a children's fable, ***The Fishers***, and a travel memoir, ***Travel Wings: An Adventure***, in addition to short stories and poetry. She is the recipient of an American Academy of Poets award in 1978; Tompkins awards for poetry and fiction in 2004, 2005, and 2007; a John Clare award for poetry in 2005; a Judith Siegel Pearson award for poetry in 2005; and a Heck-Rabbi award for drama in 2006.

CPSIA information can be obtained
at www.ICGtesting.com
Printed in the USA
JSHW051438300622
27461JS00002B/2

9 781640 661318